Peter Watt has spent time as a soldier, articled clerk, prawn trawler deckhand, builder's labourer, pipe layer, real estate salesman, private investigator, police sergeant and advisor to the Royal Papua New Guinea Constabulary. He speaks, reads and writes Vietnamese and Pidgin. He now lives at Maclean, on the Clarence River in northern New South Wales. He is a volunteer firefighter with the Rural Fire Service, and fishing and the vast open spaces of outback Queensland are his main interests in life.

Peter Watt can be contacted at www.peterwatt.com

Also by Peter Watt

The Duffy/Macintosh Series
Cry of the Curlew
Shadow of the Osprey
Flight of the Eagle
To Chase the Storm
To Touch the Clouds
To Ride the Wind
Beyond the Horizon

The Papua Series
Papua
Eden
The Pacific

The Silent Frontier
The Stone Dragon
The Frozen Circle

Excerpts from emails sent to Peter Watt

I've just finished *Beyond the Horizon* today and, apart from loving it as much as all of your other books, I can't wait to read the next instalment. Thanks again for the entertainment (and education) your books provide.

Thank you for writing books that make me proud to be Australian.

Just wanted to let you know how much I enjoyed *Beyond the Horizon*. Another fantastic read. Mum has just finished *To Chase the Storm* and Dad is about to start *Flight of the Eagle*. Can't wait til the next book in the series is released.

I've just finished reading *The Silent Frontier* and I must say that it was the best reading book that I've turned the pages of for fifty years. Fascinating and loved the story of the Duffys and Macintoshes. Being a silent warrior myself of the Vietnam War, I appreciate what you have been able to portray; great stuff, great story, good mates and a simple, hard life made difficult.

I try to get to bed by 9 pm but reading your books I find I am still trying to get to the next page or the end of a chapter before putting the book away for the night, and when I look at the clock it is often 11 pm.

Many thanks for another great read. Australia should be proud to have a writer like yourself.

Thank goodness it was too hot to attend to any housework. Once I started *The Pacific* the day just flew by.

Have just finished *Beyond the Horizon*. Brilliant. I tried to stretch it out by reading a little each day, but as usual, that didn't work. Always disappointing when the end is reached . . . My wife had a quick glance at the family tree . . . she was amazed as to how all the characters are carried forward from book to book. I think she was even more amazed that I was able to explain who they were and where they all fitted in to the saga. Keep up the brilliant storytelling.

My congratulations to you on putting together a wonderful story. My father, who served in Gallipoli, and later was promoted to a major, led his battalion at the battle of Mt St Quentin in Aug/Sept 1918. Your mention of this battle brought back stories he used to tell me just before he died . . . Again, thank you. I will now look for more of your work.

I have thoroughly enjoyed every book you have produced. You have an amazing talent with the way you introduce so many characters to your stories and keep every new character as interesting as the last. Keep up the good work as I can't wait to dive into the next masterpiece.

I just wanted to tell you how great your books are. I recently finished *Beyond the Horizon* and *The Pacific*. I took them with me on holidays and thoroughly enjoyed reading them, I got lost in the worlds of the characters . . . Thank you for writing books about our country and our history. Your books are truly wonderful.

Just thought I would drop you a line and say 'well done' on the series, it has really dragged me in. I have only become a regular reader since retiring five years ago . . . Once again, congratulations on the story and as soon as I have completed the saga of the two families, I will then venture into the others stories you have penned but I have to find out what happens to that bastard George Macintosh first.

PETER WATT

WAR CLOUDS GATHER

PAN
Pan Macmillan Australia

First published 2013 in Macmillan by Pan Macmillan Australia Pty Limited
This Pan edition published 2014 by Pan Macmillan Australia Pty Limited
1 Market Street, Sydney

Cataloguing-in-Publication entry is available
from the National Library of Australia
http://catalogue.nla.gov.au

Typeset in 13/16 pt Bembo by Post Pre-press Group
Printed by IVE

For my Aunt Joan Payne at Tweed Heads,
who lived these times.

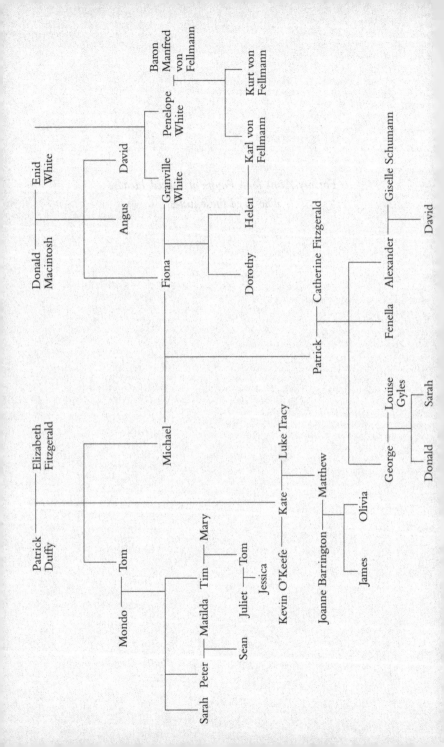

PROLOGUE

Central Queensland, Australia

My name is Wallarie; I am a Nerambura man of the Darambal people, and you stand on the place of my Dreaming, where I lived for almost a hundred of your whitefella years.

I no longer hunt in the brigalow scrub for wallaby and goanna, but I am with the ancestor spirits as a light you whitefellas call a star. Sometimes I return to soar in the blue skies over the sunburned plains as the great wedge-tailed eagle, and I look down upon the people who now walk the red earth of my ancestors.

My blood flows in the mighty warrior, Tom Duffy, and his daughter, Jessica. Sometimes I visit Tom in the dark places of the night when he sleeps and dreams his nightmares of a whitefella war. I am saddened to see my spirit brother toss and turn screaming out the name of dead cobbers in the cold and lonely night.

1

There is another generation of the two families who know nothing of me and the Old Ones. The lands are now silent of the laughter of the people who were my people. They are all gone but the whitefella who are young do not see the storm clouds gather when fire will once again fall on them.

Part One

1936

Resistance

I

Berlin, Germany 1936

The room in the Berlin government building was sombre in the Gothic style popularised by the German leader, Adolf Hitler. But it also reflected a decadent opulence, with its expensive wood panels and plush leather lounges. The mandatory portrait of Hitler had prominent place on the wall, and a clock ticked the seconds away in the silent inner office.

Two men, dressed in their finest Savile Row suits, sat sipping coffee from delicate china cups. Both were in their late middle age but the Australian was the younger of the two. The American was taller and showing the first signs of balding. Despite their different nationalities the two men shared a common link, albeit a distant one, of family.

'Sir George,' the American said, 'I hope you enjoyed the Olympic Games our hosts staged a few weeks ago.'

Sir George Macintosh returned a faint smile. 'I had little

opportunity to attend the Games due to business meetings, but my son and daughter enjoyed them enormously. Our hosts were very generous in looking after them.'

'I must confess that I, too, missed most of the Games as my time was taken up with various German bankers,' James Barrington replied. 'But we are both businessmen and the wheels of enterprise must grind on.'

Sir George Macintosh was about to comment when the door to the office opened and two men entered. Sir George and James Barrington rose respectfully for the President of the Reichsbank, Herr Schacht. His thick hair was greying and he wore pince-nez glasses and a starched white collar. George knew that Schacht controlled the finances of Nazi Germany, despite his well known outbursts against military spending by the Führer and his treatment of the local Jewish population. This was George's second meeting with the powerful German banker. The younger man with Schacht, his translator, had slicked-back blond hair and wore a pin in the lapel of his suit, proclaiming his membership of the Nazi Party.

'It is good to meet you again, Herr Schacht,' George greeted in German, a language he spoke because of his family's Prussian relatives. 'May I introduce my American friend, Mr James Barrington.' Sir George tried not to sound smug but he knew that he had just one-upped his American colleague with his knowledge of the language.

Schacht held out his hand to Barrington and the young translator turned to George. 'I did not know that you spoke our language,' he said, and George sensed a certain arrogance in his tone.

'I have relatives in this country,' George replied. 'You may know of them, the von Fellmanns, formerly of Danzig.'

'Ahh, General Kurt von Fellmann,' the translator

answered, some of his arrogance disappearing. 'A fine man, and leading member of our military. You have an esteemed relative, favoured by our Führer.'

'I didn't know you spoke German,' James said, looking at George with open curiosity.

'Given we have close connections through our two families, old chap, I thought you would have known that about me,' George said, referring to the fact that a distant cousin, Captain Matthew Duffy, was the father of James Barrington's grandchildren. The twins, James Jnr and Olivia, now nineteen years of age, had grown up with all that money could buy: luxurious homes, the best education, the finest of friends from other influential families. James Barrington had wisely seen the stock market crash coming and had been able to divest his fortune into enterprises that survived the disastrous economic tsunami that had left millions of people destitute. With the trip to Berlin for the Olympic Games, James Barrington intended to show his beloved grandchildren how the hard work of the German people, under their new leader, had dragged the nation out of a shattered postwar economy. James Barrington Snr was an ardent admirer of the new German leader for the ruthless way he had put Germany back on the world map, and the American was one of the first to invest in the Third Reich.

'Gentlemen,' Herr Schacht said, gesturing to the leather couches, 'please take a seat. We have much to discuss and I must apologise that I do not have a lot of time.' The translator interpreted for the American's sake.

'Sir George,' Schacht said, taking a seat behind his desk and adjusting his pince-nez, 'I have been informed that you have a record with the German people for your financial support during the war. I also know that your support would have proved very dangerous to you had it come to light in your own country. Our own great leader once faced your soldiers on the Western Front and was lucky to survive. I feel that our Führer has always been destined to rule our people and that fate spared him that terrible war.'

George had lost a father and brother on the fields of northern France and was aware that his investment in wartime Germany might have helped fill the exploding shells with chemicals. But the deaths of his father and brother had proved fruitful to George, allowing him to take control of the family estates.

'I am a businessman,' George replied in German. 'War is of little concern to me in such matters.'

'Fortunately the Führer is a peace-loving man who does not wish to ever see war again, and your shares in our chemical industry will be richly rewarded,' Schacht replied. 'You invested wisely.'

'Thank you, Herr Schacht,' George replied. 'The German people have a friend in my family company.' As George glanced across at James Barrington he noticed that the American was shifting impatiently on the lounge. 'I am sure that my American friend has much to raise with you, and I would hope for a future meeting in private.'

'Certainly, Sir George,' Schacht replied, 'I believe that Donald and Sarah are currently in the company of Mr Barrington's grandchildren, taking in the hospitality of our country.'

George looked at his host in surprise, although he should have guessed that German officials would have him and his family under observation while they stayed in Berlin. It was to be expected in a nation so strictly controlled by the new regime of the Nazi Party.

'Well, I will excuse myself and make an appointment with your secretary,' George said, rising from his chair.

'Herr Schacht says he will speak with you now, old chap, I hope you have fruitful outcome to your discussions with him. I will see you tonight at dinner in the hotel.'

Barrington nodded and turned to Schacht as George took his hat from the stand by the door and left the room.

★

The café garden overlooking the river was the perfect venue to laze away the afternoon after a day of sightseeing around Berlin. Numerous red flags with white circles enclosing a black swastika fluttered gently on the autumn breeze. The specialty of the house was Bavarian cuisine and the proprietor wore the traditional Bavarian dress of leather knicker-bockers and braces. A portly man in leather shorts stood behind the counter while his pretty blonde daughter – her hair in long plaits – served customers at tables located on the green lawn, bordered by tiers of colourful flowers.

James and Olivia Barrington shared the table with Donald Macintosh and his younger sister Sarah. The four of them had met during the Olympic Games and had been inseparable ever since. It had been a fun-filled day, taking in the sights and shopping in the commercial centre of Berlin, which was much quieter now that the Olympic crowds had departed.

James Barrington Jnr was of medium build with a fair complexion and looks that made him attractive to the young women he met. He was also athletic and intelligent. His twin sister Olivia was striking with long red hair, and pretty features spattered with a trace of freckles.

At twenty, Donald Macintosh was the eldest of the four. He was the tallest, too, and had a slim build. He was also dashingly handsome, which had turned many a young Fräulein's head in the past few weeks.

His sister Sarah was the youngest but already had the promise of her mother's beauty, as they sat, sipping their tea.

They were not alone in the garden as a few tables away a tall, well-built young man wearing a pair of slacks and an open-neck shirt sat drinking coffee and reading a German newspaper. He paid no attention to the little party, despite their laughter and high spirits. Sarah found herself staring at the young man sitting alone. He was not handsome in the classical sense and he had the look of a man used to hard manual labour, but his face was pleasant, despite his crooked nose and slight scar above his right eye. He had thick wavy brown hair and his skin was tanned, which Sarah thought unusual as summer was disappearing from the northern hemisphere.

'I say, old man,' Donald said. 'I think you and I should head off tonight to have a look at Berlin by neon light.' His sly smile was quickly interpreted by James, who looked away uneasily. He knew that his Australian friend was hinting that they should seek out the red-light district and this was something his strict puritan religious teachings told him was wrong.

'I think that would be a grand idea,' Olivia Barrington cut across with a wicked grin. 'Can I come with you?'

Donald scowled; he was about to dismiss the idea when the café garden was suddenly filled with a crowd of drunk brown-shirted men spilling in from the street. They slumped in chairs at the tables surrounding the four tourists and shouted orders at the Bavarian proprietor. The Barringtons and Macintoshes had started to notice these brown-shirted men more and more often in the streets once the Games had finished and the visitors had begun to leave.

One of the brownshirts stood up and raised a mug of beer he had brought with him into the café. He rambled on in a loud voice and finished with the salutation, 'Heil Hitler.' All of the troopers rose and thrust out their arms in the stiff military salute of the Nazi Party. Only the Barringtons and Macintoshes remained seated, as well as the giant sitting at his table, reading the newspaper.

The drunken man in his early twenties who had initiated the toast turned to the table of four, and shouted something, spittle flying in the air. Sarah and Donald paled and turned to the others to translate the German into English.

'We must go,' Donald muttered to his American companions, but James resisted.

'We are guests in this country and have a right to remain here,' James said.

Donald looked desperately at his American friend. 'They are drunk and want to know why we did not stand when they toasted Adolf Hitler.'

'That is because he is not *our* leader,' Olivia offered bluntly.

Just as she made her statement the German SA trooper with the beer mug pulled away from his comrades and lurched over to the table, eyes staring with fanatic anger. Donald immediately attempted to pacify the drunken soldier, explaining that they were visitors to the country and did not know all the customs. This only seemed to make the man angrier and suddenly he tipped the contents of his beer mug over Olivia's head, drenching her. His gesture was met by a chorus of jeers from his companions.

Olivia sat in shock, her face slowly reddening.

James rose from his seat. 'I say, that was not called for,' he said with as much bravado he could muster. 'I shall report this matter to your authorities. My father is a respected guest of your government.'

The German SA party clearly did not understand English and this protest fell on deaf ears.

'Leave them alone,' said a deep voice in German, and the large man with the crooked nose strode towards them, a dangerous determination glinting in his grey eyes. He was beside the table in a heartbeat, face to face with the drunken brownshirt.

'You should go and leave these people in peace,' the big man said.

'Or what, Englisher?' the brownshirt asked with a sneer, obviously detecting that the man had an accent.

'I'm not an Englishman,' the man snarled. 'I'm a bloody Australian – so shove off.'

As he spoke, the Australian was aware that the largest member of the SA party had risen from his table and was walking over. He was the Australian's size and build, and by his confident expression he clearly thought he would soon frighten off this intruder to their drunken fun. He had a scarred face that spoke of street brawling.

'Australia is nothing,' the big German said. 'You won only one Olympic medal, a bronze in the triple jump.'

The Australian shifted the weight on his feet. 'We would have won a medal in the heavyweight boxing if I'd been able to register early enough,' he said, keeping his eyes on the threatening German. There was a hush in the garden now.

'Ha! You think you could have beaten our champion?' the scarred man said with a laugh, spitting on the ground to emphasise his disdain. He took a step towards the young Australian.

Three bone-breaking blows caught the German completely by surprise, and he wobbled on his feet before collapsing on the grass with a moan.

The Australian rubbed his knuckles and hoped that he had not broken any bones. 'If you have any more punching bags for me this afternoon, I would like to keep going,' he said in his accented German, but the stunned looks of the remaining SA men told him that they would not challenge him.

Sarah could feel her heart pounding. She had never seen such violence before. When she looked up at the Australian he was looking directly at her, and his eyes were now gentle. A smoky-grey colour with flecks of gold.

'I think you should leave,' he said. 'The coppers will arrive soon and I have some explaining to do. You don't want to get caught up in all that.'

'Thank you,' James said, extending his hand in gratitude. 'We were a little outnumbered. I gather from your accent that you are an Aussie like my friends here.'

'You don't have to thank me,' he replied. 'I don't like these bastards and was itching to have a go. And yes, I am an Aussie.'

He smiled grimly as the brownshirts dragged their felled champion away to their table and slapped his face to awaken him.

'You will pay for this, Englisher,' one of them shouted from a safe distance.

'What is your name?' Sarah asked, rising from her chair. 'We must thank you in some way.'

'I'm—'

'You!'

All attention was focused on two German police officers who had entered the garden and were shouting at the Australian. 'Stand where you are,' one of the police officers commanded. 'You are under arrest.'

The mysterious Australian shrugged and turned back to Sarah. 'Time you all got out of here before they turn their attention to you.' He felt the hand of one of the police officers on his shoulder and did not resist.

'We will come with you to the police station,' one of the SA men said to the arresting officers. 'We will need to give a statement concerning the unprovoked attack on our comrade. Heil Hitler.'

The Australian looked over at the Bavarian proprietor who was wringing his hands. The man must have contacted the police, worried there would be a full-on brawl in his restaurant. His pretty daughter gave the Australian a look of frank admiration and he winked at her, causing her to break into a shy smile.

★

On the pavement outside the café James turned to Donald. 'That was one helluva guy,' he said. 'Bad luck for him that those brownshirts are going to the police station with him. I think we should find out where they're taking him, and try to help.'

'The Germans are civilised people and with a reliable legal system,' Donald replied. 'Besides, I doubt that they would dare cause any harm to a visitor. Not good for tourism if they did.'

'I'm going to inform Father,' Sarah said. 'He will be able to help the young man.'

'I don't think that is necessary,' Donald said. 'He looks like he can handle himself.'

'Does it shame you that you were unable to defend us?' Sarah countered quietly. 'Is that why you do not wish to mention the incident to Father?'

His sister's words stung with truth. Donald's face reddened. He had never felt as helpless as he had in the café garden, facing brute violence beyond the reaches of all his family's wealth and influence. He had been terrified, but fear was not something his father would tolerate. 'I think that the matter is over and we should put it behind us,' he answered feebly and saw the look of disgust on Sarah's face. They walked in silence back to the hotel.

*

The young Australian experienced fear as he felt the first blow jar his head. His hands were tied behind his back and the rickety chair he was pinioned to almost collapsed. The blow hurt; it had come from the big SA man he had felled in the café garden.

Behind the SA thug stood the two arresting officers, and they both looked nervous and frightened.

'We rule here, Englisher,' the SA thug said, stepping back to deliver another punch. Blood dripped from the Australian's split lip onto his white shirt. 'You need to learn respect for our Führer.'

The helpless prisoner's obscene reply brought another smashing blow to his head, making him wish he had kept silent. He was afraid now that this man might beat him half to death before the police officers stopped him.

'Leave him alone,' an authoritative voice called into the room. The Australian lifted his head to see a German Luftwaffe officer standing in the doorway. Through swelling eyes he could see the pilot wings on his chest. Behind the German pilot a familiar figure leaned on a cane, a cigar clamped between his teeth.

'Young David Macintosh,' Sean Duffy said in an almost tired voice. 'I wonder why I ever let you come to Germany with me.'

David spat out a mouthful of blood and grinned at the Sydney solicitor. 'Ah, Uncle Sean, it is good to see you,' he said. 'Who's the flyboy?'

'I am *Hauptmann* Fritz Lang,' the German officer replied

in English. David knew that he was the equivalent rank of an air force flight lieutenant in Australia. 'Herr Duffy has called on me to free you from custody.'

'How did you know I was here?' David asked. He glanced over at the SA man who had been beating him, who stood aside with a surly and resentful look on his face.

'Captain Lang,' Sean replied, using the English army equivalent of the German aviator's rank, 'has friends in many places and was quick to inform me of your predicament. You have him to thank for the fact that I was able to muster the legal resources to free you so quickly.'

'I didn't start this one,' David said as one of the German police officers stepped forward and untied his hands from behind his back. 'I was just minding my own business.'

Sean raised his eyebrows, then took the cigar from his mouth and rolled it between his fingers. 'Captain Lang, could you please thank the police for their hospitality towards Mr Macintosh, and let them know that we will not be reporting this incident to any higher authority.'

As Fritz translated, an expression of gratitude appeared on the officers' faces. They were men used to enforcing the law, but many police officers resented the growing power the SA had over them. Only the even more feared SS now kept the SA's power in check.

When David was on his feet he rubbed his wrists and turned to the SA man who had delivered his savage beating. 'You and I might just meet one dark night down an alley, and if that happens only I will be walking out of it,' he said in German.

The SA man glared back at David. 'I will be waiting, Englisher,' he replied.

'Calling me an Englishman is enough to get you killed,'

David countered, and followed Sean and *Hauptmann* Lang out of the dank interrogation room.

*

The three men stepped out onto the footpath. Darkness was already falling. The multitude of red, white and black flags lay against their flag poles. Fritz excused himself and left, shaking hands with both Sean and David first.

'Uncle Sean,' David said painfully through his split lips. 'How in hell did you get hold of a German officer?'

Sean limped beside David and they slowly made their way down the street. 'It's a long story that has its roots back in Palestine with your father's cousin, Captain Matthew Duffy, during the war. After the war, Matthew asked me to track down the family of a German fighter pilot he had sat with as he died. I was able to use this visit to track down the pilot's widow, and son, and to pass on a letter Matthew had written to them. The pilot's son is, of course, Fritz.'

'What happened all those years ago?' David asked. His own father had been killed in action on the Western Front, which was where Sean had lost both his legs, and his mother had died in the terrible flu epidemic of 1919. David had been raised in New Guinea by his maternal grandmother, Karolina Schumann, on a family copra plantation, but had been schooled in Australia and looked after by the family solicitor, Sean Duffy, who had no wife or children of his own. Sean had become like a father to David.

'It seems that when Matthew was shot down he stumbled on a Hun pilot who had also been shot down, but was dying from his wounds. Matthew stayed with him, and in the pilot's dying moments promised to contact his family for him. I have kept that promise for Matthew. Hence, we have at least one good friend in this country, although I do not know Fritz's attitude to Jews.'

David flinched. His mother was Jewish, which meant he was technically Jewish too. His grandmother had not raised him strictly in accordance with the Jewish faith. But David had been circumcised and he had, out of curiosity, read the Torah. He knew that it did not pay to advertise this aspect of his life in Hitler's Germany, despite the fact that he had barely stepped inside a synagogue. He was a young man who preferred the pleasures of life to thinking about the restrictions of religion.

The two men walked side by side into the dark, unaware that the simple incident in the café would change the course of both of their lives forever.

2

As Captain Matthew Duffy brought the Ford trimotor to land on the airfield at Basra, he thanked the heavens that the summer heat was losing its intensity with the advent of autumn. When the doors to his three-engined, metal-skinned American cargo aircraft were opened he would not be assailed by the oven-like heat he'd endured for what seemed like months.

Beside him in the cockpit sat his copilot, a New Zealander in his twenties, Tyrone McKee. Whenever Matthew looked at the much younger man he was reminded of how many years had passed in his own life. He had reached half a century but had retained his youthful looks. He still had a thick crop of hair greying at the edges and he remained physically fit. He was not handsome but had a strong, masculine face. Matthew had run away when he was underage to fight against the Boers in Africa as an infantryman with the

New South Wales regiment. He had flown as an army pilot in the Great War in the skies over Palestine. After the war and the loss of the woman he loved, Matthew had remained in the Middle East to form a flying company carrying cargo and passengers for the ever-expanding British oil industry.

'Cut the engines,' Matthew said to his copilot, and the rugged aeroplane trundled to a stop outside a huge hangar. 'Time for a cuppa.'

The two men left the cockpit to climb out through the side door and were met by Matthew's chief engineer, Cyril Blacksmith. Cyril was in his forties and balding, but had the tough look of a street fighter. The Canadian was the only original member left of the airline company Matthew had founded in 1919. Over the years, the others had drifted away to jobs where the heat and flies were less of a problem. The Great Depression had hit the company hard, forcing Matthew to sell off all his aircraft except the Ford.

'Good flight, Skipper?' Cyril asked as he quickly surveyed the outer skin of the aeroplane for any sign of damage. Later, he would go over the engines to ensure they were in top condition.

'Yeah,' Matthew replied. 'Young Ty did most of the flying this time. We delivered the parts to the oil people on time.'

The three men walked towards the hangar and Matthew noticed another trimotor aircraft parked on the airstrip. It was a German Junkers and Matthew felt a pang of envy for the newer, stronger German version of his own aircraft. 'Whose plane?' he asked Cyril.

'You got a visitor,' Cyril growled. 'She's someone we used to know.'

Matthew's eyebrows raised in surprise. The pilot of the Junkers was a woman, and the only woman Matthew knew with flying credentials was the one he had trained many years before. Diane Hatfield had answered his advertisement in an English newspaper to join his company in Iraq. He had been struck by her determination and her youthful beauty when he interviewed her, and she had convinced him to teach her to fly. Diane had proved a born flyer and it had not been long before she earned her commercial pilot's licence. Almost immediately she had left to fly in America on a lucrative contract.

'Diane?' he asked, although he knew it had to be her and wondered why she should suddenly appear after all the years since she had left the service of his company.

Cyril grunted an affirmative as the three men reached the hangar where Matthew had his office. They had hardly entered the cavernous structure when a woman wearing riding jodhpurs and a clean white silk shirt appeared with an uncertain smile on her face. Immediately, Matthew was struck afresh by the woman's beauty, despite the years that had passed since he'd last seen her.

'Hello, Matthew.' Matthew accepted Diane's extended hand and felt its smooth warmth. 'It's been a long time.'

'It has been a long time. Are you still flying for the Yanks you left us for?'

Diane flinched. 'I am sorry for leaving you stranded,' she replied with seemingly genuine remorse. 'I know my departure must have lost you work.'

Matthew was still angry but could see she was attempting to reconcile. It made him suspicious. 'Why are you here?' he asked. 'You're a long way from your luxurious stopovers in Hollywood.'

'Sounds like you've been keeping tabs on me,' Diane flared.

'Your name occasionally crops up in the papers in connection to your boss, who I gather is a well-known criminal of

Sicilian heritage,' Matthew retorted. 'I'm surprised to see you turn up in this godforsaken part of the world.'

'I quit my job flying for the Sicilian,' Diane said.

'Just like old times,' Cyril said, bringing two big mugs of hot tea over to them.

'Thanks, Cyril,' Matthew said and ushered Diane into his office. He placed the mug on his untidy desk, mostly cluttered with angry demands from creditors.

Diane glanced around the office. 'Nothing much has changed,' she commented, taking a sip from the mug. 'And Cyril even remembers how I like my tea – strong and sweet.'

Matthew stared at the young woman; he could see a weariness etched in her face. 'What happened?' he asked quietly and saw a fleeting expression of pain.

'I have flown here from Germany to make you a business proposal,' Diane said, deflecting Matthew's question. 'I have a contract with the German government to fly out a team of their scientists – archaeologists. It seems their boss, Himmler, has a fascination for ancient artefacts. I told them I had the contacts in this part of the world to pull off the deal.'

'You meant me,' Matthew said with a slight frown.

'I know it's presumptuous but I was desperate for a job and the Germans gave me that beautiful aeroplane to fly. You would have done the same if you'd been in my shoes.'

'What do you need from me?' Matthew asked, leaning back in his chair with his hands clasped behind his head. He wasn't agreeing but this deal might help his own company get out of financial trouble.

'I need the use of your facilities,' Diane said. 'I need the services of Cyril and your pilot, McKee, whom Cyril told me is an excellent flyer.'

'What do I get in return?' Matthew countered.

'The Germans are generous in their budget,' Diane glanced down at the scattered bills. 'I could clear all your debts and promise ten per cent on top for all services your company provides.'

'If I don't agree?' Matthew asked.

'I have nowhere else to go. I'm begging you,' Diane replied quietly, a tear welling in the corner of her eye.

'Fifteen per cent on top and we have a deal,' he said, extending his hand.

'Fifteen per cent it is,' Diane agreed, taking his hand.

'You can start our mutual enterprise by letting me take your kite up for a spin,' Matthew said, standing up. 'I've been wanting to upgrade the old Ford to one of those German machines.'

'I don't suppose you still have that lovely little house in Basra – the one with the pretty garden?'

'Couldn't afford anything else,' Matthew answered. 'You're welcome to stay there.'

'Thank you, Matthew,' Diane said, stepping forward and kissing him on the cheek. 'You are one of the last, true gentlemen.'

'Cyril,' he called loudly down the hangar. 'Get Miss Hatfield's gear from her kite and throw it in the car.'

Cyril glared down the hangar at the young English-woman and his boss standing side by side in front of the office. 'Goddamned women,' he muttered as he went off to obey.

*

The lighting in the grand dining room of the Berlin Hotel was subdued. The tables were filled with Germany's aristoc-racy, as well as a smattering of high-ranking SS officers and their partners. A string quartet played in the background while the diners enjoyed the very expensive meals placed in front of them.

James Barrington Snr sat at one table with his grandchildren. They were accompanied by George Macintosh and his son and daughter. 'I hope that your talk with Herr Schacht proved fruitful,' George said across the table as he raised a spoon of truffle soup to his lips.

'I should thank you for the introduction,' James Barrington Snr replied before sipping the tasty soup. 'You appear to have good relations with our hosts.'

George did not reply. During the Great War he had invested in German industries making chemicals for their weapons. Such a revelation could have brought him a charge of treason, but he had managed to stay one step ahead of suspicion. At least now he could be more open. Herr Hitler had much support from influential people, ranging from the English royals to the brash industrial moguls of the United States who admired the former Austrian army corporal for mobilising a nation out of the crippling world economic depression.

'Did you get the opportunity to view one of the televisions broadcasting the Games?' George said, changing the subject. 'A great achievement.'

'The Brits are working on a better system,' James Snr countered. 'I think it is an industry with potential. It could be worth investing in.'

'I agree,' George said, noticing then that the four young people remained silent at the table. 'Has the cat got your tongues?' he asked, looking at his son, Donald.

'Something horrible happened today,' Sarah blurted and received a withering look from her brother.

'What?' George asked, using the tip of his linen napkin to wipe soup from the corner of his mouth.

'Nothing, Father,' Donald answered, attempting to kick his sister's foot under the table.

'I doubt that it was nothing. I can see that your sister is upset.'

'We were having coffee in a splendid café not far from here,' Sarah said, undeterred by her brother's attempt to silence her. 'Some horrible men wearing brown uniforms spilled beer all over Olivia, and they might have assaulted us, except a wonderful young man from Australia stepped in and gave one of the bullies a thrashing and then they were too frightened to touch us.'

'Did he give his name?' asked James Barrington Snr.

'No,' Sarah answered. 'But he spoke German, and I heard him tell the ruffian that he was a boxer. The police came and took him away for no reason.'

'I think we should find him and thank him,' James Barrington Jnr said. 'Make sure he hasn't been arrested for helping us.'

'You said that the hooligans pestering you today wore a brown uniform?' George questioned. 'At least they did not have black uniforms or it may have been a lot more serious. The brownshirts have lost most of their influence since the death of their leader, Ernst Rohm. Had they worn black then it might have been the SS, and they are a damned dangerous bunch. I will make inquiries with a few friends to track down your gallant white knight.'

'Thank you, Father,' Sarah said with the brightest of smiles.

They finished their meals and the young people withdrew to a comfortable lounge, away from the boring business talk of their elders.

'I think my little sister has a crush on the man who helped us,' Donald said teasingly as they sat down on the plush, velvet lounges. 'Why would you say that?' Sarah said with a scowl. 'I hardly noticed him.'

'Is that why you told me our hero had gentle eyes?' Olivia added with a mischievous smile. 'You are only a child and should not notice such things.'

Sarah turned on Olivia. 'I told you that in confidence. Besides, you said you thought the young man was rather dashing in a brutish way.'

'Oh, ladies,' Donald said. 'How could you find anything handsome about that chap? He's probably descended from convicts, and most likely a member of one of those Sydney criminal gangs.'

'Well, he saved us from a sticky situation,' James Jnr said. 'He has my vote of thanks. Do you think that your father will be able to track him down?'

'I am sure it will not be hard to find a six-foot-something Aussie boxer who speaks German and is attractive to our respective sisters,' Donald chuckled. 'When my father finds him I bet he gives him a suitable reward.'

★

George Macintosh was a man of his word. After discreet questions of his influential German hosts, he found himself in a German police station speaking with the officer in charge – a burly man with a sweeping moustache.

'Ah, yes,' the policeman said, thumbing through a record book of arrests. 'I remember the man. The SA attempted to lay a charge of assault against him but a Luftwaffe officer interceded to have the charge withdrawn.'

George was intrigued. Whoever had been the saviour of his children was an interesting person if he wielded power through the German armed forces. 'Who was the air force officer?' George asked.

The burly policeman scratched his bald head as he flipped to another page. 'Flight Lieutenant Fritz Lang,' he replied. The name did not register with George.

'Who was the Australian man you had in custody?' he asked.

'A Mr David Macintosh. Residential address: Lae in New Guinea.'

For a shocked moment George thought he might have to sit down. There could only be one David Macintosh fitting those particulars. Over the years he had almost forgotten about his nephew, whom he'd last heard was living on a copra plantation belonging to his German grandmother, Karolina Schumann.

'That man is a dangerous Jew,' George said quietly and the policeman looked at him questioningly.

'He said that he was an Australian who had come to visit the games in Berlin,' the German said with a frown.

'I know this man,' George replied angrily. 'He is not only a Jew but also a communist agitator. I think it was a mistake that you let him go and I will be informing my friends in the government of your decision.'

George could see the big policeman suddenly turn pale and start to sweat. 'We will pick him up immediately,' he replied in a shaky voice. 'But it will not be easy as he seems to have friends in the Luftwaffe and his release was signed for by an Australian lawyer, a Mr Sean Duffy.'

At the mention of the man who had once been his wife Louise's lover, it was George's turn to pale. David was the only real obstacle to his complete control of the Macintosh empire, but getting him out of the way would not be easy while Sean Duffy was protecting him. When he turned twenty-one years of age David would inherit a sizeable chunk of the family fortune. *How old was he now?* George thought in desperation. Nineteen, twenty? No, he would be closer to twenty. And the perfect opportunity to do his nephew serious harm was at his fingertips. David was in a country where both Jews and communists were hunted down and sent to concentration camps.

'Do not be concerned about Mr Duffy,' George finally said when he had collected his thoughts. 'You have a duty to arrest the Jew, David Macintosh.'

'It will be done, Sir George,' the policeman said. 'We know where he is staying in Berlin.'

George returned to the limousine that had been provided for him by his German hosts. He was smiling grimly to himself as the vehicle pulled into the traffic. Already he was formulating a lie for his children about their mysterious saviour. Lying came easily to Sir George Macintosh.

★

'The good news is that I found your white knight,' George said to his daughter and son in their suite of rooms at the hotel. 'But the bad news is that he has already departed the country and did not leave a forwarding address.'

George noted the disappointed look on Sarah's face but the expression of relief on his son's.

'What is his name?' Sarah asked. 'It may be possible to locate him when we return to Sydney.'

'I am afraid it has been ascertained by the German police that he gave a false name when they arrested him. No one knows who he is.'

'That is a shame,' Sarah sighed. 'I so wanted to express my personal thanks to him.'

George inwardly squirmed at the thought of such an event occurring. David was, after all, Sarah's first cousin whom she had never been told existed. Never mind, George told himself, David Macintosh would soon cease to exist anyway. There was a special place he had heard about – Dachau. It was said to be a place of re-education, but many never returned from the concentration camp set up by the Führer in the first years of his dictatorship to house those he considered enemies of fascism. Germans were reluctant to talk about the establishment but George had no doubt that David would find himself behind the barbed-wire fences of the camp within days, never to be heard of again.

*

David strapped down his suitcase and glanced around the hotel room, making sure he had not forgotten any of his personal items. The door opened and Sean Duffy appeared.

'Ready to leave, old chap?' Sean asked and David replied that he was.

'You can wander downstairs and ensure that our taxi is ready,' Sean said. 'My legs are a bit wobbly this morning.'

'Not surprised, Uncle Sean,' David grinned. 'You certainly put away a bit of grog last night.'

'Ah, yes,' Sean sighed. 'I bumped into a couple of old German soldiers who spoke English – of a kind; turned out they had fought at Fromelles, just like I did. Strange how old enemies can seem like friends after all these years.'

Satisfied that everything was packed, David walked down the stairs of the modest hotel. The hoteliers had proved warm and friendly but David was looking forward to moving on to London where Sean had legal business on behalf of a client.

David bid good morning to the middle-aged hotelier's wife standing behind the reception counter and stepped out onto the street to see if the taxi was waiting to take them to the railway station.

He glanced up and down the busy road and his eyes

immediately fell on a dark car directly in front of the glass doors of the hotel. Suddenly he was aware that two men in long black leather overcoats and dark hats were behind him as a hand gripped his elbow.

'Mr David Macintosh,' a voice growled in German. 'Based on Article One of the Decree of the Reich President for the Protection of the People and State of 28 February 1933, you are taken into protective custody in the interest of public security and order. Reason: suspicion of activities inimical to the state.'

The way the man droned the statement made David think he had said the words many times before. The young Australian experienced a cold chill of fear. He knew he was in the hands of the dreaded SS. A truck pulled up then and brown-shirted men spilled out onto the street.

'I am an Australian citizen,' he exclaimed. 'You do not have the right to arrest me.'

David had hardly finished his protest when he felt himself propelled towards the dark sedan's open back door where another black-coated man sat. The brown-shirted SA men had formed a semicircle around him to back up their SS comrades. Escaping would be impossible.

David was jammed in between two SS men and the car sped away.

*

Sean waited for some minutes, annoyed that David had not returned. With a sigh he hobbled down the stairs, cursing his hangover. When he reached the small reception area he saw the hotelier's wife and immediately recognised the frightened expression on her face.

'What is it, Mrs Gottfried?' Sean asked in his limited German.

For a moment she could not answer; finally, with tears in her eyes, she said, 'The SS have arrested Mr Macintosh and taken him away.'

Sean stood staring out of the glass doors onto the street in a state of confusion. Why in hell had the SS arrested David? As a criminal lawyer he knew the Third Reich had little regard for democratic laws and he felt a terrible fear for David's life. Hadn't Karolina objected to her beloved grandson visiting Germany, and hadn't Sean given his word that David would be safe in his care? Confused and frightened, Sean tottered uncertainly on his tin legs, a legacy from a war that had destroyed a generation of his friends. Even now war clouds were gathering again, just as Winston Churchill had warned, and Sean was very afraid that the coming storm would claim the young man he loved as his own son.

3

*W*ork *Sets You Free*. David read the metal sign as the truck packed with silent men drove under the archway. The order to dismount from the truck was shouted by an officer of the SS and the men tumbled from the back to be shoved and prodded into ranks. A few former soldiers among the prisoners fell in and David thought it wise to follow their example. They stood silently while the SS officer, a man in his thirties wearing an immaculate black uniform, highly polished knee-length boots and a gleaming diagonal belt across his chest, strode up to face the prisoners.

'You are men whom the state has identified as filth,' he bellowed, hands on his hips. 'The rules here are simple. Our motto is that there is one way to freedom. Its milestones are obedience, zeal, honesty, order, cleanliness, temperance, truth, sense of sacrifice and love for the Fatherland. Our commandant, Herr Eicke, has had those very words painted in large letters on the roof of one of the buildings. We will re-educate you to take your place back in society. I warn you now that you will be hung if you politicise, give speeches or hold meetings, form cliques, loiter around with others for the purpose of supplying the propaganda machine of the opposition with atrocity stories, collect information about the camp, talk to others about it or smuggle information out into the hands of foreign visitors. You will be shot attempting to escape or disobeying any order given by a guard. That is all you have to know for now.'

David listened in despair and growing fear, finally realising that he was alone and far from the safety of home. 'Where are we?' he whispered to the man beside him.

'Dachau, you fool,' the man answered from the corner of his mouth.

The next few hours were a nightmare as the latest arrivals were processed. David was stripped naked, showered with cold water from hoses, thrown a used uniform of striped pants, a jacket and a dirty white shirt that had a hole with dark staining around it in the back. Next, his head was shaved and he was ordered to a building on the other side of the square to be interrogated.

He was forced to stand to attention in another gloomy room where he was asked his name. When he attempted to protest his detention, he felt the stinging blow of a whip across his back. David desisted and fell into line with the questioning. At the end of the brief interview he was handed a red tag indicating his status as a communist.

Eventually he was marched to a wooden barracks where he was allocated a room. Each hut was divided into five rooms, each containing two rows of bunks stacked three high that could house fifty-four prisoners. David glanced around at the other men in his living area and noticed a smattering of green labels. He knew from the processing interview that the green labels were for those prisoners convicted of criminal acts by the courts.

David stood with fifty other prisoners outside the long barracks. A prisoner wearing a green tag appeared in front of them. He was as big as David and had a vicious look about him. 'My name is not important to you swine,' he said in a loud voice. 'All you have to know is that I have been appointed the sergeant prisoner in charge of discipline for this hut. Your lives are in my hands, but know this: I don't care if you live or die. But if you put my job in danger I will personally deal with you as the filth that you are.'

The prisoner sergeant stepped forward and strode down the line of men before him, stopping occasionally as if he were a high-ranking officer inspecting a parade of soldiers. David was in the first rank and from the corner of his eye he could see the big man approaching. When he came to David he stopped and stared at him.

'What is your name, swine?' he asked.

'David Macintosh,' David replied, looking the man in the eye and hoping that he was not being disrespectful.

'You speak like a foreigner,' the sergeant prisoner said in an icy voice. 'Are you a foreign spy?'

'No,' David replied and felt a hard object slam into his solar plexus, forcing the air from his lungs. As he slowly sank to his knees, he felt a crack across the back of his skull, causing a red haze to swim before his eyes.

'Our Führer has no time for you red filth,' the prisoner sergeant said, stepping back and revealing the small hardwood club he had taken from the waistline of his trousers. 'This man will learn that communism is the scourge of the German people and must be wiped out along with Jews, gypsies, homosexuals and anyone else who threatens our great country. Heil Hitler!'

David fought to gain his breath as he knelt on the ground. His size had obviously made him a target and he had been singled out as an example to the other men that they would be foolish to even think about resisting their guards.

'Get up, prisoner filth,' the prisoner sergeant roared and David struggled to his feet to take his place in the front rank. No one dared move to help the young Australian.

They were marched into the hut where David was allocated a bottom bunk and for the first time since he had arrived he found himself alone with his fellow prisoners. A boy no older than sixteen climbed to the uppermost bunk above David, sobbing and whimpering for his mother.

'Shut up, kid,' someone yelled. The boy stopped calling for his mother, but continued to sob quietly.

It was now that a deep despair really gripped David as the stench of unwashed bodies, vomit and even decomposition assailed him. He shivered with the memory of gaunt-faced men with sunken eye sockets, their dirty uniforms hanging from skinny frames. They had obviously been in the camp long enough to be half starved to death. They said nothing at the sight of the new prisoners, but quietly shuffled away to their own bunks.

David could see that there was no mattress or blankets on the wooden slats that made up his bunk, but he was grateful to be away from the constant shouted commands of the brown- and black-shirted guards. He slumped onto his back and lay miserably staring at the slats of the bunk above him.

'Are you a foreigner?' a voice from above asked in German. David quickly snapped out of his self-pity.

'I am an Australian,' he replied and saw the head of the questioner lean over the edge of the bunk. It was the face of a kind looking man in his thirties. He wore spectacles and had a round face.

'My name is Günter Schmidt,' he said without offering his hand. 'I was a schoolteacher before I came here. I saw you were also in our truck. What has brought you to our wonderful country? Do you have a name?'

'David Macintosh,' David replied. 'I came here to see the Olympic Games and then have a look around. My mother was born in Germany and I hoped to find some of her relatives. Why are you here?'

'I questioned some of Herr Hitler's policies to my senior class and one of my students from the Hitler Youth reported me to the SS,' Günter replied. 'That is all it takes and they have given me a red label like you. I am not a communist but that does not matter to the government.'

'Silence,' the voice of the sergeant prisoner roared down the hallway. Both men obeyed. A long night passed but David did not sleep. They had not been fed. The dark hours were broken by the sobbing of the young man in the top bunk and by the itching from lice infesting the barracks.

'Appelle!' Rollcall was shouted down the barracks just as David fell into a semi-sleep. It was still pitch-black and the crashing of boots could be heard everywhere as guards fell upon the barracks.

David rolled from his bunk and onto his feet. Günter Schmidt fell in beside David and they both looked to the top bunk because the young boy had not joined them. It was then that David noticed the dark, slick liquid dripping down the side of the wooden slatted bed to the floor. He hoisted himself up to look into the top bunk and saw the boy lying on his back, eyes open and staring blindly at the dirty ceiling. His arm was extended and lay in a pool of congealing blood. Beside him was a slither of glass and David could see that the boy had slit his wrist.

Shaken, David stumbled back to the floor. 'He killed himself,' he said in a dull voice, and the former school-teacher crossed himself with a muttered prayer. They fell out onto the parade ground in front of the barracks. The order was to stand to attention, so they waited for a good half-hour in the cool early morning gloom. When a man fell from the ranks a brown-shirted guard stepped forward to deliver a terrible beating. Others joined to kick the man until he struggled to his feet and stood to attention again, blood smearing his face.

David was wondering if it could get any worse when his attention was drawn to one of the guards who had helped deliver the beating.

'God, no!' he moaned softly. David recognised the brown-shirted guard as the man he had knocked down in the café garden in Berlin. The guard glanced in David's direction and even in the semi-darkness David could see the sudden recognition. The expression on the guard's face changed from surprise to grim satisfaction.

David knew that things were about to get a lot worse.

★

Sean Duffy stood at the gates of a building that was more like a medieval castle than a house. It had taken him two days to travel to the von Fellmann estate in Prussia, and he prayed that his journey would not be in vain.

After David disappeared, Sean had managed to discover that he had been taken by the Gestapo, but no one would tell him where. As a matter of fact, no one would even admit to David being snatched from the street, and Sean had seen the fear in their eyes when he'd asked. Even the young air force officer, Fritz Lang, had not been able to help as the SS held sway over all other government departments and the military. He had apologised and it was then that Sean had realised he must seek out a senior member of the armed forces and beg for help.

Sean knew that the von Fellmann family were distantly related to David. He'd also heard that General Kurt von Fellmann had been the prisoner of Brigadier Patrick Duffy – David's grandfather – during the Great War. Kurt von Fellmann also had a twin brother, a Lutheran pastor who had ministered to the Aboriginal people at the Glen View mission station. Sean hoped these links might be enough to encourage General von Fellmann to help find David.

Sean walked across the long cobbled stoneway that spanned what was once a medieval moat but was now filled with swans and ducks gliding on the brackish water. He was met by an army officer whose uniform was decorated with braid that identified him as an aide-de-camp.

'Welcome, Mr Duffy,' the junior officer said, extending his hand in a warm fashion. He spoke English and Sean was pleased that he would not have to stumble by in his broken German. 'After your telephone call the General said he would be pleased to meet with you. Please enter.'

Sean shifted his weight on his walking stick and followed the smartly dressed officer through a maze of large, beautifully decorated rooms adorned with valuable paintings, suits of armour and deer heads resplendent with antlers. Eventually they reached an open reception area where medieval maces, swords, lances and gorgets hung on the walls. Modern lounge suites appeared a little out of place among this antique weaponry. In one corner stood a tall dignified man in the full dress uniform of a German army general.

Sean had met the general's twin brother many times and was struck by their similarity. Kurt von Fellmann turned to Sean with a grim smile; his crop of white hair was cut short in military style and he, too, walked with a limp.

'It is good to meet you, Herr Duffy,' Kurt said in excellent English, extending his hand. Sean could feel the strong grip. 'I believe that you were once a favoured officer in Brigadier Duffy's regiment.' Kurt glanced at his aide hovering in the background. 'You are dismissed, Lieutenant,' he said in German and the officer clicked his heels together, raising his arm in the traditional Nazi salute. When the aide had left the room the general turned to Sean.

'It is good to meet you also,' Sean replied, extracting his hand and hoping the circulation would return quickly. 'I knew your brother Karl very well.'

'Ah, yes, Karl,' Kurt said in an almost faraway voice. 'I was saddened to hear of his death. He was a good man and I believe God will reward him in heaven. But you have not asked to see me to discuss family matters,' the German general continued in his brusque manner.

'No, General,' Sean said, leaning on his cane. 'I have come seeking your help to find a young man distantly related to you – David Macintosh. His father was the son of Patrick Duffy. Matthew disappeared in Berlin during our tour of the country.'

'Patrick's grandson,' Kurt echoed. 'Patrick was a fine man and officer. If I can be of assistance, I will do all that is humanly possible to find his grandson. How did he disappear?'

Sean did not know whether the general had political leanings towards the Hitler regime. His journey would likely be a waste of time if Fellmann was a member of the Nazi Party. 'David was taken by the SS in Berlin to God knows where,' he said, almost holding his breath. He saw a dark look cloud the general's face.

'Those swine,' Kurt said. 'If the SS have taken Patrick's grandson, I suspect they would have sent him to Dachau.'

Sean breathed a little easier: the general was clearly a Prussian army officer of the old school and had no loyalty to the SS. 'Is it possible for you to use your influence to have David returned?' Sean asked.

'I will do all that is possible,' the general frowned. 'But first we must ascertain why David was arrested. I presume that he is not a German citizen, and even the SS must realise that such an arrest could be bad for Germany's reputation. Taking him into custody would require a strong case to counter any international protests. Do you know why he was arrested?'

Now it was Sean's turn to frown. 'I do not have a clue,' he sighed. 'David is a fine young lad with no political affiliations. I should know as I have been his guardian all these years. His grandmother was a patriot to Germany in the Great War and I suspect she worked with German intelligence at great risk to her life. David is only nineteen and too young to be involved in any political intrigue.'

'You must realise, Mr Duffy, that I and the rest of the army have sworn a personal oath to Adolf Hitler,' Kurt cautioned. 'I may not agree with all of the Führer's policies but I am a professional soldier. You Allies imposed on us restrictions at Versailles that led to the deaths of thousands of German men, women and children. When I returned to Germany after the Armistice in 1918, I returned to a country starving to death because the British continued the naval blockade after the war was over to deliberately starve us. The Austrian corporal may not be the best man for the task of our recovery, but my industrial friends assure me they have control of him, although I am beginning to doubt that. I will attempt to find David and have him released, but you must understand that my first duty is to the Fatherland.'

'Any assistance you are able to render is valued, General,' Sean replied. 'I know that your brother Karl was very fond of David when he was a toddler at Glen View.'

'I have also heard rumours that my brother was very fond of David's grandmother, too,' Kurt said with the hint of a smile on his stern, aristocratic face. 'Who, I believe, is a Jewess. Would that not make David a Jew?'

'Does it concern you?' Sean asked, 'I doubt that David even thinks about his Jewish legacy.'

'Some of my finest officers in the Great War were Jewish,' Kurt replied and Sean gave a small sigh of relief. 'David's religious beliefs are of no concern to me.'

Sean understood the delicate tightrope the senior officer had to negotiate in the current atmosphere of vilification against the Jews in Germany.

'I must caution you,' said the general, 'that finding David will not be easy. At the moment Hitler needs me – he is sending me to Spain to help fight against the communists and I am one of his favoured generals. I do not know how long that will last; he can change his mind on a whim.'

'Thank you, General von Fellmann,' Sean said. He did not want to pursue the subject of German intervention in the civil war raging in Spain. Britain and France seemed to have turned a blind eye to Italian and German involvement in a war being fought between the Nationalists led by Franco and the legitimate socialist government of Spain.

'You must stay as my guest and join my family for dinner tonight,' Kurt said warmly. 'My two sons, Heinrich and Roland, have leave from the army and will join us.

Heinrich is being posted to Spain as an advisor in armoured warfare to gain some combat experience.'

'I was going to stay at a small inn in the village,' Sean said. 'But I would be honoured to meet your family.'

'I will arrange for your luggage to be brought here,' Kurt replied and called for his aide.

*

That evening Sean joined the von Fellmann men in the dining hall. He was introduced to Kurt's eldest son, Heinrich, who wore the uniform equivalent of a major, and to Roland, who wore an army uniform with the rank of captain. Both men were of medium height but very much alike in their appearance, sporting cropped blond hair and both handsome in a straight-backed Teutonic way. Sean was pleasantly surprised to hear that both sons spoke perfect English. At dinner he was seated beside Heinrich. Roland sat opposite and Kurt assumed the place at the top of the table.

A rather bland vegetable soup was delivered by an older man wearing what could have been interpreted as a military uniform. Kurt explained that the man had been one of his soldiers in the past war.

It was Roland who stood, raised his crystal goblet of wine and said in a loud voice, 'Heil Hitler.'

Sean raised his goblet of wine but said nothing, and when he glanced down the table he noticed that the general had not responded either. Heinrich also remained silent, and Sean sensed a strain descend on the table. Roland sat down, staring for a moment at the bowl of soup.

'It will not be Herr Hitler who will one day re-establish Germany's place among the leading nations, but the military shedding their blood,' Kurt said.

'I trust that Herr Hitler is not considering starting another war,' Sean said, hoping that his comment would not cause any more tension.

'My younger son believes that one day we will confront the Bolshevik Russians and rid the western world of their threat,' Kurt said, sipping his wine. 'He believes that when that time comes Britain and France will support us. Our leader has outlined this plan to destroy communism in his autobiography, *Mein Kampf*, which I found rather boring.'

'I hope we do not see another war,' Sean said. 'Anyone who lived through the horror of the Great War would agree with me.' But when he looked across the table he could see in Roland's eyes no concern for what had gone before.

'I have to agree with my son's observation on the communist threat,' Kurt said. 'We civilised nations must face them one day and only Germany appears to have the will to do so.'

When the soup dishes were cleared away, a haunch of venison was brought to the table, along with steaming vegetables and a variety of mustards. The old soldier carved the meat and placed the plates in front of the von Fellmanns and their guest. Dinner was eaten mainly in silence, and afterwards the four men retired to the large living area to partake of port and cigars. As the evening drew on, the two sons excused themselves.

Roland came to attention and gave his father a salute before leaving the room. Heinrich followed behind to bid his father goodnight but held out his hand instead. Sean could see a restrained warmth between the two men and suddenly he missed David desperately. He hoped against hope that the young man was safe.

When they were alone, the general turned to Sean. 'Are you married?' he asked.

'No,' Sean replied. 'I never seemed to get around to it.' He knew that the general's wife had died in the influenza epidemic and he had never remarried.

The German general sipped his cognac from the balloon-like goblet. 'As you may have observed, my two sons are very different. I think that Heinrich might have chosen a path in the Lutheran church if he had had a choice. Roland is one of the generation that has fallen under the spell of the Nazi Party, with its nationalistic beliefs in Germany's supremacy.'

'Did you join the Nazi Party?' Sean asked a little too bluntly and Kurt looked away.

'No, I am a soldier and do not bother myself with politics.'

'Let us hope that our two countries never find themselves facing each other on the battlefield ever again. It was a bloody affair.'

Kurt raised his glass in a toast. 'That we never experience another war between our nations,' he said with passion and Sean responded by raising his glass.

'But, my friend, you have a busy day tomorrow, as do I, so I will excuse myself for the evening,' Kurt said, swilling down the last of his cognac.

The two men parted and Sean made his way up the wide steps to his bedroom. The old soldier who had acted as a waiter helped Sean into bed and bid him goodnight. Sean lay beneath the warm eiderdown as the chill of the night became more apparent. He feared that David would be lying on a hard bed with no blankets to keep him warm; if he was in Dachau, as Sean feared, he only hoped David had strength enough to survive.

4

'Thought you would fly back with the girl,' Cyril Blacksmith growled as he and Matthew watched the Junkers disappear into the clear blue skies over Basra. 'Those Hun crates need a second pilot for best performance.'

Matthew wondered if his chief engineer was right and he should have flown back to Germany with Diane, although his reasons were different.

Diane had shared Matthew's little mudbrick villa for the past week while Cyril worked on an oil leak on the Junkers. His house sat on the banks of the Tigris River and had a small but cool courtyard bordered by wildflowers, with a water fountain at the centre. At night he and Diane sat in the courtyard with a flute of chilled French champagne and they talked about aviation. Gradually Matthew came to realise that his feelings for her were more than two old friends sharing a common interest. He dreamed of taking her into his arms and expressing the passion he felt for her, but she was young, beautiful and successful in her career as an aviatrix. What interest could she have in him?

On the last evening they'd spent together under a night sky of brilliant stars, Diane had asked Matthew the one question he did not want to answer.

'Do you ever see your son and daughter?' she asked. 'James and Olivia. They would be in their late teens by now, wouldn't they?'

Matthew leaned back in his chair and stared at the constellations above them. 'I have only seen them once since they were born,' he answered quietly. 'They live with their grandfather in the States.'

Diane frowned. 'What has stopped you from seeing them more often?'

Matthew slumped down in his seat. 'When I travelled to the States I arranged to meet them. They were about ten and total strangers to me. They were polite, but I had the feeling my visit only caused them pain and confusion. It was as if I was forcing my way into their lives. I was never married to their mother, and old James Barrington has given them everything money could possibly buy. I could sense the embarrassment in my children at meeting me, a stranger with a funny accent. I wanted to hug them but that just didn't seem right. When I walked away I knew that I was little more in their lives than the man who had sired them. That must have been around nine or ten years ago.'

'Have you written to them?' Diane persisted

'I have sat down at my desk and tried,' Matthew said, 'but what do I say to them? That today I was lucky to survive a desert storm and forced to ditch the aircraft until it passed? You know life out here can be cut short very quickly.

I suppose it is better that I let my children forget me and get on with their lives. I have lived most of my life on the razor edge of war and frontier flying.'

'That is what makes you such a fascinating man, Matthew Duffy,' Diane said with a twinkle in her eyes.

'No, it makes me a fool,' he dismissed. 'I inherited a fortune when my wonderful mother passed on. But all I have to show for it now is the company. One pilot, one engineer and one aeroplane.'

'And two children,' Diane reminded.

'At least my mother got to see the children often enough over the years,' Matthew said with a sigh. 'I believe they adored her, and she was forever chiding me to try to make more contact. I guess I was not cut out to be a good father.'

'I am sorry to hear that your mother has passed away,' Diane said. 'From what I heard about her she must have been an incredible woman.'

'The Aboriginal housemaid said that she died peacefully on the verandah of her house in Townsville,' Matthew said, staring again at the stars overhead. 'Before she died some surveyors working out west near the Julia Creek area found scattered human and horse bones. They also found a leather pouch and a letter carefully wrapped in wax paper inside an old saddlebag. It was a letter written by my father just before he died. The team who found his remains sent the letter to my mother. They were his last words of love for Mother and me. The housemaid found it in my mother's hands when they discovered she'd passed on.' Matthew paused, staring into the stars above. 'If you don't mind, I think I should turn in early tonight. I have a run to an oil field.'

Matthew eased himself from the chair, hoping that Diane did not see the tears welling in his eyes. When Diane had raised the question about his children she had unlocked a door to his past and he had been unexpectedly swamped by a wave of sad memories.

Now he stood beside Cyril until the Junkers became a mere dot in the sky and felt the pang of jealousy again.

'They'll be back soon enough,' Cyril said reassuringly, as if sensing his boss's mood. 'And when they do we will finally be making enough money to buy one of those Hun aircraft for ourselves. Maybe even give me a pay rise for looking after two kites.'

Matthew turned to his Canadian engineer. 'You get overpaid as it is,' he said with a broad grin. 'And I even throw in the flies, heat and dust for nothing.'

As both men turned to retreat to the shade of the cavernous hangar, Matthew noticed a man wearing khaki shorts and shirt dismounting from a car that had pulled up nearby. Matthew lifted his hand to his eyes to shade the morning sun shimmering on the dry, hard earth of the airfield.

'Bloody hell!' he exclaimed softly and walked towards the car. Cyril followed.

When Matthew was within a handshake of the man he broke into a broad smile.

'Ben Rosenblum,' he laughed, taking the man's extended hand. 'Anyone ever tell you that you're a chip off the old block? How is your old man?'

In his mid-thirties, Benjamin Rosenblum had the same features and solid build as his father Saul, who was a lifelong friend of Matthew's. Benjamin had the same appealing face as his father and his grip was as strong.

'My father sends his good wishes,' Benjamin answered in his accented English. 'He says you should fly to our settlement and have a cold beer with him soon.'

The two men stood facing each other and Matthew

introduced Cyril to the Jewish Palestinian. Introductions over, Cyril excused himself. 'Got to order some parts for the crate,' he mumbled and walked away. Matthew invited Benjamin into his office for tea. Ben sat down in the old leather chair and Matthew called his Iraqi servant Ibrahim to fetch tea for his guest.

'You're a long way from home,' Matthew said. 'What brings you out here? Not bad news, I hope.'

Ben shifted uncomfortably in his seat. 'I am now a member of one of Captain Orde Wingate's Special Night Squads, fighting Haj Amin al-Husseini's Arab uprising,' he replied. 'We need your help.'

Matthew knew about the Arab uprising: protests against the flood of Jewish immigrants fleeing persecution from Hitler. The Arabs of Palestine wanted the occupying British to quell the flow of new arrivals and expel those who were already there. The uprising had escalated in violence and the British armed forces had found themselves caught between the feuding parties of Jew and Moslem. General Archibald Wavell had been sent from England to command the British forces, and an eccentric but brilliant young officer, Captain Orde Wingate, had been posted to train and control the Jewish self-defence forces. Wingate was a devout Plymouth Brethren who perceived the flow of Jewish refugees back to Palestine as one of the signs for the second coming of Christ. Despite being a Christian, he was highly respected by the Jewish fighters he led as they waged a guerrilla war against the Arab militias.

The tea was delivered and Matthew poured for them both, handing Ben a cup. 'How can I help?' he asked. 'And, if I help, will it get my company into trouble?'

Ben glanced up with a hint of a smile. 'You sound like my father,' he said. 'All this worry over a simple request.'

'I know your father,' Matthew chuckled. 'Nothing asked in the Rosenblum name is a simple favour.'

'I am also a member of the *Haganah*,' Ben said, referring to the underground Jewish militia formed to protect the kibbutzim settlements. The *Haganah* was not officially recognised by the British administration, but the British government did give tacit support to the military organisation. 'We need better weapons, and more of them, if we are to survive. We have an order with the Czechoslovakian arms traders for a supply of machine guns and ammunition. The trouble is that we need the weapons now, and the fastest way to get them is by air. That is where you come in.'

Matthew sat down at his desk and picked up a pencil. 'I suspect that your mission is not condoned by the British administration,' he said, tapping the pencil on a pad of blotting paper. 'And such a mission would cost me my licence – if not my freedom – if things were to go wrong.'

'I am authorised to pay all costs,' Ben said, ignoring Matthew's concerns. 'We will also pay a generous fee for your services.'

Matthew did not answer immediately. His mind was racing through the multitude of potential obstacles to the task of flying into Europe and returning to Palestine. But he also knew that he could not refuse a request from the young man who had risked his life to save Matthew's during the war.

'Just give me time to work out costs and we can go ahead,' he sighed and saw an expression of relief on Ben's suntanned face. For a moment, gazing at Ben, Matthew was cast back thirty-six years – seeing Ben's father, Saul, in a shallow trench at the South African river crossing during the Elands River siege, when the two men fought a desperate battle against the heavily armed force of Boers who poured machine-gun and artillery shells into their poorly defended Australian position. 'You are welcome to bunk down at my place,' Matthew said, rising from his chair. 'My last house guest just flew out for Germany.'

★

The days turned into weeks in Dachau. The work parties, the drilling and exercise parades, the lack of food – supposedly designed to re-educate the prisoners into better Germans – simply acted to wear them down and break their spirits.

At least David had somehow been able to avoid the attention of the guard he had encountered in the Berlin café. That seemed a lifetime ago now as he drilled with the others for hours, occasionally feeling the lash of a whip across his shoulders if he faltered.

At night he stared at the wooden planks of the bunk above, occupied by Günter Schmidt whom he had befriended. In his dreams David was once again on his grandmother's New Guinean copra plantation under a warm tropical sun, only to wake to the living hell of the concentration camp. He prayed that Sean was looking for him and using all his powers to extract him from the camp, but there had been nothing to indicate that this was the case and his hope was turning to despair.

In the early morning drizzle he fell out onto the parade ground in front of the barracks. The weather was turning cold as winter crept closer and the prisoners shivered miserably. The smartly dressed guards prowled up and down the ranks, occasionally delivering blows to anyone not standing to strict attention.

To David's horror, the man he had knocked down in

Berlin approached him in the ranks. He had a twisted smile on his face.

'You thought that I was not aware you were here,' he said, leaning into David's face. 'But I have been biding my time and that time has come, Englisher.'

David stood to attention, staring past the SA man's shoulder.

'To show how humane he is, the commandant has chosen to allow you swine a little sporting activity,' the SA man continued. 'In three days' time, after the morning meal parade, you will be the main attraction in a boxing match with our SS heavyweight champion to see if you are as good as you boasted to us in Berlin.' Satisfied that he had unnerved David, the SA man moved on.

David began to tremble with absolute fear.

'You cannot win,' Günter hissed. 'If you win they will ensure that you have an accident and disappear. You must lose, to prove to our guards that they are the master race, and they may just let you live.'

David thought that winning was a forlorn hope as he had already lost a lot of weight and was severely weakened by the starvation diet.

'Not much chance of winning, anyway,' David muttered, and gazed bleakly into the drizzling rain.

★

Sean Duffy had moved back to Berlin after his short stay with General von Fellmann. He was haunted by not knowing where David was or even if he was still alive. So far he had not informed David's grandmother that her precious grandson was missing, possibly a prisoner in a German concentration camp; he could not bear breaking the news to her. Sean had contacted the British embassy about David's disappearance, and they had been polite but unhelpful. One official had explained that if David had broken any German laws, then it was out of their hands.

At his hotel Sean had virtually sat by the telephone for days on end; and finally it rang late one afternoon. It was Kurt von Fellmann. He did not reveal his identity but gave instructions to meet at a certain street corner not far from the hotel. Sean grabbed his hat, cane and an umbrella and made his way to the rendezvous. When he arrived he saw the general wearing a civilian suit, standing and reading a newspaper. As Sean limped closer the general turned and commenced walking slowly down the street. Sean caught up with him and they walked side by side among the many pedestrians towards a park whose trees had lost their leaves with the coming of winter.

'The precaution is necessary,' Kurt said quietly, leading Sean to a park bench. Very few people were in the park as a chill wind puffed at the dead leaves littering the grass. 'The Gestapo have a habit of watching foreigners.'

Sean sat down beside Kurt and the two men gazed across the sea of brown leaves. 'Has it come to this in Germany?' he asked sadly.

'I am afraid it has,' Kurt replied, looking down at the open newspaper as if reading it. 'Discrete questions have confirmed David as a prisoner in Dachau,' he said. 'He is under SS control and out of my reach. Himmler does not entertain any interference in his operations.'

'God almighty,' Sean answered. 'At least he is alive, but the little I have heard about that place is that many do not return. How in hell are we going to free him?'

Kurt folded his paper and stared straight ahead. 'I am afraid that we have no chance of protesting his imprisonment as the SS are already closing ranks on his case. It seems they have evidence that David is a spy for the British communist party. They were tipped off by one of your countrymen.'

Stunned, Sean knew there was only one person with reason to lie about David being a communist.

'Sir George Macintosh,' he whispered. Sean knew that David's uncle had visited Germany for the Olympic Games and stayed on in the country on business. It had been George's own wife Louise who had told Sean about her husband's trip. 'It had to be that bastard.'

'Sir George and his children were guests of mine a few days ago,' Kurt commented with a note of surprise. 'Why would he betray one who is of his blood?'

Sean turned to Kurt with a bitter smile. 'The Macintosh family is not a happy one,' he answered. 'You see, George needs David out of the way to take complete control of the Macintosh companies. I don't know how in hell he knew David was in the country, but he has to be the one behind turning David in to the SS on trumped-up charges.'

'That is unfortunate,' Kurt said with a sigh. 'Sir George is highly thought of by the Hitler government and wields some influence. This makes our task of saving David even more difficult.'

'If I know that slimy bastard, he will have done everything he can to ensure that David does not leave Dachau alive,' Sean said bitterly. 'Time is short. I beg you to help as much as you can.'

'I have a plan,' Kurt said. 'But it is one that requires the utmost of secrecy and trust.'

'Anything to get David out of that camp,' Sean said. 'I would give my own life to save him.'

'That will not be necessary,' Kurt said. 'The only people capable of getting David out are the SS themselves. But I do not hold any influence with Himmler's men. However, I know someone who has access to their uniforms and identification papers, as well as stamped forms that would pass scrutiny. The man was once one of my soldiers in the war and I trust him. There are a lot of Germans opposed to Hitler's government but it has proved futile to openly oppose the Führer. I also know someone who would be willing to impersonate an SS officer as he has no love for them. In fact, it could be said that he belongs to the resistance, but that is no matter. What I need is another man to impersonate a military intelligence officer.'

'May I ask whom you have selected for the rescue?' Sean asked.

'My son, Heinrich,' Kurt said and Sean was stunned that Kurt would put his beloved son in peril. Sean had no doubt that if things went wrong Heinrich would also end up in the dreaded prison, or worse, tortured and executed as a traitor.

'I think I know a German officer who might help,' Sean replied. 'But I cannot guarantee his co-operation at this stage.'

'We would need at least two men to get David out,' Kurt cautioned. 'We Germans are creatures who invented modern bureaucracy. It will take two men in the guise of SS officer and army intelligence for the story to be plausible. We will meet at another place the same time tomorrow to discuss final plans for the mission. I bid you good day, Major Duffy,' the general said, using Sean's old military title with a note of respect. It signalled that they were going to war. This time they would be on the same side.

Sean stayed on the bench for a short time as Kurt strolled away, his coat collar pulled up against the bite in the wind. Sean sat reviewing the plan; he knew how dangerous this mission would be and he wondered whether German citizens would really be prepared to put their lives on the line to rescue a foreigner they had never met.

It was a matter of clutching at straws but it was time to talk to the air force pilot, Fritz Lang, again and sound out his thoughts on defying his government. Sean had spent a lot of time among men and sensed that the young pilot might be prepared to assist. If he was wrong, and Lang betrayed the plot to rescue David, Sean and Kurt were surely dead men.

5

'I will do this because my mother told me that the greatest comfort she had after the war was learning that my father did not die alone,' Fritz said. 'Captain Duffy could have left my father, his enemy, to die alone in the desert, but he stayed with him.'

'I know what great peril you are putting yourself in,' Sean told him. 'You have already interceded to help save David once before. This is dangerous business.'

'I am an airman,' Fritz replied. 'I have long learned to live with death.'

The two men spoke quietly in English. They wore civilian clothes and attracted little attention from the café patrons around them. With the German pilot's assistance, Sean knew there was at least a slim chance that the very risky mission to save David might succeed.

'You will be impersonating an army intelligence officer

who has orders to take David into your custody for interrogation,' Sean said, leaning forward and speaking even more softly. 'Your uniform and papers will be given to you and we carry out the task at Dachau.'

'What if David is already dead?' Fritz countered. 'I have heard disturbing rumours that not all those detained by the SS and Gestapo come out alive. Accidents and reports of prisoners being shot while attempting to escape are whispered on the streets.'

Sean gave a pained expression; he dared not entertain that option. 'Then the mission will be cancelled,' he said. 'You will meet the man who will accompany you on the mission to go over the plan tonight,' Sean continued, passing a slip of paper under the table to Fritz containing the address.

As the two men parted and Sean limped from the café along the street he swore that he saw a dark car parked not far away, containing two men wearing the uniform of Gestapo officers. Sean had an uneasy feeling that he was under surveillance. His fear was confirmed when the vehicle pulled out from the kerb and followed at a discreet distance. From now on Sean would have to ensure that he made no more contact with the conspirators, as his presence would mean unwanted attention from Hitler's secret police. All he could do now was live in hope and wait by the telephone.

*

The morning of the fight had arrived and David queued to receive his meagre breakfast ration. Behind him stood Günter also waiting patiently for the tiny piece of bread to be doled out.

'I have to warn you that the guards intend to kill you,' he said quietly. 'I overheard them talking about it last night when I was cleaning the floor of their barracks. They are madmen who see the boxing match as an entertaining way of watching you be executed.'

'Did they say how I would be killed in the ring?' David asked, shuffling forward and feeling the hunger pains in his stomach.

'They did not but they said your death would be a lesson to us all,' Günter replied softly. 'I am sorry for you, my friend, but at least you will be permanently free of this hell on earth.'

David tried to fight the panic rising in his chest. He was only nineteen years old and he felt cheated by life. Since that afternoon in the Berlin café garden his fate had spiralled out of control, and now he was facing execution. Where was Sean? Was he searching for him? Deep down David knew that he would be, but any assistance was going to be too late to save his life.

A tiny lump of stale bread was dropped in his battered pannikin and David moved on to eat the little nourishment he had before the fight. He had hardly finished the ration when he saw the dreaded figure of the SA man push his way towards him with a sneer on his face.

'You will come with me,' the SA thug said, pushing David in the chest with a short hardwood club. 'We get you ready for the fight.'

David followed and was taken to a large parade ground where a rope had been strung between four metal pickets. Already the guards and selected prisoners were assembling as spectators, and when David looked closer he saw the man he was obviously meant to fight enter the ring: a giant, blue eyed, blond-haired man stripped down to a pair of silk shorts.

'We have a book on how many punches it will take to knock you out,' the SA thug said. 'I say it will only take ten blows to finish the fight, so don't disappoint me, Englisher.'

David felt himself pushed towards another SA man holding a set of leather boxing gloves. He stepped forward and allowed the gloves to be fitted. When he looked over at his opponent preparing for the fight he saw with a sickening realisation how they were going to kill him. Metal knuckledusters were being fitted inside the opponent's boxing gloves. The man he was about to fight had been tasked to prove the superiority of the master race. This was not a boxing bout but a thinly disguised execution, just as Günter had warned.

When David scanned the faces of the prisoners paraded to watch the match he could see in their expressions that they also knew David had no chance of surviving. They knew they were simply here to see a legitimised killing by their custodians; it was a lesson in the futility of their resisting Hitler's Reich.

Gloved up, David ducked under the single length of rope defining the improvised boxing ring. His opponent raised his arms to the cheers of the guards. An SS officer wearing full black uniform and polished boots also climbed into the ring and David guessed he would be the referee. The uniformed man gave a short speech to the cowering prisoners, telling them the fight would demonstrate the superiority of German manhood over that of a foreign communist agitator with a supposed reputation as a world-class boxer. David stood with his hands by his sides and wondered how many hits he could take before the death blow. If he was going to be beaten to death he had nothing to lose and for a fraction of a moment he experienced a soaring flame of hope.

'The Englisher, prisoner number four thousand and sixteen . . .'

'My name is David Macintosh and I am an Australian,' David said defiantly.

'You will fight now,' the SS officer snarled.

A bell rang and David immediately went into the fighter's pose, gloves ready to deflect any punches to his head. The first blow caught him in the chest and he felt its power as his ribs cracked. David's opponent was a very strong young man and had every intention of finishing the fight as quickly as possible. *Maybe the SA thug would win his bet*, David thought through the pain. But he was determined that it would take more than ten blows to fell him, and he knew that he was fighting the greatest bout of his short life.

★

The SS officer and army intelligence officer standing in the anteroom to the commandant's office were an impressive pair. Heinrich and Fritz had produced their hastily forged identification papers and the SA clerk appeared convinced.

'Why are you here?' he asked in a surly tone.

Heinrich, dressed in the uniform of an SS major, glared at the clerk. 'I do not tolerate lower ranks addressing me without the customary "sir",' he exploded and immediately the clerk jumped to his feet. 'What is your name, clerk?' Heinrich continued, prising a notebook from his top pocket. 'It will be forwarded to Herr Himmler when I speak with him next week.' From the man's frightened expression Heinrich knew that his charade as an arrogant SS officer was working.

'The officer with me is Major Conrad Neumann, and he is here to take into military custody a foreign prisoner, Herr David Macintosh, for further interrogation. Prisoner Macintosh has been identified by our intelligence as a very valuable asset, and I know that Herr Himmler will be very displeased if he is not made immediately available to us.'

'I cannot release any prisoner without signed authority from Herr Himmler himself,' the clerk stuttered.

'If you look carefully at the papers I have produced you will clearly see Herr Himmler's signature,' Heinrich continued, pointing to the rubber-stamped forgery on the clerk's desk.

'I think that we should telephone Herr Himmler's office and ask this man here to speak with him in person if he has any doubts. I have the director's personal telephone number,' Fritz said to Heinrich in a bored voice. The clerk's eyes bulged and he went to a metal filing cabinet. In seconds he had a manila folder opened on his desk.

'Herr Macintosh,' the clerk said. 'He is a foreigner and has been identified as a communist agitator.'

'That is the man we urgently require for interrogation by our military intelligence department,' Fritz said, flipping closed the folder as if the prisoner identified was of little interest; collecting him from the camp was just one more mundane task.

'I will have the prisoner found and brought to you,' the clerk said. 'But I cannot release him to you until Major Hertzog personally clears the matter.'

'Where is Major Hertzog?' Heinrich asked.

'He is refereeing a boxing match between one of his officers and a prisoner,' the clerk replied and suddenly paled.

'Is there something you should tell me?' Heinrich asked, seeing the sudden change in the clerk's expression.

'The prisoner is Herr Macintosh,' the clerk blurted, realising that by now the foreign communist would be dead at the hands of his opponent. 'I think there will be a problem releasing the prisoner.'

Heinrich and Fritz glanced at each other. Both had a good idea what that problem might be.

*

David had been able to protect his head with his gloves but he had taken a terrible battering in the midriff. The impact of the metal behind the leather was taking its toll, and he knew he would have to bring his defence down to protect his chest and stomach before the cracked ribs punctured his lungs and he drowned in his own blood. As he had nothing to lose David went on the offensive, swinging as many blows as he could against the big German's head. They connected, and even in his weakened state, David's blows still had a lot of power, causing his opponent to reel back in surprise. The referee immediately stepped in front of David to allow his man to recover from the unexpected retaliation.

Frustrated, David stepped back but now there was a fire in his eyes: he chose to die standing on his feet.

The SS fighter shook his head to clear it and stepped forward, hands raised. David did not hesitate, striking hard at the man's now exposed midriff, causing the German to grunt in surprise. He had obviously been told that the prisoner would provide little more than a punching bag for him to practise on.

David's whole world had shrunk to this tiny patch of ground. He knew that the injuries sustained to his chest had weakened him considerably. He could hear a ringing in his ears, and saw a red haze before his eyes. He hardly felt the three blows to his head. His legs suddenly felt like jelly as he sunk onto the cold earth. *So this was death*, David thought as the inky blackness descended on him. He had given it his best and had gone down fighting to the last.

*

The Atlantic Ocean certainly appeared placid when looking from so far above in the belly of the giant airship, the *Hindenburg*. James Barrington Jnr was still impressed with his grandfather's surprise gift to them for their return to the USA. It had come as a gesture from Adolf Hitler's government in gratitude for the American banker's contract to sign bonds in support of the Reich's industry. The great floating airship that now carried out regular transatlantic flights from Germany to the USA was a prized example of the advanced technology of the new Germany under its Nazi leader.

James could hear the gentle hum of the engines and slight vibration under his feet as he stood gazing down on the grey ocean below. If he was not looking through the slanted viewing windows, he could have believed he was on the luxury promenade deck of a fine ocean liner; such were the comforts and decor. He was on A deck above B deck – where the crew's living quarters, kitchens and workshops were located. Dining rooms serving only the best food were located either side of the cabin-like accommodation for the guests while the great airship also had a reading room and lounge, displaying a wall-sized mural of an atlas of the world indicating the great explorers' ship routes. Red carpet, red chairs and cream walls adorned the dining rooms. A baby grand piano constructed of duralumin and covered in leather was also introduced for the guest's entertainment. All furniture was made from aluminium tubing to save weight for the hydrogen-filled envelope that lifted the airship into the sky.

'The captain has calculated that it will take us only two and a half hours to reach the American coast,' the young man who joined James said. 'Less than half the time of a fast steamer on the same route.'

James turned away from his observations of the ocean below to greet the young Englishman in his early twenties. They had met the day before at breakfast and introduced themselves. A bond between the men formed when they realised that the Englishman, Henry Cabot, had relatives in New Hampshire where James came from who James knew socially.

'So, we should be mooring at Lakehurst before dinner tomorrow,' James replied. 'The adventure will be over.'

Henry leaned to gaze down on the water beside James. 'I hope to return to my flying club when I return to England,' he said. 'This is the first time I have been in the sky without the joystick between my knees, and I must admit, this is far more relaxing.'

'My father . . .' James said and suddenly stopped himself.

'Your father what, old man?' Henry asked, glancing sideways at James.

'I was just going to say that my father is an Australian who flew with the army during the war. I heard that he got medals for bravery.'

'I suppose he was with the AFC before it became the Royal Australian Air Force,' Henry answered. 'Is your father still around and flying?'

For a moment James remained silent, struggling with his feelings about the man who had given him life, but had not been a part of his growth to manhood.

'As far as I know he has a flying outfit in Iraq,' James grudgingly said. 'But he has never been a real part of my life.'

'I am sorry to hear that,' Henry replied with a note of sympathy. 'If your father was decorated in the war he must be an exceptional chap. Have you ever considered taking up the art and science of aviation?'

'Not really,' James answered with a slight shrug. 'My grandfather has me destined for the banking industry after I finish college.'

'This is just a small taste of how exciting flying can be,' Henry said with a warm smile. 'I am working towards getting a commission with the Royal Air Force to fly fighters. A little more modern than those your father must have flown in the war. Supermarine are working on a new fighter aircraft they have just named the Spitfire. I saw one before travelling to Germany and I must say she looks like a little beauty. I doubt that you Yanks could match her at the moment.'

James ignored the slight against his country's aviation technology, and wished that he had not mentioned his father at all because the Englishman only seemed to admire the man who had deserted him as a child. Resentment welled up in James's chest at the almost forgotten figure in his life. Was his father one of those men the English referred to as cads – someone with no feelings for others? Why had he not attempted to join his grandfather when James was growing up with his sister, who he knew resented the almost myth-ical figure of Captain Matthew Duffy? So many complex questions with equally difficult answers.

'I say old chap,' Henry said, stepping back from the viewing window. 'Have you seen your delightful sister by any chance?'

James grinned. 'I think that she said she was retiring to take piano lessons from that suave German entertainer with the greased-back hair and pencil moustache. Looks a bit like Rudolph Valentino.'

James's observation brought a frown to the Englishman whose looks were not unappealing. 'Damned Huns,' he growled. 'Don't they know they lost the war?'

Henry walked away to leave James to continue gazing

out the window. For a moment he saw his reflection in the glass pane and saw an angry expression staring back at him. Did he look anything like his father? James wondered. Was he anything like his father, was the next question in his mind. He knew that his sister had virtually dismissed Captain Matthew Duffy as someone who was dead – like their mother. But James was now at an age where learning who he was seemed to be linked to knowing his estranged father. The anger was taking root and eating at him with an overpowering desire to meet with Captain Matthew Duffy and make him pay for his selfishness. Dark clouds skittered below the airship, covering the sea below. Rain was washing against the floating luxury liner and James finally turned away to make his way to the sumptuous dining room to join his grandfather who had raised him to represent the good name and standing of the Barrington family. At least James had a sound idea where he was going in life. All he really wanted to know was who he was.

★

Heinrich and Fritz reached the makeshift boxing ring too late. Already a couple of prisoners were dragging David's body from the parade ground to a truck assigned to remove bodies for disposal. The other inmates had been silently dispersed back to their arduous regime of drill and work.

Heinrich and Fritz saw an SS major standing in the centre of the ring congratulating a heavily built young man who sported a swollen left eye.

'Major Hertzog,' Heinrich said in a loud voice a few paces away. 'I was assigned to have prisoner David Macintosh taken to military HQ for interrogation. We believe the knowledge he has is vital to national interests.'

Major Hertzog turned to Heinrich and stared at him.

'Do you have the papers for such a request?' he asked coldly.

'I have written authority from our intelligence department,' Fritz answered, stepping forward with the falsified documents.

'You are unfortunately a little late,' Hertzog said with a sneer, glancing at the papers. 'The scum you came for just lost a boxing match against one of my officers. You can make a note in your report for your senior officers that the man died of an accident. And as for you, Major,' Hertzog continued, 'I confess that I have never had the opportunity to meet you before. As a matter of fact, your face is new to me.'

Heinrich felt a cold chill of fear: the man they were dealing with was suspicious of him. Everything was falling apart and they were too late to save David. All they had to show for their attempt to rescue him was his body, lying face down on the cold earth, waiting to be hoisted aboard a truck for removal to an unmarked grave.

'We will take the body off your hands, Major,' Fritz said, diverting the SS major's gaze from Heinrich. 'At least we can produce his corpse as evidence of the unfortunate accident.'

Hertzog turned his attention to Fritz. 'You can take him but you will sign for his release. In the meantime, I have work to do.' With that, the SS major strode away.

'At least we will be able to get the boy's body back to his family,' Heinrich said bitterly. 'If only we had been a little earlier, maybe he would still be alive.'

'Nothing we could have done,' Fritz consoled, walking over to David and rolling him on his back. 'You may as well fetch the car and we will load him ourselves.'

Fritz rolled David's body over and gasped.

'What is it?' Heinrich asked.

'I think he is still alive,' Fritz said, crouching down to put his ear against David's chest. 'His heart still beats!' he exclaimed. 'The man is still alive.'

Heinrich cast around to see if they were being watched, and was pleased to see that in this part of the camp they were virtually alone. Heinrich gripped David's wrist, seeking a pulse and found a very weak beat.

'He is – but just barely,' Heinrich confirmed. 'We must get him out of here and seek medical aid as quickly as possible. I suspect he may be just a heartbeat from death.'

★

There were voices speaking softly in German all around him and he was warm. David drifted into a world of pleasant sounds, smells and colours. When he slowly opened his eyes the first face he saw was that of Sean Duffy staring down at him with a worried expression, his eyes now filling with tears of happiness.

'Welcome back, old boy,' Sean said, gripping David's hand in his own. 'Thought you were going to just lie there and sleep away the rest of your life. You got yourself into a spot of bother.'

David tried to orientate himself in this new world, struggling against the clean sheets and warm eiderdown, but was gently pushed back by Sean. 'You have lost a lot of weight and we were worried that you might not recover from your beating. Miraculously you only have broken ribs and Dr Vogel has done a grand job healing you.'

'Uncle Sean,' David croaked. 'Where am I?'

'You are safe,' Sean said, and added, 'for the moment. As soon as you are well enough to travel we will have to get out of Germany. I am afraid the mission to rescue you didn't quite go to plan. The authorities have learned that your rescuers were imposters; luckily they already slipped back into their real roles and have not been identified. The SS are not certain of your fate and I suspect they will presume that you are alive until proved otherwise. It was an oversight by the Dachau people not to confirm your death at the camp. We are in Dr Vogel's house in Berlin. He has risked his freedom to help us. It seems that Herr Hitler is not as popular as the western press has crowed. From what I have observed there is a small but dedicated resistance movement in this country, hoping to oust Hitler and his henchmen. One of your rescuers contacted the good doctor.'

'Was I at Dachau?' David asked, confused. 'Or was that really a bad dream?'

'You were in Dachau,' Sean confirmed. 'But we got you out when the guards wrote you off as dead. Had it not been for the prompt actions of your rescuers you would have surely died. But you are now out and our next challenge will be to leave Germany before we are tracked down by the Gestapo.'

A bald, middle-aged man wearing spectacles entered the room.

'How are you feeling, Mr Macintosh?' he asked, leaning over David and removing a stethoscope from his medical bag. 'I am Dr Vogel.'

David thanked him for his care and the doctor grunted his acceptance of his patient's gratitude. After the examination he stood up and turned to Sean.

'He is young and his body is recovering well,' he said in English. 'He will need a few more days of good food and rest before he is well enough to be moved. In the meantime I must attend my practice, but you are welcome to remain here.'

'Thank you, Herr Doctor,' Sean said, shaking the man's

hand. 'We will leave as soon as David is well enough to travel.'

'You will need to make arrangements to smuggle the young man out of the country,' the doctor said. 'All train stations and airports will be watched by the Gestapo.'

'I have given the problem a great deal of thought,' Sean reassured. 'I think I may have a solution to getting David out.'

'Good,' Dr Vogel said. 'My wife will bring chicken soup. She is Jewish and believes that chicken soup can cure any illness known to man. It is because of her that I take this risk.'

The doctor left, leaving Sean alone with David, who slipped back into sleep before the soup could be delivered by the doctor's wife.

Sean sat and watched David sleep. Sean was not a religious man but he offered up a prayer of thanks to God for the boy's safety.

He had decided that he would get David out of Germany not by land or by sea, but by plane. They would fly over the German borders. All Sean had to do was contact Matthew Duffy. From the occasional letters they exchanged, Sean knew Matthew was flying out of Basra. In the meantime Sean needed to get David back on his feet. The terrible experiences in the concentration camp had left their indelible mark on the young man's body and, Sean suspected, in his mind.

Sean left the apartment building and walked to the nearest post office. He limped along a tree-lined street where people went about their day as if Hitler's dictatorship had no bearing on their lives. After all, he had provided them with a better way of life and so they ignored the injustices being committed against individual freedom so long as there was food on the table and a job to go to.

Sean reached the post office and was greeted by a jolly man with a red nose. He spoke a little English and Sean spoke a little German, so between them they were able to work out which form Sean needed to fill out in order to send a telegram.

Sean made his way to a desk to carefully compose his words to Matthew. That he was a foreigner would invite immediate interest and Sean realised that he would have to use some kind of code to the Australian flyer. Sean wrote down his words and took the form back to the counter where the postmaster took it away for transmission. Sean waited nervously for some time before the postmaster returned with a fixed smile.

'Your telegram has been sent,' he said with a heavy accent and put his hand out for the fee.

Sean paid the man and left the post office. Outside, in the sunlit street, he saw a black car pull out from the kerb. Sean felt a cold shiver of fear. Heinrich and Fritz had been able to smuggle David into the doctor's apartment building through the rear entrance in the early hours of the evening of his rescue; the building contained many flats and Sean had left it to draw away the Gestapo surveillance team. Sean guessed that the tail on him was to report who he met with and maybe the SS had not made his connection with David Macintosh. But it was only a matter of time before the Germans traced their paperwork and linked him with the Australian escapee and all Sean could hope was that the SS was a typical German bureaucracy. Every second was now beginning to matter.

Sean knew that he could not lead them to the building where David was recuperating. Instead, he made his way to a beer hall and spent the day sitting alone sipping the fine beer that Germany produced. In the early evening he slipped out and made his way along the narrow streets of the city to the doctor's house, carefully watching for anyone trailing him. He knew of a back way into the apartment building and in the dark tapped on the apartment door.

'You have been gone for a long time,' the doctor said.

'I was being watched,' Sean replied, grateful to be in the warm flat out of the chill of the Berlin night. 'But I seem to have shaken off those watching me. I think they got bored waiting for me to come out of the beer hall.'

Everything now depended on a message crossing Europe to the Middle East to Captain Matthew Duffy.

When Sean carefully pulled back the curtains to observe the street below he could see the black car had returned. The Gestapo were not even bothering to hide themselves and were parked under a street light. Sean guessed that the only thing stopping them from knocking on Dr Vogel's door was that they knew a foreign visitor was staying under his roof and did not want to cause any international protests just after the Games. At least one consolation was that they had not seemed to have made the connection with him and David or they would have already knocked down the doors to the flats in the building.

The situation was no less perilous than when Sean was serving on the Western Front those years earlier and he was no less afraid.

6

Extra fuel had been loaded and Matthew sat in the cockpit with a chart on his lap, calculating the best route to Czechoslovakia. He would fly via Istanbul and, all going well, experience good weather and friendly customs personnel there. Ben Rosenblum was eager for Matthew to get the flight underway as he was nervous, so deep in the Arab territory of Iraq.

'You got a telegram, Skipper,' Cyril said, clambering into the cockpit in his greasy overalls.

Matthew paused in his checklist and accepted the envelope from Cyril's oil-stained hand. He opened the telegram to read the few words scribbled down in English.

Urgent need to pick up package in Berlin.

The message also provided a day and time for the pickup.

It was signed by Sean Duffy.

Cyril read the telegram over Matthew's shoulder. 'What does it mean?' he asked.

'It has to be something bloody important for Sean Duffy to contact me,' Matthew said, puzzled by the lack of information in the message. Matthew could see that the date gave him two days to reach Berlin. He knew that he could be on time if he left in the next few hours but he had committed himself to the contract to pick up the munitions in Prague. Matthew made a quick calculation in his head just as Ben Rosenblum joined them in the cockpit.

'When are we leaving?' Ben asked.

'There has been a slight adjustment to my flight plan,' Matthew replied. 'We will be detouring to Berlin before reaching Prague.'

'That was not mentioned when you submitted your flight plan,' Ben frowned.

'We have to pick up a package of some kind at the Berlin airport,' Matthew explained.

'What kind of package?' Ben asked.

'I don't really know, but as the message has come from a man I consider almost a brother – then it must be important,' Matthew said.

'You are being paid to fly to Prague and pick up our cargo,' Ben reminded him, and then, although he realised that being Jewish in Germany was not a good thing, he added, 'but if it does not interfere with the mission, I cannot see any problem.'

Matthew nodded his gratitude. 'We fly out within the hour,' he said with a smile. 'Fair skies and good weather ahead . . . I hope.'

Ben left the cockpit to retrieve his duffel bag for the flight, leaving Cyril and Matthew alone in the cabin.

'I don't like it,' Cyril cautioned. 'If you want my opinion it has the smell of trouble about it.'

'Thought the same thing, old chap,' Matthew agreed. 'But family is family – even distant family – and one must recognise that.'

'Take care,' Cyril said, placing his hand on Matthew's shoulder. 'I'm getting too old to find another boss. At least the old girl is in peak condition and she should get you to Prague and back without any worries.'

'Thanks, Cyril,' Matthew said, appreciating that there was at least one person in the world who cared for him – at least for his Ford trimotor aeroplane anyway.

*

With rest, David had regained enough of his strength to leave the bed and walk around. The chicken soup seemed to have worked – along with as many dumplings as the doctor's wife, Eva, could spoon into David.,

Sean and David sat at a table, playing chess. Sean was losing.

'There's something on your mind, Uncle Sean,' David said, when Sean made an obvious blunder.

Sean frowned. 'I sent the telegram knowing that there was little chance Matthew could have answered as I could not afford to reveal any address that might lead the Gestapo to the doctor's door. But I do not know if Matthew actually got it and will be at the airport at the designated time.'

'Life is a gamble,' David said. 'All we can do is bet on the fact that Matthew will be at the rendezvous, and hope the stakes aren't too high if he's not.'

Sean glanced at David and was reminded how much he looked like his father, Alexander Macintosh, who had been killed on the Western Front. He was the spitting image around the face, but differed from his father in size. David was taller, broader, and more like the Duffy men.

'Were you ever told why you were arrested?' Sean asked.

'Nothing, not even how long I was going to be held. The only thing they said was that an informant put me in as some kind of communist agitator,' David replied, fingering a chess piece. 'For the life of me I can't think of anyone who would inform on me.'

'I think I may have a prime suspect,' Sean said. 'Your uncle was in Germany around the time you were picked up and has good cause to see mischief come to you – even to the point of your death.'

'Are you talking about Sir George?' David asked with a frown. 'My grandmother told me that he is the devil himself.'

'He is the most evil bastard I have ever known,' said Sean, 'and as a criminal lawyer I have seen a few. It has never been proven but your uncle may have been instrumental in conspiring to have his own sister murdered, and he was linked to the death of a Sydney prostitute many years ago.'

'I've never met him,' David said, pushing his chess piece across the board and picking up Sean's knight.

'You did when you were a toddler,' Sean countered. 'Your uncle made a rare visit to Glen View but departed in a hurry, for reasons never explained. Thank God he did, as I suspect he may have, even then, been planning to kill you. When you turn twenty-one you will have a third share in the family enterprises and that will make you a very rich young man. Sir George will do anything to make sure that you do not take your place in the Macintosh financial affairs.'

'I don't care much for the business world,' David said. 'I was hoping I might get a place at Duntroon, to train as an army officer – just like my father and grandfather. From what I have seen and heard I think we will be at war very soon. We have to stand up to the fascists and fight.'

'If you had seen what we saw back in the Great War you would reconsider your enthusiasm for war,' Sean cautioned. 'No sane man would want to go through what my generation did in the trenches. I think you should consider a future other than soldiering, or you might end up like me – no legs and no wife.'

Suddenly they heard the thumping sound of hurried footsteps coming up the stairs. The door burst open and Eva entered.

'The Gestapo are searching all the houses on the street,' she cried, her eyes wide. 'I do not know if they are searching for you, but you must leave immediately.'

David snatched a warm coat and Sean his walking stick. Although Sean had not understood everything Eva had said in German he could certainly read her terrified expression.

'What's happening?' Sean asked David.

David told him.

'This way,' Eva said, gesturing to the open door. 'Down the back stairs to the alley.'

Both men found themselves in a narrow alley that was open at both ends. They could hear loud voices coming from the street.

'I'm not sure if the Gestapo are looking for me,' David said, straining to hear what the uniformed men were saying. 'But we cannot stay here and put the doctor and Eva in danger.'

'I agree,' Sean said and the two men made their way to the far end of the alley. When they emerged onto a nearby residential street they could see three black cars parked in front of a house and a man being roughly manhandled towards one of the cars by a couple of black-uniformed men, while a woman was slumped at the top of her stairs sobbing her protests.

'Not us they are looking for,' David whispered. 'What do we do?'

'We walk towards the Gestapo as if we do not have a care in the world,' said Sean softly. 'That way we show we have nothing to hide.'

David shot Sean a concerned look. They stepped out and proceeded towards the cars. A couple of the Gestapo turned their attention to the older man walking with a cane, and the younger man sporting faded bruises on his face, but David bid them good afternoon with the calmness of a man with ice in his veins. The greeting seemed to work as the Gestapo returned their attention to their hapless prisoner.

When Sean and David were around the corner walking towards a crowded thoroughfare, David stumbled slightly. Sean could see sweat beading on his forehead despite the chill of the late afternoon. 'Are you okay?' he asked in concern.

'I don't know how I did it,' David said hoarsely. 'When I saw those uniforms I had a recollection of those same uniforms beating a man to death on the parade ground. I thought I might go to pieces, and start running.'

'But you didn't,' Sean said. 'You have your father's courage.'

The two men joined the pedestrians on the wide tree-lined street. They caught a tram and, with little else other than the clothes they wore, made their way to Berlin's main airport. All they could do was hope against hope that the telegram had reached its destination.

*

Ben Rosenblum had regained the colour he had lost when Matthew had lifted off from an airfield at Istanbul hours earlier. Matthew had invited the young man to take the copilot's seat for the flight and Ben had reluctantly admitted that he was afraid of flying. His journey to Basra had been on a small coastal steamer and this was the first time in his life he had actually flown. Despite Matthew's reassurance that flying was safe, they had hit bad weather before reaching the Turkish capital, and Matthew had been forced to fly around billowing thunderhead clouds flashing with lightning.

Ben had been sick while Matthew fought with the controls of his aircraft. But Matthew was an excellent pilot and had brought them through for a smooth landing at the Istanbul airstrip. In the Great War he had flown against German and Turkish pilots and the irony of landing on the old enemy's turf was not lost on the former fighter pilot.

Now Matthew was flying in the fading light of evening into the heavily built-up suburbs of southern Berlin. He was heading towards the Tempelhof area where the Germans were still constructing a huge air terminal for international travel. When Ben looked out the forward window all he could see was myriad lights in the growing dark and he thought it would be impossible to land an aircraft in such confusion. Matthew strained to make out the airfield landing lights and found them. With practised ease he set down the Ford with just a couple of rough bumps then taxied towards a vacant area under floodlights.

Government workers scurried around in the dark and Matthew prepared his paperwork, ready to identify himself if the officials questioned his purpose for the landing. Matthew glanced to his right where another similar aircraft sat on the tarmac. Even in the dim light he could see the serial number of the Junkers trimotor.

'I will be damned,' he swore. 'That's Diane's kite.'

Ben glanced at him but Matthew shook his head. 'Just a friend,' he responded to the questioning look on Ben's face. 'Someone who used to fly for me a few years back.'

The fluttering propellers came to a stop and both men unstrapped themselves from their seats to stretch their legs. Matthew led the way into the cargo hold of his aircraft and opened the door to drop to the ground below. He pulled up the collar of the worn leather flying jacket he had retained from his days with the Australian Flying Corp in the skies of Palestine, and was immediately greeted by four German officials wearing the uniforms of customs men.

'Your identity papers,' one of them demanded with his hand out, and Matthew passed his passport and cargo manifest. With a hand torch, the official scrutinised the papers and passport, while one of the officials peeled off to intercept Ben who did not understand German, but followed Matthew's example, producing his papers.

'You are a Jew, ja?' the official said in guttural English when he saw that Ben was from Palestine. Ben replied in Arabic, a language he was fluent in. The confused official glanced at his superior who was interviewing Matthew.

'My passenger is an Arab,' Matthew said in German, turning away from the man perusing his documents. 'He is a personal friend of al-Husseini, leading the rebellion against the British and Jews in his country.'

The German interviewing Ben broke into a smile, satisfied with his bona fides.

The check on their status completed, the German customs men left them alone and Matthew walked over to Ben. 'You could have warned me,' he said mildly. 'I was not aware you were travelling with Arab papers.'

'In this part of the world it does not pay to be a Jew,' Ben smiled. 'We are taking in thousands of Jewish refugees from Germany and they have told some bad stories of their treatment here. I always make sure that I have a double identity when I am away from home.'

'Matthew,' a familiar female voice called and the Australian turned to see Diane striding towards him, wearing her flying suit. 'What in Hades are you doing here?'

'Nice to see you, too,' Matthew answered when she reached him. 'We're just passing through on a contract to Prague. My passenger is Ben Rosenblum.'

'Pleased to meet you, Mr Rosenblum,' Diane said, extending her hand.

'Ben does not understand English,' Matthew quickly added. 'He is a Palestinian Arab.' Matthew could see the look of annoyance on Ben's face as he realised that Matthew had cut him off from any conversation with the very pretty lady.

'But I know that you speak Arabic,' Diane said. 'What is he doing flying with you?'

Matthew was not about to answer that question and changed the subject. 'When do you head back to Basra?' he asked.

'We're ready to fly out tonight. Our archaeologists and cargo arrive very soon. I hope to make Istanbul before morning and refuel there before returning to Basra. How long will you be gone?'

'I'm not sure,' Matthew answered. 'But I should be back before the weekend.'

'Well, safe flying and cheerio for now,' Diane said, turning on her heel to walk back to her aircraft.

Matthew watched her walk away, admiring the curves of her body.

'What do we do now?' Ben asked, rubbing his hands to ward off the night chill.

'We wait,' Matthew replied, wondering why he was doing so. What was this vital cargo he was to pick up?

While they waited Matthew carried out routine checks of his aircraft with the aid of a flashlight. He was checking the undercarriage when Ben hissed at him.

'Someone is coming towards us across the airstrip,' he warned.

Matthew strained his eyes into the dark but could see nothing. It was obvious that the Jewish fighter had good night vision as within a minute Matthew could see two figures emerging from the darkness. A tall and broad-shouldered young man was assisting the man Matthew recognised as Sean Duffy. When they reached the aircraft Sean thrust out his hand to Matthew, gripping it with as firm a grip as possible.

'Bloody hell, old boy, it has been a long time since we last met,' Matthew said, then turned his attention to the young man with Sean. 'Who is your friend?'

'David Macintosh, sir,' David replied, also extending his hand. 'It is good to finally meet you. I have heard many stories about your flying career in Palestine during the war. When we saw your aircraft land Uncle Sean said that it had to be you by the smooth way you set down. But really we just took a gamble this had to be your aeroplane,' David continued, gesturing to the Ford. 'We have had to gamble a lot lately.'

'David,' Matthew said. 'You must be the son of Alexander and Giselle. What in hell are you doing in Germany?'

'I don't wish to sound alarmist,' Sean cut in, 'but we have to get out of this country right now. We have had some bother with the local authorities who would like to see David dead. I was able to ascertain late this afternoon from a telephone call I made that the SS have somehow tracked us to the Tempelhof area.'

'What did you do?' Matthew asked with a bemused expression. 'Piss in Herr Hitler's soup?'

'Something like that,' Sean replied, and as he did so he could see a group of men running towards them from the terminal area under construction. This time they were carrying rifles and pistols. 'I think we had better leave.'

Matthew turned to see the men coming towards them. 'Get in the plane now!' he shouted, and all four men scrambled for the open door to the Ford.

Matthew was last in and immediately raced for the cockpit and slammed himself down in his seat to hit the start controls. It was fortunate that his engines were still warm and they kicked over with a reassuring roar. But when Matthew glanced out the cockpit window he could see that the men were closing fast and raising their rifles to open fire.

Matthew grabbed the controls and swung the nose around to taxi out onto the airstrip, but he had a sinking feeling that he would not make it before the men on foot were within range to shoot up his aircraft.

Ben had thrown himself into the copilot's seat. 'We're not going to make it,' he said through gritted teeth. 'The bastards will be on us before we can get going.'

Suddenly Matthew was aware that Diane's Junkers was taxiing between his plane and the pursuers, causing them to scatter lest they be caught in the spinning blades of the aircraft. The distraction gave Matthew the time he needed to pick up speed and place himself on the runway, where he opened the throttle for the shortest takeoff in his career.

'Hang on!' he shouted over his shoulder and the aircraft shuddered with the strain of the takeoff. He could hear a German voice calling to him over his radio to immediately land and hand over the two unauthorised persons who had been spotted near his aircraft, but Matthew ignored it. Ben picked up the hand piece and yelled down an obscenity in English that caused a short silence from the control tower.

Then they were in the air and Matthew glanced at his compass to correct his course for Prague. The southern suburbs of Berlin were lit up under the rising aircraft and Matthew thanked his lucky stars they were flying at night. That meant the German fighter aircraft he had noticed parked at the edge of the airfield would not be able to pursue them. He knew that his aircraft was now blacked out. When he was satisfied all was well with the aeroplane and he had enough fuel to get him across the German border and into Czechoslovakian airspace, Matthew finally let out a deep breath.

He reached for a cigar in his pocket and lit it, breathing out the smoke and reflecting on Diane's unexpected action. He had no doubt that if she hadn't placed her Junkers between the German military men and his trimotor, they would either be dead by now or in the hands of the German authorities.

'Remind me to get a very large bunch of flowers when we are in Prague,' Matthew shouted into Ben's ear. 'And see if we have any tea left in the thermos, old chap.'

Ben nodded his head and unstrapped himself from his seat to make his way into the cargo hold where he saw Sean and David sitting, ashen-faced, on the floor.

'Flying is very safe,' Ben said with the authority of a man who had spent only a few hours in the sky, and most of those in terror. 'I am Ben Rosenblum,' he introduced himself. 'We are going to Prague.'

Sean looked at Ben. 'I don't care where we're going so long as it's out of Germany,' he said. 'Just tell me when we're over the border.'

When David and Sean were alone in the fuselage of the aircraft they discussed how the SS had tracked them to the airport. Sean had an idea but did not wish to dwell on the thought that the SS were not as stupid as he thought. They must have finally connected him to David. The telegram had given the place and date for their escape and only the gambler's luck they had depended on so much had got them off the ground as the SS closed in.

7

Within the week Matthew flew his trimotor back to Basra via Jerusalem. Sean and David had left him in Prague to make their way to London via Paris. The reunion had been marked by many hangovers as the two old warriors talked over family matters and the recent past.

Matthew came to a stop outside the big hangar where Cyril waited, hands on hips, to inspect his aeroplane. Like all aeronautical engineers, Cyril felt the plane was really his by virtue of the fact he knew every valve, bolt and oil line.

Diane's aircraft was sitting at the edge of the airstrip. Matthew looked at the bouquet of colourful flowers on the copilot's seat and realised that they had wilted somewhat from the flight.

Matthew exited the aircraft with the large wad of American dollars that had been paid to him when he delivered his cargo to an improvised airstrip outside Jerusalem.

The men waiting had said very little as they'd unloaded the crates of weapons and ammunition. Ben had left with the taciturn men who had the demeanour of tough and dedicated disciples.

'G'day Cyril,' Matthew greeted. 'Much happen since I left?'

'You have a visitor,' Cyril answered, grim-faced. 'And it is not Miss Hatfield.'

No sooner had the Canadian engineer opened his mouth than Matthew saw a British uniformed officer walking towards them with a small swagger stick tucked under his arm. The approaching army officer had tanned legs below the bottom of his khaki shorts and a tanned face, suggesting that he was not a recent arrival to Basra. Matthew guessed the man was in his late twenties. When he came closer Matthew could see that he had a handsome face and a small moustache.

'Captain Duffy, I presume,' he said without offering his hand. 'I have been waiting your arrival. I am Major Guy Wilkes, army intelligence.'

Matthew removed his leather flying helmet and breathed in the desert air. Although it was a clear day, the temperature was dropping and he kept his gloves on.

'What is army intelligence doing on my airstrip?' Matthew asked.

'If we could speak in private, old chap,' Major Wilkes said.

'We can go to my office,' Matthew replied and stepped off with the British officer beside him, leaving Cyril to watch on suspiciously.

'I heard that you had a spot of trouble at Tempelhof,' the major smiled with just a touch of sarcasm. 'It appears that the German authorities are protesting to His Majesty that a British-registered aircraft made an unlawful takeoff from their territory last week. It seems you did not get the required clearances.'

'I am not sure what you are referring to,' Matthew answered calmly. 'I was at Tempelhof, but nothing unto-ward happened when I left.'

They reached the entrance to the huge hangar and Matthew saw his Iraqi servant, Ibrahim hovering nearby. He called to him in Arabic to prepare tea and ushered the British officer into his cluttered office. Matthew gestured to the battered leather chair and took a seat behind his desk.

'Well,' Wilkes said, placing his swagger stick across his knees, 'I am not here to question you about your flight into Germany, and I am sure that I can make that problem go away if you are prepared to once again fly the flag for the Empire. I have read your very impressive war record, flying with the AFC, and I also know about your work for our intelligence service during the war. I believe that you were awarded an MBE along with your MC.'

Matthew eyed off the younger man. 'I am a civilian, Major,' he replied. 'And I deny any incident in Germany.'

'I said that I was not here to talk to you about Tempelhof,' the intelligence officer said, leaning forward in his chair. 'I am here about the weapons you picked up in Prague from the Brno factory.'

Matthew began to feel uneasy. Ibrahim arrived bearing a tray and pot of tea and both men ceased speaking while he poured the tea into two cups. When he departed, Major Wilkes sipped from his cup, while Matthew left his alone.

'I thought that the British government was sympathetic to the *Haganah*,' Matthew said, realising that there was no sense in lying.

'The trouble is you do not know much about Ben

Rosenblum,' Major Wilkes said. 'Did he tell you that he belonged to Orde Wingate's boys?'

'Yes,' Matthew said, picking up his tea. His throat was suddenly dry. 'You must also know that his father was a staunch supporter of the British during the war.'

'Saul Rosenblum and his son no longer see eye to eye,' Wilkes replied. 'Ben is now with the Irgun.'

'Irgun?' Matthew asked.

'A radical splinter group whose members believe that simply defending themselves from Arab attack is not enough. Their tactics are rather brutal against a lot of innocent Arab inhabitants of Palestine, and they appear to consider us as enemies too. Those arms went to them.'

Matthew realised that he had been conned by his best friend's son and he was angry.

'Had I known I would not have accepted the contract,' Matthew said.

'I tend to believe you, Captain Duffy,' Wilkes said in a voice that was genuine in its sincerity. 'You made a mistake but have the opportunity to redeem yourself.'

Matthew could feel the wad of American dollars in his jacket; he might not agree with the Irgun but he was not about to give up the fee covering his costs and commission. 'How can I make up for my mistake?' he asked.

'A former employee of yours has recently flown in a party of German archaeologists,' the major said. 'We know that the delightful Miss Hatfield has a contract with the German government, and I have been informed that you are in partnership with her in this contract. We need someone close to Miss Hatfield to observe the Huns' movements in the country. We feel that with your impressive background serving the Empire you are the man to keep us up to date on what the Germans are doing. We would also like to know a little more about how Miss Hatfield obtained the contract with Hitler's government.'

'I suppose archaeologists simply dig holes in the ground looking for bits of pottery that they can get excited about,' Matthew said with a touch of sarcasm. 'My priority is to keep my rather small airline afloat, Major.' Matthew was about to rise from behind his desk but the British officer's proposal stopped him.

'What if I had the funds to put you on a retainer? Would that help?'

'How much?' Matthew countered.

Guy Wilkes reached into the top pocket of his jacket to remove a piece of paper, which Matthew instantly recognised as a bank cheque. He passed it to Matthew, who glanced at the figure.

'For how long?' Matthew asked, impressed.

'You would be contracted for at least the time that the Germans are running around the desert digging up bits of pottery,' the major said. 'In addition, the usual work you do for our oil companies continues without interruption.'

It was a generous offer and Matthew knew that he had little choice if he wanted to keep the company operating. 'You have a deal,' he said, standing and extending his hand to seal the agreement between himself and British army intelligence.

The British officer rose and accepted the gesture.

'Good,' he said. 'I feel that we will achieve a lot working together, old chap.'

'Do you suspect Miss Hatfield of being a Nazi sympathiser?' Matthew asked as the major prepared to return to army HQ in Basra.

'There are many Nazi sympathisers in both the USA and England,' Guy Wilkes replied. 'I hope that you find she is not one of them.'

Matthew thought about how Diane had placed her aircraft between his own and the pursuing German soldiers days earlier, risking her life. 'I doubt that Diane is a Nazi,' Matthew said.

'We will rely on you to ascertain her political sympathies,' the major shrugged. 'I will be in contact. We can meet each week at this café in Basra,' he said, handing Matthew a small piece of paper. 'In the meantime I think that you should get acquainted with Miss Hatfield's archaeologists.'

Matthew watched the British officer leave and thought about retrieving the flowers from his aircraft. A dash of water might still revive them.

*

Sean felt that the Savoy in London was worth the cost for a week's accommodation, considering all that he and David had been through in Germany. The plush and famous hotel was also close to the law offices where Sean needed to conduct his legal business on behalf of his Australian clients. He left David to enjoy the historic sites of the city on the Thames River.

At the end of the day they met in the dining room. Both men had used a substantial amount of money from Sean's London bank to outfit themselves in new clothes. Sean had built up a sound legal practice over the years, and without a wife and children to spend it on, had saved much of his substantial income. Now he could afford to spoil David in the hope that it might distract the young man from the horrors of his imprisonment in Dachau.

'I found a good gym not far from here,' David said, fork embedded in a piece of roast lamb in the Savoy's very posh dining room. 'I might get a chance to have a workout in the ring with one of the Pom heavyweights.'

'Do you think you have recovered enough to get back in the ring?' Sean asked, picking up his glass of good French red.

'I have to do something,' David replied, gazing off across the room to where he could see a very pretty young lady sitting with what he presumed were her parents. 'I can't sightsee all day, it'll drive me mad. I need to get back in training.'

'If you think you're up to it, you have my blessing to have your head knocked in by some Pom heavyweight,' Sean shrugged. Sean had booked them both on a ship back to Australia in just over a week's time. His legal dealings were going well with his learned English friends, and now it was only a matter of waiting for the slow wheels of the civil legal machine to grind over.

After breakfast the following morning, David changed into casual clothing and made his way to the gym he had identified. He stepped inside the building and the familiar pungent smell of sweat, tobacco and unguents for sore muscles assailed him, bringing back memories of the Sydney gym he trained in under the management of Harry Griffiths, a close friend of Sean's. Harry had trained David himself and he was a good teacher.

'What you want?' asked a smallish middle-aged man who had long lost his hair.

'I'm in from Sydney, Australia,' David answered. 'I wouldn't mind some time in the ring.'

'You a colonial fighter?' the little man asked, retrieving the stub of a cigar and lighting it.

'I've been with Harry Griffiths' gym for over four years,' David replied.

'Never 'eard of 'im,' the little man said. 'But young Horace over there needs a punchin' bag. You look like a 'eavyweight. You got any kit?'

'No,' David replied, looking across the room to a well-built man around his own age and weight, sparring with a boxing bag. The room had around a dozen other young men in different stages of training, and the air echoed with grunts, slaps on leather and orders roared at individuals to keep up their hands, shuffle their feet or use their shoulder with the punch. It was all so familiar to David.

'Get yourself ready over there,' the little man said, handing David a set of gloves. 'Horry,' he roared. 'You got yerself a match. Three three-minute rounds. I'll ref.'

Horry slapped his gloves together as his eyes met David's.

Sitting down on a small wooden stool inside the boxing ring, David put out his hands to be strapped by an old assistant. 'You met the boss,' he said through teeth yellowed by years of smoking. 'You must have impressed Ikey to be able to get in the ring with his best boy. You ever fight before?'

'Yeah,' David answered, flexing his knuckles when the strapping was applied. 'Last fight was back in Dachau for the heavyweight championship.'

'That near Glasgow or something?' the assistant asked without sounding as if he was interested in the answer, and David did not bother explaining.

David had stripped down to his singlet, and a leather head protection was handed to him. He was barefooted but no one seemed to mind when he and Horace stepped into the centre of the ring. A few of the fighters in training stopped their activities to watch the fight.

'Clean fight,' Ikey said, still puffing on his cigar. 'Horry, this is your opponent – all the way from the colony of Australia. Don't know 'is name but 'e reckons 'e can fight.'

David touched gloves with his opponent and the two men returned to their corners. The assistant clanged the bell, and the two young men began circling each other with hands up in defensive positions. For David it felt so good to be back on the surface of canvas, surrounded by ropes and not barbed wire.

'Have a go, Aussie,' someone yelled and David once again experienced the euphoria of being in the ring, pitted one on one against an opponent. Three rounds went quickly. David landed many good punches but his English opponent was in the prime of his fighting career, and David knew that he was receiving more than he delivered. It was a good clean fight and when the bell clanged for the finish of the third round, David collapsed on the little wooden stool thrust into his corner by the assistant. As this was not an official fight there was no need for the proclamation of a winner, but David hefted himself from the stool, walked over to his equally battered opponent, and held his hand up as a gesture to Horry being the winner on points. The gesture took the other man by surprise.

'Thanks, Aussie,' he said with a warm smile. 'You can fight. Hope we don't go too many rounds when you're in top form.'

'Name's David Macintosh,' David said and Horace extended both his hands in the boxer's gesture, which David accepted.

'Horace Howard,' Horace said. 'You can call me Horry. Fancy a drink after I finish up here?'

'Sounds good,' David replied as the other boxers drifted back to their activities. 'My shout, to acknowledge your win on points.'

'Hey! Colonial, 'ow long you goin' to be 'angin' around?' Ikey said, interrupting the conversation. 'Could do with another fighter. Wot's yer name?'

'David Macintosh,' David replied as the assistant climbed

into the ring and began removing David's gloves. 'I never got your name.'

'Smartarse,' Ikey replied. 'But you put up a bloody good fight with my best boy so I'll tell you. Ishmael Solomon. People around 'ere call me Ikey.'

David smiled and nodded his head. *With a name like that the little man was definitely not Irish*, he thought with a smile.

David waited around while Horry finished his training and found himself chatting with Ikey. David warmed to the little man and ended up unexpectedly talking about his time in Dachau.

'You need a couple of stiff drinks,' Ikey said, leading David to his office with his hand on his back. David sat down on an old chair while Ikey rummaged in a drawer of an old filing cabinet and retrieved a bottle of Scotch. He poured a generous measure into two small glasses and handed one to David.

'*L'chaim*,' he said, raising his glass.

'To life,' David replied. 'That is about the limit of my Hebrew. I'm afraid my grandmother has given up on me and says that I'm no better than a *goyim*.'

'So, you're from Australia and found yourself in Dachau,' Ikey said, searching about in the filing cabinet until he found a fresh cigar. 'I hear stories about the way Hitler is treating the Jews in Germany. Next he will declare war on all Jews – and just kill us.'

'I doubt that he would do that,' David answered, his eyes watering from the strong liquor. At nineteen he was still underage for drinking but that had not stopped him in the past, and he felt much older than his years now. 'To do that would bring the world down on Hitler.'

'The French and our own government don't have the guts to stand up to Hitler,' Ikey spat. 'You watch, my boy, they will give in to him. Fascism is going to take over the world, you'll see, and we'll just lie down and let Hitler have his way.'

The Jewish man's speech had changed now they were away from the boxers. 'I gather from the way you're speaking that you're really an educated man,' David said quietly.

'Very astute, my boy,' Ikey said. 'I was born in the shadow of the bells of St Paul's and was an actor on the stage until the Depression,' he said, lighting the cigar and puffing clouds of blue smoke in the room. 'But life is only a big stage, and I had enough knowledge of the fight game to open this gym a couple of years ago. So I went back to my old accent to fit in with the crowd around here. I've always had the knack of being a good judge of winners – and I see one in you.'

'Thanks for your faith in me,' David said. 'But I'm not sure where my life will go. I have a plan to return to Australia and enrol in Duntroon, our equivalent of your Sandhurst.'

Ikey stared at David for a moment before taking a seat at his desk and putting his feet up on it. 'You ever think about signing up to fight in Spain?' he asked, watching David's reaction through the smoky haze he had created with his cigar.

'I haven't thought much about anything since I got out of Germany,' David replied. 'But I do know that the world is asleep and we have to stop fascism now before it takes over.'

'Are you a communist?' Ikey asked bluntly.

'No, but that doesn't stop me from hating fascism. I saw what went on in Dachau; if Hitler is prepared to do that to his own people, what is he capable of doing to the rest of the world?'

'Horry is signing up with an international brigade. He sails off in a couple of days.' Ikey said. 'You could go with him and make sure he doesn't do anything stupidly brave.'

Startled at the sudden offer David found that he was almost holding his breath. Sitting in this dingy cramped office, staring at the worn soles of Ikey's shoes, David knew that what he said next would change his life forever. His rage at his imprisonment in Dachau was eating away at him, and now he was being offered a chance to fight back.

'Why not?' he replied, raising his glass. 'Where do I sign up?'

★

That evening David and Sean were seated in the dining room of the Savoy Hotel among the glittering jewellery of the wealthy matrons of the British upper-class and their immaculately dressed husbands. Sean was shocked to see the bruising to David's face, and he could smell the alcohol on his breath, although David did not act drunk.

'Did you get into a scrap?' Sean asked.

'Had a workout in a gym not far from here,' David replied.

'Did you win the bout?' Sean persisted with a slight smile.

David glanced at Sean. 'No, but I held my own.' He took a deep breath. 'I thought I might as well tell you now that I won't be returning to Sydney with you, Uncle Sean.'

Sean raised his eyebrows in surprise. 'Dare I ask what you intend to do in London if you are determined to stay? The Savoy has just about used up my travel budget.'

'I won't be staying in London,' David said. 'I've signed up to go to Spain to fight Franco's fascist rebels.'

At David's announcement Sean felt his blood run cold. 'Don't be stupid,' he said angrily. 'You don't know what war is like. It is constant terror broken by interludes of misery. You could end up dead, or worse, like me, with no legs. Do you want that at your age?'

David felt the sting of the rebuke. 'I'm sorry, Uncle Sean, but this is something I have to do. I'm not a communist, but I have experienced what fascism does to a man. Someone has to take a stand and stop the bastards now, before they grow stronger and start a war.'

'David, you are about to inherit a fortune,' Sean pleaded, realising that anger would not sway the young man. He saw in David the same foolishness that had caused him to volunteer at a similar age to fight a bloody war far from home. 'You have responsibilities to your grandmother.'

David leaned back in his chair and Sean could see that nothing he said was going to change the young man's mind.

'I leave on the train at six tomorrow morning for a ferry to France,' David said. 'I know that you do not agree with me signing on, but I hope you will understand that this is the most important thing I will ever do in my life.'

'Having a wife and family is the most important thing you will ever do,' Sean countered. 'War means nothing. It changes nothing. How many young men died in the war that was supposed to end all wars, and here we are again, less than twenty years later, facing the very same prospect. However, if you are determined to go, nothing I say will stop you. At the least you must promise to write to me every opportunity you have. Swear to me that you will, and that you will not do anything stupid.'

Sean's words touched David and he realised again how much this former soldier meant to him. David reached across the table and Sean accepted the handshake.

'I promise that I will write, Uncle Sean,' he said.

Over the meal Sean found himself chatting with David about his days as an officer in the Australian army, fighting on the Western Front. He realised that he was attempting to drum into David everything he could think of to keep him alive.

They both rose early next morning and Sean accompanied David to the railway station. There, in the chill of the morning fog, they shook hands. Leaning out of a carriage window, a young man called to David, and the Australian picked up his bag and boarded the train.

The train worked up steam and Sean found himself staring as the last carriage disappeared from the station. This place had once seen so many young men depart for war across the English Channel, never to return.

It was then that the tears flowed down Sean's cheeks as he wondered if he would ever see David again. War had a way of destroying the best of a generation.

8

Diane returned to Matthew's bungalow with three guests.

'I did not think you would mind if our clients stayed over for a couple of days before I fly them out to their dig,' Diane said in such a way that Matthew knew he would have to agree to crowding the little space he had.

'Not at all,' he lied politely, and the three German archaeologists dressed in khaki slacks and jackets were introduced to him.

'Dr Lamar Kramer, who is the head of the team,' Diane said, and Matthew accepted the hand of a shortish, slightly plump, balding man around his mid-forties whose grip was soft and weak.

'How do you do?' he said in heavily accented English.

'Dr Derik Albrecht,' Diane said and the second man also shook hands. He was tall and lean with a handsome face and a head of short cropped blond hair. His blue eyes were piercing and his handshake strong. Matthew guessed he was in his early forties.

'So, you are the man we have hired to assist Miss Hatfield,' Albrecht said in a cold tone. 'I expect that you are capable enough.'

Matthew took an immediate dislike to him for his arrogance and turned to the third member of the team.

'Miss Erika Wolfe,' Diane introduced, and Matthew had to admit that she was a very attractive woman in her late thirties. In many ways she reminded Matthew of Joanne Barrington with her titian hair and emerald green eyes. She had a smile that was almost seductive and her hand in his felt warm.

'It is a pleasure to meet you, Captain Duffy,' Erika said in educated German. 'Our wonderful pilot has told us much about your adventurous life.'

Although Diane did not speak much German, Matthew thought he caught a glimpse of jealousy flash in her eyes, but he dismissed the notion. Diane had never shown any romantic interest in him in all the times they had been together.

'Welcome to Iraq,' Matthew said in German. 'While you are in Basra you have the run of my house, which I am sure will provide a few more comforts than you will have on your dig.'

The three expressed their gratitude and Matthew indicated that dinner would be served within the hour. In the meantime he had a bottle of Scotch fetched by his servant, Ibrahim.

The evening passed pleasantly enough and Matthew found himself switching from English to German as he answered questions and asked a few of his own. He could not help but notice the attention Dr Derik Albrecht paid to Diane but was flattered by the interest Erika seemed to take in him.

'You are from Australia, yes?' she asked in English, holding her tumbler of Scotch and soda in her hands.

'Yes,' Matthew replied. 'I'm from the state of Queensland.'

'Ah, that is the place of savage natives and kangaroos,' Erika replied. 'I have read much about Australia and would love to visit in the future.'

'I hope to retire there one day,' Matthew said, but in a distracted way as he watched Diane and Derik laughing together. He noticed the German archaeologist place his hand on Diane's knee, and she did not attempt to brush it away. 'But that will not be for some time.'

'That is good,' Erika said with a warm smile. 'I will enjoy your company on our expedition.'

Matthew returned his attention to Erika and could see in her eyes a dreamy look that reminded him of a satisfied cat.

'I will be sharing the flying with Miss Hatfield,' he said. 'We may not have much opportunity to see each other. I also have another pilot, Tyrone McKee, who will stand in for me when I am not available.'

'That is sad,' Erika said, pouting, and Matthew was acutely aware that she was showing more than a casual interest in him. He had spent so long flying and keeping his business together that there had been no time to think about any romantic interludes. The pain of losing Joanne was still with him even though more than fifteen years had passed since he had held her in his arms and watched her die. Only the reappearance of Diane in his life had caused him to think of sharing his life with another woman.

Before midnight the guests said they would turn in as

Diane had scheduled an early morning flight out. Ibrahim showed each guest to their room. Matthew slept on the floor of his living room as he had given up his bed to Diane.

It was a little after midnight when Matthew awoke. An unusual noise came from his bedroom: the low moan and whispers of a man and woman. Matthew recognised Diane's voice speaking softly, and that of Albrecht. There was no mistaking what was occurring in his bed, and Matthew felt an intense pang of jealousy. But Diane was a grown woman and her decisions were her own; besides, he was far too old for her. When Matthew finally fell asleep again his dreams were riddled with images of fighting over the plains of Palestine, of burning aircraft and men's shattered bodies as his bullets cut them to pieces. His whimpering went unheard.

*

'So they belong to the Nazi *Ahnenebe* organisation,' said Major Guy Wilkes. He was wearing civilian clothing and sipping a potent thick Arabic coffee in a small Basra café. 'Albrecht, Kramer and Wolfe.'

'That's what I was told during the evening,' Matthew replied, weary from not sleeping well the night before. 'A few hours ago Diane took off in the Junkers to fly them upcountry to their dig. What do you know about this *Ahnenebe* organisation?' he asked.

'It is part of Himmler's mad obsession with proving that the Aryan race has its roots in ancient cultures,' Guy replied. 'The organisation is staffed by second-rate scientists and attached to Himmler's SS. Its full title is German Ancestry – Research Society for Ancient Intellectual History. Our intelligence sources have identified that Herr Himmler, who is the current chief of all police in Germany, is not averse to using the pseudo-science for propaganda purposes, trying to prove that the Germans are the descendants of the lost city of Atlantis, and that they have been locked in an historic fight with the evil Semites. It is all bloody tommy-rot, but no one is game to tell Himmler that. Mostly the organisation has concentrated on northern Europe for its archaeology. That is why we have suspicions about this team your Miss Hatfield has flown into Iraq.'

'Why would the Huns be interested in this part of the world?' Matthew asked.

'In my opinion they have two good reasons,' Guy replied. 'One is that the oil fields here are of great strategic interest in time of war, and the second is that they are attempting to foster Arab interest in co-operating with the German government. They have, after all, a common enemy – the Jews. I suspect that the Germans would like to see another uprising against us here, like the one in Jerusalem being promoted by their Grand Mufti, Amin al-Husseini. But I am sure that you will be able to report back on our so-called archaeologists and we will have means of keeping tabs on them. After all, I believe that Miss Joanne Barrington, herself an American archaeologist in this part of the world, worked closely with you against the Ottomans during the Palestine campaign.'

At the mention of Joanne's name Matthew experienced a pang of sadness and guilt. He had always blamed himself for her death, despite the fact that his friend, Saul Rosenblum, had reassured him that it was the fault of the war. 'Miss Barrington was an exceptional woman,' Matthew said quietly. 'And a top-notch archaeologist.'

'Sorry, old chap,' Guy said. 'I did not mean to open old wounds.'

Matthew gulped down his coffee. 'If you'll excuse me,' he said. 'I have a cargo to fly out to one of the oil fields this afternoon.'

Matthew rose from the table and stepped out onto the dusty street clogged with donkeys pulling carts and lined with stalls selling fly-covered foodstuffs. For some strange reason Matthew had trouble getting the image of Diane out of his mind. He shook his head as he made his way past the street hawkers squatting behind their stalls. What hope did he have now of expressing his desire for her when his competitor was younger and better looking?

★

Matthew returned to his airstrip to see that Diane's aircraft was already gone. Cyril was working at the bench in the hangar.

'Where is Tyrone?' Matthew asked.

'Got a phone call that he's suffering a bout of malaria,' Cyril replied.

'He's a bloody Kiwi. More like a hangover,' Matthew growled. 'Never mind. I'll take this one to the oilmen by myself.'

'I'll never understand what it is between you Aussies and Kiwis,' Cyril said, shaking his head. 'The cargo is loaded and the forecast is for good weather. Do you want me to take the second seat?'

'No, I'll be okay,' Matthew replied. 'Just get her ready. I'll fly out as soon as you give the okay.'

Cyril finished his final examination of the Ford and signalled the thumbs-up. Matthew kicked over the three motors, and when he was ready, taxied out to the strip to take off. The plane rose into the clear skies and, after reaching his elevation and levelling off, Matthew set his course north. The flying went without much incident and after an hour he settled back to eat the sandwiches Cyril had packed for him. He was reaching for the thermos of tea when he felt his aircraft being buffeted by an unseen wind. When he peered through the cockpit window his blood ran cold. A massive cloud of sand was billowing off on the horizon, stretching as far as the eye could see. Matthew swore to himself – it looked like a *sharqi* – a dry dusty wind that plagued Iraq, and thought desperately of the nearest airfield as there was no way to fly around the sandstorm. He scrabbled for the map by his side and glanced down to see a new airstrip pencilled in. It was the one used by the German archaeologists for air resupply and the only one close enough to get the plane down and secured before the sandstorm rolled in. Matthew reset his course and pointed the nose of the Ford towards the newly constructed airstrip. He brought his aircraft down on the improvised landing ground and taxied until he was a short distance from Diane's aircraft. He could see her supervising a crew of Iraqi labourers as they tied the plane down with ropes secured to the ground with steel pickets.

Diane hurried over to Matthew.

'I will get my men to help tie down the Ford,' she shouted as the wind began to pick up dust and whip it around them.

With her aircraft secured, the Iraqis did the same for Matthew's Ford. Satisfied they had done all they could, Diane ushered Matthew to an ancient stone enclosure that had been resurrected from under the desert sands by previous archaeologists. They were fortunate that the ancient enclosure had several spacious underground rooms where all the stores and tents were now dumped. Matthew was greeted by the three archaeologists whose expressions of apprehension bespoke their limited experience in this part of the world.

They had hardly settled down when the sandstorm rolled over them with its howling wind and choking fine dust. The members of the team had already wrapped cloth around their faces to keep the dust from their lungs.

Matthew sat against a stone wall and was joined by Diane.

'How long do you think the storm will last?' she asked.

'With any luck, just a few hours,' Matthew answered. But he was wrong; the storm raged into the evening without any let-up in the howling winds.

Around 6 pm Diane and Matthew began organising a meal on a little primus stove. Tinned sauerkraut and meat made a stew; afterwards coffee was boiled to wash it down.

Matthew looked around the stone walls and wondered what this ancient place had been, who had lived and died here. As if reading his thoughts, Erika came and sat down beside him.

'We were told of this dig last year when another team discovered it,' she said. 'We are not sure what this place was used for as we do not have enough evidence to make any conclusions but we think it was a trading centre built around 2000 BC. When it was built it would have been above ground level but the desert has tried to reclaim it.'

'Well, at least we can count our blessings that it's here,' Matthew said. 'It has given us good shelter.'

'I have read of sandstorms but this is the first time I have experienced such an event,' Erika said, tucking her knees up and grasping them with her arms. 'It is truly frightening.'

'They pass,' Matthew said. 'And I have a feeling this one is just about spent.'

Matthew stood up and stretched his legs. The wind sounded like an animal in its death throes. He walked to the entrance where a canvas sheet had been improvised to keep the sand out, and when he pushed it aside only a few puffs of wind remained. Above his head the crystal clarity of the stars shone with a brilliance only seen in such isolated places on earth.

Matthew stepped outside with the terrible apprehension of how his aircraft had weathered the storm, but when he made his way in the dark to the Ford, silhouetted against the starlit sky, it appeared to be intact, although its undercarriage was buried in about two feet of sand. Diane's aircraft also appeared undamaged and similarly buried. There was no doubt that he would be forced to wait for first light before the plane could be dug out of the sand and prepared for a takeoff.

He was joined by Diane, who had also slipped out to inspect her aircraft with a torch.

'Looks like we were lucky,' Matthew said when Diane ran the beam of the flashlight over both aircraft. 'But I will need your boys to dig me out tomorrow.'

'You will have them,' Diane said, turning off the light to save the torch batteries. 'You know, I have missed these nights in the desert,' she said, staring up at myriad stars. 'It was not the same in the States – except when I had the opportunity to fly over the wilderness there. Out here it is *all* wilderness.'

'You seem to be getting on with our clients,' Matthew said, his hands in his pockets against the biting cold of the night. 'Especially Dr Albrecht.'

Even in the dark Matthew sensed that the expression on Diane's face had changed.

'I am not sure what you are implying,' she said with a tone as cold as the night around them.

Matthew said nothing, only turning to walk back to the ancient structure where he could see the glow of the lanterns inside the doorway. He regretted making the veiled reference to Diane and Albrecht, but he had to admit he was hurting.

When the sun rose the camp came alive. Breakfast was served, but Diane was nowhere to be seen. Matthew wondered whether she was avoiding him. However, Erika was friendly enough and chatted with him beside the small fire of camel dung as the labourers went about shovelling sand away from the undercarriage of both aircraft.

'It is a shame that you could not remain today and observe how we carry out our work,' Erika said, sipping her sweetened coffee. 'I am sure that you would find it interesting.'

'I'm sure I would,' Matthew replied, gazing at Albrecht and Kramer carrying a small but what appeared to be extremely heavy wooden crate between them from Diane's aeroplane. So heavy that Kramer dropped his end, causing the box to hit the corner of some stonework and split. In the early morning sunrise a flash of fire glinted through the splintered box.

Gold! Matthew thought. Small ingots of gold! Erika noticed the change in Matthew, and her attention was drawn to her two colleagues quickly attempting to pull the splintered timbers together to conceal the contents of the crate.

'It is payment for our labourers,' Erika said quickly but unconvincingly. 'We have decided to hide it from them lest they get ideas to steal their pay in advance of any work.'

Matthew could see that the Iraqi labourers were preoccupied with their work and had not paid any attention to the two Germans unloading a few crates from the Junkers.

'You're very generous with your workers,' Matthew said with a cynical smile. 'I am no expert, but the little I just saw was a small fortune.'

'We have a little in reserve for supplies,' Erika said lamely, rising from beside the fire. 'I must go and assist Derik and Lamar.'

Matthew shrugged, downing the last of his coffee. He watched Erika walk over to her two colleagues and start speaking with them. When Albrecht turned to stare at Matthew he guessed that he was the topic of conversation. It made him feel uneasy but he acted as if nothing had happened when Erika returned to him by the fire.

'You will be leaving us this morning,' she said with a strained smile. 'I hope that you will be returning soon.'

Matthew thanked her for her courtesy, then ambled over to his aircraft now free of the sand that had covered its undercarriage. He began carrying out a full pre-flight examination of the external components of the aeroplane. He was checking the pressure in the tyres when Diane joined him.

'We have a good supply of aviation fuel here,' she said to him. 'I guess you might like a top-up before you go.'

Matthew stood up and faced her. 'Not a bad idea. I used up a bit finding your airfield yesterday.'

Diane smiled. 'I will arrange for the men to refuel, and if you like I'll give you a conducted tour of what our team have excavated so far.'

Matthew accepted the invitation and followed Diane to the old stone walls of what appeared to be a small settlement. Diane passed on the refuelling instructions through Dr Kramer, who then ordered a couple of Iraqis to attend to the Ford with a forty-four gallon drum of fuel.

'The team have been fortunate in finding a few small cuneiform clay tablets which will help them date this site,' Diane said, leading Matthew down into a trench that had possibly once been a small alleyway. 'Don't ask me why that got them excited,' she continued, 'but we can have a look at their find.'

There were questions that Matthew wanted to ask, but something held him back. He hated himself for doubting

Diane's allegiances as she had saved him at the Berlin airport, but he also knew she was close to the German archaeological team and Major Guy Wilkes's warning echoed in his mind.

The tour over, Matthew could see that his aircraft had been manhandled around for the takeoff. He said goodbye to Diane, went to his aeroplane and clambered in through the side door. His cargo was intact, covered by canvas sheeting, and when he sat down at the flight controls he brushed off the fine dust that had penetrated the aircraft during the storm. There were marks in the dust and Matthew shrugged off the observation with the thought that maybe someone had checked the cabin for damage. Satisfied that all appeared to be working, Matthew kicked the engines into life. They spluttered and then were roaring smoothly. When Matthew glanced out of his cockpit he saw Diane standing alone watching him. He waved and she waved back.

Matthew taxied a short distance and opened up the throttles. The airstrip was soft under the wheels but Matthew had decreased the air pressure to compensate. The desert sped past and, with a slight jolt, the plane was in the air. Matthew had a hundred and fifty miles to fly and the weather was good.

The dig below faded out of sight and Matthew was once again over the almost featureless plains where little else but scorpions and nomadic Bedouin eked out an existence. He had only been flying for ten minutes when his portside engine suddenly spluttered into silence, quickly followed by the starboard engine. Even his centre engine in the nose was coughing and wheezing as if the aircraft had a bad cold, and Matthew realised with alarm that he had only seconds to carry out emergency landing procedures. He immediately looked around for a suitable piece of ground for landing. It was not the first time in his flying career he had carried out such a procedure.

Matthew was thankful that he had not reached his flying ceiling and calculated that he was about eight hundred feet from the ground as the aircraft commenced to drop. The ground was coming up fast and Matthew could see a relatively flat stretch scattered with small stones. The engine in the nose had now cut out and the aircraft was virtually gliding. He fought the sluggish controls and the earth was suddenly under his undercarriage, the aircraft bouncing along at breakneck speed. Matthew did not know if he was praying or cursing as the Ford slowly lost speed and then came to a sudden and violent stop as it slammed into a small sand ridge. For a second the nose of the plane tipped down but the tail fell back.

Matthew blinked in his disbelief. He had not crashed but expected structural damage due to the violent landing. He could hear the crack of metal contracting in the chill of the morning, but other than that, only the silence of the desert.

Unstrapping himself from his safety harness, he left his seat, his legs suddenly wobbly from the adrenaline draining from his body. It had been a very close call.

Matthew jumped out of the cargo hold onto the desert floor and looked up and down his aeroplane. On first inspection it appeared intact. If he could get Cyril flown out to this spot to fix the engines, they could construct a temporary airstrip for a takeoff.

Thank goodness for the radio, Matthew said to himself, and returned to the cockpit. He lifted the handset and noticed with alarm that the frequency and power knobs were jammed. The radio was out of use, and it appeared that it had been sabotaged.

'God almighty,' he swore softly, still holding the useless handpiece. It seemed the failure of his engines was no accident. The disturbed dust in the cockpit now made sinister sense. Someone had sabotaged his aeroplane with the intent of killing him. Was it because he had seen the crate of gold? Diane had made sure he was away from the Ford when it was being refuelled, providing someone with the opportunity to sabotage his fuel and the radio, ensuring that if he survived the crash he would not be able to call for help.

Matthew knew now that he was in a fight for survival. He went through a mental checklist of what he had aboard the aeroplane. He had a Lee Enfield .303 bolt action rifle, and his old Webley & Scott service revolver, with a good supply of ammunition for both. He also had a drum of water along with a couple of crates of tinned meat and tinned fruit. At least thirst and starvation would not kill him immediately.

Matthew's hope was dampened by the fact that he was about the only aircraft to fly the skies to the oil field, and if Diane had been involved in the sabotage it was not likely she would raise the alarm before word got to Basra that he had not reached his destination.

Matthew peered through the window of his cockpit; all around him was a sea of stone-scattered sand broken only by the occasional rocky gully. His situation was grim and he knew it.

*

David Macintosh had visited Paris before, but for his companion, Horace, it was his first time outside London. The two young men had formed a strong bond since they had left for France. Ikey had given Horace the names and addresses of those involved in recruiting soldiers for the newly formed International Brigades to fight Franco's fascist rebels in Spain.

Their first contact was in a rather grimy Paris suburb.

'Well, here goes,' Horace said cheerfully as they stood on the cobblestoned street, gazing at the run-down tenement.

David followed Horace up the stone steps to knock on the door. Eventually it opened to reveal a short and very attractive dark-haired young woman with equally dark eyes. She looked upon the two men with an expression of suspicion.

Horace removed his cap. 'Are you Natasha?' he asked.

'Oui, yes,' she replied. 'Who are you?'

'I am Horace Howard and my friend is David Macintosh. Ikey gave us your name.'

The trace of a smile broke through the young woman's suspicion. 'Ikey sent a telegram saying you were coming,' she replied, opening the door for them to enter. 'He has informed me that Comrade David was a former prisoner of the fascists in Germany. I have great hopes that he will help us recruit with his story of enslavement at the hands of the Nazi government.'

Her English was fluent but she spoke with a heavy accent.

'You're not French,' David said, admiring her dark beauty.

'I am Russian,' she replied, leading them down a narrow hallway that smelled unpleasantly of overripe vegetables. They passed dingy rooms with rotting mattresses on the floor and finally came to a larger room that appeared to be an old library. Posters written in Russian and French adorned the walls, with pictures of worker soldiers holding rifles above their heads and words exhorting men and women to arms.

'Make yourselves at home,' she said, going to a gas stove that looked out of place in the room that must once have held books along its crumbling shelves. 'I will prepare coffee for us.'

Both men sat side by side on a couch that sagged in the middle, casting each other looks of puzzlement. They had expected something grand and noble for their recruitment but this all spoke of poverty. It did not bode well for the future if they were to go to war against Franco's professional troops.

Natasha wore a long skirt that clung to her curves with some style despite its cheap manufacture. David found himself staring at her body with open desire. She turned to catch his eye and he looked away guiltily. 'I do not have sugar and the coffee is not good, but it is hot.'

She placed two mugs in their hands and took a seat in a decrepit lounge chair opposite them. 'Tell me, Comrade David, of the circumstances of your imprisonment in Dachau.'

David tasted his coffee; she was right about it being of poor quality. It was bitter without milk and sugar. He related his experiences in Germany with as little emotion as he could. As he spoke he could see that the Russian woman was staring at him intently, leaning forward as if to hear every word.

'When you talk at our meetings your story will touch the hearts of those who listen,' she said, rising from the couch to pace the room. 'You are a living example of the cruelty of the fascist state of Germany. I thank you, Comrade David.'

Horace glanced at David with an expression of envy. David grinned in response, as if to say, *I can't help it if she finds me interesting.*

Natasha allocated the two men a room and scrounged

some moth-eaten blankets for them. She informed the two that an evening meal would be provided that night at a café sympathetic to the cause.

When they were alone in the room Horace turned to David, who was spreading his blankets on the mattress.

'I should have asked Natasha when we will be going to Spain,' he said. 'I didn't sign up to spend my time in this flea-infested dive.'

David sat down on the mattress and leaned against the damp wall. 'I wouldn't be in a hurry to get to Spain,' he said, surprising the Englishman. 'You haven't had a chance to see Paris yet.'

Horace slumped down on his mattress. 'If it is like this I may as well have stayed in London. At least the rats there understand English. What have the Froggies got that we don't have in England?'

'Nicer looking sheilas,' David replied with a cheeky grin.

'What's a sheila?' Horace countered.

'You know, a girl, a woman.'

'You have your eye on Natasha,' Horace said. 'You can forget it. Ikey told me that the Ruskies send in their spy agents to recruit, and that they are completely dedicated to Stalin's secret service.'

'Are you a communist?' David asked and Horace fell silent for a moment.

'It's the only way we're going to get our rightful share of the wealth the capitalists have accumulated at the expense of the working man. You only have to see that birth into the capitalist classes overrides hard work and intelligence to achieve a decent life. It's time for revolution. Fighting and defeating the fascists in Spain – who are so admired by the capitalists in England – will send a message to all the oppressed people of the world that the time for revolution has come.' Horace looked slightly abashed at his impassioned response. 'Why have you signed up?'

'To fight fascism,' David replied. 'But not as a communist. I'm a Jew.'

'A Jew!' Horace exclaimed. 'You don't look anything like Ikey.'

'My mother was a Jew,' he said, 'and in Germany that makes me a Jew and the Germans are backing Franco. The enemy of my enemy is my friend. So, I will go and fight the Spanish fascists.'

Horace shook his head. 'Doesn't matter that you're not a communist, you're my pal and you're prepared to fight beside me, and that's all that counts.' He held out his hand and David accepted the gesture. They shook, sealing their friendship for life.

That evening the two men accompanied Natasha to a café in a narrow cobblestoned street and entered a rather large smoke-filled room crowded with men wearing berets. David noticed that Natasha had attached a small enamel red star to her dress above her right breast. She was immediately welcomed by the large crowd of patrons and returned their greetings with salutations of 'Comrade'. Natasha had a table cleared for her and the three sat down; a bottle of red wine and glasses were placed on the table. David was hungry and a platter of crisp baked bread, cheese and an appetising soup were soon delivered. Horace poured the wine while Natasha raised her glass. 'To Comrade Stalin and the revolution!' she said. Horace echoed her words but David simply tucked into his soup.

Natasha glanced at David in surprise. 'You do not toast the revolution?' she asked, staring intently at him.

'I am not a communist,' David replied, wiping a drop of

soup from his chin with the back of his hand. 'I signed up to fight fascists.'

A slim young man approached the table and whispered in Natasha's ear. She nodded and rose from the table to make her way through the noisy crowd to a small stage. David finished his soup and was about to take a sip from his wine when he noticed the crowd had hushed. Natasha raised her arms and began speaking in French, which David did not understand, although he did recognise his name being used. The crowds turned their heads to look at him.

Horace leaned in towards David. 'I think you're the star attraction tonight,'

'Please come up and tell your story, Comrade David, and I will interpret,' Natasha called. David pushed back his chair and made his way to the small stage.

'What am I supposed to say?' he asked Natasha.

'Just tell them of the horrors you saw in Dachau and your personal mistreatment,' she replied.

David stared at the crowd through the haze of tobacco smoke. He could hardly see their faces and was nervous at speaking in public. But he began, his words were echoed in French, and soon he was caught up in his memories and did not notice his audience. When he had finished he was aware that the crowd was on its feet, calling bravo and cheering him. Natasha began to sing the 'Internationale' and the song was picked up by the crowd as they rose to their feet. David blinked. He did not think that he was such a good public speaker but the reaction seemed to suggest otherwise.

When the anthem of the workers was finished Natasha took David by the hand and led him back to the table. He experienced a sharp surge of desire for her as he felt the softness and warmth of her hand.

They sat down and the table was assailed by well-wishers

speaking predominantly in French but also a few other languages, including German.

'You are a natural leader,' Natasha said in David's ear. 'You have that rare quality about you that causes men and women to want to follow you.'

David could see that Natasha was smiling openly for the first time since they had met earlier that day. But there was something else in her smile that encouraged him to hope that she might return his feelings of desire.

That night when the three returned to the run-down apartment building, David's hopes came true. Natasha led him to her room and pulled her dress over her head to reveal a well-curved body. No words were needed as she pulled him down onto her single bed and David experienced his first full sexual encounter with a woman.

If he had any reservations about continuing with his enlistment they were all swept away in the arms of the beautiful Russian. Such was the depth of his passion that he would have gladly died for her.

9

The young woman walking beside the tall man is approaching her eighteenth birthday. She has a cherubic shaped face reflecting her French mother's looks, and the olive complexion of her father's Aboriginal ancestors.

Jessica Duffy loves the man walking beside her. Tom Duffy has a strong face and body, even as he nears his fourth decade. His thick hair is now grey with a touch of white streaks but his eyes shine with the reflections of a sad life. A man still learning about the complexities of rearing a daughter – with the help of the good nuns at Jessica's school in Brisbane where she boarded for most months of the year, returning to north Queensland in the holidays to stay with her taciturn father.

Jessica graduated at the top of her class and was taken by Tom to visit Glen View Station for the first time in her life. She knew of the property in vague terms as a place her father worked as a young man when he returned from the war. There she met the manager, an old Scot, Hector MacManus, who greeted her warmly as if she were his long lost granddaughter. Jessica could see that the Scot and her father were close friends as the evening before they sat on the verandah of the station house with a bottle of Scotch between them, reminiscing about friends now gone from this world. Jessica had finally dozed off in a big bed to be woken the next morning by the clatter of cattle station life; rising under a hot summer sun that seared the vast expanse of brigalow scrub surrounding the sprawling homestead.

After breakfast, Tom borrowed a sulky and after harnessing a horse took Jessica on a journey into the bush. When she asked her father where they were going he simply smiled mysteriously and said that she would find out soon enough.

Eventually Tom brought the sulky to a halt and dismounted, helping his daughter down to the red earth.

'We are here,' he said.

Placing her feet on the ground, Jessica looked around and could see a craggy hill dominating the landscape, rising through the tough and stunted bush.

'But I can only take you to the summit and not to the cave up there,' Tom added. 'The cave is a place where only men are allowed to enter – not women.'

Jessica frowned. 'That is silly, Father,' she said, causing Tom to smile at how much his beautiful daughter was turning into a self-willed young woman.

'It is the law of the old people,' Tom replied, removing a thick cigar from a silver holder, lighting it, cupping in his hands against the gentle zephyr of breeze drifting across the great inland plain. 'Your people,' he added.

'What do you mean by that, Father?' she asked, screwing her face up at him.

'Your ancestors on my father's side once roamed this land,' Tom replied, gazing up at the summit of the hill. 'I think that it is time you learned of your links to this land – and that hill,' he said, pausing for a moment before continuing. 'You did not know that you have Aboriginal blood in your veins.'

Some of the girls at her boarding school had whispered behind her back that she was part Aboriginal, but her two dear friends, the twins Charlotte and Sophia, had stood up to the gossip, saying that this was not true and that Jessica had inherited her complexion from Spanish ancestry. Jessica had come to believe that she was of Spanish blood. After all, Tom Duffy was a well-respected property owner from west of Townsville and his wealth had carried them through the worst of the economic depression that had seen many of Jessica's class mates' families go bankrupt. Her father's statement shocked her.

Tom glanced down at his daughter and could see the anguish in her expression at his revelation. He gently placed his hand on her shoulder.

'It is something to be proud of, Jessie,' he said quietly. 'Old Wallarie was the last full-blooded survivor of our people, and used to live in the cave on that hill. He was a great warrior in his time. I met him before I went away to the war, and when I returned he was still living on Glen View. But he is gone now and would want me to tell you who you really are. Like me, you are the child of two worlds, but while you live, so too does the blood of the Nerambura clan who used to live by the creek here in harmony with the land.'

Jessica listened to his words, still in shock from learning of her roots in a culture that was spurned by Australia's European occupiers. She reached for her father's hand and felt his warm grip as the tears flowed down her cheeks. Her emotions swirled in confusion and fear. She had heard the term half-caste from some of her friends and it had been uttered with contempt.

'I am a half-caste,' she whispered, attempting to take in the enormity of this revelation.

'No,' Tom said gently. 'You are the true child of this land, and if I can ever sway the Macintosh family to sell me Glen View we will take it back for Wallarie. Our blood is that of two proud peoples – the Irish who fought the English, and the Darambal people who resisted the whitefellas when they came to these lands with their flocks of sheep. Knowing who you are is as important as knowing where you are going in life. Up there,' Tom continued, 'do you see it?' Jessica focused on a magnificent giant eagle gliding on the thermal wind tunnels rising from the hot, dry plains. 'That is really Wallarie guarding his land,' he said and Jessica smiled at her father's observation. *He could be a bit silly sometimes*, she thought. To believe that an eagle could also be a dead man was stupid. But she did not let go of her father's hand as they returned to the sulky, looking over her shoulder with some apprehension at the great bird in the sky. He might just be right about the majestic eagle. She shuddered; it was as if it was watching her with an almost human interest, an experience that would haunt her for many years of her life.

*

George Macintosh was furious. There was little that could cause the businessman to lose his temper, but a substantial loss of money certainly could. It had been bad enough that his contacts in the German government had informed him of David's escape from Dachau and their belief that through some miracle he was still alive. And now this!

Donald stood in the centre of his library barely able to control his trembling while his father's ire was concentrated on him. They had hardly been back in Sydney a week after arriving home from Europe when George was informed that the subsidiary company assigned to his son's management had shown a massive loss.

'I was away with you, Father,' Donald said feebly. 'I did not have the opportunity to oversee the accounts.'

'You assured me that you had it all under control before we left, and I allowed you to transfer substantial funds for your enterprise,' George said, pacing the library to walk over to the huge window overlooking the driveway. 'The loss may not cause us any long-term damage, but your incompetence concerns me.'

'I am sorry, Father,' Donald said meekly. 'It will not happen again.'

George gripped his hands behind his back and stared out the window. His son was proving to be a walking disaster where financial matters were concerned, and there were rumours of gambling debts and lavish parties that might explain the company's losses. 'Did you skim off any of the money to cover gambling debts?' George asked, without looking at his son.

'I, er . . .' Donald stuttered. 'I only borrowed a small amount, which I intend to repay.'

'So, now that we know where the money went, I am partly reassured,' George said, turning to face his son. 'Gambling is a better reason than proving to be absolutely useless in managing any of the company businesses. You will promise me now that you will desist gambling from this moment onwards. Is that clear?'

'I, ah . . . Perfectly clear,' Donald replied unconvincingly. 'But I do have some debts to pay.'

George walked over to his desk and retrieved a cheque-book from a drawer. He also picked up a fountain pen and handed both to his son. 'Write out a cheque for the amount you owe and I will sign it,' he said. 'But it will be the last time.'

Donald passed the cheque back. His father raised his eyebrows at the sum but still signed.

'The only gamble you will face from here on in is that of the business world,' George said, tearing the cheque out and passing it to his very relieved son. 'From now on you will report your business decisions to me before you make them.'

George stared at Donald and remembered how the boy had always been a problem at his exclusive private school. It had only been George's influence and generous donations that had saved Donald from being expelled. The boy was not shaping up as the heir to the Macintosh empire. It even seemed at times that Donald had no real interest in the world of finance. Frowning, George shook his head. The boy had to shape up, and he would ensure that this happened, no matter what it took.

*

Donald left his father's library with the cash cheque tucked in his pocket.

'Are you in trouble?' Sarah asked, encountering her brother in the hallway.

'I was,' Donald admitted. 'But not now.' He brushed past her and hurried down the stairs. She knew it was race day at Randwick and she hoped he wasn't going to anger their father by mounting up more gambling debts.

Sarah made her way to the library and knocked on the door.

'Enter,' her father commanded, and she stepped inside to see him sitting at his desk. George glanced up at her. 'I suppose you want an advance on your allowance,' he sighed.

'No, Father,' Sarah replied. 'I just wish to speak with you.'

George always felt a little uncomfortable in his daughter's presence – she reminded him so much of her mother. His estranged wife, Louise, no longer lived in the house, but had years ago moved to an expensive apartment at Rose Bay, financed by her late father's substantial fortune. 'What, may I ask, do we have to speak about?'

Sarah sat down in a comfortable leather chair adjacent to her father's desk. 'When I finish school I wish to become a partner in the family business.'

George was taken aback by his daughter's request. He stared at her closely, as if seeing her for the first time. Despite his bias against women, he was proud of her school record at one of Sydney's most prestigious ladies colleges, where she excelled in her studies and sport. 'That is not possible,' George replied gently. 'Your late grandfather's will does not cater for female offspring. The will stipulates that your brother, myself and David Macintosh will have equal shares.'

'Who is this David Macintosh?' Sarah asked. 'All Mother tells us is that our cousin lives in New Guinea and is around Donald's age.'

'My late brother's son appears to have no interest in the family companies,' George lied. 'The little that I know of him is that he is a lazy type with little ambition. He is very much like his father.'

Sarah nodded. 'So, if this cousin of ours is not a person to be involved in the family business, why should I not take his place when I leave school?'

127

'Unfortunately, there is a solicitor, Sean Duffy, who would block any move I made to include you as a partner in the companies. However, do not be concerned for your future,' George went on. 'One day you will meet the right young man from a good family and assume your natural role as wife and mother.'

'I wish to be a part of the family enterprise,' Sarah persisted. 'Not some breeding cow.'

'Young lady!' George exclaimed. 'I do not like your language. You have to accept that this is a man's world, and your role is to support the man who becomes your husband.'

Sarah stood up and glared at her father. 'You know that Donald is useless in the business but you keep supporting him,' she said and stomped out of the room, leaving George a little taken aback. He shook his head. No woman was capable of understanding the subtleties of business, and with time Sarah would come to accept her role in life.

There was a knock at the door and the valet poked his head around the corner. 'Mr Dwyer is here, Sir George,' he said. 'Shall I tell him that you are in?'

'Yes,' George said. 'I am expecting him.'

Dwyer entered the room, clutching his briefcase and smiling. Dwyer was in his early sixties, bald and with spectacles. His sedentary life had given him a very wide girth and he was puffing from his walk up the stairs.

'How are you, Sir George?' he greeted.

'Good,' George replied, gesturing to a chair. 'You had better sit down before you have a heart attack.'

Dwyer took a seat, laying his briefcase across his lap and producing a wad of papers from it. 'We have further correspondence from Mr Tom Duffy in Queensland regarding the matter of purchasing Glen View Station,' Dwyer said, adjusting his spectacles to peer at the papers.

'Ah, yes,' George smiled grimly. 'It seems that the man is persistent. How many years has he submitted the request . . . ten, fifteen years?'

'His offer is more than generous, Sir George,' Dwyer said. 'We took some big losses in the '29 crash. I know that the property has sentimental value to the family, but it is barely making a profit. Would it not be wise to accept his generous offer?'

George glanced at the wall displaying the mounted collection of Aboriginal artefacts: long, wooden barbed spears and an array of war clubs and narrow wooden shields. 'I have heard from Glen View that the last of the black vermin, Wallarie, is gone,' George said and had a fleeting memory of his contact with the old Aboriginal warrior years earlier which had been the cause of many nightmares since.

'From what you have been able to ascertain, this Tom Duffy fellow is actually a blood relative of Wallarie, and I have no intention of ever selling to that bloodline. My dear departed grandmother, Lady Enid Macintosh, was under the deluded impression that there is a curse on the family originating from Glen View. I am not a superstitious man but I have to acknowledge our family has experienced a lot more suffering than most. Out of a sense of justice I do not believe that any trace of that black blood should ever again inhabit Glen View.'

'Very good, Sir George,' Dwyer said. 'I will draft the usual letter of non-acceptance to Mr Duffy.'

'Good,' George said. 'Is there anything else?'

'Not for the moment,' Dwyer replied and stood to leave the room.

When he was gone George thought about this man who had persisted in offering to buy Glen View. His investigators had learned that Tom Duffy was of Aboriginal blood, and had enlisted in the Great War under the guise of being of Indian blood. During the war he had been decorated for many acts of courage. He had a daughter, Jessica, to a French schoolmistress. She would be around seventeen years of age, by now. George knew which elite Catholic girls' school Jessica attended, and that she was both very pretty and very intelligent.

But it was Tom Duffy who intrigued him. The man had come back from the war to a fortune. How in hell had a blackfella made so much money? George stood to pace his library floor. He was worried because, although he really was not a superstitious man, something lingered in the deepest part of his psyche about the power of the old Darambal warrior, Wallarie. George had seen and experienced things he could not explain rationally. For some reason, he felt that the spirit of Wallarie – the last full-blooded member of the peaceful Aboriginal clan George's great-grandfather, Sir Donald Macintosh, had slaughtered – might still be in this Tom Duffy and his daughter.

George stopped pacing. 'Don't be stupid,' he chided himself. 'That's blackfella superstition.' But the fear persisted and George decided that Tom Duffy was a threat. George didn't like threats, and sometimes extreme measures were necessary to eliminate them.

*

Donald Macintosh sat in his mother's small but sunlit art studio gazing around at her paintings hanging on the wall. He was a regular visitor to his mother's harbourside apartment, but had not told his father this; he wanted to keep the peace with the man he feared most.

The apartment had been purchased by Louise from her father's estate, which had allowed her to be independent of her husband's income. This had enraged George – he could no longer control her by pulling the purse strings. With her newfound financial freedom Louise had defied social convention by separating from her husband. She did not seem to care that she had been snubbed by polite Sydney society; she had a new circle of friends, and seemed very content away from the confines, and cruelties, of life with Sir George.

Louise was a woman in her early forties who had not lost the beauty of her youth. Her skin was as smooth as when she was sixteen and her hair did not show the beginnings of her middle years; only her waistline had thickened a little. Donald thought she seemed happy, and he was glad. As he waited for his mother to bring them a tray of tea and biscuits, Donald's eye caught a new portrait of a man in his middle age. 'Who is that?' he asked when Louise stepped back into the studio.

Louise followed her son's gaze to the painting.

'That is a remarkable man,' she replied, taking her own cup of tea and seating herself in a cane chair. 'Major Sean Duffy. He was a war hero and is the lawyer who also handles the conditions of your grandfather's estate.'

'So that is Sean Duffy,' Donald said with a hint of animosity. 'Father says that he is a troublemaker. A crippled papist out to destroy us.'

Louise raised her eyebrows. 'That does not surprise me,' she sighed. 'Major Duffy is a fine and honourable man whose singular role in the family is to carry out the wishes of your grandfather. Major Duffy served with him on the Western Front and lost his legs there.'

'You must have had recent contact with this Duffy fellow. This portrait is new, I think,' Donald said.

Louise sipped her tea and placed the cup on a small cane table by her chair. 'I had almost completed the painting just before Sean travelled overseas with your cousin, David,' she said. 'I hope to one day have David sit for a session. I know his portrait would be highly valued by Major Duffy. He has been like a father to David since the death of your Uncle Alexander.'

'So you know this David Macintosh as well,' Donald said and found that he was angry that his mother had not revealed this to him before.

'Yes, he is a fine young man like you,' she replied. 'I think that you would like him if you ever met him. His mother Giselle was my closest friend. We went to school together and she kept in contact when she went to live at Glen View.'

Agitated, Donald put down his tea and stood up to walk over to the painting. He stared hard at the face looking back at him. He could see that the man was not unattractive, and a terrible thought flashed through his mind. Was this the face of the lover his father blamed for Louise leaving the family home?

'Your sister does not come to visit me,' Louise said, cutting short Donald's disturbing thoughts.

'I am sorry for that, Mother,' Donald said, turning away from the portrait. 'Her last year of schooling leaves her little time for social affairs.'

'You know that is not true,' Louise replied. 'She hates me for leaving your father.'

Donald knew that his mother was right, but he wished to shield her from any pain. He loved his mother but had been able to adjust to the domestic situation that unfolded years earlier when his mother had packed up and driven away to take up residence miles from his father. George had immediately declared to his children that she did love them but preferred to be with her lover. But over the years that Donald had skipped school to secretly visit Louise, he had never seen any sign of another man in the apartment. However, he had learned of his father's infidelities. 'I am sure that she will visit for Christmas,' Donald said lamely. 'I know that I will.'

Louise stood up and walked over to her son, wrapping her arms around him. 'You will always be my little boy,' she said gently. 'I know that your father expects you to inherit his enterprises when he is gone, but you are you, and I know that one day you will follow your heart and do what you believe is right.'

Donald was stiff in his mother's embrace. 'Mother, I am not a little boy,' he said, gently disengaging himself. 'Father needs me in the business – and I know my duty to the family.'

'But is it what you really want?' Louise persisted, stepping back to look into her son's eyes. 'I know about your indiscretions. I know you are unhappy in your current role in the company's affairs. What is it that you really want to do?'

For a moment his mother's words touched a deep part of his soul, but Donald dared not express his innermost desires. Family and duty echoed in his head. Concepts drilled in by his stern father, whom Donald both loved and feared.

'What I want is not important,' Donald replied. 'Maybe Sarah should have been born a man,' he continued with a bitter smile. 'It is she who dreams of taking control of the family's affairs.'

'Sarah is very much like her father,' Louise said. 'I think that you take after my side of the family.'

The two faced each other and in his mother's words Donald realised many things about himself. He was not like his father, and he had to admit to himself that he did not want to follow in his footsteps. He was lost in a rich world of money and privilege and could see no way out.

IO

Night approached along with low scudding clouds and a chilling wind. Matthew Duffy put on more clothes under his old leather flying jacket and used siphoned fuel to light a fire in the sand. It was not a big fire and when he applied some old oily rags it gave off a small black cloud that was immediately dissipated by the wind. At least he had a good supply of flares should any searchers be in the area.

Huddled beside his fire near the downed aircraft, Matthew rubbed his hands together to increase the circulation. The sun was on the horizon behind the clouds and it was then that Matthew looked up to see the party of men mounted on camels about a mile away. He counted at least two dozen as they sat back watching him. Matthew reached for the rifle beside him and felt its cold assurance. His experience living in the British-controlled lands of Iraq warned him that the locals were generally not sympathetic to the occupiers of their country, or else were bandits interested in what they could loot.

Matthew slid back the bolt and chambered a round of the high-velocity .303 ammunition. He slipped the sights to five hundred yards and propped himself against the wheel strut, taking careful aim at the men mounted on their camels. Matthew had selected the range as he knew any further would be a waste of time; he would have to allow them to come to him before his shots had any accuracy. Matthew's teeth chattered, and not just with cold. If they were hostile, his chance of survival was very remote. But the men out on the flat plain turned and moved away, disappearing below the horizon.

Matthew lowered his rifle in relief. All he could do now was wait, and pray. Pray that he was already missed and someone would start a search for him.

That night Matthew dozed fitfully inside the aircraft. He woke with a start at every little sound, snatching at the revolver by his hand. It was always possible that the men on camels might decide to launch a night attack on him. They didn't, though, and when he finally dragged himself out from under a pile of blankets he peered through the window to see a light cold drizzle of rain and an empty horizon.

★

'He's not returned and I haven't heard anything on the radio,' Cyril said anxiously.

Tyrone McKee stood puffing on a large cigar, his brow furrowed with worry. 'Nothing from the oil crew up north?' he asked.

'Nothing,' Cyril replied.

'I heard they had a bad sandstorm north of here,' Tyrone said. 'You think he might have gone down in it?'

Cyril shook his head. 'The skipper is too good a flyer to get caught by a sandstorm,' he said. 'He would have looked for somewhere to put the crate down and wait out the storm. According to my calculations,' Cyril continued, unfolding a map of the region north of Basra, 'Miss Hatfield and her party of Germans have a strip made up near their dig site.' He traced his finger along a pencilled-in flight route Matthew would have taken to reach the oil well. 'He could have put down there to sit out the storm.'

'Do they have a radio?' Tyrone asked, leaning over to look at the map.

'Not that I know of,' Cyril answered. 'But I bet the skipper would have landed there.'

Tyrone was a good pilot but understood how easy it was to miss a landmark in the huge expanse of rugged desert. 'He told me that if anything happened I was to seek out a Pom major by the name of Wilkes,' Tyrone said with a frown. 'Think I should head off to army HQ and find him?'

'A good idea,' Cyril said. 'He could get onto the RAF to fly out and search for the Ford. If we don't find the skipper, you and I are out of a job.'

But neither man was really concerned about losing their employment; it was their friend they were worried about.

*

'The Royal Air Force has just established a base at Habbanijah . . . here,' Major Guy Wilkes said, pointing his swagger stick at a point on the wall map in his office. 'It's equipped with Westland Wapitis.'

'I know them,' Tyrone replied, fixing the RAF squadron's location in his mind. The base was about fifty miles west of Baghdad on the Euphrates River. 'The Royal

Australian Air Force have them as well. A mate of mine in the RAAF let me take one for a spin. Good crate.'

'I presume as a civilian your flight was not authorised,' Guy said with a wry smile.

'Yeah, well, there was a bit of trouble after that,' Tyrone said with a guilty expression on his face. 'Would your RAF chappies put up a couple of aircraft to search for Captain Duffy?'

Guy Wilkes tapped his swagger stick against the side of his trouser leg and stared at the map. 'You said that the line between here and here is the most likely route he took,' he said, tracing a line from Basra heading north.

'I know that the RAF have the job of patrolling the oil lines, and the one between the Kirkuk oil fields and Rutbah Wells,' Tyrone said. 'The skipper's route is not far from there.'

'Yes, well, the flyboys of the RAF think they can do the army's job of patrolling the trade routes and keeping the sheikhs in line, so they can now earn their pay looking for Captain Duffy,' Guy said. London had decided the land was too vast for army patrols to counter violent outbreaks among the tribesmen of Persia and so had deployed the RAF to react to reported incidents. The two-seater Westland was armed with a Vickers machine gun in the nose and a Lewis machine gun mounted on a Scarff ring for the observer. It could also carry up to five hundred and eighty pounds of bombs. Rebellious villagers would have leaflets dropped over them, warning that they should evacuate their village because of its anti-British activities. The village would be flattened with bombs on the next visit by the British planes. The army had its armoured cars but the bombers proved to be most effective in their role as pacifiers of rebellious tribesmen.

'I will send a telegram to our HQ in Baghdad outlining the co-operation of our RAF brothers in searching for Captain Duffy's downed aircraft. I will keep you up to date on any progress,' he said and Tyrone thanked him.

When Tyrone drove back to the company airstrip outside Basra he felt a terrible guilt for not flying with Matthew on the assignment. But he had met a British nurse and she had proved to be more of a distraction then he had imagined.

★

It was mid-afternoon when Matthew became aware that the men on the camels had returned, but this time they had doubled their numbers. Matthew, however, had not wasted the day. He had set about utilising the many sticks of gelignite he had located in the supplies intended for the oil field. It had taken all morning to lay out the explosives with their wires leading back to the shallow trench under the aircraft; then, satisfied with his improvised minefield, he had retreated to the aircraft to wait.

Oh for a Vickers machine gun, Matthew thought, watching the men on camels moving into a skirmish formation to attack him. *Saul Rosenblum, you old bastard, why aren't you here beside me today?* So many times he had faced death and walked away, but the numbers were just too great for him to get out of this one.

Matthew placed the clips of .303 ammunition beside him and slipped into the shallow trench he had managed to scrape from the rock-hard earth. He had piled up as many large stones as he could as protection and laid out the electrically operated plunger beside him in the trench. He lay on his stomach with the rifle propped on a stone. A drizzle of rain began to fall and Matthew shivered uncontrollably – a combination of the bitter chill and nerves. Five hundred yards, Matthew calculated the group of camel mounted tribesmen had advanced. He checked his rifle sights and reminded himself to re-adjust them for the range when the attack began otherwise he would fire high. Already the war party of around fifty men had divided, with one half riding away to a flank. *It will be a two-pronged attack*, Matthew thought, and was surprised to see that only half of the large party had commenced to move towards him. They may have done so out of confidence.

Matthew took a breath and slowly released it, pleased to see that his hands had stopped shaking. He squeezed the trigger and the rifle slammed into his shoulder. One of the attackers pitched from the saddle of his camel and hit the rocky plain. Matthew quickly swung the sights on another rider as he pulled back the bolt, ejecting the spent cartridge case, and chambered a fresh round. The camels had been whipped into a trot and they came at him fast. Four hundred yards. Matthew slipped down the rear sight adjustment, fired again and watched as another rider was ripped from his saddle. Two hundred and fifty yards was the critical range.

Matthew continued firing, recharging the rifle with a fresh magazine, and the riders kept falling to his deadly aim. When he saw the bulk of the tribesmen were in his killing ground, Matthew reached across to the electronic plunger and made a short prayer the cold had not interfered with the wiring to the explosives. His prayer was answered when the ground before him erupted, tossing men and beasts into the air. The attack had been broken up and the few survivors still in the saddle wheeled their mounts around, retreating for the safety of the second party around half a mile away. They left behind them disembowelled camels thrashing about in agony and a few men attempting to rise from the ground. Matthew's rifle picked off each stunned survivor, leaving none alive. Then he turned his rifle on the badly wounded camels and put them out of their pain. The only sound now was the ringing in Matthew's ears.

The second party of tribesmen on the horizon were clearly stunned by the unexpectedly deadly welcome they had received. They would not be so confident in the future.

Matthew had used the only ace he had, and he knew that when the enemy rallied they would overwhelm him easily. When Matthew reached for his revolver he decided that he would keep the last bullet for himself; he knew what these fierce tribesmen did to unfortunate prisoners. He knew that only a miracle could save him now and he waited with bated breath for the start of the next attack. But the hostile tribesmen did not attack again that day and disappeared below the horizon.

That night he sat with his rifle cradled in his arms. The darkness was like a smothering blanket as light rain continued to fall and the Australian flyer fought off the need to sleep. He found his thoughts drifting to Diane and her possible betrayal of him. This thought alone caused Matthew to feel despair. How could she set him up to be killed after all he had done for her? Matthew found himself cursing his feelings for the woman, and his rage against the betrayal helped keep him awake. But despite his efforts, sleep crept out of the dark and took him into her arms.

With a start, Matthew awoke just before dawn. The light rain had stopped but the wind was knife-sharp, cutting through his clothing with an icy blade. When Matthew pushed himself into a sitting position he peered out the window to see that the plain was empty of tribesmen. He hoped that perhaps the cold had forced them back to their camps.

Matthew had a small primus stove and went about lighting it to prepare a hot meal. At least he had food and water for a long siege, and enough blankets. His supply of ammunition was his main concern. Just how long could he hold out?

*

Tyrone had opted to travel to Baghdad on the train and the jolting trip took him a day. When he reached the city he made his way to the British military HQ and introduced himself to a British air liaison officer.

'We received Major Wilkes's telegram,' the British officer said. 'But I'm afraid the weather yesterday was too ghastly to put any of our aircraft up. It seems we have a freakish cold front carrying snow in to the hills.'

Tyrone controlled his frustration with the thought that the weather had indeed been atrocious and even he would have had second thoughts about going up. 'What about today?' he asked, and the British officer reached for a sheaf of meteorological papers, perusing them with an expression of concern.

'I think we can take off this morning but another front is coming through,' he said. 'The planes will have to return before mid-afternoon to avoid the front.'

'That's better than nothing,' Tyrone said, extending his hand in gratitude.

*

It was midday, according to Matthew's watch, and he sat up in the cockpit, which gave him the best view of the terrain around him. He fiddled with the radio, dismantling the front panel to see if he could fix it. But when the panel came off he could see that the internal workings had been sabotaged. Wires were cut and a valve smashed.

141

'Bastards,' Matthew muttered and looked up to see almost a hundred camel-mounted tribesmen spread across the horizon. 'Bloody hell,' he moaned in despair. Armed with little more than a rifle and revolver he had no chance against those numbers. Surrender was not an option and that left only one alternative. Matthew broke open the revolver to ensure it had all its chambers loaded and clicked it back ready for use. He raised the revolver to his head and placed his finger on the trigger. But it was as if a voice was speaking to him in his mind – *Don't do it. Take a few of the bastards with you.*

Matthew lowered his pistol and turned to pick up the rifle. He still had a few sticks of gelignite and had placed them around the cargo hold. All he had to do was connect the fuse wire to the detonator device and with one downward push the aircraft would be blown to pieces – along with himself. In doing so he would deprive the tribesmen of their prize. At least he would go down fighting.

Matthew quickly connected the fuses, just as the tribesmen strung themselves out for a final sweeping attack on his position. Satisfied that he had made his preparations to blow up his beloved aircraft, Matthew took the plunger and wire out of the cargo hold and down to his shallow slit trench.

The men were hollering as they galloped their camels towards his position, but Matthew calmly stood in his trench, firing his rifle as fast as he could into the mass of men. For some strange reason he found himself reciting the Lord's Prayer, despite the fact that he was not a religious man.

Above the crash of his own rifle and the distant, ululating cries of the attacking tribesmen, Matthew heard a drone that was unmistakable. Matthew recognised the sound of the Wapiti engine.

Lowering his rifle Matthew stepped from under the belly of his downed aircraft to look up into the cloudy sky. The aircraft was overhead but above the low scudding clouds. The enemy were around five hundred yards out and Matthew knew that he had to signal his position on the ground. He had left a box of emergency flares in the cargo hold to help the aircraft burn when he blew it up. Dropping the rifle, Matthew scrambled back into the hold to rip out a couple of the tubular flares, dropped to the ground and fired one into the air above his head. Through the low cloud he could see the glow of the flare drifting to the ground. He fired another, and when he looked over his shoulder he realised that the enemy were a mere two hundred yards away, firing their rifles from the saddle. Bullets ripped past Matthew into the fuselage, punching holes in the thin metal skin of his aircraft.

Then he saw the biplane drop below the clouds over the heads of the attacking tribesmen, who suddenly faltered in their assault. Already the distinctive sound of a machine gun had entered the sounds of battle, and men fell from their mounts. The tribesmen swirled around to scatter as the deadly threat entered the battle arena. For a moment the Wapiti, flying almost at ground level, disappeared and then reappeared further away. Matthew knew exactly what the pilot was doing and he cheered.

The aircraft came down, its forward-firing Vickers tearing a stream of bullets into the confused tribesmen. Matthew saw the objects falling from under the wings. The bombs exploded on impact, spreading deadly shards of metal among the attackers. The first bomber was joined by a second, which went about strafing the tribesmen retreating desperately for the horizon.

The plain was suddenly empty – except for the dead and dying scattered across it. One of the RAF planes circled overhead, dropping a note to Matthew's position. Matthew retrieved the message wrapped around a .303 bullet. It read that his position had been noted and that an armoured column was not far away and coming to his rescue.

Matthew waved to the pilot in gratitude. Then the two aircraft were gone, leaving him alone on the rock-covered plain. Within four hours a brace of armoured cars rumbled into his location. He had already prepared a brew of tea for his British saviours, who appeared stunned at the number of dead tribesmen around the downed aircraft.

'Blimey!' an English gunner said, dismounting from the turret of his armoured vehicle. 'You had a real party here!'

Matthew was conveyed back to Baghdad while an army crew kept vigil on his aircraft. A RAF aircraft kindly flew Matthew back to Basra where he was able to pick up Cyril and Ibrahim with their Leyland truck to drive north to fix the Ford trimotor.

Guarded by a couple of British armoured vehicles, Cyril was able to make temporary repairs on the fuel system as well as the radio. None of the bullets that had passed through the fuselage had done any serious damage and were patched. After a couple of days of clearing an airstrip, the Ford engines coughed into action, taking the aircraft down the improvised strip and into the air to Basra.

When Matthew brought his aeroplane in to land he could see Diane's German Junkers sitting at the edge of the strip. When he eventually climbed out of the aircraft he saw Diane walking quickly towards him.

'Oh, Matthew, I was worried sick,' she said. 'Thank God you're safe,' she said, throwing her arms around him and holding him as if she would never let him go.

Matthew wished he could believe her feigned concern as he extracted himself from the hug.

'I have asked Cyril to arrange for you and your friends to rent a place in Basra,' Matthew said in a cold voice. 'I am sure that you will find it comfortable. We can meet at my office when we need to discuss the mutual contract we have with the Germans.'

Diane stared at Matthew, confusion written plainly on her face.

'Have I done something to offend you?' she asked in a hurt voice.

Matthew turned his back on her and walked away to the hangar.

*

Later that day Matthew received a visit from Major Wilkes, who was dressed in civilian clothes.

'Glad to have you back in one piece, old chap,' Guy said, taking a chair in the office. 'Also pleased to see that your aeroplane seems to be back in working order.'

'Thanks for the help from the RAF – no doubt the result of your intervention,' Matthew said. 'I truly thought that I was going west this time,' he added, using an old expression from his war days.

'Was the damage to your crate an accident?' Guy asked carefully.

'No,' Matthew replied. 'It was sabotage. Cyril found water in the fuel and my radio had been tampered with. Someone wanted to make sure that if I survived a crash landing I wouldn't be able to call for help.'

'Our intelligence reports about the tribesmen that attacked you link them to a sheikh who is known to be anti-British,' Guy said. 'Apparently some of his men are working on the Germans' site, and I suspect they informed him that the plane would crash. I don't know why the Germans would want to do away with you.'

'It might have to do with something I was not supposed to see,' Matthew said. 'A wooden box full of gold at the site.'

'Gold?' The major leaned forward in his chair. 'It must have been a substantial amount.'

'A lot of gold,' Matthew replied. 'Enough to make someone very rich.'

'Your observation corroborates our suspicions that the Germans will use the gold to pay the sheikh to carry out anti-British activities. Maybe even pay for arms to rebel against us out here,' Guy said with a frown. 'We fear attacks on the oil lines and drilling sites. Disrupting our fuel supplies could cause an economic disaster in Britain.'

'Why don't you just go and arrest the German archae-ologists for spying?' Matthew asked.

Guy leaned back in his chair. 'Not that easy. The damned government at home do not wish to upset Hitler and his cronies. To accuse the Germans of espionage, subversion and sabotage would cause an uproar that Whitehall does not want. No, it is up to me to counter their efforts in more subtle ways, and that is why I still need your help.'

'I doubt that I will be of much help now,' Matthew shrugged. 'I have made it plain to Miss Hatfield that her concern for my welfare was not welcome.'

'Ah, Miss Hatfield,' Guy said. 'I have finally received information on her activities in the USA. It seems that she was a registered member of the Yankee version of the Nazi Party. The Nazis have increasing support in the USA, with its large population of German immigrants. I suspect that her membership of the Yank Nazi Party would have helped secure her current contract. We will be depending on you to keep an eye on her and report back to me on the Germans' activities.'

The information about Diane being a member of the Nazi Party caused Matthew a great deal of distress. He had flown against the Germans in the Great War, and her act of joining a party of fanatics felt like a personal betrayal.

'I doubt that I will be able to convince Diane that I am still chummy with her after the reception she received from me,' Matthew said. 'I made it clear that I did not wish to see her again except on business matters.'

'Well, old chap,' Guy said, rising to his feet, 'I'm going to have to trust to your colonial charm to convince her that your coolness towards her was caused by a bump on the head,' he said with half a smile. 'It's vital that you remain in a position to monitor what goes on in the Germans' camp.'

'After they tried to kill me?' Matthew exclaimed. 'Support for the Empire stretches only so far.'

'One must remember that you are also accepting the King's shilling to work for us,' Guy said. 'Cheerio for now.'

The British intelligence major departed the office, leaving Matthew pondering his position. He was stuck between a rock and a hard place.

Later that evening he plucked up the courage to visit Diane in her new accommodation. He had brought a bottle of his best French wine and was ushered into the high-walled apartment by the servant who attended the flat.

Diane met Matthew in her small but comfortable living room. She was dressed in a long colourful cotton skirt. Matthew could see the hurt and anger in her face.

'I have come to apologise for my rudeness today at the airstrip,' he said, holding out the bottle to her.

'I don't know if I wish to speak to you outside business matters,' Diane replied. 'I was worried sick when I heard that you had gone down.'

'I'm sorry,' Matthew said, placing the bottle on a low table in the centre of the room. 'My nerves were a bit jangled from the experience and I was not myself. I value our friendship and I know I can be a bit clumsy when it comes to dealing with women. My life has been lived almost entirely among men.' Matthew could see that his plea for understanding seemed to be working as Diane's expression softened just a little.

'I was hurt more than you know,' Diane replied, taking a step towards the table and touching the top of the wine bottle. 'You have been such an important part of my life. You took me in after the war and made my dream of learning to fly come true. You know I had to move on when the company was facing financial disaster, even before the crash came in '29. I did not want to hear that you couldn't afford to keep me on as one of your pilots – so I took the position in the USA to avoid hearing those words from you.'

'I didn't know that was why you left,' Matthew said. 'I do know that I owe my life to you for what you did at Tempelhof. You did not tell me how the Germans reacted to your intervention.'

'Oh, they were as mad as hell,' Diane chuckled. 'But I apologised, explaining that I was a mere woman and was not aware that I had taxied between them and your plane. They accepted my explanation.'

As they would, Matthew thought. *If you have contacts in Hitler's government.* Matthew knew that he was once again falling under her spell, but he reminded himself that she must have been involved in the sabotage of his aircraft – what other explanation was there? He was obligated to the British government to keep close to Diane and the German scientists; he was not obligated to fall in love with her, and he would do his best to resist her charms.

'I don't think we should waste such a good bottle of wine,' Diane said. 'Would you like to join me for dinner tonight?'

'Sure,' Matthew replied, lost in her smile. 'What time?'

'Say, eight for eight-thirty,' Diane replied. 'You will have to excuse me for now, I have a lot of paperwork to attend to.'

Matthew left Diane's residence with his own confused thoughts. He accepted that he was not an authority on the ways of women but what he thought he read in her acceptance of his apology was genuine. He reminded himself that she was sleeping with the leader of the German expedition who may have been instrumental in plotting to kill him. It was like being in a spider web waiting for the black widow to come to him with death.

II

David could feel the soft curves of Natasha's body pressed against his own bare flesh and he marvelled at the feelings he had for the Russian woman who he learned was five years older than him. He had gone as far as declaring his love for her two weeks after they had first slept together, but she had frowned and cautioned him that she must put her love for the revolution ahead of her personal feelings.

Already the spare rooms were filling with recruits waiting to travel south to the French border with Spain in the Pyrenees, where they would be armed and deployed to fighting units. Horace had been a little cool towards David during their time together exploring the French capital. While sitting on the edge of a stone-covered bank on the River Seine one afternoon David had asked Horace why. Horace had burst out that David's ill-concealed affair with the Russian woman was the reason they had not yet been transferred to the border with the other recruits.

David thought about his friend's outburst, and that night in bed asked Natasha why they had not been sent to Spain when the others who had come to the house had transited through within days.

'You wish to leave me so soon?' she countered, rolling over to gaze into the young man's face in the dim candlelight.

'You have said many times that you cannot love me,' he replied. 'So why delay our deployment?'

For a moment Natasha simply stared at him and then turned away without answering. David gently turned her back to him and could see that her eyes were filled with tears.

'What have I said?' he asked, stroking her face with his fingers.

'I could not tell you my true feelings even if I wished to do so,' she said, gripping his fingers in her own. 'My masters in Moscow do not know what love is,' she said. 'Love is a bourgeois concept to weaken men and women.'

'But I love you and I think that you should leave Paris and go with me to London where I can organise for us to travel home to Australia,' David said. 'What I feel for you is more important than fighting the fascists in Spain.'

'Do not say that, David,' she said, placing her fingers on his lips. 'The revolution is bigger than you and I. Just accept that in this place and time we share our bodies while we can. That is the way of war. For now just share this moment with me.'

David was confused by her words, which did not seem to match her actions. She was a passionate woman, but it seemed much of her passion was devoted to her country and its crusade to bring down fascism. But that night they loved each other and David tried not to think that in the morning Natasha would once again recruit men for the civil war across the border.

The next week David went with Horace to watch a local soccer game and when they returned they were met by a Russian man who looked like the pictures David had seen of Lenin.

'You are the two English recruits,' he said in greeting. 'In the morning you will be driven to the border.'

'Where is Natasha?' David asked.

'Comrade Natasha is no longer with us,' the Lenin lookalike replied. 'She has been recalled to Moscow.'

'What are you talking about?' David said angrily. 'She would have told me she was going.'

The Russian agent glared at David. 'It is not your place to question orders,' he said. 'Comrade Natasha is to be re-educated for her reported corruption in France. She has been deemed to allow her personal feelings to come before her duty to the Motherland. You should know, as you should have been sent south weeks ago, with the others who have already departed.'

A cold chill ran through David as he realised that someone must have reported his affair with Natasha, and now she was being punished for it. He also knew that asking where she had been sent was a waste of time. The Russian turned his back on the two men and went inside.

The next day Horace and David boarded a van and were sent out of Paris. As they travelled the memories of Natasha swirled in David's mind. She had never said she loved him but he knew she did. He buried his head between his knees as the van bumped along country roads. He did not want his English pal to see him cry for the loss of his first love. David was beginning to see that there wasn't much difference between fascism and communism in the way individual interests were of no concern to the state. Despite his growing reluctance to travel south to fight in a Spanish civil war, he felt committed. Beside him was a man he had promised to look out for and Horry now became the only true reason to fight in the terrible civil war across the border.

★

Shouts of '*Vivan los rusos!*' came from the crowds of men, women and children cheering on the marching column of foreign volunteers in the Spanish capital of Madrid. They responded by raising their fists in salute. David experienced an unexpected burst of pride. His doubts seemed to fade away when he saw the joyful faces of the people welcoming them.

'We're not bloody Russians,' Horace Howard growled as they made their way along the Gran Via with their motley group of men from Germany, France and other nations.

'You understand a bit of Spanish?' David asked Horace.

'Enough to know that the wogs think we're Russian infantry sent by Comrade Stalin,' Horace replied.

Their journey to Madrid via the Basque country on the border between France and Spain had been guided by French communist sympathisers. The Basques had provided rudimentary training with the Mauser rifles David and Horrie now carried, but it had been cut short when Franco had moved to take Madrid from the government. Men and munitions were needed urgently to counter the assault by Franco's well-trained and well-equipped Moroccan troops. Facing them were civilians with little knowledge of warfare – and even less in the way of reliable small arms. Already the city had come under attack from

German bombers of the Condor Legion, as well as Italian and German tanks aiding the fascist cause.

As they passed through the streets of Madrid they saw signs of devastation everywhere. On the streets were dead animals. The sobering sight made them aware for the first time that they were going into combat. Many reflected death might visit them before the sun even went down.

Their section leader was a grizzled German veteran of the Great War, now self-promoted Sergeant Otto Planke, who had opposed Hitler as an avowed communist on the streets of Munich. He had taken David and Horace under his wing, as well as a young American, two Frenchmen, two Czechs and a Canadian. Otto spoke passable English and decent French and Czech. David mostly conversed with the tough former soldier in German. All except David had belonged to left-wing movements in their own countries and were bemused that someone who wasn't a communist would volunteer to fight in Spain. But David would counter with the simple statement that he had experienced at first hand the terrible truth of Dachau and thus he was accepted as one of their own.

'What's happening?' the American volunteer called to the sergeant. 'Are we going to get some grub?'

The American was a short, solid young man from Chicago named John Steed. He was twenty-five years old and had worked in the meat industry as an abattoir worker. He was single but had a girlfriend back home. John Steed always seemed to be thinking about scrounging food, and his skills in this area had already come in handy for the self-appointed section.

'*Nein*,' Otto replied. 'Ve go to fight, Comrade.'

Within the hour David and Horace found themselves in a suburb where barricades had been constructed across the streets and rudimentary trenches dug. Otto distributed his section along a small length of the trenches that covered the road, and both Horace and David shared a firing pit with one of the Czech volunteers, who once served with the French Foreign Legion in the twenties. All three men were armed with old German Mauser bolt-action rifles and a mere ten rounds each. David was familiar with the rifle as he had used one on the plantation in New Guinea and had proved a crack shot. He had shown Horace how to use his own Mauser and while handling it had found it to be defective. David had set about repairing the weapon while they had waited to travel to Madrid and he had managed to fix it. Such mechanical problems were endemic to the volunteers, who were poorly trained and ill-equipped.

David laid his rifle on the low earthen mound in front of the trench and leaned forward, adjusting the rear sight to cover the range to the end of the long street. In the distance he could hear the crackle of small-arms fire and thud of bombs exploding. Overhead he could see the occasional aircraft seeking out targets. David realised they were the targets those Italian aircraft sought to strafe and bomb. It hit him then that he was very far from home and family. Until now he had been caught up in the cause of fighting fascism, but now he truly realised that there was no going back. The bittersweet memory of Natasha was still with him but the reality of facing possible death made her a distant figure in his life at this moment. Horace had put forward the idea that she had been recalled to Moscow because someone in Paris had reported her sleeping with a non-communist. From what Horace knew, that was reason enough to have her recalled from Paris, such was the paranoia of the Russian regime. Although Horace was aware that the system being exported by Stalin was full of dangerous inconsistencies, he rationalised that all revolutions had their casualties until the system settled down. David didn't agree, but there was no use arguing now.

'Get down as low as you can in the trench if you see the Italians fly down against our position,' the Czech said in German. 'Tell your English friend to do the same.' His name was Jaroslav Zeravek and he was a handsome man in his early thirties, strongly built and around six foot tall. His presence in their trench gave David and Horace a small amount of confidence as the former legionnaire had seen much action in North Africa against the fierce Bedouin tribesmen.

When David next looked up he saw a lone Italian fighter circling overhead.

Suddenly an armed volunteer tumbled into the trench beside him and David was shocked to see that she was a young girl, barely sixteen. She was a striking, grim-faced beauty with olive skin, long raven black hair and large eyes, wide with fear. David guessed she was from the city's local militia and not the International Brigade. She found herself next to David, and when he turned to her he found that he was smiling as if to reassure her that she would not join the ranks of dead in the forthcoming battle. The young woman returned his smile and said something in Spanish.

'Check their rifles,' Otto called from down the line.

David reached over to the girl and gently took her rifle. He slid back the bolt and noticed that there was no bullet in the chamber. He pushed the bolt forward to ensure that the rifle was ready for action, and handed it back. *Does she even know where the trigger is?* he asked himself in despair.

'Damned amateurs,' Jaroslav grumbled beside David, who wondered if he was included in that list.

'She's a real looker, your one,' Horace said to David with a note of envy.

'I don't even know her name,' David replied, a little embarrassed at his own attraction to the girl. 'Besides, she's a soldier and we treat her as such.'

Otto dropped into the trench to take stock of their preparations.

'What's the situation?' David asked him.

'From what I know we have twice as many fighters,' Otto said in German, reaching for the packet of cigarettes he had in the top pocket of his battle jacket. 'The Manzanares River is an obstacle to the Nationalists for a direct assault on the city centre. But if I were the Nationalist commander I would try to avoid street fighting by launching an attack through the Casa de Campo Park on this side of the river. But the Republican idea of keeping secrets is not so good – I heard that the Nationalist commander's plan was found on a dead Italian tank crew member yesterday. We're smack in the middle of a diversionary assault while the Nationalists attempt to establish a bridgehead just north of the city centre around the university. We are on the south-west. You can expect to use up all your ammunition when the time comes for Franco's assault.'

David was impressed with the sergeant's professionalism. 'What do we do if it looks like we're going to be overrun?' he asked as the sergeant lit his cigarette and took a long puff, smoke curling into the clear chilly air.

'The Republicans are broadcasting a slogan over their radio station,' Planke replied, gazing down the deserted street where only a skinny dog sniffed through bomb-damaged homes. '"*No pasaran!*" Which means, "They shall not pass." That means we're supposed to stay at our posts to the death.'

David felt a cold chill of fear. He had never seen combat but he had seen death and he instinctively looked to the beautiful young woman in the trench beside him. It was beyond comprehension that such beauty and innocence could be killed.

Otto could see David gazing at the Spanish girl. 'Don't worry,' he said, puffing on his cigarette. 'You and the boys stick with me and none of us will die. I have never been a great believer in standing to the last man.'

David found some reassurance in his words. He was recognising that he was only nineteen and that he had a whole life to live ahead of him. He needed every fragment of hope to prevent his hands shaking and his bowels loosening. The gunfire and crump of bombs was getting closer and the earth shook with small jolts under his feet. The sergeant finished his cigarette and flicked the stub down the street before departing for the left flank of their section.

David returned to his position, leaning on the edge of the trench, rifle forward on the small earthen mound. He thought that he could smell the freshness of the young woman beside him, distracting him from thoughts of what lay ahead. The waiting was terrible but it ended within a few minutes when movement down the street caught everyone's attention. They were uniformed men with skin as black as pitch. They came forward, crouched low, bayonets fixed.

'The Moroccans!' Jaroslav yelled and David had one square in his sights. He squeezed the trigger and saw the man collapse. His shot was followed by a crackle of deafening fire on either side of him. David did not have time to realise that he had just killed a man for the first time in his life. All that mattered now was that the enemy be held back – or they were all surely dead.

On that chilly day in Madrid blood ran as rivers in the streets of the old city and death came to attacker and defender alike.

12

David's world had come down to the feel of the rifle butt against his cheek and the shape of the figures moving in front of him. His fear was forgotten as he fired and worked the bolt to chamber another round of the high-velocity ammunition. He sensed that most of his bullets were hitting their mark on the advancing Moroccan troops, who now retreated to the safety of street corners out of the line of fire.

'Get out, pull back!' Otto yelled.

The young Australian glanced over to the Spanish girl and suddenly felt sick in the stomach. She lay in the dirt at the bottom of the trench, her face smashed by an enemy bullet. Her wide eyes stared at the clear sky and David thought he could see utter surprise in them.

'Get her ammunition,' the sergeant yelled at David, who stood transfixed by horror. 'Snap out of it, Comrade,' Otto shouted, shaking his shoulder. 'Just get her weapon and ammunition, we need every round.'

In a daze David crouched down to search the pockets of her trousers and found eight loose rounds. Her rifle lay by her side and David could see that it had not been fired – the safety catch was still on. He picked up the weapon and scrambled from the trench, following the rest of his section back up the street just as an artillery round exploded behind him. Red-hot pieces of steel took chunks out of the buildings either side of the narrow cobblestoned street, and over his shoulder David saw one of the French volunteers throw up his arms, dropping his rifle. David's instinct was to keep running, following the example of the experienced German soldier, but instead he stopped, turned back and ran to the Frenchman lying on his stomach. Wisps of smoke hovered over the Frenchman and blackish blood spread across the back of his tunic. David bent down and rolled the comrade over to see that he, too, stared with vacant eyes into the Spanish sky.

'Macintosh, get over here!' Otto bawled just as another artillery shell slammed into the street, exploding with enough force to bowl David over from the blast. He lay winded for a moment and wondered if he had been hit, but after a few seconds realised he was still intact. Scrambling to his feet, he snatched up the two rifles but noticed that the Frenchman's weapon had been severely damaged by shrapnel. It was useless. With all the strength he could muster, David sprinted down the street towards the doorway of a small residence and was hauled through the door by the sergeant.

'Damned fool,' Otto snarled at David. 'You can't help the dead.'

David passed the spare rifle to the sergeant and looked around to see his comrades huddling against the stone walls as if they could be absorbed by the bricks, protected against the artillery shells now raining down on the neighbourhood. Houses were blasted to rubble either side of the street.

'The girl . . .' David said, not knowing why.

'The girl is dead,' the sergeant said harshly. 'And we just might join her if you don't snap out of it. Make sure that your rifle is ready for the next attack.'

David knew that he had used all his rounds defending the trench and so felt in his pocket for the Spanish girl's spare rounds. He reloaded with them and had a strange thought that they were like some kind of jewellery of death. The brass cases were new and shined like gold.

'What's happening, Comrade Sergeant?' the remaining Frenchman asked, clutching his rifle and staring with wide eyes at the doorway. 'Are they going to kill us?'

'Not if I have my way,' Otto Planke spat. 'They will follow up the artillery barrage with another attack down the street, and we will be waiting for them again. You will find places on the level above us to take up sniping positions, while a couple of us cover downstairs. Listen to my orders and you just might live until at least tomorrow.'

The men of the section listened and obeyed. Had their self-appointed leader not pulled them out of the defences when he did, they would have been killed by the Nationalist artillery shells. It was obvious that Otto knew war and what to expect. He saw no sense in holding an exposed position in the street when they could use the buildings as shelter to retain the ground they had been tasked with defending.

'You, Macintosh,' Otto said as a few of the men made their way up a wooden staircase to the second level of the house. 'You stay down here with me. I can see that you are good with your rifle, and I want you to cover the street from here.'

David nodded and pulled over a rickety wooden table and set it up as a barricade just inside the window. He guessed that if he poked his rifle out the window he would indicate his position to the enemy. But by keeping back and covering the street for a short distance, he felt that he had more of a chance. Otto noticed his preparations.

'You have the instincts of a soldier,' he said with a note of grudging admiration.

The shelling had stopped and an unnerving silence fell on the street.

'They will come at us with grenades,' Otto said to David and Jaroslav. 'But they are not used to fighting in towns. The Nationalists are about to learn how dangerous urban warfare can be. We will make them pay for every brick in this town.'

David was aware that the terrible, almost crippling fear had returned as the adrenaline drained from his body. 'God, what am I doing here?' he groaned under his breath and used the back of his hand to wipe dirt away from his face. When he looked around the room he could see that it was simple but clean. Just four wooden chairs, a table, and religious icons adorning the walls. A sideboard contained a few kitchen utensils and a set of crockery, most now smashed on the floor from the earth-shaking explosions.

Jaroslav had taken a position covering the open doorway. He had placed two of the chairs as a prop to rest his rifle and had also set himself back in the room.

'You did a brave but stupid thing on the street going back for the Frenchman,' the Czech said in German, laying his cheek against the wooden butt of his Mauser and swivelling the rifle barrel to ensure a good field of fire across the limited area he could see from inside the room. 'You have to learn that you leave the fallen until we have the chance of recovery later – or you will join the dead. It is the way of war.'

'They are coming!' a voice warned from upstairs. 'They have a machine gun!'

The words had hardly echoed in the ears of the men downstairs when the machine gun opened suppressing fire, raking the street.

David's heartbeat quickened and he stared down the barrel of his rifle at the empty space beyond the window frame. His heart almost stopped when the machine gun ceased firing and a figure loomed in front of him. David fired and the enemy soldier fell, dropping the grenade on the outside of the windowsill. After a couple of seconds it exploded, hurtling shards of shrapnel through the window and smashing into the table in front of David. Around him he could hear the crash of small arms and the yells of men fighting and dying.

Above the ear-splitting noise David thought he heard John Steed yell that their comrade, the Canadian, was dead. *So much for Otto's promise to keep us alive*, David thought with a sense of despair as the machine gun opened up again, now raking their shelter in a hail of bullets. All David could do was wait, and pray that he would not join the Canadian.

★

The door to Sean's office opened and a tall, broad-shouldered man with thick greying hair stepped through. Sean rose from his chair and limped around his desk to extend his hand to the Queensland millionaire and former soldier.

'So we finally meet again,' Sean said, beaming a smile and feeling the man's strong grip. 'The last time was with the battalion on the Western Front in 1916. It is so good to see you, Tom Duffy.'

'Good to see you again,' Tom said. 'I heard you lost your legs, but at least we're both still alive, which cannot be said for a lot of good cobbers.'

'Take a seat, old chap,' Sean said and glanced past Tom to the clerk hovering at the door. 'Inform any other clients who may be waiting that I will not be available for the rest of the day. I'm sure that they can be rescheduled.'

Tom sat down, glancing around the walls displaying military photos of Sean's days on the Western Front in the same battalion that Tom had served with. Sean could see his interest and both men soon found themselves swapping stories of their time in the trenches. There was a brotherhood in such conversation and both men recalled the good times – and bad.

After some time of reminiscing Tom brought up the reason for his visit – his latest bid to buy Glen View Station.

'I am aware that you have made many attempts to purchase Glen View from the Macintosh companies,' Sean said. 'Maybe you should have looked me up earlier. I'm sure that Sir George Macintosh has deliberately dismissed your rather generous offers because of your name. We know that over the past sixty years or so there has persisted an animosity between the two families. From what I can gather the seeds of the antagonism relate to a character, Michael Duffy, who had a romantic interest in the daughter of the Macintosh family. Rumours persisted that Patrick Duffy, the grandfather of David Macintosh, was actually the son of that Duffy–Macintosh union. But for some inexplicable reason old Lady Enid Macintosh took Patrick in. Sadly, time has muddied the reasons for that, and what we have today is a continuing tradition of resistance to anything attached to the Duffy name.'

'As you know from our time in the battalion I am the

descendant of the same family line – but with Aboriginal blood,' Tom said quietly. 'Life is a strange thing when a man is judged by his race and not his humanity.'

'At this stage I feel that your continuing offers will be a waste of time and money,' Sean said. 'George Macintosh rules alone, but that will change in a couple of years when his son and the son of Alexander Macintosh come of age and take their places on the board as part owners. I am sure that Alexander's son, David, will be sympathetic to an offer to sell Glen View. It has always been the one part of their empire that seems to have been cursed, and that may also influence George's son. Of course, once George dies, matters will be easily resolved, but the bastard seems to lead a charmed life.'

'I know,' Tom said quietly. 'Wallarie has told me of the curse.'

'Wallarie!' Sean exclaimed. 'The old bugger can't still be alive!'

'Not in the whitefella sense,' Tom said. 'But his spirit is well and truly hanging around Glen View – along with the rest of his clan – and no one will be at peace until I'm able to take the land back for them.'

Sean stared at Tom but could not read anything but seriousness in his statement. He reminded himself that Tom had the ancient blood of the original inhabitants of the vast continent. 'Tom, I know that you're a very wealthy man with other cattle properties in Queensland and other enterprises,' Sean said with a frown. 'Why waste your time and energy pursuing the purchase of this one property?'

'Because that's what Wallarie always wanted,' Tom answered. 'He wanted our blood to have continuance with the land he was born to. It's where I should die, and my daughter's children walk.'

Sean was taken aback by Tom's answer. Sean lived in a world where the bottom line of life was measured in pounds, shillings and pence. The man sitting opposite him did not appear to hold the same values. 'Well, until I hear from David, I cannot influence him on any future decision about Glen View,' Sean sighed. 'The stupid young man is somewhere in Spain fighting for the Republican cause against Franco's fascists.'

'How old is he?' Tom asked.

'He would be twenty by now,' Sean replied. 'If he is still alive. God knows why he didn't listen to me in London and return home. His grandmother is sick with worry – he's the only flesh and blood she has left.'

'I have a daughter, Jessica,' Tom said, 'and she is of an age where she thinks she knows what's best for her and I'm only an old, silly man who knows nothing.'

'That sounds like David,' Sean sighed and realised that he was in a conversation between two concerned fathers, albeit that Sean was not really David's father by blood. There was not a day that went by without Sean looking to the mail to see if David had written from Spain. But no letters arrived, and Sean found that his nights returned the terrible old dreams of the trenches. He often cursed himself for not working harder to keep David from volunteering with the International Brigades.

'We still have a lot to catch up on,' Sean continued, changing the subject. 'And I think that you and I should retire for the day to meet an old cobber of mine, Harry Griffiths. He was with another battalion that served alongside our own in 1916.'

The two men left to go to a place where old soldiers could continue talking about times past – the local pub.

★

The defenders of the house had exhausted their meagre supply of rifle rounds, and all they had to show for the expenditure were the bodies of the black Nationalist troops outside the building and the spent cartridges at their feet.

Night was falling and the battle for the street had been sporadic. David knew that he had accounted for many of the dead and he now sat back against the rear wall, staring with blank eyes at a wooden crucifix on the wall. Should a night attack be launched, then they would have to fight with rifle butts, knives and fists. Although he had been engaged in the fighting for a mere few hours, it felt like a lifetime.

Horace joined him and he noticed his friend's uncontrollable shaking. The two men sat side by side with their backs to the wall, rifles between their knees.

'Do you think we'll live to see tomorrow?' Horace asked, attempting to light a cigarette.

'I don't know,' David replied quietly. 'I always thought that it would be someone other than me getting killed, but now I see it is all some kind of lottery. You don't know when your number will come up.'

'If I don't make it, old pal,' Horace said, 'there is something I have to get off my chest. I think it might have been me talking about you and Natasha sleeping together that got her sent back to Moscow.'

David did not look at his anguished English friend but at the smashed window opposite them. 'I don't think you should trouble yourself with that,' he answered in a tired voice. 'It is the bloody system that you put so much stock in. As far as I have learned, Comrade Stalin is not much better than Herr Hitler. Your revolution is not going to make the world a better place, and it was your communist system that decided Natasha had to be recalled, not you.'

Horace stared down at his feet, tears welling in his eyes. 'I just wanted to get that off my conscience,' he said. 'I didn't want to die carrying that to my grave.'

David reached out and placed his hand on his friend's shoulder. 'We are both going to get out of this alive, and return to London where you can buy me an ale at that pub around the corner from the gym. That is, after I belt your head in.'

Horace attempted to laugh in his relief but broke into a sob. David's hand remained on Horace's shoulder and he wished that he, too, could express his true feelings, but he was aware the German sergeant was watching them. David was not going to break down in front of him.

'It will be okay,' David soothed. 'We will get out of this hellhole and be eating breakfast behind the lines before the sun comes up.'

David's soothing words had an impact and Horace stopped sobbing, wiping his tears away with the back of his sleeve. Without another word he stood up and walked stiffly over to join the rest of the small group awaiting the next move. When David glanced over at Otto, the tough sergeant gave a small nod of approval before moving among his men, auditing their ammunition supply. When he got to David he crouched.

'None left,' David answered in German. 'What happens now?'

'We get the hell out of here under cover of darkness, and fall back to the main body of the Brigade,' Otto answered. 'You all did well today.'

The tough, solidly built old soldier inspired hope in the tiny house, and without any other option to cling to, David placed his life in the man's hands.

'When?' he asked, and the German glanced out the window at the fading shadows.

'When it is dark enough to make our escape. I will tell you when.'

So they waited, counting the minutes and living in fear that the Nationalists would launch another attack. David had heard the rumours that Franco's forces did not take prisoners, shooting the captured where they stood. He glanced at the watch he had purchased in London before setting out on his journey to Spain. The watch his grandmother had given him as an eighteenth birthday present had been taken from him at Dachau, and the replacement watch was a reminder of why he was now in this bullet-riddled room. He remembered how he had spent his twentieth birthday in Paris getting drunk with Horace, but that now seemed a lifetime ago.

Jaroslav, the Czech, joined him and passed a flask of wine he had found in the house kitchen. 'Are you old enough to drink?' he asked with a wry smile.

David took the flask and gulped down the red wine to quench his raging thirst. It was bitter but it wet his dry mouth and throat. 'What was it like in the Legion?' David asked, passing back the flask.

'Tough,' Jaroslav grunted and took a long drink from the flask. 'I missed the green fields of my country when we were in North Africa. But the men I served with were my brothers and the Legion my family.'

A bullet cracked above their heads and David instinctively ducked. He noticed that Jaroslav hardly flinched.

'Are they coming again?' David asked.

'I don't know, but they are positioning snipers to keep us pinned down,' he replied. 'That is what I would do. But the German is a good soldier and we will get out of here back to the Brigade.'

Reassured, David held out his hand for the flask, the wine

helping to sooth his nerves. At home he would not be allowed to drink but here there was only one rule – fight or die.

That evening, when the night had arrived with a blanket of blackness, Otto moved among the men and gave his orders for the escape.

'We will leave here in twos – a minute apart,' he said, squatting in the downstairs room where all the section had gathered. 'Pick a man to go with you and remove your boots. We can't make any sound on the cobbles of the street. You keep going until you strike our main force HQ, which should be about four blocks to the north.'

Jaroslav placed his hand on David's shoulder and volunteered for them to be the last to leave.

The order was given and Horace left with the American, the first two to depart, leaving the rest to wait in absolute silence, straining to hear if the first pair out had struck any trouble. There was no sound and the next two departed. Finally, only David, Jaroslav and the sergeant remained.

'Time to go,' Otto whispered and they slipped out the door onto the street, acutely aware that the enemy forces were still close. It was dark but a glow above the roofs indicated some of the shattered houses were burning.

At first they moved cautiously, clinging to the walls of standing houses until a voice yelled at them in Spanish from a rooftop not far away.

'Run!' Otto said loudly and the three began a sprint along the cobblestone street. David's boots were tied around his neck and they banged against his face and chest. He was aware that they were being fired on as bullets smacked into the street, splintering chips of stone. David hurtled around a bend and straight into three shadowy figures armed with rifles. As startled as David, the three men hesitated, and David barrelled into the one raising his rifle. Both David and the man went down hard, while behind him he could hear Otto shout something.

'Don't hurt him! He's one of us.'

David recovered his feet. 'I'm sorry,' he said in English and the other man also stood up, brushing himself down in the process.

'You ever play rugby?' the well-educated English voice asked, surprising David.

'Yes, I did,' he answered.

'You must have been a front row forward,' the unknown Englishman said with just a hint of amusement. 'I played breakaway. I gather from your accent that you're a colonial from Australia. May I introduce myself: I am Archibald White. I believe I once had relatives living in Australia about fifty years ago. Call me Archie.'

'Pleased to meet you,' David said, extending his hand. 'David Macintosh.'

'Funny thing,' Archie said. 'I believe that one of my long-lost relatives married a lady by the name of Fiona Macintosh in Australia. Not relatives of yours by any chance?'

'I don't know much about my family,' David replied.

'I think it's time we left this street and got back to the lads at HQ,' Archie said and the defenders moved away. The Nationalists had been held back that day by international volunteers and a ragtag army of poorly armed factory workers prepared to resist until the end. But the Nationalists were already bringing up reinforcements for another assault on the Spanish capital.

That night Otto's section found brigade HQ and were treated to a meal of salami, cheese and bread. Flasks of wine were passed around and the section gravitated to the rubble of a house that had been smashed by an exploding bomb. It was hard to remember how only hours earlier they had been showered with the joyous greetings of the Spanish Republican supporters as they marched through the streets. So much had happened in one day that the hours felt like years.

'I got these,' John Steed said, handing out cigars to the survivors of his section. David took one from the American, although he did not smoke, and slipped it into the top pocket of his jacket. No one asked where the Yank had found the precious tobacco. David was exhausted and he soon fell asleep. That night he experienced his first nightmare of combat. He could clearly see the blood-drenched face of the beautiful young Spanish girl, whose face was now a meaty pulp. She was begging him in English to save her.

The next morning the section was resupplied with ammunition and orders were issued for their part in the defence of Madrid. David glanced around at the survivors from the day before and wondered whose face would come to his nightmares that night, or whether he, too, would be experiencing the sleep of the dead.

In the distance he could hear the crump of artillery shells exploding and the pop of rifle fire alongside the chatter of machine guns.

'Section, move out,' Otto commanded, and the men fell into a single file to make their way towards the front lines defending the city. The noise grew louder and David experienced the rising fear once again. Suddenly an Italian fighter plane swooped on the column making its way towards the front. Bullets smashed into the cobblestones, spraying the volunteers and Spanish militia with splinters of rock. Men screamed in their death agonies and the smell of blood filled the air. This was now the Australian boy's world, far from the peace he had once known growing up in New Guinea.

13

The private investigator's report on Sir George's office desk caused him to explode in fury.

'Damned worthless cur!' He picked up his telephone and called his secretary.

'Have my son report to me – now!' he roared and slammed the receiver down. Within minutes Donald appeared.

'You wanted to see me, Father?' he asked cautiously.

George rose from behind his desk and walked across to his son, waving the report. 'Do you think I am some kind of fool?' he asked, nose to nose with his son.

'I'm sorry, Father, but I don't know what you mean,' Donald replied, backing away.

'I employed a private investigator to look into your life,' George said, turning on his heel and walking away from his son. 'You gambled the money I gave you to wipe your gambling debts, and it appears you would rather indulge in alcohol and women of dubious virtue than live in the upstanding manner I expect.'

Donald's face reddened. 'What I do in my personal life has nothing to do with my role in the company,' he spluttered.

'It does when I have SP bookies ringing my office, demanding that I cover your gambling debts, and when you're fiddling the books to pay for your extravagant lifestyle.'

Donald hung his head in contrition.

George returned to his desk and slumped in his chair. 'You leave me with just one choice,' he sighed, toying with the report in front of him. 'I am sending you to Glen View for a couple of years, where you will learn how to manage cattle properties. At least out in the scrub you will have little opportunity to spend our money, and it will get you out of the grips of the bookies in Sydney. I am prepared to sign off on whatever you still owe those people, but I swear it will be the last time.'

Donald heard the name Glen View and was horrified. From what he knew of the cattle station it was stuck in the middle of nowhere. 'Father . . .' he attempted but George simply raised his hand and glared at him.

'There is a doddering old Scot, Hector MacManus, who currently manages the property, and I have been considering firing him,' George said in a calm manner. 'I feel that you are the man to replace MacManus until the time comes for you to return to Sydney and assist me with the management of our companies. It is not a life sentence and, who knows, you might even find the challenges of rural life satisfying.'

'How long, Father?' Donald asked despairingly.

'Two years – if you stay out of trouble,' George replied.

'I want you to leave on one of our coastal traders which is sailing for Brisbane this week. So, you can have time to make your farewells and pack for your new career. Are we both in agreement?'

'Yes, Father,' Donald replied meekly. 'If I could, I would like to take the rest of the day off.'

George stared at his son standing in the centre of his office. 'You may,' he replied. 'Now, go and pack for your trip.'

Donald walked from the office like a man walking to his death. George watched him go and wondered how he could have sired such a worthless son and such an ambitious daughter. It was a pity women could never assume the helm in the Macintosh companies. It was well known that women were the weaker sex and not capable of rational decision-making. But then he thought about his grandmother, Lady Enid Macintosh, who had defied that image of women, and he wondered. Maybe Enid Macintosh was a freak of nature who had the ability to match any man in the ruthless world of high finance. He tried to dismiss the idea of his daughter ever taking a managing role in the family business. She would find a suitable husband and be a good wife, bearing children and fading into obscurity in a genteel way. As for Donald . . . who knew what went through his vacant head? The boy was a waste of time.

★

'Is there nothing you can do to change Father's mind?' Donald asked his mother at her flat.

Louise stood before a large canvas on her easel, filling in bright colours of the harbour below. Her landscapes were shaping up well, and a friend had promised an exhibition in one of the city's most reputable galleries.

'My darling Donald,' Louise replied. 'It is only for two

years, and I have always wanted to visit Glen View, so you will not be altogether alienated from your family.'

Donald found a chair and sat down, hardly glancing at his mother's work of art but noticing that the damned portrait of that odious Sydney solicitor, Sean Duffy, was now hanging in pride of place on her studio wall. 'Isn't there a curse on all Macintoshes who visit the property?' he asked in the hope that his mother would show some sympathy and go into battle for him against his father.

Louise put down her palette and her brush and wiped her hands on her paint-stained apron. 'That was when Wallarie was alive,' she said. 'But only if you believe in such superstitions.'

Donald shrugged his shoulders. 'Maybe the curse still exists and I would be tempting fate to go up to Queensland and work on the property,' he said, desperate to remain in Sydney with its bright lights and sinful living.

'You, the son of the mighty Sir George Macintosh, should be the last to believe in old Aboriginal stories,' Louise said with a definite note of sarcasm. She walked across to her son and placed a hand on his shoulder. 'I think the break from Sydney will do you a lot of good. I remember when Giselle was living there, she wrote that the country has a magic you have to experience first-hand. Her own son, David – your cousin – lived his first years at Glen View before going to New Guinea with his grandmother, Karolina Schumann. I promise to visit you. I have always wanted to see the magic Giselle wrote about.'

With his last hope dashed, Donald resigned himself to travelling north. Two years was a lifetime to a young man, and the thought of such isolation frightened him. The only thing he knew about cattle was how to choose a good steak at a restaurant.

★

That evening Louise lay in the arms of her lover, Sean Duffy. They curled together, absorbing the soft warmth of each other's bodies. Sean puffed on a thick cigar, content after an evening of good food, wine and lovemaking.

'Sean, my love,' Louise said gently, waving away a cloud of rich-smelling smoke. 'You must give up smoking or it will hasten your demise.'

Sean stubbed out the cigar and kissed Louise on the lips.

'The war tried to kill me but it could only take my legs,' he said. 'The rest of me still works – as you damned well know.'

Louise giggled and snuggled closer to the man she had rediscovered in the last couple of years when she'd finally accepted her love for him.

Sean untangled himself, secured his artificial legs and hobbled across to the large window leading out onto the balcony with its spectacular view. He leaned on the door-frame, staring out at the harbour twinkling with lights from ships and boats lying at anchor.

'You're distracted this evening, my love. Are you worrying about David?' Louise said, leaning on her elbow and sipping from a flute of champagne.

'I've not had a word from him since he stupidly enlisted in the International Brigades,' Sean said without turning around. 'He could be badly wounded in some Spanish hospital or . . .' Sean did not finish the sentence. Louise padded across the room and joined Sean in the doorway. She placed her arm around his shoulders. 'I am sure that in some way or other if anything were to happen to David you would be informed. From what you have told me he is a remarkable young man, and very independent. Your worrying won't keep him any safer.' She laid her head on his shoulder. 'I love you, Sean Duffy.'

Sean turned to look at her and she lifted her face to his. 'Why don't you divorce George and marry me?' he asked.

'We have a wonderful situation, which, I am afraid, would be ruined by George if I sought a divorce,' she replied. 'He does not bother himself with me when he believes that you and I are not lovers. If I sought a divorce, George would make our lives miserable.'

'He's only a man,' Sean scoffed. 'We could cope with anything he threw at us.'

Louise reached up and touched Sean on the cheek. 'I know that, but I like my life as it is,' she said. 'It's not that I don't love you, but I feel at this stage in our lives our love is enough to give us the happiness we deserve. We are together because we wish to be, not because a piece of paper declares us man and wife.'

'You present a good argument,' Sean said with a smile. 'I'm glad that I don't have to go up against you inside a courtroom.'

'Then we will agree to love each other until death do us part,' Louise said with her own smile. 'Because that is the only thing that would take me from you.'

'Agreed,' Sean answered, taking her in his arms and holding her tight.

★

On the other side of the world Captain Matthew Duffy stomped his feet and blew warm air into his gloveless hands. The biting cold wind had dropped the thermometer below freezing and all aircraft were grounded. The collar of his fur-lined leather jacket was pulled up and he gazed at his own Ford trimotor sitting forlornly on the tarmac, covered in an icy sheen.

But at least one vehicle was moving. Matthew saw an army staff car drive up to his hangar. Major Guy Wilkes alighted, walking quickly towards the shelter to get out of the wind.

Matthew hurried after Guy and invited him to his office where a brazier burned, warming the small room.

'I didn't see Miss Hatfield's kite when I drove in,' Guy said, warming his hands over the small flames.

'She had an assignment in Germany,' Matthew answered, locating a bottle of good whisky to share with the British officer. 'I would say she is probably grounded with similar weather.'

Guy sat down on an old lounge chair and accepted the tumbler Matthew passed him.

'Cheers, old chap,' he said, raising his glass.

'I doubt that you came all the way out here to freeze your arse off when you could have remained in your much warmer office in Basra,' Matthew said, sitting down opposite the major.

'I missed your colonial hospitality,' Guy responded with a smile. 'And thought that you should know I would like you to wrangle an assignment to visit our German friends up on their dig – as soon as the weather clears.'

'What in hell for?' Matthew countered.

'We need to find out more about what the Huns are up to,' Guy replied, sipping his drink. 'Our department has reports that a couple of tribal leaders in the north who usually spend their spare time killing each other have suddenly united. It does not bode well and we think that they have done so with the prompting of German gold, and a promise of arms and explosives to be flown in from Germany in the very near future. As a matter of fact, we have access to certain intelligence that Miss Hatfield may be bringing back the said arms and munitions.'

At the mention of Diane being involved in such a treacherous act Matthew experienced mixed emotions:

betrayal and sorrow, and yet he couldn't change his feelings for her.

'Do you have definite proof of the delivery?' Matthew asked.

'Fairly reliable, old chap,' Guy replied. 'That's why we need you to be with the Huns when her aircraft arrives. I suspect that she will unload her cargo at their site before returning to Basra.'

'You do realise that the bloody Germans have already attempted to kill me,' Matthew said rather than asked. 'What are my chances they won't succeed a second time around?'

'You are a man with an impeccable reputation for getting out of tough scrapes,' Guy said lightly, raising his glass to stare at the golden whisky. 'I am sure that you will take all precautions necessary.'

'Okay, I'll do what you want,' Matthew agreed with a sigh. 'I'll take Tyrone with me as copilot. I'll have to brief him on our real mission at the Germans' camp.'

'That's a good chap,' Guy said, swilling the remainder of the whisky. 'But I would caution you that he is only briefed on what he needs to know, and nothing more. I'm sure you're aware how sensitive things are between Berlin and London. Our government will do anything to appease Herr Hitler in order to avoid a conflict with the Germans.'

'You can depend on my tact, Major Wilkes,' Matthew reassured. 'First break in the weather we will fly up north with the excuse that we're just checking on their welfare after the latest bout of blizzards.'

'See, you already have everything in hand,' Guy said, rising from his chair and slipping on his fur-lined gloves. 'I look forward to catching up with you in the officers' mess when you return. It will be my turn to supply a round of drinks.'

Matthew watched the British intelligence officer leave and wondered what the hell he had got himself into this time.

*

The following day the weather cleared enough for a takeoff.

'We're flying to the German camp,' Matthew told Tyrone when they were both in the cockpit carrying out pre-flight checks.

'I didn't notice any cargo when I came aboard,' Tyrone said, buckling his harness.

'There are a few things you need to know about this flight.' Matthew went on to explain that they were actually carrying out an espionage mission for the British army, without elaborating on who was behind the request. When Matthew explained that Diane was a suspected Nazi sympathiser, Tyrone uttered his disbelief.

'I don't believe that for one minute,' he said with a frown. 'She's too decent a lady to be tangled up in Nazi politics.'

'Well, she is,' Matthew said, checking the oil pressure gauges when he kicked over the three engines. 'I also have to warn you that our lives will be in danger when we land at the German camp, so carry a pistol at all times and watch my back.'

'Bloody hell, Skipper!' Tyrone exclaimed. 'I didn't sign on to get myself killed by a bunch of archaeologists!'

'You won't,' Matthew replied as the engines roared into life and their vibrations shook the Ford trimotor. 'I promise that no harm will come to you.'

Tyrone shrugged and adjusted his harness as Matthew taxied onto the airstrip and roared down the dry, concrete-like earth. The aircraft climbed into the clear cold sky, and Matthew set a course north of Basra. After a relatively short flight they saw the earthen strip below and made their landing.

When the aircraft came to a stop they were met by a puzzled Derik Albrecht.

'What do we make of your unexpected visit, Captain Duffy?' he asked as Matthew and Tyrone emerged from the cargo door.

'We were just flying north to Baghdad and thought we would drop in to ensure that your party had weathered the recent blizzards okay,' Matthew lied. 'We wouldn't mind a good hot cup of tea and a stopover tonight, Dr Albrecht.'

'You must realise that we are very busy here, Captain Duffy,' Albrecht said with a note of hostility in his voice. 'But you are welcome to stay for the night – if you are prepared to look after yourselves. I have not yet expressed my regrets for the unfortunate incident of your crash after you left us last time.'

'Oh, just one of those things that happens to flyers from time to time,' Matthew said casually, seething inside. He suspected that the man standing before him was the architect of the crash landing intended to kill him. Or was Matthew really angry at the handsome German scientist because he had slept with Diane?

Albrecht led them to a small encampment away from the archaeological dig and had one of the Iraqi workers prepare a pot of tea. He excused himself and left Tyrone and Matthew sitting on wooden crates under the canvas shelter, sipping the hot tea from tin mugs.

'What do we do now?' Tyrone asked, gazing across the flat land at the mound where the ancient buildings were slowly being exposed for the first time in three or four thousand years.

'We wait for Miss Hatfield to fly in. If the weather holds, that should be tomorrow morning,' Matthew said.

'Then I must be hearing things,' Tyrone said with a wry smile. 'Because I swear I can hear Junker engines.'

Matthew strained to hear the sound as Tyrone rose with his mug of tea to stare at the horizon. Eventually Matthew caught sight of Diane's aircraft descending in preparation for landing. She was a day early and, if Wilkes was right, she was carrying arms and ammunition for the Iraqi rebels. Such a cargo would seal her guilt as a collaborator with the Nazis. Matthew prayed that she was not, but his prayer seemed to be whisked away on the desert wind.

Diane's aircraft taxied to a stop beside Matthew's and within minutes she jumped down from her aeroplane.

Matthew gazed at her and felt a strange regret that this time all his suspicions might be confirmed. He could read the expression of shock in her pale face. It was obvious that she was not pleased to see him. *Yes*, Matthew thought. *She has the look of a guilty person caught in the act.*

'Matthew, Tyrone, what are you two doing here?' Diane asked.

'Just passing through,' Matthew answered with a forced smile.

14

That evening Matthew and Tyrone joined the archaeological team in their main tent. By the light of kerosene lanterns they shared a hearty meal of hot soup and sausage, followed by a bottle of schnapps.

Matthew noticed that Diane seemed to be keeping her distance from him, although she was polite. Erika made it a point to sit close to Matthew and engage him in conversation. He sensed her desire and under different circumstances he might have considered letting the rather pleasant situation develop into something more interesting.

Outside the cold winds blew. Matthew finally made their excuses and he and Tyrone retired for the night. Both men left the tent and were buffeted by the chilling winds as they struggled over to their aircraft to make an inspection of its vulnerable sections. A seal had been placed on the fuel tank inlet. As they passed Diane's Junkers, Matthew noted that a man was huddled under the wing, a heavy cloak covering him and the barrel of the rifle poking from the cloak.

Satisfied after their careful inspection, they climbed aboard the Ford. Matthew and Tyrone wrapped themselves in heavy blankets in the freezing cargo hold to wait out the night. Although they had been invited to remain in the shelter of the excavations Matthew had declined saying that they had adequate warmth in the Ford.

'Did you notice that they didn't unload whatever is in the Junkers?' Matthew said and Tyrone nodded.

'I have a feeling I know why – our unexpected arrival,' Matthew mused. 'And sometime in the early hours of the morning we are going to have a look inside the Junkers.'

'What about the sentry?' Tyrone asked.

'I strongly suspect he will desert his post to join his fellow workers inside the warmth of their tent,' Matthew replied.

'What if he doesn't?' Tyrone countered.

'Then we kill him,' Matthew replied. Tyrone winced as Matthew withdrew a razor-sharp hunting knife from a sheath on his belt. Both men dozed fitfully until around 4 am, when Matthew shook Tyrone awake.

'Time to go,' he said. 'Make sure you have your revolver.'

Tyrone struggled reluctantly from under his pile of blankets and they slipped out into the pitch-black night, carrying hand torches with them. Matthew was pleased to see that the wind had dropped. The night was still and the air was sharp. Matthew flicked on his torch and swung it to where the guard had been posted. He was satisfied to observe that the guard had indeed sought a warmer place to pass the night. Matthew switched the light off and both men moved cautiously towards the German aircraft. Tyrone was behind Matthew as they made their way to the side cargo door.

Matthew helped Tyrone up inside the fuselage and crawled inside with the help of his copilot, where he turned on his torch to play it over neatly stacked wooden crates stencilled in German to indicate what they held: rifles, grenades and ammunition.

'What do we do?' Tyrone questioned in a whisper. 'Blow the cargo?'

Squatting, Matthew turned off his torch leaving them both in the dark. 'No, my orders were simply to confirm the contents of the cargo,' Matthew answered in a low voice, feeling crushing despair. It was now clear that Diane was working with the Nazi scientists to incite rebellion against the British in Iraq.

'Our job is done,' Matthew said. 'Time to get back to our aircraft.'

Tyrone let out a sigh of relief. It had all gone off without incident and they could take off in the morning for a return trip back to Basra. They made their way in the dark to the cargo door and exited. Both men were on the ground when Matthew suddenly became aware that they were not alone. A shape loomed up in front of them and Matthew instinctively knew that the sentry had returned to his post. He stood frozen only a matter of inches from Matthew, who had his hand wrapped around the handle of his knife. Without hesitating Matthew threw himself on the Iraqi, plunging the knife with as much force as he could into where he guessed the startled man's throat was. With more luck than skill Matthew found his target and the knife cut through the tough cartilage, choking off any cry of alarm. Warm blood splashed over Matthew but he continued to drive the man into the hard earth, twisting the knife as he did to inflict maximum damage. Matthew continued to hold him down until his thrashing ceased.

'Bloody hell!' Tyrone hissed only feet away. 'Is he dead?'

Matthew found that his hand was shaking uncontrollably. In all his years of warfare, from Elands River in South Africa to the skies over Palestine, he had never killed a man so intimately before, with the dying man's last breath on his face. 'He's dead,' Matthew replied in a flat voice, pulling the knife from the Iraqi's body. 'We have to get rid of him and cover any trace of what has happened here.'

He glanced around to see if the short, violent episode had attracted any attention. He dared not use the torch again to survey the scene and was desperately attempting to think of a way to dispose of the body.

'We get him back to our kite and wrap him in blankets,' Matthew said finally. 'We spread rocks on the blood and pray the evidence is not found. The Huns will hopefully think that their man deserted his post and went walkabout. If we do a good job of cleaning up we will be out of here before any evidence of our involvement turns up.'

No sooner had Matthew uttered his instructions than they were suddenly lit up in the strong beam of a torch.

'Matthew?' a female voice asked in a puzzled tone. 'What are you doing over there?'

Matthew realised that he still held the knife in his hand. Diane was advancing towards them and was only a mere ten paces away when she gasped in horror.

Never before had Matthew faced such a decision and suddenly his mind flashed back to a hilltop so many years earlier when he had held the life of his beloved Joanne in his hands. He had delivered a lethal dose of morphine to alleviate her terrible pain from a gunshot that left no hope of salvation. Now he was forced to deliver death to the woman he secretly desired.

'What are you doing out here?' Matthew asked and realised how inane his question was.

'You taught me a long time ago to always ensure the condition of your aircraft,' Diane replied, standing with her torch shining in Matthew's face.

From the corner of his eye Matthew saw that Tyrone stood with his pistol levelled at Diane.

'I'm sorry that you chose to follow my instructions this time,' he said sadly, still struggling with the next step. He should kill her – he'd confirmed her complicity in the Nazi plot to arm rebellious tribesmen.

'I know what your cargo is,' Matthew said. 'Why, Diane?'

'Not everything in life is etched in black and white, Matthew,' she replied quietly. 'I suspect that within a very short time what you have done will be discovered, and neither you nor Tyrone will get out of here alive.' Her words held enough threat for Matthew to take a firm grip on the handle of his knife. He had no other choice than to kill her. He could not risk the loud sound of a gunshot from Tyrone.

'Nor is the situation as it appears,' Diane continued, switching off her torch and leaving the three standing beneath a canvas of brilliant starlight. 'I wish I could explain but all I can do is give you and Tyrone a chance to get out of here alive,' she said.

'You tried to kill me with the sabotage of my plane,' Matthew countered. 'Why would you try and help us now?'

'I was not aware of what had been done to your kite,' Diane replied sadly. 'I believe that Albrecht was behind the sabotage.'

'You expect me to believe that?' Matthew scoffed. 'I know you're a member of the American Nazi Party and that you and Albrecht are lovers.'

'Why would my relationship with Albrecht concern you?' Diane asked. 'You've never shown any romantic interest in me.'

'I don't want to be a bother,' Tyrone said quietly, 'but the longer we stay out here, the greater the risk of being found out.'

Matthew knew his copilot was right. 'You said that you would give us a chance to live,' he said. 'What do you mean by that?'

'You should take off now,' Diane answered. 'I know it's risky without airstrip lights, but you're one of the best flyers I know. I will tell the team that I suggested you leave before the weather turned bad. As for the dead man at your feet . . . his absence will not be missed for some hours.'

'You would do that?' Matthew questioned, his mind reeling.

'I stopped the Germans at Tempelhof, didn't I?' she countered. 'Go now and take the body with you,' she continued urgently. 'You do not have much time and I will need to get back to the tent to explain to Albrecht why you are leaving so early. By the time the absence of the guard is discovered you should be back at Basra having morning tea.'

Matthew turned to Tyrone, who was already dragging the body of the Iraqi back to their aircraft. He turned to follow his copilot, confused at what had just transpired.

The body was pulled aboard and both men took their seats in the cockpit. After a quick check Matthew fired the engines and they coughed into life. Already Diane was gone from view and when the engines were warm enough to take off Matthew could see the lights in the main tent go on. No doubt Diane was explaining their unannounced departure to Albrecht.

Even in the dark Matthew was able to find the strip, and with his engines at almost full power he took off. Within a minute the undercarriage was free of the earth and they were climbing into the sky, plotting a course back to Basra.

Matthew went over and over every word they had exchanged on the airstrip. What was not black and white? She was a confirmed member of the Nazi Party. She had smuggled arms to the German team for distribution to the rebels. That was certainly black and white.

Matthew made his way further back into the cargo hold to the body of the man he had killed, and for the first time had a clear view of him. He could see that he was a young man, probably in his early twenties. His beard was clotted with blood and his eyes the opaque colour of death. He felt great sadness for this stranger who had not been his enemy but a threat to his mission. Matthew felt that he'd had no choice but to kill him; he was back to the old days of kill or be killed.

He pulled the body to the doorway and with great caution opened the door and slid the body from the aircraft as the wind howled past with its mournful song. The body fell towards the earth and Matthew said a quiet prayer, unsure whether he was praying for the Iraqi or himself.

*

In Basra it was breakfast time in the officers' mess and Major Guy Wilkes sat down with his cup of tea in a comfortable chair in the anteroom to peruse a week-old copy of the *Times*. He glanced up from the pages when he noticed his orderly-room clerk hovering at the door to the mess with an anxious expression.

'What is it, Corporal Starthorne?' he asked.

The corporal remained in the doorway, not daring to

enter the holy place of officers. 'There is a decoded message that has been signalled to us, sir,' he said. 'I think you should see it now.'

With a sigh, Wilkes placed his fine china cup on a small table and followed his clerk to the signals building. He entered and went to the room that encoded and decoded top secret messages from London. The signaller on duty had his headphones on and was intent on scribbling down messages on military forms.

The corporal clerk went to a clipboard and retrieved a lengthy decoded signal, passing it to the intelligence major. Wilkes signed the message as a record that he had received it, and commenced reading. It was from Military Intelligence Department Six in London and had been relayed after an intercept on the American communications station in Britain. Although the view that gentlemen did not read other gentlemen's mail was often echoed in the intelligence world, they still did. Being an ally did not exclude listening in to each other's top secret messages.

'Damn!' Guy muttered, passing the form back to his clerk. 'Ensure this message is destroyed ASAP. Do we know where Captain Duffy is right now?'

'The last report was that Captain Duffy was on his way to the German camp,' he answered. 'That is all I know at this stage.'

'Get my car ready, Corporal Starthorne,' Guy Wilkes said. 'You and I are going to drive out to Captain Duffy's hangar and pray that he has returned in one piece. I also want you to make an appointment with our foreign affairs chap in Baghdad as soon as possible. You can inform him that we require an urgent meeting.'

'Yes, sir,' the clerk replied. He delegated the appointment for the foreign affairs representative to another clerk on the way out of the office and rushed to get the car ready.

★

Matthew's Basra airstrip was in view and the weather had held to a clear, crisp day as the aircraft came in to land smoothly. Even from the air Matthew had spotted Major Wilkes's staff car waiting by the hangar, no doubt there to take his report on what he had found.

Tyrone taxied the Ford to the hangar where they were met by Cyril, who stood shivering with his hands in his pockets.

'Hope you've been looking after my kite,' he said by way of greeting and waved over his shoulder to Major Wilkes. 'The major says he wants to have a wee word with you.'

Matthew thanked Cyril and asked Tyrone to chase up Ibrahim to prepare breakfast and tea. When Matthew approached Guy he could see the strained expression on the British officer's face.

The major extended his gloved hand. 'Hope all went well, old chap,' he said, shaking Matthew's hand firmly. 'I have received a spot of intelligence this morning that has changed everything around here. But first, did you make it to the Hun camp?'

Matthew briefed him on all that had occurred up until his confrontation with Diane. For reasons unknown and he himself did not quite understand he did not inform the British officer of that strange meeting, but he did tell him that he had been forced to kill a sentry.

'Did you speak with Miss Hatfield while you were at the camp?' Guy asked with a trace of a frown on his face.

'Only during the evening meal,' Matthew lied. 'Why, is there any significance in that?'

'I could do with a good hot cup of tea,' Guy replied. 'My morning brew was rudely interrupted today.'

'Tea is being prepared even as we speak,' Matthew answered, leading Guy towards his office in the big hangar. 'I sense that there is a connection between you missing your cup of tea and Miss Hatfield.'

'There is, old chap,' Guy answered. 'And I think you will need a strong brew, too, when I tell you why.'

15

It hurt when Donald Macintosh hit the earth of the dusty yard. The horse continued to pigroot, and the men leaning on the wooden railings of the circular enclosure sneered at Donald's discomfort. The stockmen knew he was the son of the property's owner and harboured the working man's dislike of those in the boss class.

Donald had now been a resident of Glen View for two weeks. In the last three days he had attempted to master the art of riding a horse, something he had never done before. Old Hector MacManus, leaning on a walking stick, shook his head in despair. Today Hector had allowed one of the half-broken horses to be saddled, hoping that his protégé might have learned enough to handle the frisky mount. Up until this moment Donald had thought he'd learned plenty about horse riding, but lying winded on his back on the ground, he admitted to himself that he had a lot to learn if he was going to gain the respect of the men watching.

Although Donald still yearned to return to the bright lights of Sydney he knew that he would just have to make the best of a bad situation. He listened carefully to the old Scot as he attempted to teach him how a cattle station worked. Donald had found himself in a world of men who spent their whole lives working the tough and often dangerous plains as stockmen and who respected a man for his character rather than his income. They were no-nonsense workers who believed in giving all a fair go, as long as they pulled their weight. In the end, Donald knew he would just have to accept their scorn.

He rose to his feet, dusting down his trousers, and went in search of his wide-brimmed hat. It lay at the edge of the yard. When he walked over to retrieve it he looked up and came to a sudden halt. Standing behind the rails was a young woman whose dark beauty immediately caught his attention. She was watching him with the trace of an amused smile.

'Hello,' she greeted when Donald was only a few paces away. 'You seem to have trouble sitting on a horse.'

Donald could see that the young woman watching him had an inherent intelligence in her liquid black eyes, observing his every movement. She had a golden sheen to her skin and appeared to be just a few years younger than he. Where she had come from baffled him.

'Oh, I was okay yesterday,' Donald replied with a self-effacing smile. 'I actually got to stay in the saddle for at least an hour.'

'You will need to learn to remain in the saddle for a lot longer if you wish to ride with the Glen View mob,' the young woman said.

'Let me introduce myself,' Donald said, dusting off his hat and holding it in his hands. 'I'm—'

'You're Donald Macintosh,' the girl interjected. 'I already know that from Mr MacManus. I am Miss Jessica Duffy, but you may call me Jessica, Mr Macintosh.'

'In that case you can call me Donald,' he replied, warming to the young lady on the other side of the fence. 'I am very pleased to meet you, Jessica Duffy, and dare I ask what such a beauteous sight in this desolate land is doing laughing at the dilemma of a novice?'

Jessica laughed softly and stepped back from the fence. 'My father and I are guests of Mr MacManus,' she said. 'Every chance my father gets he stops over here. Sometimes I'm free to travel with him, and I am pleased to say that this time I had the opportunity to see the son of Sir George Macintosh fall on his arse.'

Donald smiled at her use of a word one would most definitely not hear from the lips of a Sydney lady. It was obvious from the cultured tone of her voice, however, that she had been well schooled. She was wearing jodhpurs and a clean silk shirt – the way she was dressed spelled money.

Satisfied that the owner's son had learned a lesson in horsemanship, the stockmen drifted away from the horse-breaking yard, leaving Jessica and Donald alone.

'Mr MacManus has prepared morning tea at the homestead and I was sent down to invite you to meet my father,' Jessica said, turning on her heel and obviously expecting Donald to follow. He could not help but notice the way her round backside filled her tight pants.

They reached the verandah of the homestead, stepping through the open gauze door to enter the spacious dining room beyond the kitchen. Donald saw a tall, broad-shouldered man standing talking to the old Scots station manager. When the stranger turned to greet his daughter, Donald was slightly taken aback by his dangerous demeanour. There was something behind the eyes that spoke of a wild animal ready to kill.

'Daddy, this is Mr Donald Macintosh,' Jessica said with a genuine note of love in her voice. 'Donald, this is my father Tom.'

Tom held out his hand to Donald, who was almost too frightened to accept the gesture. Donald did not know why he was so frightened of a man he had never met before – even though he had heard Tom's name in company circles as both a distant relative and the man who wanted to purchase Glen View Station.

'Pleased to meet you, Mr Duffy,' Donald said, feeling the iron strength in the other man's grip.

'A pleasure, Mr Macintosh,' Tom said, balancing his cup of tea in one hand. 'No doubt you have heard my name mentioned before.'

Donald felt decidedly uncomfortable at the comment. Tom Duffy was looking him directly in the eye.

'My father has mentioned that you have shown an interest in purchasing Glen View,' Donald replied after clearing his throat.

'Tea, Donald?' Jessica asked. Her familiarity brought a disapproving glance from her father, which did not deter her at all. 'I found Donald making an examination of the soil,' she continued. 'I think he may have been thinking about ways to improve the pastures.'

'You mean you found Mr Macintosh face down in the round yard,' Hector exploded with a laugh. 'My fault, I allowed the lads to saddle a half-broken mount so we could see how young Mr Macintosh was going. In actual fact he is doing very well in his horse handling. I might let him off mucking out the stables today.'

Donald could see a slight smile on the stern face of Tom Duffy, and suddenly his apprehension melted in the warmth that came into those same dark eyes.

'I appreciate your generosity, Mr MacManus,' Donald said graciously, knowing full well that Hector would not have ordered the son of his boss to do such a menial task as mucking out stables. 'It is certainly far more pleasant being in such august company as Mr Duffy, whom I remember was decorated for great bravery in the war.'

Tom looked with surprise at the young man. 'I am flattered that you have any knowledge of my war experiences,' he said.

'My father has a very comprehensive dossier on you, Mr Duffy. If I remember correctly, you were awarded a Distinguished Conduct Medal along with a Military Medal, and at one stage it is rumoured you were actually recommended for the Victoria Cross. I also know that you had a fearsome reputation as a sniper on the Western Front.'

'You're well informed,' Tom said. 'Do you also know that we are distantly related, and that Aboriginal blood runs in my veins and those of my daughter?'

The obvious challenge caught Donald off guard. He had heard both those pieces of information. He realised Tom was watching him carefully for a reaction.

'Ah, yes,' he replied. 'But the colour of a man's skin does not measure his worth.'

The sudden chill in the warm air seemed to dissipate at this answer and Donald glanced at Jessica to see her reaction. She appeared unfazed, and bent to pick up a scone, eating it with great delicacy.

Donald was fascinated by her. She was both a lady and

someone who could express vulgar words in the yards. Donald had known a lot of young ladies in Sydney and he found himself comparing her with them. He decided she would definitely be able to hold her own in any society – despite her heritage. He admitted to himself that he had been raised by his father to believe that black people were incapable of joining civilised society. But in this room, in the presence of the impressive Tom Duffy and his beautiful daughter, Sir George's views did not seem to hold much weight.

'Are you staying over for a while, Mr Duffy?' Donald asked.

'Mr Duffy usually spends a week when he visits Glen View,' Hector answered. 'Although your father may not approve, I consider Mr Duffy a friend. He worked for me just after the war, and knows these lands as well as any man, and Miss Duffy is probably one of the most accomplished horse riders I know.'

'I can assure you, Mr MacManus, that I am not about to inform my father of Mr Duffy's visits,' Donald said. 'I would like the honour of riding with Miss Duffy tomorrow. I am sure that she can prevent me from pursuing a career as an agronomist. And, Mr Duffy, I am fully aware of your reputation with a rifle.'

All in the room broke into a soft laugh at this.

'It is up to my daughter, Mr Macintosh,' Tom said, glancing at Jessica whose face had broken into a broad smile. 'Looks like she will accept your offer. Just be back before last light.'

That night at dinner, Donald shared the table with Hector and his guests. The conversation centred around running a cattle station: cattle prices, diseases and pastures. Donald sat opposite Jessica and every now and then he would catch her eye and she would smile at him openly. Donald had to admit that he was smitten by this unusual young lady.

That night, as Donald lay on his back staring at the dark places in the room, he became aware that the curlews' song was louder than usual, and that there was something disturbing in it. He finally dozed off, but for some reason a nightmare came to him. He dreamed of a hill that had a life of its own, guarded by an old grey-bearded Aboriginal warrior holding a long and deadly spear. The nightmare was a warning, but Donald had no idea what it meant when the sun rose to warm the brigalow scrub once again.

Donald got up and snatched an early breakfast from the kitchen. Jessica was already saddling up her horse when he walked out to the round yard. She had selected a steady and reliable gelding for him.

'I will give you a tour of this land of my father,' she said, tightening the girth to her horse. 'You may be the owner of Glen View, but you do not realise how much of my history is in these lands.'

Donald swung himself into the saddle while Jessica flung over canvas water bags along with a picnic she had organised with the kitchen staff. He allowed Jessica to lead the way and they set off at a comfortable pace.

Just before mid-morning they arrived at a grove of small trees and Jessica dismounted, leading her horse to tether it. Donald did the same. The oppressive heat of the day was already present in the stillness of the grove.

'What is here of historical importance?' he asked when Jessica passed him a water bag to drink from.

'Over there,' Jessica said, pointing to what Donald could see were three small, almost indistinct mounds of earth with a few rocks sprinkled on them. Termite-rotted wood lay at the head of each mound.

'Those are the graves of Patrick Duffy – who is our mutual great-great-grandfather,' she said, gazing at the three graves laid out in the little shade of the stunted grey trees. 'One of the other graves belongs to my grandfather's brother, Peter Duffy, and we do not know whom the other grave belongs to. My father thinks it might be Patrick's faithful Aboriginal servant who came from the Murray River region.'

Donald stared in awe at the graves and wondered at the fact his great-great-grandfather was under the ground in one of them. 'No one in my family has ever told me about Patrick Duffy,' he said softly. 'It is as if I have no ancestry other than Sir Donald Macintosh, my namesake.'

'Patrick was murdered on Glen View, and so was Peter,' Jessica said with a note of sadness. A soft, hot breeze swirled small eddies of dust around the grove. 'I just wanted you to know who I am,' she added unexpectedly. 'I'm sure you know my father wishes to purchase Glen View for sentimental reasons, and because he made a promise to Wallarie when I was born.'

'Wallarie,' Donald said. 'I have heard his name so many times in my family. He seems to haunt my father, but I gather he is dead by now.'

'Wallarie can never die,' Jessica said with a smile. 'He has just changed into another being, still living on his traditional lands.'

'I thought you had the best schooling a young lady could receive,' Donald said, looking at Jessica. 'I believe you went to an exclusive Roman Catholic college, so how could you make such a statement?'

'Because in my blood is that of Wallarie's people,' Jessica said with a serious expression.

Donald was taken aback by her certainty. She seemed

suddenly much older than her years. Most of the girls he knew in Sydney society were only interested in the latest fashions, parties and gossip, but this woman walked with a deep spirituality.

'I think it is time for us to visit Wallarie, and then we will eat,' Jessica said.

Donald followed her back into the saddle and within the hour they came in sight of a craggy, extinct volcano looming above the brigalow plains.

'That is the sacred hill where Wallarie resides in a cave,' she said, dismounting. 'But it is a place for men only.'

Donald couldn't hide his scepticism. 'Surely you don't believe in all that?'

'I do,' Jessica replied. 'But I don't think there are any rules preventing me climbing the hill with you.'

David was starting to be intrigued. 'Here, let me take your hand. The track is rough,' he said, indicating the path, which looked as though it had been worn down by bush animals.

Jessica took Donald's hand, although he knew that she did not need his help. Together they climbed the narrow twisting trail until they reached the summit with its magnificent panoramic view of the vast sun-baked plain. For a moment they stood side by side and Donald noticed that Jessica had not let go of his hand. Behind them was the opening to the cave under an overgrown old gnarled tree whose roots curled into the face of the overhang above the cave entrance.

Jessica turned to gaze at the entrance. 'Wallarie still lives in there,' she said and for a moment Donald felt a chill when he remembered the strange nightmare from last night.

'I bet I go in there and don't find anyone,' Donald said and Jessica let go of his hand.

'I don't think Wallarie would want a Macintosh to go into his cave,' she said with an expression of deep concern. 'It was your great-great-grandfather who slaughtered Wallarie's people here so many years ago.'

'But that was not me – although I might bear the same name,' Donald replied.

Before Jessica could stop him Donald turned and walked quickly towards the cave. He plunged inside to be assailed by the musty smell of ages. The sun was shining through the entrance, illuminating the centre of the cave and evidence of fires long extinguished. Donald's eyes adjusted to the gloom and he realised that he was alone despite Jessica's warnings. His act of bravado was only intended to impress Jessica, but suddenly he was gripped with an unexplainable fear that rooted him to the earth. The hair on the back of his neck was sticking up and he was afraid to turn around lest he see who was watching him with an intensity he could almost touch. It was as if the watcher was questioning his right to be in the cave and yet rationally Donald knew he was alone in the cave.

Suddenly a ghostly voice was whispering in his ear, 'You got any baccy?'

Donald mustered all the strength he had then and found the use of his legs. He backed out, wide-eyed and frightened, into the reassuring light of day.

'You saw him?' Jessica asked. For a moment Donald was speechless. No doubt Jessica's talk of the old Aboriginal had caused him to imagine things, but the voice had been so real.

'I . . . I don't want to discuss the matter,' he said in a shaky voice and Jessica smiled.

'I told you Wallarie still lives,' she said.

'I think it's time we went back to the horses and had our

picnic,' Donald suggested, still trying to shake off the eerie experience in the cave.

This time Jessica slid her hand into his and they walked together down the hill to the horses. As much as he hated to recognise it, Donald grudgingly admitted to himself that there were mysterious things beyond the world of the living.

'Ah, Wallarie has flown away,' Jessica said happily, gazing up into the cloudless blue sky at an eagle floating on the thermals. Any other time Donald would have scoffed at such an observation but this time he did not.

16

Double agent! The words kept going through Matthew Duffy's mind.

Major Guy Wilkes had explained how a British intercept of an American diplomatic cable had revealed that a British citizen, Miss Diane Hatfield, was working on behalf of the US domestic intelligence service, the Federal Bureau of Investigation. The FBI under Hoover was only allowed to carry out intelligence on American soil, so the nature of Diane's international movements had required some legal negotiations with overseas diplomatic posts – and hence the intercept to brief American diplomatic staff. Wilkes had surmised that the Americans had kept her recruitment quiet from the Brits as it was known the US President, Franklin D Roosevelt, had no love for British imperialism. America did not have a formal overseas intelligence service and outside the military intelligence departments, Roosevelt could only rely on a close group of wealthy and diplomatic people to provide him with the information he required when they travelled to foreign lands. Diane was seen as a coup as she was slowly but surely gaining the German government's trust and was moving closer to the inner circles of the Nazi dictatorship.

Matthew sat alone in his office going over all that the British major had been able to put together from the report he had received from his own people in London. How Diane had been recruited by the FBI was not known, nor why she would agree in the first place. What Matthew did know was that she had once flown for an American gangster of Sicilian heritage who was rumoured to be closely allied with the Italian dictator, Mussolini. *Therein was a clue*, Matthew thought. Mussolini and Hitler were very close allies.

Matthew knew Diane lived on the razor's edge. What if the Germans were also intercepting American coded traffic? The thought chilled Matthew. Someone was bound to slip up, and Diane could find herself facing the Gestapo. He had heard they were ruthless and cruel and he had no doubt they would torture and likely execute her.

'You are ordered not to make contact with Miss Hatfield,' Wilkes had said at the end of his briefing to Matthew.

Perhaps he could extract Diane from her dangerous double life. He had little faith in the Americans being able to protect her if things went wrong. They were too far from this part of the world controlled by the British and French. Matthew stood up and walked over to the map and stared at it. How could he make contact with Diane without endangering her life? For the moment there was no answer.

★

Sir George Macintosh sat in the Macquarie Street special-ist's surgery on an expensive leather chair, staring at the white walls with their clinical bareness. His symptoms had persisted and he had had a round of tests, the results of which he would know in a moment.

The door opened and the doctor – a distinguished man of science who was also a knight of the realm for his services to medicine, and who belonged to George's own exclusive club – walked in. He wore a dark suit and held a sheaf of papers. He took a seat at his desk and George waited for him to speak. The worried expression on the doctor's face was bad enough but the silence of waiting for the results was even worse.

'George, old chap, I am afraid I have bad news,' the doctor said finally. 'It is confirmed that you are in the tertiary stages of syphilis, and from what the tests say, it appears to be neurosyphilis.'

'Are you damned sure that your tests are right?' George exploded. 'Other than losing my balance a little bit lately, and shooting pains in my lower body, I feel as well as anyone.'

'I am sorry, George, but the tests were thorough. You may have contracted this disease years ago, and the only signs then would have been a chancre at point of contact and around ten weeks or so later some non-itchy rashes. The disease becomes latent before reaching a tertiary stage, which you are now in. I'm afraid there is no cure.'

'Does that mean I am about to die?' George said, unable to believe it.

'No,' the doctor replied calmly. 'But it does mean you may drift into a state of dementia as time goes by.'

'You mean madness,' George replied bitterly. 'What have I done to deserve this?' As if an echo to his question he suddenly remembered the face of a very pretty girl he had murdered years earlier. What was her name? Maude Urqhart. It was just after her death that the ulcer had appeared, and a few weeks later the rashes. George had ignored the signs and he shuddered now when he thought that the girl he had murdered was reaching out from her grave to seek revenge. George paled and realised that his hands were trembling. He knew now that he was cursed.

'If it is any consolation,' the doctor said, 'your disease is no longer infectious, and we have a variety of painkillers if you find you are suffering.'

George looked up with a haunted expression. 'How long do you think I have before I go mad?'

'It can be many years before the sickness takes hold,' the doctor attempted to reassure. 'I cannot say how long, but I feel you should get your affairs in order. It pays to be prepared, old chap. I am sorry that I cannot offer any more hope than I have.'

George rose from the chair with great difficulty. He did not bother to say goodbye but left the doctor's consultation room as if he had been told of his imminent execution.

*

They had followed the Russian tanks into Boadilla del Monte in central Spain amid fierce fighting against Franco's Nationalists and captured the town.

After months of fighting the weather was bitterly cold and David Macintosh was vaguely aware that Christmas was not far away as he huddled against a low stone wall cradling his Mauser rifle in his arms. So much had happened since he'd arrived in Spain and already he had lost his friend, Horace Howard, in the fighting in Madrid. The artillery shell had exploded directly where the young Englishman had been bunkered down, and when the smoke cleared nothing remained of him. The blast had virtually vaporised him with its direct hit, leaving nothing to mourn except the memory of his smiling face.

The former German soldier of the Great War, Otto Planke, moved along the wall where David huddled with others watching the low hills to their front and the enemy lines beyond. 'Time to go back and get some food,' he said in German. Of the original section only Jaroslav, the Czech, and John Steed, the American, remained. The Englishman who had joined them in Madrid, Archie White, was still alive; the others had either been killed or evacuated with wounds back to France.

The men eased themselves from the shelter of the stone wall. They followed Otto back to the house in the town where they were billeted. Inside the warmth of the stone house the men sat down at an old wooden table. China plates, cracked with age, were placed in front of them by the elderly widow who resided there. She was dressed in a long black woollen skirt with a woollen shawl around her shoulders. She ladled vegetable soup into bowls and handed them around; the men ate the hot soup with a slab of cheese and some home-made bread. The old widow muttered about the war and how hard it was to get cheese with the siege on the town. Archie could speak Spanish and he promised her that the siege would soon be lifted, and she would get all the cheese she wanted, although he knew along with the others defending the town that the enemy was actually bringing in fresh forces, ready for an all-out assault, probably early in the new year.

With their stomachs full, the men retired to huddle around the big open fireplace staring at the glowing coals. Archie had four cigars left from his precious stock, and handed them to each man with the exception of David, who did not smoke.

They lit up and enjoyed the nicotine rush that soothed nerves and took them away from the cold and anxiety.

'It feels like we have been marching and fighting forever,' Jaroslav said in German to no one in particular.

'God in heaven!' Otto said, puffing on his cigar. 'It was worse in the war when we were fighting the Frenchies at Verdun. At least Franco hasn't used gas on us yet.'

David stared into the small, flickering flames and let his mind drift to more pleasant moments. He had found fleeting love only three weeks earlier, in the arms of a young Spanish girl in the back of a shelled-out factory. Living with sudden and savage death had a way of bringing men and women together. Whether it had been love or lust David experienced he did not care. He lived day to day now. Although David could not speak Spanish it did not seem to matter; flirting between the two young people quickly turned into a passionate act of lovemaking among the deserted machines. For those moments there was no war or death, just the warmth of two bodies entwined in desire. All that David knew about the young woman was that her name was Cristobel and Madrid was her home. Regretfully, David had been transferred out to his current posting and since then there had been no contact. Such was the manner of war.

Weary from the long hours posted to the front line of the town, the men eventually lay down on the stone floor, wrapped in blankets, to snatch sleep. But in the early hours of the morning the door opened, bringing David awake. Two men had entered and shook Otto awake, speaking in low voices before leaving.

Irritably, Otto awoke the others.

'Get your things together,' he said. 'It is our turn to go out into no-man's-land, and carry out a recce on the Nationalists. Brigade HQ has ordered the mission.'

The men shook off sleep, picked up their rifles and fell out into the bitterly cold darkness. Together they made their way to the front line at the edge of the township, and there they were met by a leader of the Spanish Republicans. He briefed them in Spanish and Archie translated. In turn David spoke in German for Jaroslav and Otto's sake. They were to go as far forward as possible and attempt to snatch a Nationalist soldier for interrogation. This would not be easy. The Spanish commander handed Otto a small coil of rope along with half-a-dozen hand grenades. All the men were armed with their rifles and deadly knives honed razor-sharp. Passwords were given and then it was time to wend their way down the hill into a small valley until they came to the forward positions of the enemy, marked by the flickering lights of numerous campfires.

David had been posted to lead the section, as Otto considered that he had the best night vision of their group. As they had descended into the valley David felt how tight his stomach was. He had a bad feeling about the mission. Within a couple of hours they had advanced close enough to actually hear the voices of the enemy on the forward edge of a low hill. Otto signalled that they go to ground to make a decision on how they would make the next leg of their journey across no-man's-land. Just as they settled on their stomachs on the wet and icy earth a star shell exploded over them and a parachute flare drifted slowly to earth, lighting up the countryside. It was sheer luck for David's section that they were already crouching out of sight of any enemy observer. David clutched his rifle to his chest and fingered the safety catch. Had the flare been fired by an alert sentry? Or was it simply a random act? The bad feeling he had in the pit of his stomach grew worse and he wished that he could grow wings and fly away until he found some place where the sun shone to warm his chilled bones. There was such a place – and it was called home. But questioning why he was lying out on the slope of a foreign hillside did little to change the reality of his situation. The flare finally settled onto the earth and went out, pitching the country into almost total blackness, broken only by the glow of campfires ahead of them.

'Over there,' Otto whispered. 'I can see the outline of a sentry.'

The four men followed the German's observation to see the silhouetted head and shoulders of a careless sentry.

'We take him,' Otto said.

Easier said than done, David thought. How many others would be with him in the trench?

Another flare went up but this time it was followed by a long burst of machine-gun fire that raked the ground around David's section. It was obvious that they had been spotted and death was coming for them. David hugged the earth, whimpering a prayer over and over again. He did not care which God heard it so long as the bullets did not find his body and rip him apart.

*

A white Christmas was coming to the US state of New Hampshire. In the Barrington home the traditional Christmas tree had already been erected and decorated by the staff.

Young James Barrington stood with his back to the great log fire in the spacious living room, warming himself after returning from gridiron practice. He had bathed and changed his clothes and was wondering if his grandfather would notice if he took some of the fine bourbon from the liquor cabinet on the other side of the room. Football practice had gone well and in the new year James would be playing in the much-followed college league as one of the star players.

Olivia entered the room dressed in a fashionable skirt and blouse. She greeted her brother, who was very much the favourite of her girlfriends. They often pestered her with questions about her twin with a view to getting closer to the handsome and eligible young man.

'Have you ever wondered what our father is doing right now?' he asked.

His question took Olivia by surprise. She took a book from the library shelf that occupied one complete wall of the room.

'I rarely think about him,' she replied. 'I doubt that he even thinks about us at all.'

James frowned. He did not know why but as the last year had passed he had come to think about his estranged father more and more. Maybe it was because he was on the verge of pursuing his own life as an adult, and he wondered if he was anything like the man who had sired him.

'We have not seen or heard from him since we were little children. I wonder if he's even alive,' James continued. 'Grandfather never speaks of him, and I know there's no love lost between the two of them.'

Olivia placed the book on a polished sideboard and sat down in one of the great leather chairs facing the open fireplace.

'There were times when I was just a little girl I would hope our father would come riding in on a big white horse and sweep me up in his arms,' she said bitterly, staring into the flickering flames of the fire. 'But it did not happen, so I try not to think about him any more. As far as I am concerned he died when our mother did.'

'Maybe he has had a reason not to see us,' James defended. 'I think I would like to meet him now that we're older.'

Olivia looked up at her brother. 'And how could we do that when we don't even know where he is, let alone if he is still alive? From the little I have been able to get out of Grandfather, our father lives – or lived – a very precarious life in the Bible lands, flying aeroplanes.'

'That's just it,' James said. 'He's had such an adventurous life, and was once a fighter pilot in the war. I think he was even a Brit ace.'

'How do you know all this?' Olivia asked.

'I remember when Grandmother used to visit us when we were young. She told me the stories about Father,' James said, a note of eagerness creeping into his voice. 'When he was much younger than we are now he ran away from Australia to fight the Dutch farmers in Africa. He must be a truly adventurous man.'

'You're our football star,' Olivia answered, noticing her brother's wistful expression. 'And one day you will take control of Grandfather's business.'

James slumped into a leather chair beside his sister and watched the fire. 'Do you know, I would give anything just to meet with him once and ask him why he has not kept in contact with us,' he said sadly.

'I have thought the same thing,' Olivia said quietly. 'There's so much he could tell us about our mother. It must have been so romantic the way they met. But I do not know even that detail of their lives. Was it at some grand ball, or did they meet in a French café on the Seine?'

'I'm going to find him,' he said and Olivia looked sharply at him.

'You don't even know where to start,' she scoffed.

'I'll approach Grandfather and speak with him.'

'He won't help you,' Olivia said. 'He hates our father.'

'If Grandfather won't help me, I'll do it on my own,' James said stubbornly. 'I'm no longer a child. I'm free to do as I will.'

'I wish you luck,' Olivia sighed and picked up the book beside her chair and rose. 'If you ever find our father, ask him why he has been absent from our lives for so long. I'm sure he will have no excuse to offer. He's just a selfish man who only thinks about his own needs.'

James watched his sister leave the room. They were very close and James often growled at his pals who showed more interest in Olivia than he thought appropriate. His thoughts drifted back to the conversation that he dared share only with Olivia, wondering how he would find the legendary Captain Matthew Duffy, hero of the war and daredevil pilot. Since their holiday in Europe, James had found himself thinking more and more about finding his birth father. There was so much he wanted to know from him. With or without his grandfather's assistance, James was determined to go in search of Matthew Duffy. All he needed was money and that was not a problem as his doting grandfather had opened a generous account for him.

The fire crackled softly as James once again thought about stealing some of his grandfather's good bourbon.

17

Christmas had come and gone. Sir George Macintosh sat in his library staring blankly at the wall opposite, with an open bottle of Scotch on the desk. He hardly saw the array of Aboriginal weapons that had been collected after the massacre of the clan that had inhabited Glen View lands for thousands of years.

A gentle knock at the door was followed by the entry of his daughter Sarah.

'Father,' she said softly. 'You have not taken any meals for the last two days.'

'I'm not at all hungry,' he answered in a flat voice.

Sarah walked over to her father and placed her arms around his shoulders. George had not encouraged affection from his children, and the fact that Sarah had hugged him took George by surprise.

'If there is anything wrong I would like you to tell

me,' she said.

'Nothing is wrong,' George lied. Only that he had exiled his worthless son to Queensland and he had an incurable disease that would eventually kill him.

'With Donald away,' Sarah said, 'I was hoping that you might consider me for a place in the family business. I know that I am able to be an asset to you, Daddy.'

Heaven forbid that a woman could run such a vast financial concern as the Macintosh companies, and yet he could not ignore the success of Lady Enid Macintosh. He knew that she had been the iron fist in the velvet glove, and the rumours were that she, in fact, established their financial success while her husband and eldest son were off carving out Glen View from the northern wilderness. Had his daughter inherited her character? Was she ruthless and ambitious in a way he hadn't realised?

Sarah moved from behind her father and suddenly sat in his lap as if she were a little girl. She placed her arms around his neck and leaned against his chest. George softened, comforted in his loneliness. Here was one person in the world who loved him, yet George also knew that his daughter could manipulate him with her love.

'I will think about your proposal and possibly find you a position in my office,' he said gruffly and Sarah looked up into his eyes.

'Thank you, Father,' she said with a broad smile. 'I promise to help you lead the companies into a bigger and better future.'

George had a strong feeling that she could, although Donald would remain the token head of the Macintosh companies.

But he also remembered with gloom that David Macintosh, the son of his brother, would also take a share in the running of the companies. *This is a matter that has to be resolved before the boy reaches twenty-one*, George thought. There were legal ways of ensuring Sarah took his place should David not survive until he was of age.

★

David felt the crack of machine-gun bullets close to his head as he dug with every ounce of his strength in the cold earth beneath his body. He wanted to shrink to the size of an ant and scuttle away. He dared not raise his head to see where the machine gun was firing from, and behind him he knew that the rest of the section was also clinging to the earth. The machine gun had been firing in disciplined bursts to ensure that the barrel did not overheat, which indicated that the men in the trenches ahead were well trained. But then the gun ceased firing and another flare went up into the night sky.

'They are changing belts,' Otto said behind David. 'See if you can locate them.'

David raised his head a fraction – enough to see the outline of the trenches – and noticed that the enemy had not as yet completed sandbagging the forward edge. In fact, he could see the outline of the two-man crew working the machine gun silhouetted against the light of the drifting flare. He calculated that they were about forty yards away.

'Try and take out the gun crew,' Otto said as rifle rounds continued to crack around them from the Nationalist positions. The machine gun was still the most dangerous threat. They all realised that they were pinned down and when the sun rose they would be fully exposed to any sharpshooter with a rifle.

David slid his rear rifle sight to forty yards and dug the butt into his shoulder. Breathing as calmly as he could, he sighted the upper half of the soldier who was feeding a new belt of ammunition into the breech of the machine gun. The flare gave him plenty of illumination so when David squeezed the trigger his shot was true. He saw the soldier throw up his arms and disappear from sight.

Quickly ejecting the empty cartridge, he swivelled just a tiny bit to place the man behind the weapon in his sights. They had been foolish not to have their prime weapon sand-bagged and now they were paying the price. David fired again and saw the soldier drop.

Satisfied that David had temporarily put the machine gun crew out of action Otto gave the order that it was every man for himself on the deadly dash back to their own lines.

When the flare had fizzled out, each man rose, turned and ran as fast as he could, leaving the night as black as the entrance to hell.

David hefted himself from the earth and ran in as much of a zigzag as he could. Bullets from rifles still zipped around them but they were being fired blindly into the night. The hope was that the fleeing section could put enough distance between themselves and the Nationalist lines to cause the enemy shooting to become inaccurate. In the dark Archie suddenly grunted and fell in front of David, tripping him.

'I'm hit,' Archie groaned with David sprawled over him.

'Where are you hit?' David asked.

'In the bloody arse,' Archie answered and David slung his rifle over his shoulder, scooped up the Englishman and continued towards their own lines, now only about five hundred yards away.

Archie was not a big man but the struggle up the slope to the town took a toll on the young Australian.

'Just drop me off here, old chap,' Archie protested. 'I'll make my own way back.'

David ignored him and continued to sweat his way towards the dim lights he knew marked their lines. Finally a voice called out a challenge. David responded with the correct password and he was helped past the barricades by a couple of Spanish militiamen who laid Archie out on the cobblestones of the street.

David collapsed to his knees beside Archie, fighting to get his breath as the Englishman reached up to grip his shoulder.

'You should not have put your life in danger like that, David,' he said gratefully. 'You still have many long years ahead of you.'

David tried to smile but was getting his strength back when Otto came over to him and shook his hand.

'Well done,' he said, then walked away, leaving David to reflect on just how close they had all been to getting killed. His action had helped save the section and he realised that they were like his own family: the German, the Czech, the Englishman and the Yank. David now knew that he no longer fought for a cause but for the men he served with. Not that he had much choice: when the volunteers signed on they forfeited the right to walk away.

The section returned to the widow's billet and fell into troubled sleep.

David was shaken awake after noon and given a meal of cheese, coarse bread and olives. Very little was said but Otto made a point of sitting beside David when he took a seat by the open fireplace.

'You are a strange one,' Otto said, chewing on a piece of cheese. 'You are not a communist and yet you fight along-side us.'

'I am here because I have experienced what your Nazi government does to people in Dachau,' he replied, staring at the hot, glowing coals of the fire.

'You were in Dachau?' Otto repeated. 'I have had many friends sent there – not to come back.'

'I joined up to kill fascists, and you don't have to be a communist to do that,' David explained. 'If we do not stop the fascists here, then we will be facing a war in the near future.'

'You are very wise for one so young,' Otto said. 'And I fear it will be my country that you will be fighting.'

David glanced at the tough German sergeant. 'My father died on the Western Front in the war,' David said. 'He was fighting your countrymen.'

'Then you have reason to hate us,' Otto said, finishing the cheese and searching in his pockets for the stub of a pre-smoked cigar.

'Strangely, I don't hate you – or your country,' David answered. 'Just the people in your government running things.'

'Then we have that in common,' Otto said, finding the stub of his cigar and lighting it with a small stick he found by the side of the fire. 'The German people are not bad but they are being led blindly into another war.'

'We can both agree on that,' David said with a small laugh. 'But for now all we have to do is survive here in Spain.'

They fell into silence as the distant crackle of small-arms fire drifted on the winter wind to the little house in the town where men from five nations waited to take their place on the front line.

*

James Barrington Jnr stood in his grandfather's study, a defiant set to his jaw.

'I need to find my father,' he said.

'Why?' James Barrington Snr asked. 'What do you hope to achieve searching for a man who has shown little or no concern for you and your sister?'

James knew that his reasons were not easily explained – he even had trouble understanding them himself. It was as if he needed to see what he might become, and at the same time make Matthew hurt for his neglect of his children.

'I am not deserting you, Grandfather,' James answered sincerely. 'It's something I just need to do.'

James Barrington Snr leaned back in his great leather chair and gazed at his beloved grandson. 'I have always dreaded this day coming,' he said. 'But I will not deter your plans. You need to face your father and see the worthless man that he is.'

James blinked at how easily his grandfather had acceded to his wish. He had stepped into his grandfather's study expecting a fight.

'Thank you, Grandfather,' he said. 'I promise as soon as I have found him I will return home.'

'Your journey should commence in Iraq,' James Barrington Snr said, leaning forward and pulling out the drawer of his desk. 'I would suggest that you travel to Basra, and there you will find Captain Matthew Duffy. He owns an aviation business that I have heard is suffering hard times. I will even organise for your travel to Basra, but on the proviso you spend no more than a week there. I will arrange for you to take a passenger liner to Europe, and from there you can make your way to Basra. The costs will be debited against future earnings, so that you don't leave under the impression that I condone your search for your father. You can leave on the first available liner.'

James stepped forward and extended his hand. 'Thank you, Grandfather,' he said, his head swimming with the adventure ahead. 'I accept that the cost will be mine to incur.'

★

It was time for Tom Duffy and his daughter Jessica to return to Townsville. They had spent Christmas at Glen View and in that time Donald had decided he was in love with the big man's daughter, although nothing more than the occasional stolen kiss and holding hands had occurred between them.

Neither had mentioned the word 'love' and Donald was frightened to express this feeling lest Jessica reject him, although from what Donald could perceive she was attracted to him. Promises were whispered that they would keep in touch by letter as Tom loaded the sulky for their long journey across the plains back to Townsville.

Old Hector MacManus stood leaning on his walking stick to farewell his guests, and Donald could have sworn that the tough Scot had a tear in his eye as he waved them goodbye. Donald and Hector stood side by side until the sulky had disappeared into the scrub, and only the cawing of crows remained to break the silence.

Hector finally turned to return to the house. 'Time you got back to work, laddie,' he said to Donald. 'Your leave is over.'

Donald was about to remind the station manager that in most terms he was really Hector's boss as he was the son of the owner, but bit his tongue. He had come to like this man he at first rejected as incompetent, influenced by his father's opinion, but soon learned just how capable the Scot was running such a big enterprise. Donald had quickly learned that Hector had the respect of the stockmen – Aboriginal and European.

'Right, boss,' Donald replied with a grin, replacing his wide-brimmed hat and striding across to the stockyards where the men were branding cattle. They greeted Donald with indifference – except for one of the stockmen – a tall, lean man tanned by long hours under the sun.

'Had a good holiday, Mr Macintosh?' Mitch asked with a sneer. 'While the rest of us took on all the work?'

Donald felt the sting of the rebuke and felt the eyes of half-a-dozen other men burn through him. He climbed through the wooden rails of the yard and walked towards the tall stockman who was holding a red-hot branding iron over a beast that had been brought down on its side in preparation. Donald could feel a knot of fear in his stomach. He was backed into a corner – he knew that the other men watching would be considering his reaction to the slur. Donald walked over to Mitch and stopped a few feet away.

'I didn't realise that I was carrying you,' Donald said with all the calmness he could muster. 'Thanks for telling me.'

Mitch straightened his back and stared, nose to nose with Donald. 'If you weren't the boss's son you wouldn't even be here,' Mitch said with a slow smile. 'This is no place for sissy city boys like you.'

'Maybe you should put down the branding iron and find out just how sissy I am,' Donald said, issuing his challenge in front of the men sitting on the rails and standing around the downed beast. He wondered at his own confidence; perhaps it had something to do with Jessica. She was a country girl and such acts of bravado were expected from men working close to the land.

Mitch dropped the branding iron and lashed out with a right hook. Donald was taken unawares and the blow rattled his head. He stumbled, falling back to raise his hands in a defensive posture. He had never learned how to box but had seen enough fights to know the basic moves. Mitch stepped in and threw three more punches, each one striking Donald's head with stinging force. Donald was aware that a cheer had gone up from the men watching; one voice was even yelling, 'Have a go, sissy boy.'

The expression hurt as much as the blows from Mitch, and the young man suddenly felt a cold rage rush through his body. He could see Mitch grimly smiling as he took another pace towards him, an expression of victory in his eyes.

Donald was a half-head shorter but had a well-developed body inherited from both his Scots and Irish ancestors. He snapped a punch directly into Mitch's face and was aware there was a sudden silence in the stockyard as Mitch staggered back, blood gushing from his broken nose. Donald took two paces forward, balanced himself and delivered another two blows into the face of his opponent. Suddenly the cheering commenced again with his name being shouted by the spectators who only seconds earlier had jeered him.

But Mitch was a seasoned fighter. He recovered from seriously underestimating his opponent and spat a glob of blood onto the hot earth. The stockman rallied and waded back into Donald with a series of lightning-fast blows that hammered the sense from Donald, causing him to see a shower of red stars and sink to his knees, blood running from his split lips.

Donald realised that he had no answer to the stockman's years of experience brawling in country pubs, and expected to be pulverised by feet and fists. He wanted to gain his feet but the other man's fists had knocked all sense from him and Donald knew he was beaten.

A hand reached down and he was hefted to his feet. 'Yer fight pretty good for a sissy boy,' Mitch said, wiping his broken nose with the back of his hand and wincing. 'No one else has been able to bust my nose before. I suppose yer goin' to tell the boss I gave you a hidin' so he will sack me.'

Donald was regaining his senses, trying to focus on the other man's face. He could not see any animosity and was confused. His father had always taught him that you make sure your opponent was ground into the earth in business affairs – and in life. No mercy should ever be shown to the defeated.

'You hit bloody hard,' Donald said weakly, and thrust out his hand to the stockman. 'I concede you won, and hope you might teach me a thing or two while I'm here.'

A look of surprise fell across Mitch's battered face. 'Yer not goin' to tell the boss about what happened here?'

'No,' Donald said. 'You and I fought a fair fight and you won,' he replied. 'It's all over.'

Mitch shook Donald's hand and a cheer went up from the watching stockmen. Some even slapped Donald on the back and said, 'Good fight.'

Both men went over to the water trough and washed the blood from their battered faces. In the act of challenging Mitch it seemed Donald had won the respect of the tough men he worked alongside.

That evening Donald dined with Hector in the homestead.

'Fall off your horse again?' Hector said across the table, and Donald sensed the humour in the statement.

'Yes,' he replied. 'Fell into a wooden rail.'

'Down in the stockyard, I heard,' Hector said. 'The boys tell me it had a name, the stock rail – Mitch.'

'I started it,' Donald said defensively. 'Not his fault.'

Hector took a sip of the soup in front of him. 'You did well, so I have been led to believe. I think you did the right thing. In this part of the country, a man is judged by his toughness and fair dealings – especially in a fight. We are not like your city friends out here. We don't put the boot in.'

'Luckily for me,' Donald snorted as the hot soup stung his split lips. 'I realised out there today that I still have a lot to learn.'

'I have to say, Mr Macintosh . . .'

'I don't deserve the title of Mr,' Donald cut in. 'I think hearing Donald from you would sound more appropriate, Mr MacManus.'

'A fine Scottish name it is too,' Hector said. 'I was going to say that you are not the man I first met when you arrived. If you are not careful, you might even come to love this harsh country with its tough but simple life.'

'You might be right, Mr MacManus,' Donald said. 'But eventually my father will want me back in Sydney to assume the role of co-owner of our companies. I do what my father wishes.'

Hector shrugged. 'You'll be doing that with your cousin, David Macintosh, who is also a fine young man.'

'My father has a different opinion,' Donald said. 'From what I have been told, Cousin David has been under the wing of that damned Sydney lawyer, Sean Duffy.'

'It's a pity you've never met David,' Hector said, wiping his mouth with a linen serviette. 'I think you might like him.'

Donald did not reply, and the two men continued the meal in silence. Already the moon was rising over the brig-alow scrub, and the curlews combined with the dingos to sing their mournful songs of the night.

Part Two

1937

Life and Death

18

Major Guy Wilkes of army intelligence fumed at the reply he had received from London. Despite the overwhelming evidence of the German archaeological team's subversive role in the Middle East, he had been cautioned not to take any overt action. Suspicion of British involvement in any unfortunate fate that might befall the German scientists had to be avoided at all costs. London did not want an international incident with Berlin.

The major paced his office in Basra and wanted to shoot the lot of them – except Miss Diane Hatfield, of course, who was obviously working for American intelligence. But why she should be doing that was a mystery. Her first loyalty should have been to the British government.

The coded message Wilkes had received said that there was to be no overt action carried out, and he smiled grimly. It did not mention anything about covert operations.

Guy Wilkes slumped into his chair behind his desk. He had an ace up his sleeve and that ace was Captain Matthew Duffy. All that was needed was an unfortunate accident to occur to the Germans – with no links to himself and the British government. Guy Wilkes thought that he had such a plan. Aeroplane accidents were not uncommon and, after all, hadn't the Germans attempted to kill Captain Duffy in such a way?

*

It had been just after the New Year that Diane flew in to Basra for resupplies.

Matthew saw her land and left his hangar to greet her. The weather was still cold and she was rugged up in leather flying jacket and leather pants.

'Hello, Diane,' he said. 'I think that you and I need to talk.'

Diane frowned, but followed him to the office where she sat down in the old leather chair. Matthew called for a pot of tea and remained silent until the tea had been delivered and Ibrahim had left them alone.

Matthew poured the tea and handed a cup to Diane.

'I know about your role with American intelligence,' he said quietly and Diane looked sharply at him.

'I don't know what you're talking about,' she retorted.

Matthew slumped into a chair behind his desk. 'There's no point in denying that you are working for the American FBI,' he persisted. 'I cannot tell you how I know, but a lot of things are making sense now. I don't believe you were involved in the sabotage of my kite, and now I understand why you saved us at Tempelhof.'

Diane placed her cup carefully on a small side table beside her chair and appeared deep in thought.

'If anyone else had asked me of my involvement with the Americans I would have denied it,' Diane said, gazing around the office. 'But it has been hard to hide the truth from someone I care about as much as I do you,' she continued. 'As you may know I was hired in the States to fly a well-known gangster around the country but he got into a spot of bother with Mr Hoover's G men. Because of my association I was threatened by the FBI with imprisonment. They accused me of complicity in his operations despite the fact all I did was fly him around the country. But when they found out that the man I was working for was a friend of Benito Mussolini, they made a deal with me. I had to join the American Nazi Party and report to the FBI on their activities. My membership led me to Berlin where I was given my current contract. I was trapped and had no other choice but to go along with the Americans. I'm glad that you know because I felt as if I was betraying you more than anyone else. So now you know.'

Matthew softened at Diane's confession. 'Is that why you slept with Albrecht?'

Diane looked away before answering. 'Only partly,' she said quietly. 'You have always acted the gentleman, completely unaware of the crush I had on you when you were teaching me to fly in those years after the war. You don't know how much I yearned to have your arms around me.'

'I didn't know,' he managed to say.

'You men are so ignorant of what we women are saying to you,' she said sadly. 'If sleeping with Albrecht made you jealous, I'm glad. But I didn't sleep with him for that reason. It was a mistake. But my life is always on the line around the Germans and you had never indicated how you felt about me.'

'Diane, I'm a man over fifty with no real fortune left – and two estranged children. I have so little to offer any woman – let alone one as young and beautiful as you,' Matthew said with a sigh. 'If I lose the only aircraft I own I will lose my sole source of income. What have I got to offer a woman?'

Diane rose from the chair and went around to Matthew, sitting down in his lap and placing her arms around him. 'I'm thirty-six years old and have spent my life doing things many women would envy,' she said. 'But even I dream of the love of a man I want to spend the rest of my life with, and maybe even have children with before it is too late. I have always hoped that man would be you, Captain Duffy.'

Matthew found that he was having trouble taking everything in. Diane's declaration of love had come at the same time as her confession to working as a double agent. The moment was overwhelming and the tough Australian flyer was at a loss for words.

Just then Cyril appeared in the doorway and raised his bushy eyebrows at the sight of his boss with his former employee sitting on his lap.

'Ahem,' Cyril said, clearing his throat. 'Major Wilkes is here to see you, Skipper.'

'Hello, Cyril,' Diane said, slipping from Matthew's lap. Behind the engineer Guy Wilkes appeared wearing a suit of civilian clothing. Clearly he did not want to attract too much attention.

'Miss Hatfield,' Guy said with a wide grin. 'I see that you and Captain Duffy have made yourselves comfortable. I hope that I am not intruding.'

Matthew glared at the British officer whose timing could not have been worse. 'What is it, Major?' he asked, and Guy put on a hurt expression.

'I thought that we were on a first-name basis, Matthew,' he said. 'I was just passing by, and thought that I might drop in for a cup of tea and a chat with my favourite colonial flyer.'

'Diane has told me about her service with the Yanks,' Matthew said and watched the amused expression on Guy's face disappear.

'Then I think Miss Hatfield should join us in a conversation regarding the contract she has with the Nazis.'

Diane looked to Matthew, who nodded his head for her to stay. She sat down across from both men.

'Miss Hatfield,' Guy said. 'I know that you are actually working for Mr Hoover and the FBI, but I am going to stick out my neck and appeal to your patriotism towards your own country. I had not included you in my planning but it seems that circumstances have changed. I confess that I have little experience working with double agents, but I also sense that Matthew would vouch for your reliability.'

'If you mean am I loyal to my country and king,' Diane answered, 'then you can depend on me. My work for the Americans is under duress but I do believe in their anti-fascist stance. I don't think it matters whether I work for the Americans or my own country – fascism is a threat to the free world. What do you want me to do?'

'Firstly, you cannot tell the Americans you are now prepared to work for His Majesty,' Guy said, leaning forward and fixing Diane with his eyes.

'Does that make me a triple agent?' Diane asked with a short laugh.

'I suppose so,' Guy replied. 'But now you are working for the right people.'

'I don't think Diane should be working for anyone –

except herself,' Matthew protested. 'You know how dangerous espionage can be.'

'Thank you, Matthew,' Diane said. 'But I have come this far and feel my contribution has been of some good in the war against the Nazis. When I return to Berlin I am to be received by Herr Himmler himself, so I have been told. That is a considerable step towards learning the inner workings of the government in Germany.'

'Himmler,' Guy uttered, impressed by how far the FBI-recruited agent had progressed. 'I can see why the Yanks value your role for them.'

'I would rather see Diane extracted from her current spying activities. It just takes one small slip and she could end up in some shallow, unmarked grave.'

Diane reached over and touched Matthew on the arm. 'I'm reassured by your concern but I can handle myself.'

Matthew was not convinced. He'd had similar reassurances almost twenty years earlier from Joanne, and she had not lived to see the end of the war. This time he would not take the chance of losing Diane.

'What can you tell me about your current contract with the German government?' Guy asked.

'About as much as I presume you have already deduced,' Diane replied. 'Their primary mission is to supply the rebels up north with funding and arms to attack British interests in this part of the world.'

Guy nodded. 'How successful have they been?'

'I think Matthew has been able to tell you that they have distributed the gold they had and the arms I brought in from Germany,' she answered. 'I can tell you at least which of the sheikhs has received the guns and money. Herr Albrecht is a favourite of Himmler and is his prime agent in this part of the world, so he is trusted to run his own operation in Iraq.'

'I can pass on that intelligence to our air force and army units. They can strike against the sheikhs before they operate against us. Your information will be invaluable,' Guy replied.

'I can also tell you that I am to fly the team to Palestine for an archaeological dig there,' Diane continued. 'We are scheduled to fly out next week, but from what I have been able to learn they are planning to make contact with the Arab leaders fighting the Jews.'

'That certainly makes a difference to what I had planned,' Guy said, leaning back in his chair. 'I had hoped to sabotage your aeroplane and bring it down.'

Diane looked with horror at the British officer. 'Were you planning to kill me?' she asked.

'No,' Guy said, shifting in his chair. 'I was hoping to have Matthew replace you as pilot and have him parachute from the aircraft before it crashed.'

Shocked, Diane stood up and glared at Guy. 'Of all the hare-brained plans,' she snorted. 'There is no way that could have worked.'

'Under the circumstances it was the best I could think of,' Guy replied sheepishly. 'I am under orders that anything I do must not reflect in any way on the British government.'

'If they are going to Palestine,' Matthew said, 'then I can be of help there. I have a grudge to settle against the bastards who tried to kill me.' Both Guy and Diane looked at Matthew curiously. 'I have friends in that part of the world who have no love for the Nazis. Just leave it with me and there will be no repercussions to the British government. But I will need to fly to Palestine – and that costs money.'

'I am sure that I can divert funds to pay your costs,' Guy said. 'One way or the other, while those three are operating in this part of the world, British interests are threatened.'

'I am afraid I have to arrange supplies and be back at the camp before sunset,' Diane said. 'I only wish that you and I could talk some more,' she continued, looking directly at Matthew with a mischievous glint in her eye.

She excused herself, leaving Matthew and Guy alone in the office.

'You are sure that you are able to eliminate the Germans without any suspicion falling on the British government?' Guy questioned.

'How much do you wish to know about how I plan to go about it?' Matthew countered.

'I would rather know nothing, old chap,' Guy answered. 'That way the government I represent can deny any knowledge. But if you are able to carry out this mission I think I can promise that you will be suitably rewarded. There is another oil company intending to carry out exploration here and in Iran. I'm sure that you would win the tender and it would probably be generous enough to upgrade your fleet to more than one plane.'

Matthew understood the under-the-table offer and extended his hand. The mission was sealed with a handshake, and the British intelligence officer departed the office leaving Matthew to mull over his plan. However, while he toyed with the idea he excluded one person from the list of those to be executed – Erika. When he looked deep in his soul he realised that killing a woman was something he was not prepared to do – despite her political leanings. He was sure Major Wilkes would have no trouble killing Erika, but that was the nature of a man sworn to protect his country's interests at any cost. So, how was he to eliminate the two men and spare the woman while not raising any suspicion of an organised execution of German citizens?

★

James Barrington Jnr had finally arrived in Basra after a boat trip via the Suez Canal and then up the river to the port city. The sights and smells of this very alien land were so unlike those he had experienced on his European holiday with his grandfather and sister. *This is a land of intrigue and mystery*, he thought as the cargo ship steamed up the mighty river that had cradled the birth of civilisation.

When the ship docked James went ashore with the little luggage he had and found a taxi blowing volumes of smoke from its exhaust. James had learned from his grandfather the name of his father's airline and where it was located. He slipped into the taxi and gave the name of the airstrip, which thankfully the driver knew. It was only as they drove out of Basra that it hit James he was about to meet his father.

The taxi arrived in the cold afternoon at the airstrip, and James paid the driver, hefting his single carpet bag from the taxi. He saw that he was only around a hundred yards from a lone aircraft sitting on the tarmac. James recognised the American-built trimotor aeroplane from those he had seen in the USA, and he spotted a man standing on a ladder tinkering with one of the engines. From the distance he could not make out the man's features. He took a deep breath and strode towards him. When he was at the bottom of the ladder he looked up as the man turned to see who the visitor was. Immediately James knew that this man was not his father.

'What can I do for you, lad?' the man asked, holding a spanner and glancing down at him.

'I am looking for Captain Matthew Duffy,' James said.

'You're a Yank,' Cyril said. 'Why would a Yank be looking for the skipper?'

'And I deduce from your accent that you are one of those damned Canadians,' James retorted. 'Just tell me if Captain Duffy is here, and where I could find him.' James found that his patience was wearing thin with the anticipation that any moment he would confront the man who he would normally have called father. Cyril climbed down from the ladder and wiped his greasy hands on his overalls.

'No need for bad manners, young man,' he said. 'The skipper is in his office, but he has a flight out within the hour so he might be a bit busy to see you.'

'I think he might just have time for me,' James answered.

'Why would that be?' Cyril asked, cocking his head.

'Because I am his son.'

Cyril's expression of bemusement at the appearance of this cocky young American changed to puzzlement. 'I'll take you to him,' he said, slipping the spanner into a back pocket, and James followed the Canadian engineer towards the hangar.

They stepped inside and walked towards the company office in the corner of the hangar. Cyril stopped at the door and opened it without knocking.

Matthew was behind his desk filling in forms and hardly glanced up at Cyril.

'Got someone to see you, Skipper,' Cyril said as James stepped forward from behind the Canadian.

For a moment Matthew stared at the face of the young man, as though there was something vaguely familiar in his features.

'Who are you?' he asked without rising.

James remained standing in the doorway. 'You don't recognise me?' he asked.

'You look vaguely familiar,' Matthew replied. 'Are you the son of someone I do business with?'

'My name is James Barrington Jnr and it seems that I am your son . . . Captain Duffy.'

Cyril rolled his eyes and walked away, leaving the reunited father and son to experience this awkward moment alone.

19

In that moment, face to face with Matthew, it dawned on James that his father was in all respects a total stranger. The only thing they shared was blood and now he wondered if the long journey across the Atlantic to Europe and then on to the Middle East was in fact a waste of time.

'I'm not sure how I am to react to your visit,' Matthew said. 'I notice you have adopted your grandfather's family name, and I am Captain Duffy to you.'

'What did you expect?' James said. 'My sister and I last saw you when we were little children.'

Matthew rose from behind his desk. 'How is your grandfather?' he asked.

'He is well,' James replied. 'He wonders how you could run down your business the way you have.'

'Not everything in life is about making money,' Matthew flared. 'I am still flying, and that's all that matters to me. So, now you've seen me, what else do you want from me?' he asked.

'I have run out of money,' James lied. 'I was hoping that you might be able to give me employment so that I can save enough to return home.'

Matthew sat back down behind his desk while James found the big leather chair and made himself comfortable.

'I can barely pay my copilot and engineer,' Matthew said. 'What skills do you have?'

James frowned. 'I do a lot of tinkering with my grand-father's cars.'

Matthew stared at his son for a moment. 'You can work with Cyril,' he said. 'But Cyril is your boss – and you do what he says.'

'Hot dog!' James said, a smile lighting his face. Despite his misgivings about his father, the idea of working on an aircraft had great appeal to the young American.

'For the moment you work for bed and board, until Cyril tells me you're up to scratch. In the meantime you can bunk down at my place. It's nothing fancy.'

'Thank you, Captain Duffy,' James said, rising from his chair. 'When do I start?'

'First thing in the morning. Today I have a flight north to an oil field,' Matthew said.

'Would it be possible for me to go with you so I can see what the Ford is like?' James asked eagerly.

Matthew frowned. 'Why not? I suppose a flight will give you an idea how the kite performs. Leave your bag here and I'll see if Cyril can rustle up some gear for you.'

With the meeting over Matthew went in search of his engineer, and informed him that he now had an apprentice. He also organised flying gear and brought James into the hangar to go through the spare kit.

Watching James burrowing through the big wooden crate caused Matthew many emotions he had not known before. He was standing in the presence of the human being he and Joanne had created so many years earlier. It was hard to take in that this tall, well-built young man was actually his own flesh and blood. Matthew regretted his coolness in the first moments of their meeting, and was also experiencing the guilt of not making more of an effort to keep in touch with his children.

'I can't find a jacket big enough for me,' James said, turning to face his father.

'I have a spare jacket from my days flying in the war,' Matthew said and recovered it from another wooden crate. He held it up and thought that he saw a look of pure joy on his son's face when he took the heavy leather jacket with its fleece-lined collar and sleeves. The jacket bore the marks of much use. It fitted perfectly and James was ready to fly.

'C'mon, boy,' Matthew said. 'Time to start earning your keep. You can take the second seat in the cockpit.'

And so father and son, total strangers to each other, flew out of Basra.

*

Matthew was flying low enough for James to be able to pick out the detail they passed over on the flight north to the British oil fields. He was fascinated that in the vast expense of semi-arid lands, away from the mighty river system that fed the country, he could still see signs of life below: tiny mudbrick villages and the tents of Bedouin leading camels across the sandy wastes.

James had made up his mind not to allow himself to get close to his father. But the well-worn leather jacket made James squirm just a little as he sat in the copilot's seat beside his father – it reminded him that Matthew had been only a little older than James when he had flown the dangerous skies as a fighter pilot.

'Do you want to take the controls while I go back and get some coffee for us?' Matthew shouted to his son.

Startled, James did not know how to reply. Matthew leaned over to provide basic instructions on how to handle the aircraft's guidance system of rudder and yoke. James gripped the controls and placed his feet on the rudder pedals. Immediately he realised that the pulsing he could feel through his body was the life of the aeroplane sliding though the freezing air outside.

'Just keep it straight and level on the magnetic bearing you can see here in front of you,' Matthew said, indicating the needle moving very slowly from side to side. 'I won't be long.' With that, he unbuckled his harness and slipped from the pilot's seat, leaving his son frozen with trepidation in control of the aircraft's flight. The nose dipped a little and James desperately tried to remember what his father had said about straight and level. He pulled on the control stick gently and the nose rose again.

Matthew stepped behind the doorway to the cockpit and grabbed the thermos on a small rack, along with two metal mugs. He ensured that he was only seconds from his own seat in case he was required to take charge, but his son seemed to have the Ford flying on a level course and Matthew felt a swell of pride that the boy appeared to show signs of being a natural flyer.

Matthew remained standing back in the doorway, watching his son's intense concentration on keeping the aircraft straight and level. After a long five minutes Matthew strapped himself back in his seat, and passed James a mug of hot, sweet coffee from the thermos.

James reluctantly let go of the controls when his father took over, but gratefully accepted the coffee while staring ahead through the perspex window at the horizon beyond. He sipped his drink while his thoughts swirled about the experience of flying the aeroplane; that his father had given him so much time without showing any great concern for his competence said a lot.

Within the hour Matthew spotted the tall oil rigs in the desert and the airstrip not far away. James was impressed with how smoothly his father brought the aircraft down onto the hard-packed earth, then taxied to a lorry where two men stood waiting for the engines to be shut down.

Matthew unbuckled his harness straps and James followed suit.

They climbed down from the aircraft and one of the men wearing a hard hat marked *Boss* greeted them. When the giant man spoke, James recognised his Texan accent.

'I see you have a new copilot, Captain Duffy.'

'Not yet,' Matthew replied. 'He's still a rookie, but he shows promise. One day he might just make a flyer. Mike, meet my son, James Barrington. James this is Mr Mike Halata.'

'Pleased to meet you, sir,' James said, accepting a bone-crushing hand shake from the jovial Texan.

'I didn't know you had a son,' Mike said as another lorry arrived to unload the cargo of mail, rig parts and fresh rations.

'I also have a daughter,' Matthew said. 'But she is back in the US with her grandfather. It's a long story, Mike, and it would cost you one of your best bottles of bourbon to hear it.'

James noticed the respect between the two men working on this dangerous frontier, and as they chatted James looked up to see a flight of four British RAF biplanes skimming overhead with bombs under their wings.

'I heard the Brits had identified some tribesmen north of here as recently being armed with German rifles,' Mike said. 'No doubt the Limeys are on their way to sort them out. We got a call to expect a column of Brit armoured cars through here tomorrow to mop up what the flyboys miss.'

'Well, no time to stand around enjoying ourselves,' Matthew said, extending his hand to his old friend. 'Got to get back before the light fades.'

James followed his father to the aircraft where a couple of men using hand pumps had just finished refuelling the Ford from forty-four gallon drums. For some strange reason James felt an eerie sense of belonging as he trailed the man he had set out to punish, although he refused to let him off the hook – yet.

On the flight back Matthew gave James more instruction on the controls, but there was so much information that it did not all sink in. The most important part was that his father allowed him to take the controls for over an hour. The dimming skies were clear and still, with only occasional buffeting, and James could have sworn that his father actually closed his eyes while James held the controls. The young man felt a flush of pride that his father had so much confidence in his skills.

*

David's section was now reduced to the German sergeant, the Englishman who had recovered from his wound in the buttocks, and the tough Czech. John Steed had fallen to a Nationalist sniper bullet. They trudged across a bleak landscape of scattered stone houses and a hill where they could see a church and a living complex nearby. The section had been tasked with joining a Republican militia unit at the nominated rendezvous, and warily they continued their march as the cold wind and drizzle whipped around them.

When they finally struggled up the hill along a well-beaten track David began to sense that something was wrong. He was leading the small section and signalled a halt.

'What is it?' Otto asked, clutching his rifle ready for use.

'I thought I heard a woman screaming,' David said.

'Maybe the wind,' Otto replied and signalled to push on until they entered a wide courtyard. There they froze at the terrible sight before them.

Three Spanish militiamen stood over the bodies of five women, lying among their torn clothing. David could immediately see from the clothing that the women were Catholic nuns. A few feet away, the body of a man still dressed in the cassock of a priest lay in a blood pool and it was obvious that he had been shot.

The three militiamen were smoking cigarettes and leaning on their rifles when the section entered the yard. One of the women was still alive and reached up with her hand, imploring the militiamen to let her go. One of the men raised his rifle and shot her between her breasts. Her hand fell back and her head lolled to one side.

'What the hell is going on here?' David hissed to Otto, who was staring with anger at the horrific scene.

'They have a rule to execute any priests or nuns they find,' he answered bitterly. 'The Church is on Franco's side, and religion is viewed as the opiate of the masses.'

'Those women were raped,' David said. 'Does Karl Marx insist that innocent women be raped?'

'It is war,' Otto said. 'Those people there were enemies of the revolution.'

'It was cold-blooded murder,' David countered and felt his rage rising as the three Spanish militiamen greeted them with grins.

'You have come just a little late, my friends,' said one of the Spaniards. 'Had you been earlier you could have had some virgin brides of Christ.'

His face suddenly twitched with fear as he stared behind David and Otto. A rifle shot rang out and the Spaniard fell with a bullet through his head. Without questioning who had fired the fatal shot, David swung up his rifle and fired at one of the militiamen attempting to bring his weapon to bear on him. David's shot took the man in the stomach and he dropped his rifle, pitching forward to his knees and groaning in his agony. The third shot came from Otto's rifle and his bullet took the third Spaniard in the chest, forcing him backwards onto the cold earth. David chambered another round and fired at the head of the man he had shot in the stomach. A silence fell on the courtyard and Otto turned to the Englishman, Archie White, standing beside the Czech who was covering the bodies with his rifle lest they show any sign of life.

'You damned fool, did you fire the first shot?' he questioned in heavily accented English.

Archie nodded. 'They were animals and deserved to be executed for their crime.'

Otto stomped around the yard in frustration and anger. No matter what the militiamen had done, he knew that his section would not receive a friendly reception from other militia who would not be far away. Even as he pondered on their situation he looked across the courtyard to the valley below to see a column of Republican soldiers winding its way towards the church and small convent. From the corner of his eye he spotted a fourth militiaman in the doorway of the church building gaping at the bloody scene.

'We have to get out of here,' Otto barked. 'There may be others of these goddamned militiamen around who might have seen us kill their comrades.'

The rest of the section did not need any further prompting and quickly made their way out of the courtyard, retracing their route back to the town where they had been billeted. They were now hunted by both sides of the civil war.

★

It was night-time when David and the others approached the town and a challenge from a sentry was answered with the correct password. David's section filed through the Republican lines and were met by the town's commander, a small wiry Spaniard with cold dark eyes.

'You were ordered to join our battalion at the church,' he said to Otto in German. 'Why have you returned?'

Otto was an old soldier and always had a story ready for any situation. 'We ran into a Nationalist patrol between us and the church. I decided to pull back until it is safe to head out again.'

The Spaniard glared at Otto but appeared to accept his story. 'Go to your billet and be prepared to leave before dawn,' he said.

They slung their arms and made their way back to the house where the old widow greeted them with a bowl of rich vegetable soup flavoured with a dash of goat meat. The men were grateful for the hot meal, and Otto kissed her on the forehead. She giggled like a young girl and brushed him away bashfully.

When the meal was over, the four men gathered around the open fireplace in the kitchen.

'It will only be a matter of time before we are identified as the men who killed those bastards back at the church,' Otto said. 'I think we should scrounge as many provisions as we can and get out of here. It is time we made our way back to France.'

He received no argument from the other three and they quickly set about packing the cheese and bread the old lady offered from her meagre larder. Rugged up, they bid the old lady goodbye, and the section slipped into the darkened streets and back alleys of the town. It would be a long journey back to neutral France and they would have to pass between the lines of both sides.

They passed small groups of militiamen sitting around fires in the street but they did not pay them attention. At the edge of the village they came upon the forward defences manned against a sudden night attack, and any defenders seeking to desert.

Otto brought his men to a halt.

'Once we get past the guards we will split up,' he said to David. 'Jaroslav will travel with me, and you and the Englishman will travel together. We will attempt to meet in Madrid at the cathedral in five days' time. But first we have to get through our defences. When I signal you will rush the guards. The signal will be me lighting a cigar.'

The men acknowledged the plan and Otto approached the four men standing guard, while the other three stayed in the shadows of a building facing the outskirts of the village. They watched as he chatted with the guards in a casual manner. When Otto lit up a cigar the three of them rushed the surprised guards. David used his fists to knock one of the guards unconscious, while the butt of Otto's rifle knocked another man onto the ground. The remaining two were overwhelmed by the sudden attack, and stared into the barrels of the rifles held by their attackers without any sign of resistance. Otto glanced around and was satisfied that they had not been seen.

'We take these men with us,' he said, indicating the two who were still standing. 'Far enough away we let them go. Good luck.'

David and Archie took one of the guards, while Otto and Jaroslav took the other at gunpoint into the night. They were now deserters and expected no quarter if caught by either side.

Deep in the valley Archie and David told their prisoner to make his own way back to the village, and the grateful Spaniard thanked them for sparing his life. He scuttled away, leaving the Australian and Englishman somewhere between the two lines of trenches.

'Well, old chap,' Archie whispered. 'Time to go and seek out the pleasures of Madrid before Paris offers up its delights.'

'Yeah, but which way,' David queried and Archie withdrew a prismatic compass with a luminescent dial.

'We go north,' he said, turning the compass to orient them. 'A souvenir from my brother who served on the Western Front,' Archie added. 'Poor chap lost his sight to a Hun artillery round, and he gave me this as a lucky talisman when I told him I was enlisting in the International Brigades.'

The two set off in the dark as a cold wind scattered the clouds across a splatter of stars. By dawn they had made good progress, but when the sun rose everything changed. They found themselves in the middle of the Nationalist army's front lines. Freshly dug earthworks and the figures of men moving around in trenches on a hillside opposite and behind them indicated the dire predicament they were in. Even from a distance David could see the black and white crosses on the side of German tanks. These were professional soldiers assisting Franco's forces, and both men knew that the enemy would shoot first and ask questions later.

*

Dr Derik Albrecht had earned his doctorate in archaeology but had also become a dedicated Nazi at the German university where he taught. Membership had ensured rapid promotion and when he had been invited to meet Herr Himmler personally, his aspirations towards chancellorship of the university had soared. The head of all German police forces had asked him to carry out an important mission for the Fatherland. Albrecht would use his cover as a scientist and lead an archaeological team to the Middle East to make contact with Iraqi rebels, and act as a liaison officer for the Third Reich and Himmler himself.

Albrecht was not a professional spy but had accepted the role with a promise that if he was successful he would win an important place in the new government's scientific section. His two colleagues had also received a similar offer and were also dedicated Nazis.

But Albrecht had received some training in espionage, sabotage and subversion techniques, and one part of that training was in the use of codes. He now sat in his tent on the Iraqi dig, waiting for Diane to return and fly them out to Palestine. The mission to Iraq had proved a failure as the British armed forces had struck at the tribesmen Albrecht's team had recruited. It had been a costly loss to the German government and they had decided it would be more successful if his team could establish links amongst enemies of the hated Jews in Palestine.

In front of him was a letter he had received from his supposed uncle in Berlin. It was an innocuous letter about fictional family affairs, and the German agent reached for a copy of his English version of a popular Agatha Christie crime novel, flicking open the pages to the one he sought. With the book open beside him he commenced to decode the letter, and as he did so he found himself holding his breath. German counterintelligence had broken the American diplomatic code and learned that the Englishwoman, Diane Hatfield, was a double agent working for the Americans.

Albrecht ensured that he had decoded correctly and, convinced that the information was correct, proceeded to burn the letter on the sandy floor of his tent. As he did he felt sick with the thought of all he had said to the Englishwoman when he had bedded her. Pillow talk, the English called it, and when he looked back on Basra and the times since at the dig he realised that he had said more than he should. If it got out that he had been loose with his information he would no longer bask in the warmth of Himmler's good graces. In fact, he might find himself being sent to Dachau. The thought chilled Albrecht. The sooner he could silence Diane the better. The message from Berlin had also finished with the instruction *eliminate the double agent.*

He rose from his camp stool and went in search of his fellow agents. As he trudged against the howling wind he considered his orders and realised that he could not kill her out in British territory, as that would cause the British to carry out an investigation. He would have to ensure that Diane disappeared or had an unfortunate accident that could not be linked to him.

Albrecht had hardly briefed his colleagues on Diane's treachery when they heard her aircraft in the distance.

'What do we do?' Erika asked.

'Nothing for now,' Albrecht replied. 'We continue to Palestine where our mission is of greater importance, and then we must act to silence the traitor.'

20

The sun filtered through low scudding clouds while the wind swirled around David and Archie lying on their stomachs, observing the trench system a mile away on the grass-covered forward slope.

'German all right,' David said. 'Looks like they're with a Nationalist unit.'

'We have company,' Archie added and David turned to see what the Englishman had spotted behind them.

'Bloody hell,' David swore. There was a patrol of Franco's Spaniards winding its way up their hill, apparently after a night patrol. The enemy patrol, being led by a German NCO, was only around two hundred yards away and it was obvious they could not miss the two hiding at the crest.

'Well, old chap,' Archie said. 'I don't think we have too many options left.'

David knew what Archie meant. Resigned to discovery,

he groaned in despair before rising stiffly to his feet, hands in the air. Archie followed his example and the two men stood, whipped by the cold wind on the crest of the hill, in full sight of the approaching patrol. It came to a sudden halt and the soldiers pointed their weapons at them.

'Just pray they don't shoot us down,' David said, his rifle at his feet.

The German NCO and four men from the ten-man patrol moved towards them cautiously, while the rest of the patrol took up defensive positions, looking outwards for a possible attack. David noted the practised battle tactics and this gave him hope that the men taking them prisoner were well-disciplined soldiers. As they grew closer David recognised the uniforms and insignia of Spanish Foreign Legion troops.

'We are English,' Archie shouted, and David grumbled, 'Speak for yourself. I'm a bloody Australian.'

The German NCO was the first to them with his pistol pointed directly at David.

'We have surrendered to you because we are deserters from the Republicans,' David said in German. The NCO was surprised by the young man's use of his language.

'You are not German?' he queried, recognising David had a foreign accent.

'No, I am an Australian citizen,' he replied. 'My comrade is English.'

The German was a man in his late thirties with a hard face. 'We will search you and take you back for interrogation,' he said, turning and giving orders in Spanish to one of the men with him.

The Spaniard stepped forward and patted down both Archie and David, going through their pockets and ordering them to remove their boots.

'You're a Yank!' David exclaimed, hearing him deliver an order in English as he searched them.

'Yeah, I joined the Legion a couple of years ago. My home town is El Paso,' he replied.

David was reminded that it was not only the French who employed mercenaries from other nations in foreign legions.

'What will happen to us?' David asked and the legion-naire shrugged, stepping back.

'Pick up your boots and do what you are told,' he said.

Archie and David were marched in silence to the Nationalist lines where the troops hardly glanced at them. They were taken to a barbed-wire compound, which was little more than a tiny enclosed paddock able to hold around twenty men. They were not alone as it was already holding five dispirited prisoners who wore civilian garb and had the appearance of peasant farmers.

Inside the compound David put on his boots, aware that his feet were frozen and praying that he would not get frost-bite. The other prisoners, exposed to the elements, huddled together for body warmth and hardly gave the new arrivals a second glance.

David and Archie removed themselves from the pris-oners and sat side by side in a corner of the compound. 'What happens next?' David asked, his teeth chattering.

'I suppose we will not be shot outright,' Archie said pessimistically, blowing into his hands. 'Our nationality will need a bit of consideration before they execute us. On the other hand, I don't think Franco's people care much about that.'

'You're a cheerful bastard – full of optimism,' David said, staring at the German soldiers mixing with the Spanish legionnaires behind the trenches. He could see a mobile field-cooking wagon, and steam rising from a great pot of something he figured was meat stew from the aroma that drifted over to them. Soldiers were lining up with tin mugs and pannikins to receive breakfast, and David realised just how hungry and cold he was. No move was made to feed the prisoners.

They were only in the compound for a couple of hours when the German NCO and two legionnaires came for them. Under guard, David was marched to a tent in the field, surrounded by German light tanks.

He stood waiting outside the tent where the German NCO had disappeared and when he popped out he gestured to David to enter. David did so and found himself standing before a German officer in field grey. The man had a monocle and a duelling scar and David could see from his rank that he was the equivalent of a captain in the British army.

'I am told that you claim to be an Australian and that you also speak reasonable German,' the officer said coldly. 'How is it that you speak German and what is your name?'

'David Macintosh, and I have German relatives,' David replied. 'It has always been a family tradition that we learn German.'

David's answer seemed to warm the stern German officer, who gestured for the NCO to leave them. When he did so the officer leaned forward and spoke quietly.

'Who are your German relatives?' he asked.

'My family is related to the von Fellmanns from Prussia,' David replied. 'I believe that I have distant cousins in your army. Count von Fellmann is highly placed, I gather.'

'God in heaven!' the officer exclaimed. 'Major von Fellmann, the count's son, is my commanding officer. It is a small world that we should capture one from the International Brigades who is a distant cousin from Australia and yet in this country fighting with the communists. I doubt that the major would approve of your actions, Herr Macintosh.'

The news that Heinrich was the commander of the German unit attached to Franco's army both made his spirits soar and at the same time brought back the realisation that he was probably still wanted by the Gestapo in Germany as an escapee from Dachau. Heinrich's involvement in his escape also put him in danger from the Gestapo.

'Is it possible for me to speak with Major von Fellmann?' David asked as politely as he could. 'I am no longer a member of the Republican army – I am a deserter from their ranks.'

'But you are a communist,' the German captain countered. 'That is just as bad as being a member of the Republican movement. I expect you know the fate of any communists taken prisoner.'

David knew that he was alluding to the policy of the Nationalists to execute any persons suspected of being communists. The civil war was as bitter as any ever waged and no quarter was asked or given by either side.

'I am not a communist. Ask the man I was captured with,' David pleaded. 'I foolishly joined for adventure and have now realised the error of fighting with the communists. As a matter of fact, my English comrade and I were involved in the killing of Spanish militiamen who had raped and killed nuns not far from here. It was then that we decided to switch sides.' David's story was a desperate effort to save his life, and Archie's too.

'Sergeant, come here,' the officer called through the tent flap, and the NCO stepped inside, snapping off a smart salute.

'In your patrol report I noticed that you included information from some peasants living near a convent not far from here that some Spanish soldiers killed their comrades over a barbaric massacre of Catholic nuns and priests. What else can you add to the report about the identity of the Spaniards who turned on their Republican comrades?'

'All the peasants could tell us was that they thought the men were from the International Brigades,' the sergeant answered.

'Thank you, sergeant, you are dismissed.'

The German officer leaned back in his camp stool and stared at David. Outside, David heard a ragged volley of rifle shots. It sounded like a firing squad and he felt his stomach knot with fear. Within a minute the German sergeant returned to the tent, saluted and delivered his report.

'The prisoners have been executed, sir,' he said.

'Thank you, sergeant,' the officer replied. 'Keep the firing squad on alert for another execution. You may return to your duties, sergeant.'

'My comrade – the Englishman . . .' David said hoarsely, his mouth dry.

'He has not been executed – yet,' the officer replied. 'The decision remains with the commander but I have reservations that he should ever learn a relative was captured supporting the communists. It may be better that I make the decision to dispose of you both without embarrassing him.'

The statement chilled David and any hopes he had that he would see the sun set today rapidly disappeared.

'Sergeant,' the officer called loudly and the German NCO appeared in the tent again. 'Return the prisoner to the compound and guard the two men closely.'

David was marched back and shoved inside the compound. Archie looked up at him with despair.

'They just shot them,' he said in a whisper. 'They were just farmers suspected of harbouring Republican forces.'

David sat down and gazed at the guard left at the barbed-wire gate. It was the American legionnaire. David walked over to him.

'Hey, Yank, do you have a cigarette for my cobber?'

The American searched his pockets, producing a packet of English cigarettes. He took one, lit it and handed it to David, who passed it to Archie huddled against the wire.

'My name is David Macintosh,' he said. 'I just need a very small favour.'

The legionnaire looked at him suspiciously. 'I don't do favours for commies,' he said.

'I have a cousin here who is your commander, Major von Fellmann,' David persisted. 'If you could just get a message to him that his cousin is currently his prisoner.'

The legionnaire stared at David, blowing smoke into the cold air. 'He's not my commander. He is an advisor to assist General Franco's liberation from the communists.'

David glanced around at the German tanks lined up and the many men wearing German army uniforms. 'Your Franco seems to have a lot of advisors,' David said facetiously and the legionnaire did not comment.

Resigned to the fact that he was unable to call on the help of his distant German relative David fell into a conversation with the legionnaire. He learned that the man's name was Jose and he had enlisted four years earlier after hearing about the Spanish equivalent of the French Foreign Legion, which had been in existence as long as its French counterpart but was less publicised.

Jose was a Mexican, born on American soil into poverty. To feed his wife and three children, he had jumped a ship as crew to enlist in Spain. As he already spoke Spanish and was not a citizen of the country, he was accepted and had seen service overseas with the Spaniards. David could see that he

261

was a gentle man whose only concern was sending back the meagre pay he received to his family in El Paso.

When Jose was relieved of his sentry duties, the guard who took his place refused to enter into any conversation.

Archie and David sat the afternoon out, shivering in the cold until near sunset when the execution squad came for them.

'Well, old chap,' Archie said, rising stiffly from the earth. 'It has been an honour serving with you in this damned wasted cause at the arse end of the world.'

Two Spanish soldiers tied David's and Archie's hands behind their backs and led them away from the camp. David guessed that their execution would be done out of sight so as not to raise any questions. A half-mile from the camp the execution detail came to a stop under the command of the German sergeant, whose expression demonstrated some sympathy for his unfortunate prisoners. He ordered his men back twenty paces, leaving the three standing on the edge of the hill.

'I am sorry, my friends,' he said, checking that the rope around their wrists was still tied. 'I do not take any comfort in executing fellow Europeans for these dago bastards – communist or not.'

David stared over his head at the firing squad of six men already lining up and checking their rifles.

'Would you prefer to kneel and be shot in the back of the head, or would you prefer to face the rifles of the squad?' he asked. 'We do not bother with any cover for your eyes so I suggest you close them before I give the order to shoot.'

David felt that he was really just having a nightmare and that he would wake up on the plantation back in New Guinea, to see the smiling face of his wonderful grandmother, Karolina. He fought his terrible fear by retreating to another place and time.

'I prefer to be shot facing my executioners,' David finally said in a flat voice. 'I am sure my English comrade would prefer the same.'

'You are brave men, my friend,' the German sergeant said. 'Maybe Herr Himmler is right and there is a Valhalla, and you will be welcomed as warriors.' With his final statement, the sergeant turned and marched back to his firing squad.

David and Archie stood as erect as they could to hide their fear. There was nothing else they could do as the final seconds of their life ticked away. At least they would show the enemy that they could die bravely.

David felt the bitter wind curling around his body as the sun began to set before his eyes. His final thoughts were of regret that he had not told those he loved how much they meant to him. That he had not written to the man who had become a father to him and that he would never experience the meaning of love for a woman who would bear his children. He was only twenty years of age and had barely begun living life. He could hear Archie muttering the Lord's Prayer beside him, and he became aware that he was trembling uncontrollably.

'Shoot straight, you dago bastards!' David cried out to his executioners. 'See how an Aussie dies without any fear.'

David's rousing words were carried by the wind. It was his last act of defiance as the volley of shots from the firing squad echoed off the hillside and he felt the bite of the bullet. The two men slumped to the earth as the sun began to descend into the Spanish hills.

*

It was a hot day on the other side of the world. Sean Duffy sat at his desk perusing a sheaf of legal documents for a forthcoming matter in the court of petty sessions.

He had ignored the dull pain in his chest but it suddenly became like a giant vice crushing him, and spread to his jaw. Sean began to sweat as he clasped his hand to his chest and attempted to rise. He staggered for the door but toppled over his desk, scattering an ink well and the legal papers. He did not know if he cried out in his pain but when he looked up he could see the shocked face of a clerk staring down at him. Then the pain went away and Sean Duffy lost consciousness.

★

Sir George could feel the pain rack his body and he reached for the vial of pills. He knew that the insidious disease was reminding him that death was around the corner. With the glass of water on his desk he swallowed the pills and waited in his library for the pills to take effect.

George had summoned Clement Woods, his leading director, for a meeting and wanted to be clear-headed when the man arrived. If all went well George might just be able to ensure his empire survived in the future, should he not live out the year. Already he had come to the conclusion that there would be no future if his son was able to squander all George had built over the years.

He glanced at the painting of Lady Enid Macintosh; the artist had captured her determination. Maybe his own daughter had inherited her spirit and even if he allowed Donald to take nominal head of the Macintosh companies it would be Sarah who would really rule behind the scenes. Maybe the next generation sired by Donald would be able to put the management back into male hands.

'Your visitor is here,' the valet said at the doorway.

'Send him in,' George said, slipping the vial of pain-killers into a desk drawer.

'Ah, Sir George,' said Clement Woods, a man in his fifties and the most influential director of the board. 'I hope that you are well.'

'Yes,' George replied. 'Take a seat, Clem.'

Woods sat down opposite George's desk with his hands in his lap.

'I would like to speak with you about the future management of the Macintosh companies,' George said.

'Certainly, Sir George,' the director answered dutifully.

'I am going to propose that my daughter, Sarah, be granted a seat on the board when she turns twenty-one,' George said and watched his director's expression carefully at this radical announcement. The man blanched.

'I believe your daughter is only around sixteen years of age,' he replied awkwardly.

'She is now seventeen and I said when she turns twenty-one,' George countered. 'Not now, although I would like her to have a responsible position in the head office so that she can commence learning about the workings of the companies. She is very bright and a quick learner.'

'It is highly unusual to have a woman on a company board,' Woods replied. 'I personally would support any suggestion that you put to the board, but I am afraid I am but one voice.'

George rose from behind his desk to tower over the man. 'I also know that you carry the most influence and I expect you to lobby the board before the next meeting.'

'But you have Donald to take the reins when you choose to step down,' Woods attempted.

'My son will take his place in the company when he returns from Queensland but I am talking about the future. It would not be until 1941, when Sarah turns twenty-one.'

'I will do my best to convince the other board members to accept your wishes,' Woods said in a resigned voice.

'It is not simply a wish but an order,' George said in an icy tone. 'Make sure it happens. I can promise all who accept will be richly rewarded. Maybe it is time that some generous bonus packages be paid to you and your fellow directors. Now, I am sure you have a lot of telephone calls to make and you will be wanting to be on your way.'

Clement Woods rose from his chair, nodded to George and left the library.

George knew that Woods would do the job, and that at the next board meeting the request for Sarah to take a seat on the board would be unanimously endorsed by all in attendance. He smiled to himself. What Sir George wanted, Sir George got.

*

Sean was confused when he opened his eyes and felt his hand being held by someone close by.

'Where am I?' he asked and felt tears splash his face. He smelled the familiar perfume of the woman he had always loved.

'Oh Sean, my love,' Louise sobbed. 'You are still alive, thank God.'

'What happened?' Sean asked, focusing on the sterile white world around him, noticing the antiseptic scent of a hospital ward.

'You had a heart turn,' Louise answered, dabbing at her eyes. 'They rushed you in an ambulance to hospital and the doctors did not think that you would recover. But by some miracle you're still with us.'

Sean struggled to remember having the heart attack, and a strange memory came to him. He was not sure if he had been imagining it but for a fleeting moment he'd been somewhere very cold with a view of the sun setting. The pain had been like being shot in the chest.

'When you are allowed to leave the hospital I insist that you stay with me at my apartment where I can tend to your recovery,' Louise said.

'I have a law firm depending on me,' Sean tried to protest, but from the serious expression on Louise's face he knew that this was a battle he would never win. 'All right,' he said. 'But just until I'm on my feet again.' Then Sean laughed. 'Funny, I have no feet to stand on anyway. The Huns took care of that.'

And then the eerie memory returned. It was near night and the sun was setting across a grassy hillside, and for some reason Sean felt a terrible anxiety that caused him to break into tears.

'Oh my love,' Louise said, stroking away the tears. 'There's no need to cry. Soon you will be well and your old self. What is making you cry?'

Sean fought the uncontrollable feeling of dread. 'I don't know,' he whispered, holding Louise's hand. 'I just don't know.'

21

Two weeks had passed since James had turned up, and in that time Matthew had ensured that his son work hard for his bed and board.

James showed a great interest in learning to fly but Matthew reminded his son that his job was to work with Cyril on the maintenance of the airfield and the Ford. The weather was turning and the sun shone over the ancient and arid lands of Iraq. At least this made working outdoors a little less uncomfortable when Cyril and James pulled apart the engines to repair them. The desert sands played havoc with moving parts and the heavy, dirty work seemed to James as though it would never end.

Finally, he'd had enough. Splattered in oil and grease he marched to his father's office and, without knocking, walked in.

'What is it?' Matthew asked, barely glancing up at his

son standing with his hands on his hips.

'You said that you would teach me to fly,' James blurted. 'I've been working with that cranky old Canadian from dawn till dusk and I have not had a single flying lesson.'

Matthew looked up with a bemused expression. 'Must I remind you that I am running a business and making very little money? Most of the time just bloody sandstorms and swarms of flies. I don't have time to play nursemaid to you. And from what you have told me you will be due back in the States soon enough to return to your law studies at Harvard. I am sure you will make a fortune in your grand-father's business when you graduate.'

For a moment James stood uncertainly, mulling over the reality of what his father had stated. He knew that he must soon return to the USA to commence his studies as he had promised his grandfather that he would do so and it was already past the time he had said he would return. But James had contacted his grandfather and already furious letters arrived from him in New Hampshire.

'Are there any books that I can study about flying?' he asked quietly.

'Why?' Matthew asked. 'I'm sure you can take flying lessons back home if you want to be a weekend flyer.'

'If I had something to start with I might be able to learn a bit more from you,' James swallowed. 'I have heard that you're one of the best.'

Matthew reached into his desk and removed a dog-eared manual. He stood up and walked over to his son, passing it to him.

'This is a manual on meteorology, aerodynamics and just about everything else you have to know before you can take the controls of an aircraft on your own. Read that, and if you can pass all the questions I throw at you, then I will take the next step and put you in the cockpit. Normally you would learn to fly on smaller aircraft, but if you're good enough, we'll go straight to the Ford.'

James stood holding the manual as if it were a holy book. He glanced up at his father, who had a faint smile on his face.

'Thank you, Captain Duffy,' he said.

'You know, there has not been a day that has gone past in my life that I did not think about you and your sister, although I don't expect you to believe that,' Matthew said, gazing at his son.

'Goddamn!' James exploded. 'Why couldn't you just have seen us more often? Or even written? My friends would ask about my father and I would lie and say that he was killed in the war. Olivia told the same lie to her friends.'

'You can see how far Basra is from New Hampshire, and you can also see how other people depend on me being here to keep them employed. Sometimes a man has to face up to responsibilities to others outside the family,' Matthew said calmly.

'I would think that your family came first,' James replied bitterly. 'Grandfather was right about people with Irish heritage – they are selfish and care for no one but themselves.'

'You have Irish blood through my side of the family,' Matthew reminded with just the faintest of smiles. 'Your grandfather seems to have accepted that – albeit grudgingly.'

'Goddamn you!' James said and turned on his heel.

*

'What's up with him?' Tyrone said as James brushed past him out of the office.

'Nothing to be concerned about,' Matthew said, returning to his desk to retrieve a flight plan. 'The young fellow is just a bit confused about his identity.'

'He is a fine young man,' Tyrone said. 'Don't you think you're being a bit hard on him? I heard Cyril say James just wants to learn how to fly, and you have him day in and out up to his elbows in grease.'

'When the time is right I will keep my promise to him,' Matthew said. 'But he is due back in the States in a couple of weeks, and it takes longer than that to become a competent pilot. You and I both know that. Besides, I am Captain Duffy to him – and little else.'

Tyrone did not make any comment. 'I have the mail,' he said, passing Matthew a pile of letters.

Matthew took them reluctantly, knowing that most would be invoices but at least he was making that pile disappear with the income from Diane's contract and the money from the British government. One letter addressed from Palestine caught his eye. He recognised Diane's handwriting.

'Thanks, Ty,' Matthew said. 'Cyril said he needed a hand loading the cargo.'

Tyrone took the hint and left the office. Matthew eagerly opened the letter and began reading.

Diane had written that she had wished more time with him but her contract had taken her to Palestine where the German team were undertaking another dig on a site not far from Jerusalem. But it was a sentence about their time together in London that caught Matthew's eye. He had never spent time with Diane in London, and immediately he recognised it as some kind of distress code. It was signed off with the words *I hope that we can meet soon* underlined for emphasis.

Diane was in trouble. He had to approach Wilkes with his planned mission to Palestine. There was no time to lose.

Matthew hurried out of his office and jumped into the company vehicle. In Basra he sought out Guy Wilkes at the military headquarters, letter in hand.

'An unexpected pleasure,' Guy said when Matthew brushed past the orderly-room clerk and into his office.

'She is in deep trouble,' Mathew said, waving the letter in front of Guy. 'I just received this today, and I swear she's trying to tell me that she needs help.'

The British officer rose from behind his desk and took the letter from Matthew. 'We suspect that our equivalents in German intelligence may also be reading the Americans' mail,' Guy said, passing back the letter. 'In that case they may have learned of Miss Hatfield's duplicity.'

'I can fly out tonight for Jerusalem,' Matthew said. 'All I need are papers from you authorising the flight for an urgent humanitarian matter.'

'By the time you return to your crate I will have the proper papers for you,' Guy promised. 'You just ensure that whatever you do, it does not come back to us. I am now going to officially wash my hands of the matter, but unofficially I wish you all the luck in the world. Safe flying.'

Matthew returned to the airstrip and found his son and Cyril in the hangar with a stripped-down piece of the Ford's engine.

'If that's fixed, how long will it take for you to get the old girl ready for a flight?' Matthew asked.

'An hour at the most,' Cyril replied. 'I didn't know we had any flights scheduled for today.'

'Not one on the list,' Matthew replied. 'But I want to be off the ground before sunset.'

'Can I come with you, Captain Duffy?' James asked eagerly, sensing something dramatic was occurring.

Matthew looked at his son. 'I'm sorry, James, but this is something you have to stay out of.'

Crestfallen, the young man returned to cleaning the metal pipe in his hand. 'Son of a bitch,' he muttered, but Matthew did not hear him.

'Tyrone flying with you?' Cyril asked and Matthew shook his head.

'I'd like to see you in private,' Matthew said to Cyril, who followed him a distance into the hangar, away from James.

'I'm going on a job that might be a bit dicey,' Matthew said awkwardly to the man he considered more a best friend than an employee. 'If anything happens, I want you to look after James and make sure he gets home safely. Will you promise me that?'

'You know I will, Matthew,' Cyril answered. 'He's a good lad, and a lot like you must have been at his age.'

'Thanks, old friend,' Matthew answered, extending his hand in farewell. 'I have every intention of returning in a few days.'

'It wouldn't have something to do with Miss Hatfield, would it?' Cyril said with a sly smile. 'I can see it in your face.'

Matthew didn't reply, only walked into his office, deep in thought.

*

'What did the captain speak to you about?' James asked when Cyril joined him.

'Nothing in particular, young Jim,' Cyril lied. 'Just that we have to get this bit back in the engine and make sure it's working.'

'Don't ask me why but I think my . . . Captain Duffy is up to something dangerous.'

Cyril looked hard at the young man. 'Your father's whole life has been spent living on the edge. I could tell you things that would make your hair stand on end. And why don't you use the word he would so desperately like to hear you say?'

James glanced down at the cement floor of the hangar with its oil stains and patches of sand blown in with the desert winds.

'He could never find time to visit me and my sister,' James tried to explain, although he realised his words were falling on deaf ears. The Canadian obviously kissed the ground that Matthew walked on.

'Get over it,' Cyril growled. 'We have work to do.'

James obeyed and the engine piece was expertly put back in place. Even as they worked James found himself thinking confused thoughts about his father. He had come to Basra to punish him with the guilt of deserting his children, but now he was having trouble keeping up his outrage. His father had been kind and even understanding towards him. Whatever his father was planning, James knew that he should be beside him in case he needed a hand. Needless to say, his father would not agree with this, but James also had the Barrington cunning in his blood that had made that side of his family very successful.

'Is there any cargo to be loaded for the captain's flight?' he asked.

'We already have the crates aboard,' Cyril replied from the top of the ladder where he was working with a spanner to secure the engine part.

James remembered the big wooden crates being loaded by some Iraqi workers. From what he knew, one of the crates was packed with army blankets. He broke into a broad smile.

*

Dusty, sore and tired, Donald slid from the saddle of his horse in front of the Glen View homestead. For the last three days and nights he'd been assisting with rounding up stray cattle in the property's back blocks. The work had been from dawn until dusk each day. But when the sun set over the plains a fire was lit and food prepared and the cattlemen sat around the fire, joking, laughing and telling tall stories. Donald had been accepted into their circle for the way he had been able to take their banter about being the boss's son; they could see that Donald was a fast and willing learner prepared to take falls from his mount and still get back into the saddle.

Now he had returned to the station house he looked forward to a hot bath followed by the roast dinner he could smell cooking. He was met by Hector on the front verandah, holding a letter for him.

'This came today,' Hector said, handing the envelope to Donald.

Mail was a precious item out here. Donald glanced at the handwriting and his face reflected his disappointment. It was not from Jessica but typed. He could see from the letterhead that it was from his father's office.

Donald secured his horse to a rail in the homestead yard, knowing that he was expected to attend to the sturdy stock-horse the moment he finished reading the letter. He ripped the envelope open and read the one page correspondence typed by one of the company's secretaries.

'Bloody hell!' Donald swore.

'Bad news?' Hector asked, leaning on his walking cane.

'If you'd asked me a couple of months ago,' Donald answered, 'I would have jumped for joy, but since then . . . well, things have changed. My father is directing me to return to Sydney to celebrate my twenty-first birthday. That means I assume control alongside him and, frankly, I do not relish such a position.'

'Your birthday is next week, according to the station records,' Hector said. 'I told the boys and they planned something for you, which I would think was your first official drink. Maybe it's a good thing that you're returning to Sydney – the boys party hard when they have an excuse.'

Donald shook his head. He walked over and undid the reins of his mount, then walked the horse to the round yard for a brushing down and thorough examination of its hooves, and anything else that might require checking after the three days in the scrub.

As he worked he thought about leaving Glen View. He had initially resisted the exile, but he had eventually grown to love the rugged life so far from civilisation. The nights camped out under the stars and the serenity it brought to his soul was something he had never expected. He had fallen for the spirituality of the land, and was well and truly in its clutches. Besides, while he was at Glen View he was closer to Jessica in Townsville, and he had calculated that he could travel there to see her after the mustering was done. But the directive to return to Sydney had put a halt to all that.

When he did return he would put it to his father that he should be given the family's cattle stations to manage. He thought Hector would put in a good word for him.

After leaving his horse in the yard, Donald walked past the graves marked with engraved stone tablets. He knew that an aunt he had never met was buried in one of the graves, alongside Patrick Duffy's faithful servant of many years. Donald's mother had told him that his father had exiled Giselle and her son David to Glen View. Giselle had died in the influenza pandemic of 1919, leaving her son in the care of her mother. For a moment Donald thought about his cousin. In a year David would also turn twenty-one and the companies would be overseen by the triumvirate of his father, himself and David. Donald wondered where his cousin was at this very moment.

★

Sean had convalesced at Louise's apartment for as long as he could stand sitting around and doing nothing, but after a week he was desperate to return to his office and catch up on his backlog of cases.

He sat at his desk going through a pile of papers, the occasional head popping around the corner to express how happy they were to have him back. Sean knew that he was popular with the staff and his colleagues, as he ran the office like that of a company commander in the army. He was firm, fair and friendly to all, regardless of whether they were the tea lady or office boy or one of the junior partners.

Sean worked his way through the mail until he came to a telegram. He was annoyed that it had not been delivered to him when it arrived, but reminded himself that he had told no one of his stay with Louise. When he saw that it came from the Swiss Red Cross, his hands started to shake.

Sean ripped open the telegram and read the few lines on it. For a moment he sat staring at the string of words, and then the tears began to roll down his cheeks. According to the Red Cross, it was ascertained through Nationalist sources that David Macintosh, a member of an International Brigade, had been killed in action weeks earlier.

'Oh David,' he whispered. 'You were far too young to die so far from home.' For several moments Sean was taken back to all those other young faces he had seen in death on the battlefields of France and Belgium. 'And we are not even in a bloody war.'

Sean eased himself from his desk and called to his articled clerk to tell him that he would be leaving the office for the rest of the day. In fact, Sean would find Harry Griffiths and tell him the bitter news and then the two of them would go to a pub and get roaring drunk, raising their glasses to the memory of the young man who was precious to them both. After that, he would find Louise and fall into her arms in his grief.

22

When Matthew was ready to fly out for Palestine he looked around for his son.

'Have you seen James?' he asked Cyril, who replied that the boy had said he was going with Tyrone in the lorry to fetch supplies from the docks at Basra. Matthew could see that the lorry was gone and felt disappointment that his son had not chosen to see him fly out.

All checks done, Matthew fired up the three engines; when they were at their maximum revs for flight he taxied out onto the strip to wave goodbye to Cyril before turning the nose into the wind and taking off. The aircraft lifted from the ground and Matthew set his course west for the Holy Land.

A couple of hours into the flight he peered through the cockpit window to see a dark cloudbank ahead of him. He realised that it was a storm front that had not appeared in the meteorological report. He looked left and right but could not see any break and glanced at his fuel levels. He was too far into the flight to turn back, and already the aircraft was feeling the first buffeting of the storm ahead.

'Well, here goes,' Matthew said loudly. It would be rough but the Ford was a hardy aircraft. The aircraft plunged head-long into the storm and Matthew immediately regretted that he had chosen to tough it out. The swirling winds alter-natively lifted the aircraft and dropped it while Matthew fought with every ounce of strength to hold the controls and steer his aircraft. The physical strain began to take its toll, Matthew wished he'd taken his Canadian Cyril's advice and brought Tyrone along as copilot. Another vortex hit. The Ford dropped a couple of hundred feet and one of the engines almost stalled. Matthew desperately tried to read his dials but in the dim light of the cabin this was almost impossible.

Suddenly Matthew was aware that James had appeared at his shoulder and was already strapping himself into the seat beside his father.

'Where the bloody hell did you come from?' Matthew exploded angrily, guessing that James had stowed away and recovering from the shock at seeing his son.

'I thought sitting back there you might need some help,' James replied calmly, shouting to be heard over the roar of the engines and the raging storm. Outside the sky was punctuated by brilliant flashes of lightning coming danger-ously close to the little plane.

'You can keep your attention on the dials,' Matthew said, grateful for his son's help, but afraid that if anything happened they would both go down together. This thought alone made Matthew determined to use every bit of flying skill he had. So long as the aeroplane remained in one piece he would get them through the fierce storm.

'What am I supposed to see?' James asked, staring at the panel.

'You make sure all those needles stay where they are,' Matthew shouted. 'If any vary dramatically, you tell me. You can also keep an eye on the horizon for any breaks in the storm.'

James nodded and alternated between watching the vital dials and searching the blackness for any sign of light. Suddenly he grabbed his father's shoulder and pointed out a tiny break in the storm. Matthew nodded and heeled over his aircraft to fly it towards the opening his son had spotted. Although the wind still buffeted the aircraft, Matthew could see the sun beyond and continued flying into the break until the storm was behind them and they were in clear skies again.

Matthew was exhausted but quickly calculated a new route to bring the aeroplane back on course. 'Take the controls and keep her straight and level on the bearing you can see on the compass there,' he said and James immediately placed his hands on the controls.

Matthew unstrapped himself from the seat, stretching his weary limbs before going to fetch the thermos and sandwiches Cyril always packed aboard. He returned and was satisfied to see that his son was competently keeping them on course. Through the cabin window the sun was setting across a vast region of sand dunes, and on the horizon they could see rocky hills.

Matthew unwrapped the sandwiches and handed one to his son. 'Curried egg,' he said with a wry grin. 'Not the best choice in a confined cabin, I'm afraid.'

James accepted the sandwich with one hand and bit into it.

'I'll take the controls and give you a chance to have a coffee,' Matthew said.

'Okay, Father,' James said, reluctantly letting go of the controls and taking the mug of hot coffee offered by Matthew.

For a moment Matthew wondered if he had heard his son properly. Had he actually called him 'Father'? Matthew did not want to say anything in case he had heard wrong. Still, it would not get his son out of a severe reprimanding for choosing to stowaway on Matthew's dangerous mission. The rest of the flight went without incident and just after sunset Matthew saw the lights of an airstrip outside Jerusalem. They had arrived and the vital stage of extracting Diane and at the same time eliminating the German agents was at hand.

★

Sir George Macintosh had been informed that his hated nephew, David Macintosh, was reported killed in the Spanish civil war. A news reporter wanted his reaction to the young heir's tragic death.

Needless to say George expressed his view that it was a terrible thing such a promising young man had been killed in the prime of his life, but he could not help adding that it was a shame his nephew had elected to fight for the communists against the freedom-loving forces of General Franco. It was well known that the Republican forces were massacring members of the Spanish church along with many innocent men, women and children; however, little was being said in the local newspapers about the Nationalists executing men, women and children with their aerial bombardments and firing squads.

And now Donald had arrived home to take his rightful place as one of the heirs to the financial empire. The illness was progressing in George's body and despite his reservations he knew he must mentor his only son. George was surprised to see how much the months at Glen View had changed his son. He had lost the softness of the easy life and was tanned and lean. He sported a faint scar over one eye and his hands were toughened by the long hours of hard manual work expected of a stockman.

'Take a seat,' George said by way of greeting. 'We have a lot to talk about now that you have turned twenty-one. I believe that you chose to go out to dinner with your mother instead of attending the event that your sister and I organised for you.'

'I didn't want you to go to any trouble for the occasion,' Donald replied and his father sensed defiance in his excuse for missing the dinner George and Sarah had organised that included business acquaintances and prominent members of Sydney society. George had fumed when his son had not shown although he had been informed of the function. George had lied to those who sat around the table that his son had taken sick but had wished them all his thanks for attending. Not that those at the party minded as a bountiful and excellent meal was provided – along with copious amounts of alcohol and cigars.

'I will not abide such obvious rudeness in the future. If you choose to act petulantly you will experience my real wrath. Do you understand?' George reprimanded sternly.

Donald, sitting across the library from his father, stared back. 'I am sorry if my behaviour did not meet your high expectations, but I have not seen my mother for some time, and I felt that she had first claim to celebrating my coming of age, Father.'

'Your first duty is to the family's future,' George retorted. 'Duty first and personal feelings second. On Tuesday the board meets and you will take your seat alongside me. Sarah is doing fine work for the company and I expect the same from you.'

'I will be at the office on Tuesday,' Donald said, rising to his feet.

George watched his son leave the room and sensed that his plan to send Donald to Glen View had changed him in ways that were not entirely desirable. His son seemed to have a more confident air about him, which might make him difficult to control. Still, under George's firm hand, he just might shape up to be a worthy captain of the family's financial enterprises.

★

True to his word, Donald appeared in the boardroom on Tuesday and was warmly welcomed by the company directors.

'Thank you, gentlemen,' he said as he took his seat beside his father at the head of the long table. 'I will once again express my sincere apologies for not attending the party my father organised for my twenty-first birthday. I believe most of you attended and had a good time.'

'Hear, hear,' was chorused in the room. 'Jolly good show.'

George was pleased at the way his son had shown contrition to the board members and settled back to review the matters before the monthly meeting. Each item was announced and votes were taken. George was pleased to see that Donald seconded his suggestions. Maybe exile to Glen View really had matured Donald, George mused.

'Mr Tom Duffy has yet again entered a tender to purchase the Queensland property, Glen View,' the secretary said, drawing attention to a matter on the agenda. He was an older member of the board and had served under

Patrick Duffy before working exclusively for George. 'It is an extremely generous offer and according to our stock and station agent well worth accepting.'

'I propose that we accept Mr Duffy's offer,' Donald said quietly and suddenly all eyes were focused on him.

'That will never happen,' George snapped and turned to his son with fury in his eyes. 'Why would you even entertain such a thing?'

Donald had already guessed that his proposal would not be seconded by anyone on the board, given his father's long-standing antipathy to the idea. But he felt motivated to stand up for Tom Duffy, whom he had been deeply impressed by. Or perhaps it was to gain Jessica's attention. Either way, Donald knew that his would be the only dissenting voice.

'I have had the honour of meeting Mr Duffy,' Donald replied. 'And he has good reasons to wish to purchase Glen View. Although the property made a modest profit in the last financial year, Mr Duffy's offer is more generous than anyone else is likely to offer. I feel that the money obtained from the sale might help a couple of our other companies that need an injection of capital at this time.' Donald could see a couple of heads nodding in agreement.

'No Duffy will ever own Glen View,' George snarled. 'Not so long as I am alive, and if anyone is foolish enough to second my son's proposal, I will use my position as chairman to veto any attempt to vote on the issue.' George's outburst elicited the obedience he desired. Those who had nodded their heads at Donald's proposal looked sheepish and stared at the highly polished table top.

'Father, it is well known that you have sentimental concerns about the property,' Donald piped up. 'But I was under the impression that business overrides sentimentality.'

George glared at his son. He had underestimated his cunning; he could see now that having him by his side might prove more dangerous than he could have anticipated, especially if his son's behaviour encouraged other board members to speak out. 'We will move on to the next item on the agenda,' George said, returning his attention to the board members spread down the table. 'I will speak with you after the meeting,' he said to Donald.

Donald did notice that there were one or two members who seemed to be in sympathy with his views, and from that he took heart. No longer would his father rule his life.

'Before we finish for the day,' George said in a solemn voice, 'there is one other matter that has repercussions for the future of the Macintosh administration. I received tragic news that my brother's son, David Macintosh, was killed in action in Spain fighting for the communist cause. As you know he would have taken a seat on this board if he had lived. As much as it pains me to say this about my nephew, it may have been a blessing for the company that he did not survive. He was an avowed communist and I'm sure would have had used his position on our board to disrupt our business practices.'

Although Donald did not know David, he felt sickened by his father's sanctimonious speech. He had welcomed the idea of his cousin coming onto the board; fresh blood was what the business needed. He was wary of Sarah's new role; he had always known she was ambitious and he felt sure she would scheme to back her father if it suited her. Now, with David's death, it would be two against one in the family management.

★

The house in the Arab quarter of Jerusalem was not known to British intelligence. But it was known to the German agents posing as archaeologists. Albrecht and Kramer sat cross-legged on brightly coloured carpets, sipping strong coffee from small cups while their host smoked foul-smelling Turkish cigarettes. Both Germans spoke fluent Arabic.

'We have a common cause,' Albrecht said to the Bedouin-dressed Arab. The man had a long black beard and dark brown intelligent eyes. His age was hard to determine, but Albrecht guessed him to be in his early fifties. He sported the traditional curved dagger as a symbol of his high position in Arab society. 'We need to rid the world of the insidious Jew.'

'My friends, on this we do not disagree,' the Arab leader replied. 'But your government has not come out in support of our sole claim to this country. Every day the British turn a blind eye to the Jews who land on our shores from your country, and yet Herr Hitler has not condemned this illegal immigration. Not only do we need money and arms to support our rebellion, but we also need political support from a country as strong as your own. Each day the Jews grow stronger and they have the tacit support of the British.'

'I am merely a lowly servant of our Nazi cause,' Albrecht answered. 'It is not a good time for my government to confront the British and French. We must first consolidate by bringing in the Germanic people of Austria and the Sudetenland to our new Reich. Only then will we resume our true role as leaders of Europe. However, we expect a shipment of gold very soon, which will be given to you to assist your cause.'

The Arab nodded his head with satisfaction.

'We have one small problem, which I feel you are well placed to assist us with,' Albrecht continued. 'We have a traitor in our ranks whom we must eliminate.'

'Then why is it not done already?' the Arab frowned, fingering his bushy beard.

'It is a delicate matter as the traitor is an Englishwoman. Her death must not be traced back to the German government,' Albrecht said. 'We would call on your expertise in these matters.'

'If you can produce a generous advance on the gold you promise I am sure I can deal with this woman in such a manner that her death appears to be at the hands of our enemies,' the man said slowly. 'Give me the woman's name and everything I should know about her.'

Relieved, Albrecht calculated that it would be two days before the first of the gold was smuggled into Palestine. If that was so, Diane had less than forty-eight hours to live.

*

James felt the grip of the man as his father introduced him.

'So you are young James Barrington,' Saul Rosenblum said, releasing his hand. Matthew took his pipe from his pocket and filled the bowl while the three men stood at the edge of the airstrip outside Jerusalem. It was little more than a flat field lit by small drums filled with sand and soaked in fuel to light a path for incoming aircraft. It was used by the *Haganah* for covert operations.

'It is fortunate that the telegram from our mutual friend in Basra arrived today or you might have landed in the Dead Sea,' Saul continued with a wide smile. 'It is good to see you after all these years.'

'I had the good fortune to see Benjamin not so long ago,' Matthew said, and in the gloom of the airstrip lights he could see a dark expression cross Saul's face.

'I do not see my son any more,' he said. 'He has sided with the extremists who do more harm than good for our cause to establish our homeland. But for now, let us forget that. I have accommodation at my cousin's place in the city, and you and I will tell mostly true stories for your boy to hear of how his father has been a warrior all his life.'

Matthew laughed. "I'm sure that my son does not wish to hear a couple of old men recall the mistakes of their past.'

'Then we will get your son drunk and he can tell us stories of pretty young ladies he has met,' Saul said.

'James is too young to drink,' Matthew cautioned.

'If he is old enough to fight,' Saul countered, 'then he is old enough to drink.'

Matthew glanced at his son and saw the expression of pleasure on his face. Suddenly he remembered he was hardly fourteen when he killed his first man in South Africa fighting at Elands River. *Has the world changed so little*? he thought sadly, and realised that his own days of killing were about to begin all over again.

23

There was a definite change in attitude from Albrecht and Diane sensed it. Since arriving in Palestine at the new dig she had noticed that he was keeping his distance. Not that she minded now. She had finally confessed her love and desire to Matthew, and shuddered at the thought of being intimate with the German but it worried her nevertheless. The alienation had actually been apparent before they left Iraq and this had touched off a terrible suspicion that maybe her cover had been blown. She sat on a wooden crate of canned foods by the side of the airstrip, basking in the warmth of the early spring day. Only a hundred yards away stood the team's tents and she could see Albrecht in a huddle with Erika. Then Albrecht left his colleague and walked towards Diane with a fixed smile.

'I have just been discussing a pickup of some artefacts the local villagers have for us,' he said. 'Erika is unable to make the drive to the village because of her work commitments. Can you go in her place?'

'I do not want to leave my aircraft unattended out here,' Diane protested.

'The Junkers will be safe with us,' Albrecht reassured. 'We really need to have those artefacts in our care as soon as possible.'

'I would like a guard to go with me then,' Diane said, knowing that the troubles between the local Arabs and Jews made the roads a dangerous place.

'I can organise for one of the Arab men we have on site to accompany you, although he will not be armed,' Albrecht answered. 'You could leave first thing in the morning and be back by suppertime,' the German archaeologist suggested. 'I am sure that driving the lorry is far safer than some of the past flights you have carried out.'

Again, the forced smile, and Diane wondered if her coded letter had reached Matthew. She knew Albrecht would have read anything she sent and was smart enough to pick up on any code, so her words had to be carefully chosen to alert Matthew that something was wrong. She had a bad feeling about the drive to the local Arab village. But everything around her was causing paranoia, she attempted to console herself. Maybe all she had to do was pick up the artefacts and was she reading more into the job than was there.

'Okay,' she sighed. 'I'll leave first thing in the morning. Who do I have to contact in the village?'

Albrecht briefed her.

★

'Diane is located here,' Matthew said, leaning on the table and pointing to a spot on the unfolded map. 'It is essential that we get her out of the Germans' clutches and eliminate the two men.'

'I thought that you said there was also a woman working with the Germans,' Saul queried, looking up from the map. James was occupied by the company of Saul's seventeen-year-old niece in the garden courtyard.

'There is,' Matthew said. 'But I do not condone the killing of women – despite their activities.'

'You are far too sentimental,' Saul said sadly. 'It could get you killed.'

'Can you do it?' Matthew asked, ignoring Saul's comment.

'I can organise to get Miss Hatfield away from the Nazi agents, but my group cannot be seen to be involved in killing the Germans. It may cause repercussions for Jews in Germany,' Saul said.

'Could it get any worse for them?' Matthew asked.

'I do not know, but I am not willing to risk the possibility,' Saul answered, standing straight and stretching his aching bones.

'If you cannot help me with the Germans, then I will do the job on my own,' Matthew said, attempting to keep the annoyance out of his voice.

'No, no,' Saul said. 'I said that we cannot be seen to have any responsibility for killing the Germans, but I know a man who is more than capable of carrying out such a covert operation, and I believe he is currently in Jerusalem.'

'If you know such a man I would like to meet him as soon as possible. Time is critical in this operation,' Matthew said.

'It is my son, Benjamin, and his comrades in the Irgun,' Saul replied. 'They are expert at such missions.'

'Ben?' Matthew echoed. 'I thought that you and he were not talking to each other.'

'He and I have taken different paths but I know Ben has a great respect for you. My cousin is in contact with him and he tells me how he is faring. I love my son deeply, even though we have different ways of going about building a Zionist nation. I will tell my cousin Micah to contact Ben and arrange for you to go to him with your plan. I feel that he owes you for risking your life getting those weapons out of Czechoslovakia last year.'

'Whether Ben agrees or not, I will be going on this mission myself,' Matthew said.

'You are a fool, Matthew, if you think that you are necessary to any operation my son plans,' Saul said with a touch of anger in his voice. 'We have fought our wars and it is time for the next generation to take up the sword.'

'I have to go along to ensure that Diane is safe,' Matthew said. 'I don't know if I can lose her as I lost Joanne all those years ago.'

Saul softened at the mention of Joanne. He had witnessed his old friend administer a lethal dose of morphine to the woman he loved to put her out of her agony. It was during the Great War and they had been on a hilltop deep in Turkish territory; there was no way Joanne would have survived long enough to reach a hospital. Saul reached out and put his arm around Matthew's shoulders.

'I understand,' he said.

Matthew folded the map and Saul picked up a bottle of Scotch just as James entered the room, a broad smile on his face.

'Zelda is a lovely young lady,' he said to Saul. 'She has entertained me with stories about her parents' escape from Russia to settle here, and how you saved their community from destruction before she was born, Mr Rosenblum.'

'Ah, that was a long time ago,' Saul waved off.

'What have you two been discussing while Zelda has been entertaining me?' James asked, looking at both men and obviously sensing the tension between them.

'You should learn that it's not good manners to ask such questions,' Matthew reprimanded.

'You will have to excuse my New England bluntness, Mr Rosenblum,' James said. 'It is something I have learned from my grandfather.'

Saul broke into a broad grin. 'I met your grandfather a long time ago, and I can see that there is a bit of him in you.'

'My grandfather has never mentioned meeting you,' James said, mildly surprised that James Barrington Snr would have any social contact with a Jewish person. 'When was that?'

'At the end of the war, and I doubt that your grandfather would have any good stories to tell of our meeting,' Saul replied, winking at Matthew, who was smiling.

James looked perplexed by the answer.

'Oh, well, I will ask my grandfather one day,' James shrugged. 'But it would be nice to know why my father has flown here to meet with you. It all seems so hush hush.'

'You ask too many questions, boy,' Saul growled. 'Maybe one day your father will tell you.' James glanced at Matthew who remained silent, still listening to the echo of the word 'father' his son had used referring to him.

*

It was in the early hours of the morning that Ben Rosenblum arrived, waking his cousin who in turn went to Saul and Matthew. Matthew joined Saul and Ben in the kitchen.

'It is good to see you, my son,' Saul greeted Ben, whose face sported a few days' growth of whiskers.

'It is also good to see you, Father,' Ben replied, accepting Saul's hug.

'You know that I cannot condone your role in the Irgun,' Saul said, disengaging from the embrace. 'But you will always be my son, no matter what.'

'I accept that,' Ben replied and turned to Matthew. 'I never thanked you properly for the help you provided us,' he said, holding out his hand. 'I have been informed that you may need the assistance of my comrades for a mission of some sensitivity.'

'I need to extract an Englishwoman who I believe is in mortal danger, and at the same time eliminate a couple of German agents working with the Arab rebels,' Matthew said. 'But, we need to do so without drawing any attention to your cause or to me. And we need to do it soon.'

Ben rubbed his face and frowned. 'Give me all that you can and I will decide tonight whether we can carry out what you ask.'

Matthew briefed Ben while Saul stood in the background. When Matthew had finished his briefing he ceased speaking and waited for Ben's decision.

'If time is that important I think that I can organise a team straightaway, and the mission will be complete before the sun goes down tomorrow,' he said.

Matthew broke into a relieved smile. 'Thank you, Ben,' he said. 'It is a bit like old times when you were young and we were fighting together against the Ottomans.'

'My father taught me so much,' Ben replied and Matthew could see the expression of pleasure on Saul's face.

'There is one other matter,' Matthew said. 'I will be going on this mission with you.'

Ben was about to protest but Saul spoke.

'It is important, Ben,' he said. 'Miss Hatfield is special to Matthew – as was Joanne.'

Ben simply nodded his understanding and did not argue. After all, he too had been on the hilltop when Matthew had administered the lethal mercy dose those many years earlier.

*

The camp awoke with the rising of the sun and Diane rose and washed herself in her tent with a wet cloth. She dressed in long pants and a shirt, over which she wore her flying jacket against the chill of the morning.

Breakfast had been prepared but the three Germans were not to be seen and the camp's cook explained in broken English that they had already left for the dig site. Diane was joined by her escort – one of the Arab workers who spoke reasonable English – and Diane was surprised to see him wearing almost European dress instead of his usual flowing Arabic garb and headdress.

'I am ready to leave,' he said. 'Better we go now and return before the sun sets.'

Diane followed her escort, whose name was Mohammad, to the camp's lorry and pulled herself into the driver's seat. Beside her Mohammad sat silently. He was not carrying a firearm but Diane could see the knife tucked in his belt. She hoped he would not have to use it, but she felt a deep sense of foreboding as she drove away from the camp.

*

Matthew found himself in the back seat of the car jammed between two burly Irgun fighters of Georgian heritage. Ben was driving, and beside him sat a young man not much more than a boy. The team of three men had been selected because they could all speak Arabic and had proved their worth in other dangerous covert operations. From what Matthew had gleaned, the Georgian Jews were brothers, and the young man beside Ben had proven, despite his youth, his ability to engage in risky operations. None had given their names, and Matthew had not asked.

The car left the outer suburbs of Jerusalem just after 9 am and was en route to the dig location identified by Matthew. They drove in silence and Matthew could feel the tension in the vehicle.

When stopped at British army roadblocks Ben produced papers for clearance and soon they were in the country. They passed a few houses and flocks of goats being shepherded by young boys.

Just after midday Ben drove off the road to a clearing where they all disembarked, stretching limbs and relieving themselves against rocks.

'We are a half-mile from the site you indicated on the map,' Ben said to Matthew. 'It is time to lay up now; we make our raid in the early hours of tomorrow morning.'

Matthew had not been told the full details of Ben's plan but he noticed the Georgian brothers were already pushing the car into a shallow depression out of sight of anyone who might be driving to the dig. Then they took bundles of Arabic clothing from the boot of the car. One of the men approached Matthew, holding out a long robe.

'Here,' he grunted and Matthew guessed that he, too, was to disguise himself as a desert Bedouin.

Ben walked over and handed Matthew a revolver. 'You might need this,' he said. 'As you have probably guessed by now, when we make our raid we will be speaking Arabic and acting as bandits. Any Arab workers who see us will tell others that we were unknown Bedouin on a raid. I am going to make the executions appear to be the result of a robbery. We will need to get Miss Hatfield out first so that she does not get caught in any cross fire.'

Matthew liked the simplicity of the plan; the less complicated, the less likely something was to go wrong. He and
Ben walked up to a crest with a view over the archaeological site. He lay on his stomach, scanning the camp through
binoculars Ben handed him. He could see the Junkers sitting
on the airstrip.

Ben lay down beside him, while the rest of the party,
now armed with rifles, sat in the hollow smoking cigarettes
and playing cards.

As Matthew swung the binoculars across the campsite he
picked up the figures of Erika and Kramer sitting at a table
outside a tent. Matthew passed the binoculars back to Ben.

'The woman you can see sitting at the table is to be
spared. She would be able to verify to her people that they
were attacked by Arab bandits.'

'That is reasonable,' Ben nodded. 'I do not see Miss
Hatfield.'

Matthew frowned. He hadn't seen Diane either. *Maybe
she is inside her tent*, he thought doubtfully. Once Ben was
satisfied that he had identified the two targets he told
Matthew that he would give his final briefing just after
sunset and at 1 am they would strike with the speed of a
desert scorpion.

'It is time for us to eat now,' Ben said, rolling away from
the crest. 'I have a meal of bread, dates and cheese for us all.'

Matthew was reluctant to leave his spot on the hill as he
had not yet seen Diane in the camp. Already his sense of dread
was growing. Had the Germans already disposed of her?

★

Diane's feeling of unease was growing by the minute. They
were within sight of the village now and nothing had gone
awry, so she could not explain her intense discomfort.

She turned a corner and braked suddenly as three men dressed in European style stepped into the middle of the road, gesturing for her to stop. Every instinct told her that she was in an ambush, and her intuition was confirmed when the men produced pistols. Diane had survived many dangerous flights by making split-second decisions and her instincts screamed out that the man sitting beside her was part of the trap. With all the strength she had she turned to shove at the Arab, whom she could see from the corner of her eye had reached for the knife tucked in his belt.

Her attack had been so unexpected that Mohammad fell against the rickety side door and fell to the ground.

With a grinding of gears she went on the offensive and drove directly at the men spread across the road. They flung themselves out of her path, firing wild shots at the truck. Diane picked up speed. When she glanced over her shoulder she could see the men, Mohammad included, running along the road to catch up with the truck. She gathered pace and slowly drew away until the ambushers were out of sight. Her mind was working frantically. Why were the men attempting to pass as Jews? Clearly they intended her harm; she suspected they had intended to murder her, and by all appearances she would seem to have been murdered by Jewish men. Diane knew that if she attempted to turn back she would be driving towards her ambushers. She was deep in enemy territory; for all she knew the men who had attempted to stop her were from the village directly ahead. It was a case of out of the frying pan and into the fire with only one dangerous option left.

24

Diane sat behind the steering wheel, the lorry parked by the side of the road. Ahead of her was the village and behind her the men she was sure were tasked to kill her.

'Right, girl,' she said. 'Time to figure a way out of this mess.'

No doubt the ambush had been planned by Albrecht; her cover was obviously blown. She had not seen Matthew since Basra and now despaired that she would ever see him again.

Diane rummaged around in the cabin of the truck and found a water bottle and a tin toolbox. Inside was a large screwdriver, which she appropriated as a weapon, and a flashlight. It was time to leave the truck, it was too easy a target and Diane guessed that the ambushers might have even blocked the road. She would make her way into the arid hills overlooking the dirt track. She would need every navigation skill she possessed in order to work her way back to the campsite and her plane. She did not know how she would avoid the Germans but she decided to worry about that when the time came.

Taking her meagre supplies she exited the truck and set a course directly north into the hills. She was half a mile away from the truck when she heard the shouts of angry men drifting on the wind. She hoped they would not be able to track her footsteps. For the next five hours Diane kept a course travelling north, using the sun as her compass guide. When night fell she would change course and travel west in the series of rocky hills and sandy gullies.

It was near sunset when Diane stopped to get her breath. She heard the faint sound of male voices; she recognised one of them and her blood ran cold. It was Mohammad. Through luck or intention, he had taken the same path as Diane. *To head for the high ground was a logical choice*, she thought bitterly. Maybe she should have gone south, but that would have exposed her to anyone on the road above the valley. All she could do now was pray for the sun to set and use the night as a cloak to keep her hidden. She guessed that the men were used to harsh conditions and could easily overtake a woman who spent a lot of time seated in the cockpit of an aircraft.

The wind brought the voices closer. They were closing the gap and Diane began to shiver. She gazed to the west and could see the red ball slowly descending towards the ridge of low hills. Now it was time to change course and hope that the men chasing her would continue north. But Diane made a critical mistake and set off on her western course just as the party of killers led by Mohammad appeared on a ridge and saw her alteration. They, too changed course and picked up their pace.

★

The sun was below the horizon and Matthew could feel the chill of the night settling over their surveillance position above the Germans' campsite.

'I still have not seen Diane,' Matthew said when Ben took up position beside him. He put the binoculars down and rubbed his eyes

'She means a lot to you,' Ben said. 'I think I understand why it was important for you to be on this mission.'

'You were there when Joanne died,' Matthew answered quietly. 'I don't want that ever happening again in my life.'

'We will find her and she will be safe,' Ben replied, remembering that terrible day on the top of a hill when he was still little more than a boy with a gun fighting the Ottoman enemies of the British.

'Your boy James seems to hold promise of a good future,' Ben continued. 'I think my cousin Zelda is a little smitten by him.'

'I have to thank your father for looking after him,' Matthew said. 'I am sure Zelda will take his mind off my unexplained absence.'

'Does James intend to follow in your footsteps?' Ben asked.

'I have a feeling James has come to understand why I love flying, and has the potential to become a good pilot,' Matthew answered, realising just how important his son was to him, and regretting the years they had been apart. But the past could not be altered and only the future planned.

The two men lay side by side as the sun finally disappeared beneath the hills of the Holy Land.

*

Diane could feel every muscle in her body ache with the strain of forcing herself up the hills and down the slopes.

She had consumed the water and discarded the bottle; now she gripped the long screwdriver and focused the flashlight on the ground ahead. She thanked God that it was a moonless night as every now and then she could hear the voices behind her shout to each other and each time they were a little closer. She knew now that it was impossible to outrun them. Even in the dark they would probably find her and it sounded as though the party had spread out in a line.

For a moment she stopped and stared directly ahead. She thought she could see a darker shadow in the rocks ahead. She crawled forward and found a narrow opening leading to a small space in the rocks. She was afraid of what may be inside but she knew she was physically spent and could not go on tonight. Closing her eyes she cautiously slid inside, praying that the space did not harbour snakes, spiders or scorpions. Nothing bit or stung her, so she settled down on her back to wait out the night. With any luck, her pursuers would overshoot her hiding place and think she'd escaped them.

*

It was just after midnight and Ben, who had taken the watch, shook Matthew awake from his slumber.

'The lights are out in the tents,' he said. 'The workers have a fire going on the western side of the campsite. I counted fourteen workers located about fifty yards from the German tents. Most have retired and only two are sitting by the fire. Both are armed.'

Matthew rubbed the sleep from his eyes. 'Which tent did the woman go to?' he asked, and Ben indicated a smaller tent in the cluster of canvas.

'Is there any sign of Diane?' Matthew asked, and Ben shook his head. Matthew tried not to panic but all he could think was that he was too late; the Germans had killed her already. The rest of the team joined them at the top of the crest and Ben briefed them in Hebrew, which Matthew did not understand.

'The Georgians are going to take care of the workers by the fire,' Ben explained. 'They are both very good with knives. Myself and my young friend will take the two tents where we know Albrecht and Kramer have retired. We will shoot them. If the Arab workers attempt to interfere in our mission the Georgians will take care of them, but I predict they will flee into the night if they think we are Bedouin bandits. We will leave the German woman alive.'

'I will have to question her on Diane's whereabouts,' Matthew said.

'Then you will have to kill her as she will inform her government and the British authorities that you were involved. We would be wasting our time impersonating our enemy.'

'I think I can get her promise to remain silent on the matter of seeing me,' Matthew answered, but even in the dim light he could see the expression of doubt on Ben's face.

'We will see,' the young man said evasively. 'You will follow me down to the camp and stick close,' Ben instructed, before giving the signal to the rest of his team to leave.

Matthew, Ben and his young partner moved cautiously, acutely aware of making any sound in their stealthy advance on the camp. They were guided by a lantern light from Erika's tent, and Matthew thought that she might still be working. Within minutes they had reached the tents of Kramer and Albrecht. When Matthew cast about him he noticed that the two Arab men by the fire were gone and guessed their fate. For big men the two Georgians moved liked cats.

Ben eased open the flap of the first tent and the young man disappeared inside. Ben slid his rifle barrel through the opening of the second tent and stood quietly for a moment, then fired once. He entered the tent and fired again. Next door Matthew heard the half-strangled cry of a man cut off from life by the blade of a knife.

'Albrecht,' Ben said, lighting the interior of the tent with a flashlight. Matthew could see the German agent lying on his back. Both bullets had gone through his chest, and he had died without waking.

A woman screamed. Matthew recognised Erika's voice and hurried across the campsite. He could hear voices calling, 'God is great!' in Arabic. He suspected it was the Georgians trying to add to the impression that the raid was being carried out by Bedouin bandits.

Matthew burst into Erika's tent and saw her sitting up, clutching blankets to her chest. Her eyes were wide with fear that turned to confusion when she saw him. The confusion was soon replaced with a glimmer of hope.

'Oh, Matthew, what is happening?' she gasped, throwing herself at him. She was wearing a slip that hardly covered her nakedness and Matthew could feel the warmth of her body as she trembled in his arms.

'Arab bandits,' Matthew replied lamely.

'What are you doing here?' Erika asked, standing just a little way back from him now. 'Are you with them?' she asked, her face suddenly contorted with fear.

'Where is Diane?' he asked.

'What has happened to Dr Albrecht?' Erika countered, anger creeping into her voice.

'I promise that if you answer my questions honestly, no harm will come to you,' Matthew said. Suddenly Erika spun around and grasped an object from under her pillow, turning around to point a pistol at him. He could see fear and anger in her face now.

'Put the gun down,' he said. 'If you kill me, the others out there will kill you.'

'What is going on?' Erika demanded. 'Dr Albrecht,' she called out.

'He is dead, Erika,' Matthew said. 'I am aware of your true role as agents for the Nazi Party.'

Erika looked about as if seeking an exit.

'If you answer my questions you will be spared, as long as you give me your word that you never saw me here tonight,' Matthew said.

'How can I accept your word?' she asked bitterly.

'I wish that we had got to know each other better,' Matthew lied, hoping to appeal to her emotional side to cement a tentative bond between them. 'I have to know where I can find Diane.'

'She is dead,' Erika spat. 'Albrecht sent her to an Arab village east of here. As she has not returned, I can only presume that the man we sent with her has successfully completed his task and killed her. We knew who she was working for.'

'Where did you send her?' Matthew asked, feeling sick to his stomach with despair.

Erika provided Matthew with the name of the village, which he remembered from the map. Suddenly the room seemed to explode and Matthew saw Erika's head jerk back as she crumpled to the floor. The acrid smell of cordite filled the tent and Ben stepped through the entrance, reloading his rifle. Blood flowed from Erika's head and was soaked up by the sand floor. Stunned, Matthew did not react.

'She could have killed you,' Ben said in a flat voice. 'I had no other choice. Our mission is complete and we need to get out of here. The workers have disappeared into the desert, but by sunrise the place will be crawling with British army and police.'

'She . . .' Matthew tried to find the words to describe his sadness for the news from Erika about Diane's fate.

'We have to get out of here before the sun rises,' Ben said harshly. 'She was a Nazi sworn to carry out Hitler's work. She would not have hesitated to kill you.'

'Erika told me that Diane was driving to an Arab village east of the site,' Matthew said, staring at the body of the woman at his feet. 'We have to go there and find her.'

'If she has not returned, then I fear we can presume she is dead,' Ben said a little more gently. 'I would be putting my team in unnecessary danger if we were to travel to the village.'

Matthew turned to face Ben. 'Then I will go alone,' he said.

'That will not be necessary,' Ben sighed. 'We will go back to our car and drive to the village,' he said. 'It is just fortunate that my men can pass as Arabs. But we cannot remain in this territory for very long before the enemy work out who we really are.'

'Thank you,' Matthew said.

They made their way back to the hidden car, where the young man and the two Georgians were waiting. Already they had changed back into European clothing and discarded the Arab dress. Matthew and Saul slipped out of the dress of the Bedouins. Ben briefed them on their new mission and Matthew could see some reluctance on their faces. Still they agreed, and soon the car was bumping along the track east towards the village. Three hours passed and suddenly the headlights picked up a lorry parked off the road. Ben brought the car to a stop.

'This has to be the truck Diane was driving,' Matthew said to Ben, and they bundled out of the car with their rifles, wary of any Arab militiamen.

'It appears she is not here,' Ben said. 'Where do we go from here?'

Matthew gazed up at the stars. 'If I were Diane I would have headed north if I'd had to abandon my vehicle for some reason,' he said.

'How do you know that she was not killed here and her body dumped close by?' Ben countered.

'I don't,' Matthew answered. 'I just know that she is one tough and resourceful lady, and I owe her some measure of hope. At the worst we may find her body when the sun rises, but in the meantime I can set out north in search of her.'

'It will be like searching for a needle in a haystack,' Ben said.

'I don't expect you to stay here – I know that you are responsible for your men,' Matthew said, removing the map from inside his jacket and spreading it out on the bonnet of the car. He illuminated it with a hand torch he carried with him for the night mission.

'You can go back and organise to pick me up at this location,' Matthew said, indicating a point on the map halfway back to the Germans' campsite. 'If I have not found her, then I will return to Jerusalem with you.'

'According to my calculations,' Ben said, staring at the map, 'you should reach that point by midday. We will meet you there but will not remain in the area long as our mission tonight will have stirred up a hornets' nest.'

'I understand.' Matthew folded the map and slipped it inside his jacket.

Ben passed Matthew a rifle with three full magazines. 'You might need this out there,' he said.

Matthew accepted the rifle, a Lee Enfield .303 – a weapon he was very familiar with. Ben also scrounged up a bottle of water and some cheese and coarse bread wrapped in a cloth, which Matthew accepted gratefully.

'Take care, my friend,' Ben said. 'My father will kill me if anything happens to you.'

'We've faced worse together in the past,' Matthew reassured when he shook Ben's hand. 'I will be at the RV at midday.'

Matthew struck north just as the sun was beginning to show itself on the horizon. He knew deep down that his quest was futile but he also knew that he must try to salve his conscience. He could not simply stand by and do nothing, not with the memory of losing Joanne so vivid in his mind. He would attempt the impossible and find Diane – either dead or alive.

*

Diane was surprised that she had dozed off and was aware that a streak of light penetrated her confined space between rocks. She lay on her back listening to the early morning sounds. She could hear no sound of humans. With any luck her would-be executioners would have given up by now. She was about to crawl out and stretch her body, stiff from the cramped conditions of the last few hours, when she thought she heard a man cough. She froze and strained to listen. She could now hear the voices of men grumbling only a short distance away, as if they, too, had just come awake.

Very carefully, Diane peered out of her hiding place to see the heads of the men just a few yards away down the slope from her. They must have decided to camp there, waiting for the sun to rise. To her horror, one of the men ambled over towards her to relieve his bladder. He stood only ten paces from Diane's hide with an expression of satisfaction on his face as the stream of urine splashed on the rocks. As he did he glanced over at where she was attempting to conceal herself. Diane knew immediately that he had spotted her as his face lit up in utter surprise. Within seconds of him shouting to his comrades the rest of the pursuers were dragging her out and hollering with joy.

Diane knew that there was nothing else she could do but face her death with as much courage as she could muster.

25

Sarah Macintosh stood by the library window of her home, looking out over the beautifully manicured gardens. She held back the long curtain and gazed down on her father sitting on one of the stone benches set against a cascading series of flower gardens.

'The old man has been like that all morning,' her brother said behind her. 'What's going on?'

Sarah turned from the window. 'You should know,' she snapped. 'I heard you opposed Father over the issue of selling Glen View to that horrid Duffy man.'

'Sarah, you've never visited Glen View,' Donald replied with a sigh. 'Nor have you met Mr Duffy, so why should you have any interest in what happens to the property?'

'It's important that we be loyal to Father on this,' she said. 'I don't know why he should wish to keep hold of the property but I respect his choice to do so.'

'I happen to disagree with him. I think it's time Glen View was transferred to the man whose native ancestors lived there.'

'You what!' Sarah said in a stunned tone. 'You think that because this Tom Duffy is part black he has a right to Glen View? I cannot believe that you would side with any member of the Duffy family.'

'What is wrong with the Duffys?' Donald asked, his anger rising.

'Don't you remember all the stories Father has told us of the trouble they have brought to this family over the years?' she said. 'They are Irish papists.'

'You may not have heard it from Father but when I was at Glen View Hector told me that our ancestor – a man called Michael Duffy who was an Irish Catholic, and our grandfather – was illegitimate but fostered by Lady Enid Macintosh, so that means we have Irish blood.'

'Stop it, Donald,' Sarah flared. 'Those stories are lies. It is no wonder Father wants to fire Hector MacManus. I have never heard of Michael Duffy as a member of this family.'

'Well, technically he wasn't,' Donald continued. 'But his son, Patrick, was born to great-grandmother Fiona Macintosh, despite her marrying a man called Granville White.'

'I do not wish to hear these terrible lies,' Sarah said, her face reddening. She placed her hands over her ears and glared at her brother. 'You hate Father and make up these stories to hurt him.'

Donald shook his head sadly; he had seen the written evidence in the records of Glen View and it had opened his eyes to many things. The family had dark secrets; his father had tried to expunge any version of the family tree that did not comply with his place in polite society. When

Donald looked closely at his sister he could see many aspects of their father in her and he felt sorry for her. She lived in a closeted world of privilege and rigid principles. 'I do not hate Father,' Donald replied. 'But I am not him, and I have my own views.'

'Father should have left you to rot up in Queensland,' Sarah said hatefully, and the venom in her rebuke stunned Donald.

'I think it's time I moved out,' Donald said quietly.

'Where will you go – to Mother?' Sarah said angrily. 'The woman who betrayed us for a crippled lawyer who is not half the man Father is?'

'Maybe I will,' Donald replied. 'At least until I get my own digs.'

'Good,' Sarah said coldly. 'Father and I do not need you here.'

Sarah turned on her heel and walked from the room, leaving Donald to stare down at his father sitting alone in the sun. There was something definitely wrong with Sir George. Donald had been home for over a month and was puzzled by his father's seeming lack of rationality. Donald wondered if he should go down and speak with his father but decided against it. It was time to pack up his belongings. In the morning he would call for a cab and move out to his mother's apartment.

*

Sir George Macintosh stared at the sparkling blue waters of the harbour. Soon winter would come and the water would change to a green-grey under the cool sun and blustery winds of the season. The disease was slowly taking hold of him and he was frightened. He found it hard to sleep; an old Aboriginal warrior would come to visit in the dark hours and taunt him with the curse of his ancestor, Sir Donald Macintosh.

Even as he sat staring at the harbour voices began in his head telling him that his own son was plotting to kill him and take the family enterprises for his own. George smiled. No one – no son or Duffy – would ever take the family business away from him. Even if it meant killing his own flesh and blood. Oh, if only Jack Firth were still around. Jack would have been able to dispose of the treacherous son who had been born of a viper. But George had experienced the thrill of killing that worthless girl during the last year of the war. How good it had felt to watch the life go from her eyes when he had administered the deadly dose of heroin. He knew now that it was his holy mission to kill his son for the sake of the Macintosh name. George swore that he would choose the time and place to carry out this sacred task. Thankfully, his wife, Louise was back in the house and when he was ready he would go to her and bed her and they would bear more children. Louise would resist but that had not stopped him in the past.

'Father,' a voice called, and George knew it was Louise, his estranged wife. 'You should come in and have a cup of tea.'

George slowly rose from the stone bench and walked towards the house. Louise was standing in the doorway, shading her eyes against the glare of the sun. How remarkable it was that she had not aged a year since he'd first met her. She was still young enough to have many more children, and this time she would get it right and bear a truly worthy son to inherit the Macintosh empire.

*

The café in Jerusalem was a favourite place for Zelda, the dark-eyed beauty and daughter of Micah. It was crowded with students from her school while outside the dangerous streets of the city seemed a world away. She was sixteen and boys were a great interest to her. James was both a little smitten and confused in her company. She was a Jew and his grandfather had so often told him that the Jews were the true evil in the world. So why was it that this young and beautiful woman opposite him at the rickety table in the café sipping coffee was so attractive? Not only physically desirable; but also intelligent and fun loving. In fact, she was like no other girl he had met back at college. Her English was not perfect, but it was obvious her intellect was far beyond that of his own and she was studying to enter medical studies with the aspiration of one day qualifying as a doctor. Zelda could jump from one subject to another with ease, and when the dark eyes stared into his own he found himself lost in a world far beyond that he had known in the leafy suburbs of New Hampshire.

'You are . . . how you say it . . . far away, James,' she said.

'I was wondering where my father is right now,' he replied. 'He just seems to have disappeared.'

'He is with my cousin, Ben,' Zelda said. 'I think they are on a mission.'

'Mission?' James queried. 'What mission?'

Zelda glanced away and greeted a school friend who had entered the café. James suspected that she was avoiding the question he had asked.

'Please, tell me if you know something,' he said, leaning forward across the table and almost taking her hand.

'I hear . . . heard my father talking to Ben,' Zelda replied, dropping to an almost whisper. 'It is dangerous. We don't talk such things here. The British look for Ben – and he go to prison when . . . if they catch him. Maybe hang him.'

James frowned. All his father had told him was that he had to go and meet with some business friends, and would leave him with Saul and his cousin while he was gone. For a moment the coffee tasted like acid in his stomach. James had come so far to meet and punish his father for his years of neglecting him, but had come to understand him as a loving father.

'Do you know where my father has gone?' James asked and Zelda shook her head.

James remained with Zelda for the rest of the day as they toured the areas she deemed safe under British military guard, although they were stopped on the streets by British army patrols, and forced to identify themselves to the soldiers, attempting to quell the daily violence in the city between Jew and Arab. Once or twice James heard gun fire in the distance and Zelda would look around fearfully. Once he took her hand to reassure her and she had not let it go as they made their way back to her father's residence in the Jewish quarter. Only outside the door did she let go of James's hand and flash him a warm smile.

James was made to feel as if he was a member of the family, and was still confused by this treatment he was getting from the people his grandfather had told him were scheming to take over the world for the Zionist cause. All he had seen to date was a small group of people in an Arab sea, attempting to hold on to the only place they could call home. And then there was Zelda who seemed to delight in teasing him for his American ways. His journey of self-discovery had taken him beyond the search for his father. He was being challenged about everything he had come to learn in New Hampshire from his waspish grandfather.

The following morning when James awoke he suddenly experienced a feeling of danger as he lay staring at the ceiling, and listening to the sounds of the house coming alive for the day. He instinctively knew that his father was in a perilous situation – and there was nothing he could do about it.

★

Diane found herself down on the ground as the men formed a circle around her, pointing their rifles at her. Mohammad smiled behind his beard.

'So, we find you and the Germans will pay well for us to dispose of a traitor,' he said. 'But first, we have fun before we kill you.' The Arab leader turned to the youngest of his men, a boy of around sixteen years, and said something. The boy broke into a smile and commenced loosening his belt.

Diane watched from the ground in horror. The screwdriver was in her belt at her back and she slowly reached around to grip the handle. The boy knelt down and grabbed the bottom of her trousers to yank them off, and it was then that Diane struck with all the speed and strength she could muster, driving the point of the large screwdriver into the boy's stomach.

He jerked up, screaming, and immediately Diane felt the crash of a rifle butt to the side of her face. She saw a spray of red haze, before falling back to the sandy ground.

'You will pay for this,' Mohammad hissed in her ear. 'The boy is the son of the village head and you have caused him a severe wound. I will not kill you now but we will take you back to the village so that your execution can be carried out under shari'a law before all the people to witness – that is after the men of the village have had their way with you first.'

The boy was whimpering as the screwdriver was

withdrawn from his stomach and a cloth placed over the bleeding. He stared with eyes of hate at Diane and was refrained from shooting her on the spot with a promise that he would throw the first stone when she was buried up to her neck in the village square.

Yanked to her feet, Diane was forced to retrace the path she had taken in her attempt to escape. For the rest of the morning she stumbled ever closer to her degradation, torture and death. If only the death could come first, she prayed. The situation was hopeless and she knew it.

*

Matthew Duffy gazed at the desolate panorama of sand, rocks and hills. He had been lucky to find the slight trace of a man's footprints. When he cast about he found more and finally ascertained the prints belonged to at least four men. He had already guessed they were trekking west into the arid lands beyond the horizon, and the fortunate finding of the tracks gave him hope that they may belong to a party searching for Diane.

A couple of hundred yards out he swore he could see the figure of an Aboriginal warrior pointing with a spear to the west. 'Wallarie!' he said softly, remembering how the old warrior had always been like a guardian angel in his life. But when he came closer to the figure standing on the crest he was disappointed to see he was actually looking at a solitary stunted tree growing in a rock crevice.

Then Matthew froze. He could see five figures moving towards him and he immediately went to ground, snatching for the binoculars Ben had given him. He focused on the group and gasped. He could see Diane, half stumbling half walking between the men escorting her. They were not dressed as Arabs but an instinct told Matthew that was a deception. Their firearms were German and they had the bushy beards of devout Moslems.

Matthew calculated that they were about five hundred yards away and on their present course they would come very close to him. He unslung his rifle and waited, desperately formulating a plan. Four armed men was too large a number for him to take on, and even if he killed one or two the others might automatically execute Diane. Matthew knew his accuracy with a rifle was second to none, but the problem remained of how to separate Diane from her captors before they could kill her.

From the map he guessed from the route they were following that they were connected to the Arab village only about five hours' walk from where they were now, which meant they would arrive at their destination well before last light. Under the cover of darkness he might have had a chance to extract Diane from her captors, but clearly that was not going to be an option. The party was growing closer and all that separated him from Diane was four armed men and a slight gully. He had to make a decision. The only thing he could think of was to get in as close as he possible and spring an ambush.

He slithered away from the crest and ran down the gully behind him. He searched about for a place to conceal himself, and found a low depression behind a crumbling ledge jutting from the side of the slope.

He could hear the voices of the men as they drew closer and every nerve in his body was strung out to breaking point. He wrapped his hands around his rifle and realised that he was both sweating and trembling. Then the men and Diane came into view a mere twenty yards away. He could see the bruising to Diane's face. It was a desperate gamble but he had no other options. Matthew acted – despite the odds of his plan being successful. A quick death would be better for Diane than the fate Matthew guessed awaited her at the village.

★

Sarah Macintosh sat at her father's desk in his library, perusing the business papers he had left for her. The complexities of the company structures fascinated the young woman and she soon found herself absorbed in her reading. Engrossed, she barely heard the gentle knock on the library door.

'Yes,' she called.

The door opened and the old valet came in, clutching a small dilapidated wooden box in his arms. 'Miss Macintosh, I found this when I was going through the family papers,' he said, placing the box on the desk in front of Sarah. 'It seems to have been put away for many years and I was not sure if you wished to go through it before it is disposed of, according to Sir George's instructions.'

'Thank you,' Sarah said. 'I will see if there is anything we should keep.'

The valet retreated, leaving Sarah with the musty-smelling box. She looked inside, and among the age-stained papers found a large leather diary embossed with the name of Lady Enid Macintosh. Intrigued, Sarah took out the diary and wiped it down. She guessed it must be almost seventy years since the diary had been used by her ancestor and flipped open the book to see that the entries were dated to the 1860s. The writing was a strong copperplate style and Sarah was hardly aware of the time that passed in the library as she read the story of the long-dead Lady Enid Macintosh.

As she read the secret thoughts of the colourful and strong woman, Sarah paled. It was Enid's story of an Irish rogue by the name of Michael Duffy that turned Sarah's world upside down. She gasped when she read of his intimate involvement in their staunchly Protestant blood line. Everything her brother had told her was true and this was a bitter thing to learn. She was tainted with Irish papist blood! This was more terrible in her upper class world than she felt she could dare face. Before she closed the diary she decided that some things from the past should remain in the past.

26

Matthew could see that the men with Diane had stopped to examine one of their party. He looked very young, little more than a boy, and his front was covered in a large blood stain; he was clearly in a lot of pain. Diane stood a few paces away, a man guarding her. Matthew carefully lined up in his rifle sights. He squeezed the trigger and a split second later the man fell back, a bullet hitting him just below his throat.

'Diane! Run!' Matthew shouted as the echo of the shot rolled around in the shallow valley. Without hesitating, Diane broke into a sprint away from Matthew's position, while at the same time the remaining two men scrambled for cover behind a ledge halfway up a slope, leaving the wounded boy in the open.

Matthew had chambered another round but the men were now out of sight and Diane had disappeared over the slope. Matthew swung his rifle onto the beardless youth, but could see that he was not an immediate threat. The boy stood holding a pistol and staring uncomprehendingly in Matthew's direction before eventually making his way painfully up the slope to join his comrades.

It was time to move and Matthew considered getting above the men he had pinned down, but when he exposed himself briefly a couple of shots cracked rock over his head. It was obvious that both he and the Arabs were at a stalemate.

Suddenly a figure appeared from the enemy's conceal-ment and dashed up the slope to disappear on the reverse side. The sprint had been so quick Matthew did not have time to bring his sights on the fleeing figure and his shot went wild.

'Englishman, you should not resist us,' a voice called from the enemy position. 'On my word I will not kill you if you surrender to us.'

'Yeah, and pigs will fly,' Matthew muttered, and responded by yelling, 'Go to hell, Abdul.'

'My name is Mohammad, not Abdul. That is an Ottoman name. We have no fight with you.'

Matthew lay back and considered his position. It was near midday and all he could do was stay alert until the sun set and then make his move. He prayed that Diane had escaped towards the road where Ben had promised to be waiting and hoped she would be safe.

The day passed with the occasional demand from Mohammad for him to surrender, and just as the sun began its slow descent in the west Matthew became aware that he could hear voices, and his hopes were dashed. They were speaking Arabic and, from what he knew of the language, they were looking for him. To confirm his dashed hopes he heard Mohammad call out to the voices. It was obvious that the man who had escaped had gone for reinforcements.

'You are a dead man, Englishman,' Mohammad called triumphantly. 'If you are not already dead I will be there to see you die slowly at the hands of my brothers.'

Matthew knew that if the villagers were approaching they would probably appear on his open side or behind him. The situation was looking bleaker by the second, and all he could do now was hope that he went down fighting, because he knew of Bedouin torture methods from his experiences in the war.

A rifle shot hit the ground near his knee, spraying Matthew with dirt. The reinforcements were already taking up positions to pick him off. He swung around and levelled his rifle at a head he could see on the opposite side of the low ridge line, and fired. The bullet missed but forced the man to take cover. Suddenly Matthew felt a terrible thump to his upper left arm and a searing pain as if a red-hot poker had been inserted into his flesh. He was aware that his arm was dangling like a useless lump of meat, as the bullet had obviously shattered the bone. Another bullet struck the butt of his rifle, smashing it from his hands. He was now almost completely helpless as his rifle slid down the slope. He attempted to reach for his revolver with his right hand, but a figure loomed over him and a rifle butt blow to the head was followed by darkness.

When Matthew finally came around he was aware that his hands were secured behind his back and a circle of fierce-eyed, bearded men glared down on him. The Australian was consumed by the agony of his wound and simply hoped that his death would be quick. However, he knew that a merciful death would be denied to him and tears of pain and rage at his situation welled in his eyes.

'You will wish that the bullet had killed you,' a man wearing western clothing said in English. 'You killed my brother, and I am the Mohammad that you insulted as an Ottoman.'

★

Sarah could hear the door knob to her bedroom rattle and a voice she knew call softly, 'Louise?'

She struggled to sit up and shake off sleep. The door opened, and outlined in the light from the hallway she could see her father. Her horror rose when she saw that he was naked.

'Father,' Sarah said in shock, 'you must return to your room.'

But George sat on the end of her bed and reached to pull down the bed sheet Sarah had drawn up to her chin.

'Louise,' George muttered. 'We need to have another son.'

Then George ripped the sheet from his daughter and rolled on top of her.

Sarah screamed, struggling with all her strength to extricate herself, but her father was strong and she could feel his hands gripping the top of her nightdress and smell his breath on her face.

Suddenly her father was ripped backwards, and in the half-light Sarah could see her brother with his arm around her father's throat, wrestling him from the bed. Both men fell to the floor, and George curled into a foetal position when Donald released his grip.

Stunned, brother and sister stared at the naked man on the bedroom floor.

'What in hell happened?' Donald asked Sarah, who had retrieved the sheet to cover her flimsy nightdress.

'I don't know,' Sarah gasped. 'I think Father has gone mad. He thinks that I'm Mother.'

'Bloody good thing that I was here tonight,' Donald said with a shudder. "Who knows what might have happened if I'd already moved out.'

'What do we do with Father?' Sarah asked in a frightened voice.

'We call a doctor to see if he should be committed to an insane asylum,' Donald replied. 'I don't know what happens after that.'

The family doctor arrived an hour later and examined Sir George still curled up on the floor of Sarah's bedroom, whimpering like a child.

'Your father may have had a nervous breakdown,' the doctor said to Donald, wary of revealing the true cause of George's mental state. 'I will have an ambulance take him to hospital, where he can be treated for his condition.'

'Shouldn't he be locked up in an asylum?' Donald asked.

'For the moment I think that a stay in hospital with suitable treatment is the best option,' the doctor answered. 'Your father is an important man in Sydney and has great responsibilities. I think he should be treated first before we consider any incarceration in a mental institution.' The doctor remained until the ambulance arrived. Sarah and Donald watched as it drove away with their father.

'I know that Father will get the best treatment possible and be home soon,' Sarah sighed.

'You want him back after what happened tonight?' Donald asked incredulously. 'He almost raped you.'

'But he's sick in the mind,' Sarah defended. 'I know that he'll get better and be his old self soon enough.'

Donald stepped back from his sister and stared at her. How could she defend him after what he had done to her?

He shook his head in disbelief. *She is definitely her father's daughter,* he thought.

The following day Donald did not move into his mother's apartment as planned but appeared in the company office where he had a memo sent out to explain that his father had been hospitalised with a minor heart condition. The same memo called for a meeting of directors to address the issues that would arise, stating that he would take charge in his father's absence.

'Very good, Mr Macintosh,' the old secretary said when Donald had dictated his memo for circulation. 'Will you be using your father's office?'

'I think so, Mr Berriman,' Donald replied. 'I will trust that you are able to guide me in any complicated matters that may arise.'

Donald's response brought a smile to the old secretary's face. 'Welcome to the company, Mr Macintosh,' he said with genuine warmth.

'When you are preparing the agenda for the board meeting I would like you to include the sale of Glen View to Mr Tom Duffy,' Donald said, opening the door to his father's office.

'Very good, Mr Macintosh,' Berriman said. 'That will be done.'

Donald walked into the spacious office and sat down in his father's chair behind the big teak desk. He would write to Jessica in Queensland and inform her of his decision. He only wished that he could be a fly on the wall when she received the news. It would certainly prove his devotion to her and maybe unleash the passion he knew she felt for him.

★

Captain Matthew Duffy gritted his teeth and forced back the scream when the men staked him out on the earth in the gully. He had been stripped naked and they had wrenched his shattered arm deliberately, but Matthew was not going to give them the pleasure of showing his pain. Sweat was like an oily sheen on his face as he continued to fight the excruciating agony. From the corner of his eye he could see some of the group gathering dry grass and twigs. He guessed that they would slowly burn him alive, as they pushed the material beneath him with wide grins on their bearded faces and muttered curses upon his life in the next world.

Matthew forced himself to imagine the faces of Diane and James to distract himself from what was coming – but that did not work. The fear of feeling his flesh sizzling cut across his thoughts, and he knew it would do no good to beg for mercy – or a quick death.

He had counted at least nine men around him, and closed his eyes when he saw the man who called himself Mohammad pass the younger, wounded boy a twist of burning grass to apply to the tinder stacked around his body. The others broke into a chorus of encouragement to the boy as he approached with the burning torch. Although Matthew did not want to scream his agony he knew that he would when the flames began searing his flesh.

A volley of shots suddenly cut short the cries of encouragement. Matthew opened his eyes and saw the boy with the flaming torch collapse, his head shot away and the flames falling harmlessly into the desert sand.

Others of the party were desperately seeking shelter, but the well-aimed rifle shots picked them off until there was silence, broken only by the groans of a wounded man. A shot quickly followed and the moaning stopped.

Matthew twisted his head around and could see Ben approaching him down the gully, accompanied by the two Georgian brothers and the younger man. Behind them was Diane, who broke into a run, collapsing on her knees beside Matthew.

'Oh, Matthew,' she cried. 'What have they done to you?'

Matthew tried to smile, but the pain was too great. 'I'll be okay after a hot shower, a cold beer and big plate of steak and eggs,' he gasped.

'We found Diane not far from where we were supposed to pick you up,' Ben said, leaning over and untying the bonds securing Matthew's wrists, while Diane untied those around his ankles. 'She was stumbling out of the wilderness. She told us of your situation. Sorry we were a little late.'

Very gently, Ben assisted his father's old friend to sit up. Matthew's arm dangled at an odd angle. Blood welled from the wound but the artery did not seem to be damaged – a stroke of luck. The movement caused a terrible spasm of pain. The last thing Matthew remembered was the sound of his own scream before he blacked out again.

*

When Matthew finally came to again he could smell chloroform or ether. Whatever it was, it reminded him of a hospital, and as his eyes focused he could see that he was indeed in a hospital bed. The first two faces he saw were those of Diane and his son, James, staring down at him with expressions of concern and happiness.

'You're awake, Dad,' James said and Matthew could have sworn that he could see a tear in his eye. Diane leaned forward and kissed him.

'See you two have met,' Matthew croaked, a dull pain throbbing in his left shoulder.

'I should have been with you,' James said. 'You need me, Dad.'

Matthew was touched by his son's concern and delighted that he had gone from calling him 'Father' to 'Dad'.

Matthew attempted to raise his left arm to reach out for Diane's hand, and it was then that the shock hit him. His arm was gone!

'The doctors were forced to amputate just below the shoulder,' Diane said gently. 'They couldn't save your arm, but the most important thing is that you are alive.' She paused for a moment. 'And that you're able to marry me.'

'Do you really mean that?' Matthew asked, forgetting about his arm for a moment.

'Well, I have seen you naked, so I suppose I'll have to marry you now.' Diane tried to laugh while wiping away her tears with a handkerchief. 'Of course I mean it, you old fool.'

'Then I accept,' Matthew answered and this time he raised his right arm to reach out and take her hand.

★

Within a week Matthew insisted on discharging himself from the Jerusalem hospital and was driven by Diane to Saul's cousin's residence, where he was given a warm welcome by his old friends, Saul and Ben. James was also at the house and a small party was thrown in Matthew's honour, with the wine flowing freely.

Matthew drank sparingly. The phantom pains of his missing arm still nagged him and he fought to keep at bay the depression that he would never fly again.

'You know I lost my kite,' Diane said, joining him in the small courtyard away from the merriment of the party. 'The German government have already seized my crate. I was hoping that you might have a position for a pilot with your airline.'

'So, you have no intention of settling down after we are married?' Matthew teased.

'James has asked me to help him get his pilot's licence,' Diane answered, taking Matthew's hand. 'He's a good boy and you can be proud of him,' she continued. 'With your permission I will take over his flight training. After all, I was fortunate to have had the best instructor in the world when I was learning all those years ago.'

'I know I will never be able to take the controls again,' Matthew said glumly, staring at the potted flowers resting on a stone shelf in the courtyard. 'But I still have the Ford, so at least you have an aircraft to fly and I can fly a desk managing the company.'

Diane leaned forward and kissed Matthew on the lips. 'Is there anywhere we can go for some privacy?' she asked with a sly smile.

'It just happens my old cobber Saul told me of a good hotel not far from here,' he replied.

No one noticed the couple disappear.

27

The sadness was apparent. Matthew Duffy stood on the wharf at the Palestinian port of Acre with his son, waiting for him to board for his voyage to France, where he would take passage on a ship back to America. James had promised his grandfather that he would return, albeit many weeks overdue, and his studies at Harvard would not wait.

'I'm pleased that you're returning to finish college,' Matthew said half-heartedly. 'Before you know it, you'll be a wealthy and successful lawyer.'

'Grandfather wants me to join the family business,' James said. 'I don't know if that's what I want.'

'I hope you're not aspiring to be a pilot – you might end up flying some out of the way airline like me.'

'Diane kindly offered to teach me to fly,' James replied. 'But I'll take lessons back in the States. One day you might need me to help out.'

'I appreciate your offer, but your life is back in the States. That's where you belong,' Matthew said.

A voice called for all passengers to embark. 'Looks like it's time to go aboard. I'll miss you, Dad.'

Matthew wrapped his arm around his son's shoulders and forced back the tears. They'd had too short a time together and there was still so much to say, but they'd been through a lot in the last couple of weeks and that had brought them so much closer.

'Give your sister my love,' Matthew said.

'I don't think she will be so forgiving,' James laughed. 'She's missed having a father in her life but at least now I will be able to tell her all about you.'

Matthew dropped his arm away and James picked up his carpet bag. He turned and walked quickly to the plank where others were embarking. Matthew remained on the wharf as the ship pulled away, James standing on the upper deck, waving. Matthew stood watching the ship disappear from the harbour, and finally turned to walk away, wiping tears from his face.

Diane was waiting for him by the car.

'He'll return one day,' she said, wrapping her arms around Matthew.

Matthew hoped she was right, but the hollowness in his heart remained. James was a fine young man and he had missed out on so many years with him. He'd just started to get used to the idea of being a father and now his son was gone again.

He kissed Diane on the cheek, grateful to have her to ease his sorrow.

★

'He's done what!' Sir George Macintosh exclaimed from his hospital bed. 'I will crush him.'

Sarah wondered if she had done the right thing informing her father of Donald scheduling Glen View for sale to Tom Duffy. Her father appeared to have recovered his senses very quickly; he seemed back to his old self again.

'I have been told by the doctors that I am well enough to be discharged today, and intend to return to work immediately to displace Donald,' George said. 'He needs to be taught a strong lesson about who is really running the Macintosh empire.'

That evening George was brought by taxi back to his harbour residence where he was met outside by his daughter and the household servants.

'Welcome home, Sir George,' they said dutifully.

George brushed past them and walked through the front door to his home.

'I have had your favourite meal prepared, Father,' Sarah said, following him. 'It's good to have you home with us.'

George mumbled his thanks and went directly to his office and locked himself away. *For better or for worse*, Sarah thought, *he is my father*. He had not been in his right mind when he'd attacked her, and now he was himself again, things could go back to normal – although as a precaution she had had a lock installed on her bedroom door.

That evening Donald returned home and was met by his father at the door.

'You do not enter these premises ever again,' George said, barring the entrance. 'I will organise to have your personal effects sent to you at your mother's apartment.'

Stunned, Donald looked over his father's shoulder at his sister, hovering in the background. 'What about Sarah?' he asked.

'Sarah and I have settled any problems that may have arisen between us, and she knows of my decision to bar you from this house,' George smiled like a cat eyeing a wounded bird. 'One day she will take your place and I will do everything in my power to have you removed from the board. Oh, and as for your decision to sell Glen View, you can forget that, because tomorrow I will be resuming the chair. If you wish to resign from the family companies I will accept your decision. That is all.' George closed the door firmly against his son.

*

Louise was happy to have her son stay until he found a place of his own in the city.

'I have prepared a beef stew for dinner – I know it's your favourite,' Louise said, fussing around her son. 'But I must warn you that a dear friend of mine, Major Sean Duffy, will also be staying for dinner.'

'That's fine with me,' Donald answered in a flat voice, not caring if the devil himself was coming to dinner. He could still see the rage in his father's face as he stood in the doorway barring entry to the house. It had hurt more than Donald was prepared to admit right now.

That evening Sean arrived for dinner.

'Pleased to meet you, Major Duffy,' Donald said, extending his hand stiffly to the man he knew was his mother's lover.

'A pleasure to meet you, Donald,' Sean said, accepting the gesture with a firm grip. 'Your mother is very proud of you.'

The three sat at the table and the beef stew proved as good as Donald remembered. It was Louise's speciality, based on a French recipe she had acquired. Conversation was light and pleasant but there was a certain tension between Sean and Donald.

'I heard that you were in the chair while your father was hospitalised,' Sean said, sipping a glass of hock. 'I also heard from reliable sources that you had all intentions of selling Glen View to a client of mine, Tom Duffy.'

'That is a moot point now,' he replied. 'My father has assumed control again. He has even suggested that I should consider resigning.'

'How dare he!' Louise flared. 'It is your birthright to take control when your father passes on.'

'He thinks that Sarah will make a better job of it,' Donald sighed. 'She can have it for all I care.'

'What would you do instead?' Sean asked.

'If I had my way I would return north, and hope that I might get the chance to manage Glen View one day,' Donald said.

'I'm sure that if Tom owned the property he would offer you that opportunity,' Sean said with a smile. 'I have spoken to him recently and he told me that Mr MacManus spoke highly of your potential, and it seems that Jessica Duffy would also give you a good reference. In fact, Tom does whatever his daughter asks. She has him wrapped around her little finger.'

Donald was taken aback at the mention of Jessica's name. When he looked at Sean he could have sworn he had a gleam in his eye.

'I truly appreciate the interest, Major,' Donald said. 'But I am not about to resign just to spite my father.'

'Good for you, young man,' Sean said. 'I only wish David had lived to stand by your side. I think that the two of you could have done great things with the Macintosh empire.'

'I was so sorry to hear of David's loss in the Spanish war,' Donald said with genuine sympathy.

'He was one of the finest young men who ever lived,'

Sean said, looking away to hide his pain. 'I don't even know where they have buried him – probably some unmarked grave in the middle of nowhere.'

'I think that we should turn to more pleasant things,' Louise said noticing how hard it was for Sean to reflect on the loss of his beloved David. 'I will clear away the table and we will go onto the balcony to take in the night life on the water. It is a beautiful night and I have a bottle of champagne to mark this moment you two have finally met.'

The evening passed pleasantly and Sean bid them good night as he left to return to his flat in the city, leaving mother and son alone.

★

The wedding in Basra was a private affair. The little Christian church stood in a sea of Moslem holy places; rarely had it seen an English-speaking couple married within its very old walls. An Eastern Orthodox priest officiated; Cyril was Matthew's best man, and Major Guy Wilkes and Tyrone McKee were the only guests. Saul was unable to attend as he'd had to flee the city. The Arabs in Jerusalem suspected Saul and Ben of being involved in the killing of the German archaeologists.

Diane wore an elegant white silk skirt, while Matthew had scrounged up an old dinner suit. Guy Wilkes had invited Matthew and Diane back to the officers' mess for the bridal dinner and had arranged for a boat trip up the river to Baghdad for their honeymoon.

At the dinner Guy read a telegram from America.

'*Congratulations on the wedding. Wish I was there*,' Guy read out. 'And it is signed, *James Duffy*.'

For a second Matthew was confused as to who James Duffy was; when it dawned on him he broke into a broad smile. James had reverted to his father's family name. He truly had a son and it was the best wedding present he could have received.

Just before the honeymooners were ready to board the boat, Guy took Matthew aside.

'I know you're wondering how the British government views Diane's work for the Americans,' he said, holding a flute of champagne. 'It has all been swept under the rug and her work for the Yanks forgotten, considering the wealth of information she provided us here. Besides, she also had an indirect hand in dealing with the problem of the Nazi agents. I heard that they were murdered by Bedouin bandits at their dig.'

'I heard that too,' Matthew replied with a serious expression. 'Terrible thing to happen to Himmler's finest.'

'Well, my wedding present is the contract you now have with the new oil men exploring out here,' Guy continued. 'You're fortunate to have Diane and Tyrone as pilots, although I suspect that you will still find yourself in the cockpit as a one-armed pilot – despite flying regulations.'

'I would find it necessary to go along from time to time,' Matthew grinned. 'I may not be in complete control of the aircraft, but I'm not out of the sky yet.'

'Well, good luck, old chap,' Guy said, extending his hand.

Matthew shook his hand warmly and glanced over Guy's shoulder. He could see Tyrone chatting with Diane. It was time to take his bride on their honeymoon. They had many years to catch up on, and Matthew was not growing any younger.

★

For Sean Duffy it was just another day at the office. Court briefs on his desk and clients to interview. A large pile of papers awaited his attention, and yet he found himself standing by the window of his office and gazing out at the life on the street.

'Major Duffy,' a clerk said at the door. For years Sean had attempted to discourage the use of his former military rank among those who worked for the firm, but it had become almost a term of endearment. He knew they were proud of his war record and the decorations he had been awarded by the king.

'What is it?' Sean asked.

'Mr Harry Griffiths is here to see you,' the clerk said. 'He does not have an appointment but insists on seeing you on a very important matter.'

'Send him in immediately,' Sean said.

'Very well, Major Duffy,' the clerk replied, ducking away. Sean waited for his old friend to appear.

Harry walked through the door and Sean's face broke into a smile, only to crash into an expression of absolute shock. Harry was not alone. The second man to enter the office was David Macintosh.

For a moment Sean thought that he might faint. Was he hallucinating? He felt himself begin to sway.

'Better sit down, boss,' Harry said. 'Young David turned up this morning at the gym, and I had the same reaction.'

'Uncle Sean,' David said, stepping forward. 'I'm sorry that I couldn't contact you earlier, but I just arrived home.' David stood uncertainly, and Sean could see the changes in him. He knew immediately that the young man had suffered a great deal.

It was Sean who hobbled forward and embraced David, tears flowing down his cheeks.

'It is so good to see you again, my boy,' Sean said, gripping the young man as hard as he could lest he vaporise as a mere illusion. 'I was told you'd been killed in Spain.'

'If you sit down I will tell you all about it,' David said gently.

'Well, I'll leave you two,' Harry said. 'I have to get back to the gym. How about the three of us meet after work at the pub on the corner? Our boy has one hell of a tale to tell.'

Sean nodded and sat down in the chair behind his desk as David pulled up a chair of his own.

David then related all the events that led up to that terrible day when the volley of shots from the firing squad had killed his English comrade but left him alive, a bullet in his shoulder.

'The Spanish were lousy shots,' David said. 'So the German in charge of the firing squad was walking up to me with his pistol to deliver a killing shot to my head, when Major Heinrich von Fellmann drove up and stopped him. It seems a message I gave to one of our guards got to him, but too late to stop the firing squad. At great risk to himself, he was able to arrange for me to be smuggled out of Spain and into France. I was given medical attention by his own staff while I was waiting to leave the country. His second-in-command was a devout Nazi so Heinrich had to keep my real identity from him. Because I can speak reasonable German I was disguised as a wounded German soldier and put on a convoy away from the front lines. Heinrich then organised for me to be spirited out of the hospital and across the frontier between Spain and France with a group of Basques. So, that was it – except I had to work my way back to Sydney as crew on a freighter. I did not know if I would ever get home, so I chose not to tell anyone I was alive until I could actually see Sydney Harbour. I'm sorry for the grief this caused you, but I could not trust that I was safe until I was able to set my feet on Australian soil again.'

'I don't care about any of that,' Sean said. 'All I care

about is that you are safe and well and back home with those who love you. Does your grandmother know you're alive?' Sean asked.

'I sent her a telegram as soon as I arrived, and I will see her as soon as I can,' David answered.

'Good,' Sean said. 'I cannot tell you how happy I am to see you again.'

'I don't suppose I could stay with you for a while – until I get my life together?'

'I would be offended if you stayed anywhere else,' Sean replied. 'You may not realise it, but you have returned from the grave at a very critical moment. I think it's time for you to meet your uncle, Sir George, and your cousins. I have to admit that I will love being there to see the expressions on their faces.'

'I suppose it is time,' David said. 'I'll be twenty-one next year, and according to the terms of my grandfather's will I am supposed to take a share in the managing of the family business.'

'You don't know how important that is,' Sean said with an enigmatic smile. 'But we are taking the day off, and I will vouch that you are twenty-one when we go for a beer with Harry. I'm sure there's so much more you would like to talk about with a couple of old soldiers who understand what you've be through.'

David thought about Sean's statement. Now he knew why Sean had been reluctant to talk about his life during the war but with the two men he most loved and admired he realised that he had become what they were – a man who had experienced combat and survived with the memories of friends lost and the importance of living.

28

Major Guy Wilkes signed for the classified signals and took the folder to his office in army HQ. He was in a good mood – the wedding reception had gone well and London had sent a message to congratulate him on the unspecified matters that had occurred in Palestine. Guy knew they were aware of the elimination of the German spy cell and that this would be attributed to his intercession. It was a good mark on his service record.

The decrypted intercepted German message marked for his attention was vague. He frowned, as all it seemed to suggest was that an appropriate response was to be made in Baghdad for the loss of the German archaeological team in Palestine. The message had originated from deep within Himmler's Berlin department and forwarded to an unknown agent in Cairo, Egypt. The killing of the three Germans had been investigated by the British authorities and reported as death at the hands of unknown Bedouin bandits. Although Guy knew his counterparts in the German military intelligence probably did not believe the findings, they did not have any proof of a covert British operation. He read on and the intercepted message from the German Gestapo HQ talked about a revenge killing of a target known to be at the centre of the case. It would be a covert message to the British to leave their agents alone in the future or retaliation would be swift and deadly.

What response could Himmler have envisaged? Guy pondered. *What target?*

Then it hit him. They had failed the first time to eliminate a double agent, and the Nazis probably held Diane responsible for the deaths of her former comrades. The encrypted message was suddenly clear.

Guy sprang from his chair and immediately went to the great map of Iraq on the wall of his office. From what he could guess Diane and Matthew would have reached Baghdad by now.

'Damned stupid!' Guy swore, remembering the small item in the local newspaper about their marriage and honeymoon destination. It all seemed harmless at the time as the matter of the Nazi spies appeared to be behind them. Anyone hunting Diane would be waiting in Baghdad for her – it was a perfect place for an assassination. It was a city full of anti-British sentiment and no doubt there were many prepared to harbour a killer of a European infidel.

Guy realised that he had no way of contacting Matthew to warn him of the potential threat. He didn't even know which hotel the newlyweds were staying in, but he could at least telephone Baghdad military HQ and ask them to track down the one-armed Australian and his English bride. One thing that did reassure Guy was that Matthew never travelled without his old service revolver.

'Corporal Harrington!' Guy bawled. 'Report to my office.'

★

Matthew could not remember a happier time in his life – the pleasure yacht sailing up the ancient river past quaint little villages that could have been four thousand years old; the spectacular bird life living along the reed-covered swamps off the Tigris River; sharing the serene evenings with Diane on the rear deck, sipping gin and tonics.

They both regretted leaving the yacht at Baghdad, but the hotel also promised a luxury that would make the honeymoon even more memorable. Because Matthew's grasp of Arabic was fairly good, the two of them were treated with utmost courtesy by the owner, who ensured they received a room with a view over the river.

'Oh, Matthew,' Diane said, bouncing on the big double bed in their room. 'I think I've died and gone to heaven!'

'Funny you should say that,' Matthew grinned. 'Those are my sentiments.'

Diane reached up for Matthew and drew him down onto the bed beside her.

'I would dream at nights about you ravishing me,' she said with a wicked smile. 'You men can be so dull-witted when it comes to subtle signals.'

'Well, let the ravishing continue,' Matthew said, reaching for the belt on his trousers.

Diane wriggled off the bed and planted her feet on the floor.

'Not until we go to the markets and I have the opportunity of buying something made of silk,' she laughed. 'Then we can spend the rest of the afternoon back here.'

'Then I had better be prepared to hock the airline,' he sighed.

Reluctantly, Matthew slid off the bed and tightened his belt. He was getting good at doing things with one arm.

'I'm not that kind of woman, Matthew Duffy,' Diane replied with mock hurt. 'Let's go, my love.'

Matthew picked up his hat and followed his bride out of the room.

Within minutes of them leaving, two burly British military police entered the hotel and were able to ascertain that Captain and Mrs Duffy were registered guests. As far as the owner knew they had just departed for the local markets. The two soldiers hurried out of the hotel to catch up with Matthew and warn him of the threat to his wife, and to him.

★

The market was crowded and the stalls sold everything from fresh fruit and delicious-smelling snacks to jewellery and clothing. The majority of the customers were Iraqis, but there were one or two Europeans among the busy throng. Matthew stood back patiently as Diane fingered the silk headscarfs, all the while making little sounds of delight. Matthew smiled to himself and felt a warm surge of love for this beautiful creature who was fascinated by the touch and colour of the silk.

Diane slipped a red silk scarf over her head and turned to Matthew.

'What do you think?' she asked.

'It's almost as beautiful as you,' he said, meaning it. She was the most beautiful woman in the whole world, and he was lucky enough to have earned her love.

Matthew suddenly grew aware that a nervous young man

was approaching. There was something about the stranger's demeanour that caught his attention. He glanced at Diane, still preoccupied with the scarf. When he looked back the young Iraqi had a pistol in his hand, pointed directly at Diane.

Matthew reached desperately for his own revolver, which he kept in a leather pocket holster. But in a split second he knew that he would not have it out before the stranger fired his own weapon.

Matthew flung himself between Diane and the assassin just as the young Iraqi fired. Matthew felt the bullet rip into his chest.

Matthew could hear screaming as he finally retrieved his own pistol, raising it and firing three shots from the ground into the startled young man. The assassin crashed back into a stall displaying clay pots, scattering the goods and bringing down the flimsy shelter. Each of the three rounds from Matthew's revolver had found its target and the young Iraqi was dead when he hit the ground.

Matthew was aware that he was on his back. He could see Diane's horrified expression above him, as panicked people fought to get away from the scene. Two burly British military police pushed their way through the fleeing customers to Diane's side as she knelt by him.

'I couldn't let it happen again,' Matthew gasped, gritting his teeth against the pain. 'I love you too much.' For a moment Matthew was not sure if he was seeing Joanne or Diane hovering in the receding view he had of the world. But he could feel Diane's grip in his hand and was being washed with her tears.

Then Matthew died in her arms.

★

David had spent the last few nights at Sean's Sydney flat, and his days at Harry's gym building up his strength. The bullet wound to his shoulder had caused enough damage to put him out of heavyweight contention but he still sparred with partners Harry found for him.

At the end of a tiring day he showered, changed into a newly purchased suit and tie, and joined Sean on the street outside the gym.

'I fancy a good steak tonight,' Sean said with an evil grin. 'Care to join me – my treat?'

'Sure thing, Uncle Sean,' David said, feeling good after a rigorous workout.

The two men caught a taxi and were driven to a posh hotel in the city. David expressed his surprise.

'Hope I'm suitably dressed,' he remarked as they left the taxi.

'You are, my boy,' Sean said. 'I'm hoping that we'll bump into someone I think it's about time you met.'

'Who is that?' David asked as they made their way through the hotel's grand entrance.

'All in good time,' Sean said mysteriously.

Sean was known to the maître d, an Italian who had once claimed to be a count on the run from Mussolini and had come to Sean for legal assistance when he had used his alias to pass bad cheques. Sean had helped him out of a tight spot and the man had never forgotten it.

'Major Duffy,' he said with a bright smile of welcome. 'I have kept the best table for you.'

'Thank you, Giuseppe,' Sean replied after handing his hat to a pretty young lady behind a tiny counter, who kept casting David admiring glances.

The Italian ushered them to a table to one side of the busy dining room and Sean ordered a bottle of white wine.

David took his seat and noticed Sean looking around the room as if seeking someone.

'Ah, there he is,' he finally said. 'I see that he is dining with his daughter.'

He rose from his chair. 'Time I introduced you. Come on, young man, meet your illustrious uncle, Sir George Macintosh, and his very pretty daughter, Sarah.'

David rose and followed Sean across the room. When George saw them approaching his smile turned to a scowl.

'Sir George, Miss Macintosh,' Sean said, smiling charmingly. 'I thought I might finally introduce you to your long-lost brother's son, David Macintosh.'

David hardly heard the introduction. He was too busy staring at Sarah; their mutual recognition was almost instantaneous.

'It's you!' Sarah gasped. 'You are the young man who saved us in that café in Berlin.'

'And you are cousin Sarah?' David replied, almost at a loss for words. 'I guess protecting family was worth the trouble that followed that incident.'

The two young people continued to gaze at each other, locked in a moment on the other side of the world. For David it seemed a lifetime ago; that afternoon that had led to the series of events that found him on the battlefields of Spain. Finally he became aware that his uncle was glaring at him.

'We finally meet, Uncle George,' he said without any warmth.

'We were led to believe that you had been killed in Spain,' George spluttered. He turned to Sean. 'How do I know this man is not an imposter? I would not put it past you to attempt such a thing.'

'Look at him, Sir George, and you can see that he is your brother Alexander's son. You need to try better than that. Oh, did I forget to mention that David is only mere months from turning twenty-one and assuming an equal third share in the management of your family's companies?' Sean enjoyed seeing the business tycoon's face redden with frustration and fury.

'If you have any courtesy, you will leave me and my daughter to enjoy our meal in private,' George said.

'Well, Sir George,' Sean said, a smile still plastered over his face. 'We will leave you in peace. Miss Macintosh, I hope that our uninvited call on your table did not cause you any distress.'

Clearly still stunned at recognising David as the handsome young man from the Berlin café, Sarah could hardly find words to reply. 'No, Mr Duffy,' she said eventually. 'I hope to meet with David in the future to personally express my gratitude.'

This brought a disapproving scowl from her father and Sean and David turned to make their way back to their own table, where the bottle of wine was waiting for them. Sean expected to have the best steak he had ever consumed.

*

The same people who attended Matthew's wedding attended his funeral service in Basra. Major Guy Wilkes stood by Diane on one side of the grave dug in the hard earth a short distance from Matthew's airstrip, and on the other side stood Cyril and Tyrone.

'The skipper always said that he wanted to be buried here,' Cyril said, reaching for a handful of sand to throw on the simple wooden casket in the grave. 'He was a man of vast horizons and desolate lands. Rest in peace, old friend.'

Diane cried for the man she had finally found, loved and lost so soon. She, too, reached for a handful of desert sand to throw on the coffin. Tears rolled down her pale cheeks, as the Eastern Orthodox priest who had officiated at their wedding now performed the last rites of burial. When the burial was over, Diane remained by the grave, staring at the coffin for a long time, then she turned and walked away to the staff car Major Guy Wilkes had provided. Matthew's Ford trimotor aeroplane was standing forlorn on the tarmac, as if a faithful hound mourning the loss of its master.

'What will you do now?' Guy asked gently.

'Matthew left the company to me and his children, James and Olivia,' Diane said. 'I have already mailed a letter to James explaining the circumstances of his father's death.'

'So you will continue operating the airline?'

'Yes, but I have spoken with Tyrone and Cyril and we have decided to relocate to the Pacific region after our oil field contracts are up here,' Diane replied. 'I think it will put me out of the range of the Nazis.'

'We will miss you,' Guy sighed. 'As it is, though, I'm being posted back to England to a staff job. It's a promotion for my work here.'

'Congratulations,' Diane said. 'I know that Matthew was very fond of you. He always considered you both a friend and foe.'

Guy gave a short laugh. 'I considered him a friend, and I regret very much inducing him to help us out. He would still be alive if I had left him well alone.'

'Don't blame yourself,' Diane consoled. 'If I had not been in his life, my dear Matthew would still be alive. He sacrificed himself to save me, and I have to live with that for the rest of my life.'

'It seems we both will have a burden of guilt,' Guy said, opening the rear door of the staff car as Tyrone and Cyril walked over to join them.

'We're going to have a wee wake at the hangar,' Tyrone

said. 'Hope you can join us, Major Wilkes, and raise a glass to one of the finest men who has ever flown the skies of this part of the world.'

'Now the boss is flying somewhere high – with both arms intact,' Cyril added. 'I'll miss you, Skipper.'

Guy drove them across the bumpy ground to the hangar. Diane was vaguely aware that she felt ill, the nausea seemed to come to her each morning she woke up. But she dismissed the feeling of nausea as the effect of extreme grief for the man she loved and lost.

29

David celebrated his twenty-first birthday quietly. He joined Harry and Sean at the pub around the corner from Harry's gym, and Sean shouted him his first legal drink. The three spent the afternoon drinking, and before David knew it, the walls of the hotel had begun to spin. He was bundled into a taxi back to Sean's flat, where he promptly threw up.

The next morning he groaned as he realised that he was still alive – the way he felt, death might have been a better option. In the kitchen Sean prepared a big plate of fried eggs, bacon and grilled tomatoes.

Bleary-eyed, David slumped in a chair at the table, and Sean pushed a plate in front of him.

'Eat up, it will do you good,' Sean said cheerily, already dressed for work. 'Tomorrow I believe you have an appointment to be introduced to the board of directors.

Today, you will get to formally meet your cousin Donald.'

David stared at the fried food and reached for a slice of toast, which he nibbled on slowly. There was a glass of freshly squeezed orange juice by the plate, and David sipped on this between bites of the toast.

'I'm not sure if I should thank you and Uncle Harry for my birthday party,' David said, 'because I don't remember much after the first shout.'

'What you will remember,' Sean told him, 'is how rotten you feel now, and you'll make sure you never drink enough to feel this bad again. When I returned from the war I hit the bottle to try to wipe out the things I'd seen and done, and I used to wake up feeling as you do now. I was a slow learner, but I know you're much smarter. My birthday present to you is, hopefully, a life free of alcoholic binges.'

David raised his hand. 'I swear, Uncle Sean, I will respect the bottle for the damage it can do to a man.'

'Good lad,' Sean said. 'This afternoon Donald will drop in to introduce himself. I guess you can sleep off your hangover until then.'

David took Sean's advice and retired to his room to snooze for a few hours, allowing his body to dry out. Around 3 pm he heard a knock at the door and eased on a pair of slacks and a clean shirt.

'We finally get to meet under more civilised conditions,' Donald said, thrusting out his hand to David when he opened the door. 'I guess this is my opportunity to thank you for your intervention that day in Berlin. Major Duffy has told me what that help cost you. I was mortified to hear that you attracted the attention of the German police and were sent to Dachau. I wish that I could have turned back the hands of time and changed the events of that day so that we did not accidentally cross paths.'

'No need for apologies or speeches,' David said. 'Come in and I'll make us a cuppa.'

Donald was dressed in an expensive suit and looked as though he had come from work at the Macintosh offices in the city. David prepared a pot of tea and invited Donald to take a seat at the kitchen table.

'Nice bag of fruit,' he said as he placed a cup in front of Donald, who sat stiffly in his chair. 'Do I get one like that when I start tomorrow?'

'I suppose with the allowance you will be granted you will be able to afford a decent suit,' Donald replied. 'I will have the honour of introducing you to the members of the board, as I doubt my father will do so.'

David sat down at the table and poured the tea, pushing the milk jug towards Donald. 'I don't know if I want to put on a suit and go into an office every day,' he confessed. 'I think I need a bit of time to just head off and have a look around.'

'I know what you mean,' Donald said, sipping his tea. 'I would have rather remained at Glen View learning how to manage a cattle station.'

The two young men looked at each other and in their simple statements recognised a commonality of shared aspirations.

'What's stopping you?' David asked.

'Something that has been drilled into me since I was a child – something called family duty,' Donald frowned. 'While my father lives, I need to be close by to counter some of his increasingly mad ideas. He is not a well man, and I have been quietly approached by members of the board saying they fear my father is showing signs of madness. They want me around to balance any decision making.'

'Fair enough,' David replied. 'Uncle Sean has a very high opinion of you.'

'I am flattered to know that,' Donald replied with a note of genuine pleasure. 'I think you have been fortunate to have Major Duffy guiding you. He has told me that you are a top-class heavyweight fighter who might have turned professional. I envy you your prowess. The last fight I got into I lost badly.'

David smiled. 'Maybe you should come to Uncle Harry's gym, and I'll get him to train you,' he said. 'You have a pretty good build, and I figure you would be around my weight division. I think it must be in the blood and that we Macintosh men are born to fight.'

'From what I can gather,' Donald said, 'we get that from the Irish blood we are not supposed to have, thanks to one Michael Duffy. According to an old diary, he was a soldier of fortune, and a champion bare-knuckle fighter. His sister, Kate Tracy, passed away at a ripe old age in Townsville a few years ago. I wish that I'd known all this before she died, because I feel she could have told us so much about who we really are.'

David nodded and sipped his tea. 'Uncle Sean told me that you have recommended Glen View be sold to Tom Duffy,' he said quietly. 'I guess you know that I would oppose such a sale.'

Donald placed his cup on the saucer and gave a pained expression. 'There is so much more you don't know of the family history,' he said. 'Major Duffy told me that you do not wish to lose the property because your mother is buried there. I can understand that as many of our ancestors are buried in the soil of Glen View, but Tom Duffy's side of the family have more roots in the soil than we do.'

'I'm prepared to consider the matter,' David replied. 'But for now I am forced to side with your father – as much as it irks me to do so.'

'So you are not saying outright that a future sale is beyond consideration?' Donald said.

David rubbed his face with his hand as if to wash away the last of the remnants of his hangover. 'Maybe one day,' he said.

'Okay, we will leave it at that,' Donald said. 'In the meantime I can say that I feel it a real honour to know that you are my cousin. I never had a brother, and hope that we get to be close friends.'

David eyed his cousin carefully but could not see any falseness in his statement. He stood as did Donald and the two men shook with firm grips.

'Welcome to the family – for better or worse – David Macintosh,' Donald said.

'I think it's time that we cemented our relationship with a drink down at the corner pub with some friends,' David said with a broad grin. 'It will be a quiet drink as I have learned a good lesson last night. My uncles, Sean and Harry, might not be real uncles by birth, but from the little you have told me about Michael Duffy, I don't think a bit of bastardry really matters in the Macintosh family.'

★

Two weeks later Tom Duffy and his daughter, Jessica, stood by the grave of Hector MacManus on Glen View. Beside them was Donald Macintosh, wearing a suit that made him feel just a bit out of place when he glanced at the stockmen wearing their cleanest work clothes out of respect for the tough old Scot.

When the funeral was over the Presbyterian minister, who had travelled such a long distance to conduct the service, looked relieved to finally be able to escape the heat.

'It would have been better if the pastor had conducted the service,' Tom said. But Pastor Karl von Fellmann was long dead and his mission station deserted; a place of dust, termites and crumbling buildings, inhabited only by snakes and goannas.

'The pastor was Lutheran,' Jessica reminded her father.

'Karl was one of Hector's best friends,' Tom countered gently.

'Hector was a truly remarkable man,' Donald said. 'He taught me so much.'

'Are you staying?' Tom asked.

'I wish I could but I have to return to Sydney. We will be employing a new manager for Glen View,' Donald answered.

'Jessica told me that you attempted to pass a motion to sell me Glen View,' Tom said. 'I just want you to know how much your gesture meant.'

'It is not the end of the business,' Donald replied as the three of them walked back to the homestead. 'Give me time and I hope to change the board's thinking about the sale.'

Behind them the rest of the Glen View stockmen and staff, Aboriginal and European, straggled along to partake in the wake organised by the head cook.

Donald felt a little guilty that Hector's death had provided him with an excuse to travel to Queensland. He had flown to Brisbane and then taken a coastal steamer to Townsville; from here he had journeyed by a lorry over rutted dirt tracks until he reached Glen View. His trip had taken a total of four days, but the funeral had been postponed until he arrived. At last he was in the company of the young woman who had remained aloof to his flow of passionate letters. When he was able to manoeuvre Jessica to a quiet place in the back-yard under the shade of a big old pepper tree he decided it was time to lay his cards on the table.

'Jessica, you must know how I feel from the letters I

have sent you,' he said. 'But you have not made your feelings clear.' Jessica looked away avoiding his eye. 'Just tell me that you do not feel the same way about me, and I will cease writing.'

Jessica turned to Donald. 'Donald, my personal feelings are something that I must learn to control.' He could hear the anguish in her voice. 'I have made a decision, and my life is no longer mine to decide.'

'What on earth do you mean?' Donald countered. 'That is a ridiculous thing to say.'

'Not if you have been called to become a nun,' Jessica said quietly.

For a second Donald thought he had misheard. 'That's crazy,' he blurted. 'You're far too beautiful to be locked away in a convent. The world needs you – I need you.'

'Donald, I do not expect you to understand my decision, but it has a lot to do with this land around us,' Jessica said. 'It has been the times that I have walked this ground and felt the spirit of old Wallarie calling to me that has led me to choose a life in the Church. I pray that one day I will be able to return and build a mission station here. I feel that as a nun I can devote my life to helping my people.'

'Bloody hell,' Donald swore softly. 'You knew this all the time that I was writing to you – pouring out my feelings on paper?'

'I wasn't sure,' Jessica replied gently. 'I didn't want to tell you until I was certain. I think I could have loved you, Donald, had I chosen a different path.'

'What does your father think of your decision to enter a convent?' Donald asked bitterly.

'Father is not very enthusiastic about my decision,' Jessica admitted. 'He said that I should allow myself time to see more of the world before donning the veil.'

'Sounds like a damned good idea to me,' Donald said, staring at the haze shimmering over the endless sea of scrub beyond the fences of the homestead. 'You're so young, and you have plenty of time to decide. I know that my arguments are selfish because I would like you in my life. Why don't you give yourself some time to consider your decision?'

'Father has said the same thing,' Jessica said. 'If it is any consolation, then I will wait a year before making a final decision,' she said and Donald's face lit up.

'And if you choose not to become a nun?'

'Then you will be one of the first to know,' Jessica laughed.

As much as Donald had the desire to kiss Jessica he knew he must hold back. The best he could do was to keep working towards passing ownership of Glen View to Tom Duffy and his daughter. He remembered the nights in the scrub when the stars shone brightly and the curlews called in the dark. It was as if the voice of the old Aboriginal warrior was speaking to him of injustices that had to be rectified somehow. He knew that Wallarie was always out there in the vast spaces of the ancient and sacred territory of the Darambal people.

*

Sir George Macintosh sat in the garden of his house and stared at the blue waters of the harbour. The world was upside down and he felt power slipping from his hands. His son defied him at every turn and now his brother's son had joined the board of directors. At least George found he had one thing in common with David Macintosh, and that was they both opposed the sale of Glen View. No member of the Duffy family would ever own Glen View while George was alive.

'Father,' Sarah's voice called and George looked up. Oh, how beautiful his daughter was growing, and how strange it was that the girl he had long ignored might yet be the saviour of his dreams. Times were changing and even Sir George had to admit women were stirring for more independence. Could it be that she might rule the family as Lady Enid Macintosh had?

'Yes, my dear,' George answered. 'What is it?'

'Time for you to come inside and have dinner,' she said. 'The weather is changing for the worse.'

Rolling over the harbour were billowing storm clouds and another thought entered George's devious mind. They were like the clouds of a war he knew was coming – as did many others who had watched world events unfold across Asia and Europe. The Japanese, German and Italian fascists were in ascendency as they rolled their armies across the map. It was a time when young men foolishly volunteered to lay down their lives for their country, while men such as himself reaped the financial rewards of war.

Sir George rose stiffly from his favourite stone bench where he had been surveying the ships at anchor that were part of the Macintosh line of island traders. As he walked back towards the house he had the fleeting thought that perhaps fortune might be good to him once again and both his son and nephew might die before he did.

EPILOGUE

My name is Wallarie, and although I am gone from the world of wind, fire, earth and water, I still live in the world of my ancestor spirits. I see Tom Duffy standing on the sacred hill of my people, looking out at the land of horizons that stretch to the end of the world. He is alone and deep in thought for the young woman who is his daughter, now one of those nuns working at a missionary station in a land north of where he stands called New Britain. Tom is sad because he promised to take back our lands so that the spirits of my people could once again hunt the brigalow scrubs. But the one who was born to give back the ancestor lands has defied us, and so the place they call Glen View still belongs to the whitefella family called Macintosh.

Sometimes I soar across the plains as a great wedge-tailed eagle, and in those times I see into the lives of the children scattered across the earth, whose blood mingles with my own people. I see James Duffy in a land across the sea, stepping from his aeroplane wearing the wings of some mob called the United States Marine Corp. His grandfather is angry because James identifies with his father who is now an ancestor spirit with us.

I see Donald and David Macintosh standing in a room of a house in Sydney. They are listening to that whitefella thing called a radio, while a bigfella boss is telling them they are at war with that bloke, Hitler.

Fellow Australians, it is my melancholy duty to inform you officially, that in consequence of a persistence by Germany in her invasion of Poland, Great Britain has declared war upon her and that, as a result, Australia is also at war. No harder task can fall to the lot of a democratic leader than to make such an announcement.

Donald and David are like brothers rather than cousins and they talk about signing up to fight. The young woman, Sarah, watches her brother with concern, and gazes at David with adoring eyes. She is very beautiful for a whitefella girl.

In a land to the north of Glen View called Singapore, I see Matthew's missus, holding a little boy in her arms as she watches one of her aeroplanes taking off. She is a smart missus and has many aeroplanes. Beside her is a cranky old bloke called Cyril, who comes from a place where the water goes white in winter. She is happy that her son is only a toddler, and too young to be a soldier in the war ahead in faraway place called Europe.

Ah, but there is evil in the world. He is a whitefella called George Macintosh whose heart is dark with desires to rid himself of others: his son and nephew. By and by the madness come to him, but Sarah looks after him when that happens. She is almost one of the Macintosh bosses now.

I see things in time, now that I have the old people's spirit in me. I see terrible things in the years ahead. They are starting to forget the curse – all 'cept Sir George – and they will pay for that mistake. I could always see beyond the horizon, war clouds gathering, and next fire will fall.

The ancestor spirits do not know 'bout baccy. I miss my baccy in this spirit world. But I will always be here, as this is the place of my people's dreaming.

Not the End

AUTHOR NOTES

The Spanish Civil War 1936–39 could easily be called the curtain raiser to World War Two. A democratically elected government was deposed by the military under General Franco, who reinstated the Spanish royal family and the power of the aristocrats and the Church. The government was socialist in philosophy and it was opposed by ultra-conservative Carlist and fascist Falange groups supported by the army. The idea of land distribution, and other acts designed to assist the poor, was a threat to the wealthy establishment. The country was split militarily and politically into a very bloody civil war.

When called upon by the besieged elected government, Britain and France chose to remain neutral while the fascists of Spain were aided by the armed forces of fellow fascist countries Italy and Germany. However, the Spanish government was able to gain Russian and Mexican aid.

Many people of the time could see the threat fascism posed to world peace and volunteered in what were known as the International Brigades to assist the elected government.

The war had no quarter. Government forces were guilty of crimes against priests, nuns and innocent peasants suspected of being on Franco's side. In return, Franco's forces executed peasants they considered loyal to the government and used aerial bombing against civilians in towns and cities. The fascist forces of Germany and Italy could see that the two major European powers – Britain and France – were avoiding any confrontation with them. So, when Franco's fascists eventually won the war in 1939, the Second World War broke out the same year.

A number of Australians joined the International Brigades to fight fascism. The 1930's were a time that saw a terrible world-wide economic recession and many in the Western world were sympathetic to communism as a way out of the catastrophe believed to have been caused by capitalism.

A forgotten part of history is the resistance movement in Germany prior to the war. There were German's who opposed Hitler's policies. Dachau concentration camp was set up to deal with these Germans. There were attempts against Hitler's life before the war and one almost succeeded. Armed resistance became impossible when Hitler passed laws disarming private citizens of the possession of firearms. Stalin did the same in Russia.

All the rest is story telling.

ACKNOWLEDGEMENTS

The production of this book is in many ways a team effort. At the publishing level I would like to recognise my publisher Cate Paterson of Pan Macmillan Australia, my editor Vanessa Pellatt, and the cover designer Deb Parry. My thanks go to Julia Stiles who has painstakingly stripped away the fat from the story. From the publicity department, thanks and congratulations to Tracey Cheetham. A thank you also to Roxarne Burns, who toils away counting the books sold so that I can get paid each year and keep writing the novels.

A special thank you to my agent, Geoffrey Radford of Anthony Williams Agency.

I would also like to thank *Get Reading* for my national tour in October 2012. That thanks is extended to Alison Crisp who coordinated the tour for me, with the opportunity to meet one or two of my readers, and hopefully recruit one or two for the future.

There are other people in my life who have contributed in small and large ways to helping me produce the books. They are: John and June Riggall, Graham Mackie, Bruce and Laurie King, Jan Dean, Kevin Jones OAM and family, Kate Evans, Kristie Hildebrand, Dr Louis and Christine Trichard, Mick and Andrea Prowse, Tyrone McKee, John and Cheryle Carroll, John and Isabel Millington, Peter and Kaye Lowe, Bill and Tatiana Maroney, Nerida Marshall from STARS, and Robert Harper and family. In Queensland two old soldiers: Laurie Norgren and Larry Gilles.

Within my own family: my brother, Tom Watt and family, my Aunt Joan Payne, cousins Tim Payne, Luke Payne and Virginia Wolfe and not to forget the Duffy side.

A continuing thanks to Brett and Rod Hardy for their continuing work on the *Frontier* project and a special mention to a wonderful lady connected to the project in the USA, Ms Suzanne de Passe.

My life has now come down to six months writing and six months fighting bushfires. To all members of the Gulmarrad Rural Fire Service, I extend my thanks for your wonderful camaraderie. That thanks is also extended to all members of the volunteer emergency services I have had the honour of working alongside of; from Coonabarabran to the Clarence Valley during the last fire season. They are the forgotten heroes of this country who put their lives on the line for no pay. My condolences to the friends and families of those who lost loved ones during the last fire season. Sadly, there will be more in the future – without a national memorial in Canberra to recognise their ultimate sacrifice. I hope that changes.

I would also like to thank a few of my writer friends: Tony Park, Simon Higgins, Dave Sabben MG, Greg Barron, Karly Lane and Katherine Howell – and all my readers.

Last but not least, all my love and thanks to Naomi.

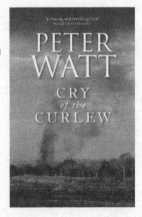

Peter Watt
Shadow of the Osprey

On a Yankee clipper bound for Sydney Harbour the mysterious
Michael O'Flynn is watched closely by a man working
undercover for Her Majesty's government. O'Flynn has a
dangerous mission to undertake . . . and old scores to settle.

Twelve years have passed since the murderous event
which inextricably linked the destinies of two families, the
Macintoshes and the Duffys. The curse which lingers after
the violent 1862 dispersal of the Nerambura tribe has created
passions which divide them in hate and join them in forbidden
love.

Shadow of the Osprey, the sequel to the best-selling *Cry of
the Curlew*, is a riveting tale that reaches from the boardrooms
and backstreets of Sydney to beyond the rugged Queensland
frontier and the dangerous waters of the Coral Sea. Powerful
and brilliantly told, *Shadow of the Osprey* confirms the
exceptional talent of master storyteller Peter Watt.

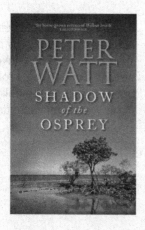

Peter Watt
Flight of the Eagle

No-one is left untouched by the dreadful curse which haunts two families, inextricably linking them together in love, death and revenge.

Captain Patrick Duffy is a man whose loyalties are divided between the family of his father, Irish Catholic soldier of fortune Michael Duffy, and his adoring, scheming maternal grandmother, Lady Enid Macintosh. Visiting the village of his Irish forebears on a quest to uncover the secrets of the past, Patrick is bewitched by the mysterious Catherine Fitzgerald.

On the rugged Queensland frontier Native Mounted Police trooper Peter Duffy is torn between his duty, the blood of his mother's people – the Nerambura tribe – and a predestined deadly duel with Gordon James, the love of his sister Sarah.

From the battlefields of the Sudan to colonial Sydney and the Queensland outback, a dreadful curse still inextricably links the lives of the Macintoshes and Duffys. In *Flight of the Eagle*, the stunning conclusion to the trilogy featuring the bestselling *Cry of the Curlew* and *Shadow of the Osprey*, master storyteller Peter Watt is at the height of his powers.

Peter Watt
To Chase the Storm

When Major Patrick Duffy's beautiful wife Catherine leaves him
for another, returning to her native Ireland, Patrick's broken
heart propels him out of the Sydney Macintosh home and into
yet another bloody war. However the battlefields of Africa hold
more than nightmarish terrors and unspeakable conditions for
Patrick – they bring him in contact with one he thought long
dead and lost to him.

Back in Australia, the mysterious Michael O'Flynn mentors
Patrick's youngest son, Alex, and at his grandmother's request
takes him on a journey to their Queensland property, Glen
View. But will the terrible curse that has inextricably linked the
Duffys and Macintoshes for generations ensure that no true
happiness can ever come to them? So much seems to depend
on Wallarie, the last warrior of the Nerambura tribe, whose
mere name evokes a legend approaching myth.

Through the dawn of a new century in a now federated
nation, *To Chase the Storm* charts an explosive tale of love
and loss, from South Africa to Palestine, from Townsville to
the green hills of Ireland, and to the more sinister politics that
lurk behind them. By public demand, master storyteller Peter
Watt returns to this much-loved series
following on from the bestselling *Cry of
the Curlew*, *Shadow of the Osprey* and
Flight of the Eagle.

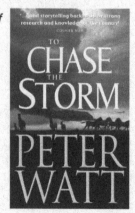

Peter Watt
To Touch the Clouds

*They had all forgotten the curse . . . except one . . . until it
touched them. I will tell you of those times when the whitefella
touched the clouds and lightning came down on the earth for
many years.*

In 1914, the storm clouds of war are gathering. Matthew
Duffy and his cousin Alexander Macintosh are sent by
Colonel Patrick Duffy to conduct reconnaissance on German-
controlled New Guinea. At the same time, Alexander's sister,
Fenella, is making a name for herself in the burgeoning
Australian film industry.

But someone close to them has an agenda of his
own – someone who would betray not only his country to
satisfy his greed and lust for power. As the world teeters on
the brink of conflict, one family is plunged into a nightmare of
murder, drugs, treachery and treason.

PHOTO: SHAWN PEENE